Praise for *Secrets of the Highlands*

The Beacon Hill series just keeps getting better! *Secrets of the Highlands* is a sequel worth the wait.

JESS CORBAN, author of *A Gentle Tyranny*

As with *Hunt for Eden's Star*, this next installment in the Beacon Hill series promises a continuation of characters quickly becoming fast favorites for my bookshelf! The intoxicating story takes me places I didn't expect to go with intense adventure, supernatural allegory, and characters that resonate with a warrior's soul. This sweeping series will enthrall readers of all ages and give you a serious book hangover. Get ready!

JAIME JO WRIGHT, author of *The Vanishing at Castle Moreau* and *The House on Foster Hill*, winner of the Christy Award and Daphne du Maurier Award

Praise for *Hunt for Eden's Star*

An imaginative, immersive story with strong characters worth rooting for. I honestly couldn't put it down!

JESS CORBAN, author of *A Gentle Tyranny*

SECRETS OF THE HIGHLANDS

D. J. WILLIAMS

wander™
An imprint of
Tyndale House
Publishers

Visit Tyndale online at tyndale.com.

Visit the author online at djwilliamsbooks.com.

Secrets of the Highlands

Designed by Eva M. Winters

Published in association with Pape Commons: a gathering of voices, www.papecommons.com.

For manufacturing information regarding this product, please call 1-855-277-9400.

For information about special discounts for bulk purchases, please contact Tyndale House Publishers at csresponse@tyndale.com, or call 1-855-277-9400.

Library of Congress Cataloging-in-Publication Data

A catalog record for this book is available from the Library of Congress.

ISBN 978-1-4964-6270-1 (hc)
ISBN 978-1-4964-6271-8 (sc)

Printed in the United States of America

29 28 27 26 25 24 23
7 6 5 4 3 2 1

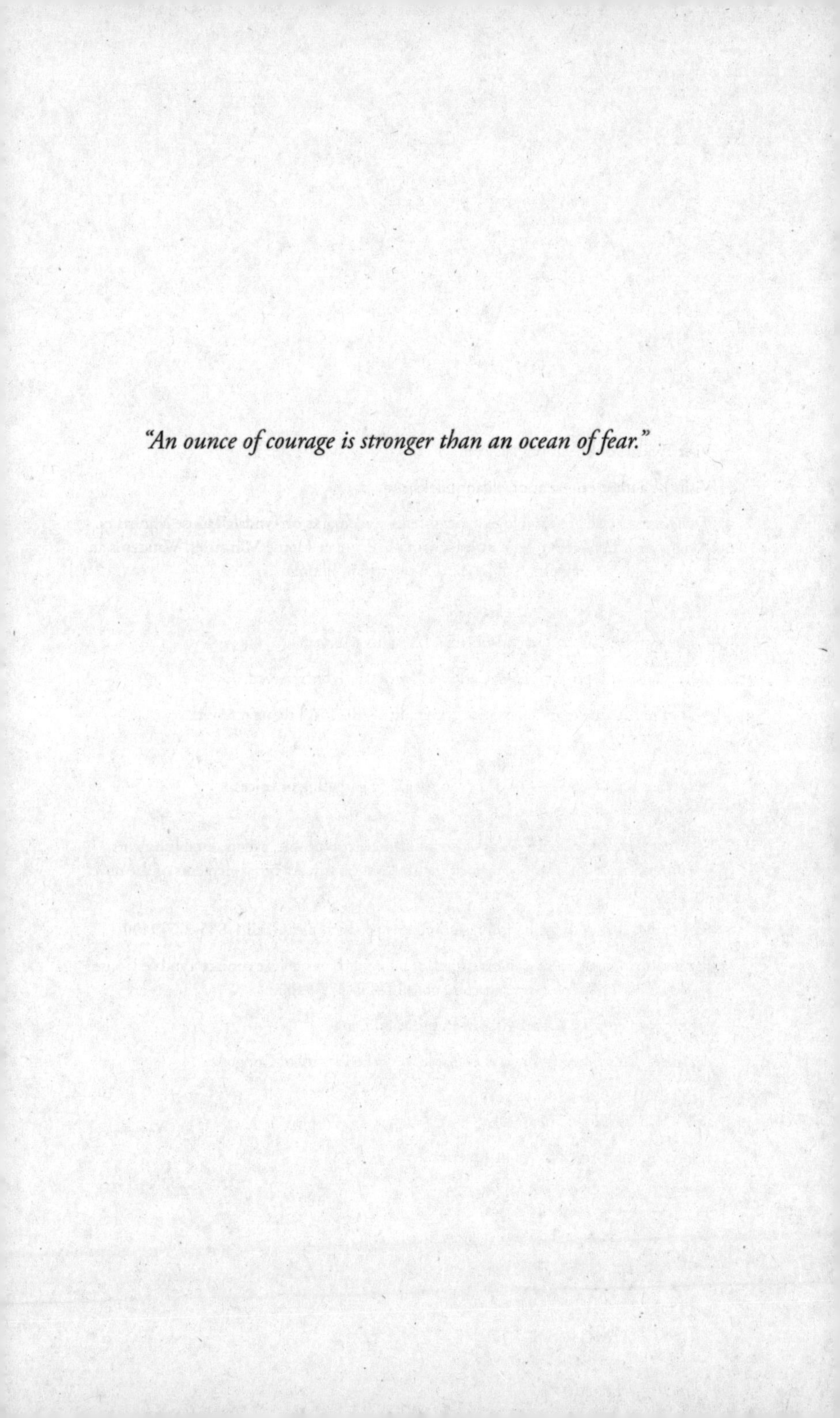

"An ounce of courage is stronger than an ocean of fear."

1

KARACHI, PAKISTAN

EMMA AND AMINA EMERGED ONTO a balcony of a clock tower steeple looming over brightly colored umbrellas scattered around a market square. An armed security guard in plain clothes casually stood near an entrance to the square while the two girls peered down on pushcarts and stalls. Pakistanis bustled and bargained for almonds, pistachios, cashews, chickens, lambs, goats, and fresh fish.

A bronze haze hovered over the City of Lights, muting the sea of stark-white high-rises. Nearly a month had passed since Eden's Star blazed within the chapel on Karābu Island, transporting them to these streets only a few miles from the Arabian Sea.

"No fruit left here either," Amina pointed out. "Maybe some garlic, if we are lucky."

"When I prayed over Jack in Nightingale, it was out of desperation—and Elyon heard my prayer. But since we arrived in Karachi, he has not gotten better." Emma's amber eyes scanned the marketplace. "He needs an experienced healer."

"We have traveled here daily since we arrived. No one has appeared."

"Healers are known to linger near gateways." From her pocket, Emma retrieved a silver coin etched with a moon and stars. "It is time we revealed ourselves."

Amina squeezed Emma's arm. "You have more to consider."

"Today, we try to save one—then tomorrow, we worry about the others."

From the steeple they took a flight of stairs down to the market square. As they walked between pushcarts and stalls, their dusty boots kicked up dirt. Emma glanced between vendors and shoppers bargaining for the best deal. Without her gifts, she'd become more cautious, yet strangely her connection to Jack had only grown stronger. She felt his pain and guilt. And she was willing to risk revealing herself as one of the chosen, knowing there was more at stake than losing him. As a child, she'd been taught by the highest Cherub to believe in miracles. But she worried that before her eighteenth birthday, Eden's Star would vanish in death before the compass led them to the light.

Amina asked under her breath, "Who do we give the coin to, then?"

"Many Cherub follow in the rituals of old." Emma nodded toward a stall where young goats and lambs were corralled in a pen. "The Eternal speaks of unblemished atonement."

Amina's nose wrinkled. "Animal sacrifices are a horrible idea."

"Most are symbolic these days." Emma approached a weathered

elderly man with a thick graying beard, who was busy tending to one of his goats. "Peace be upon you."

"Peace also be with you." His curious stare narrowed as he nodded toward the clock tower. "You never buy, only watch."

"We are searching for our brothers and sisters." Pulling her sleeve up, Emma turned her wrist and revealed a symbol. 勇氣. *Courage.* At the same time, Amina turned her head sideways to reveal an identical tattoo behind her left ear. Watching the man closely, Emma held out the silver coin in the palm of her hand. "Perhaps you are one of us."

He eyed the silver coin, then stepped back. "I cannot help you."

"Then make an introduction to someone who will," Amina pressed.

"A dangerous request." He glanced past them and continued in a lowered voice. "Since the great Elder's death, most have remained in Kati Pahari." He gazed at the coin long and hard. "You must be more careful—Merikh rule Karachi."

Emma slipped the silver coin into her pocket and leaned in close. "We need a healer."

"A healer?" His brows raised as he shifted uncomfortably. "You speak of Faizan Khalid."

"Will we find Faizan in Kati Pahari?" Amina asked.

The man nodded slowly. "He is the one you seek."

A weak high-pitched noise interrupted them as the young goats and sheep grew agitated in the corral. Emma's eyes darted around before she noticed two men talking with the security guard at the entrance. The guard pointed in her direction. Stepping back from the stall, she grabbed Amina's arm and pulled her alongside. They walked briskly through the market, neither one looking back.

"How could anyone possibly know we are here?" Emma whispered.

"This way," Amina urged. "Quickly."

A commotion erupted behind them as goats and sheep escaped the corral and scurried through the crowd, the elderly man chasing after them. Emma glanced over her shoulder at the bottleneck where their pursuers struggled to force their way through. Taking advantage of the distraction, Emma and Amina darted between stalls and climbed a rickety wooden ladder. Reaching the top of a wall, they moved swiftly across a ledge as the two men appeared below.

Amina blurted, "We forgot the garlic."

"That is the least of our worries."

Concrete exploded behind them, sending fragments scattering across the marketplace. Emma and Amina sprinted along the top of the wall, their steps creeping closer to the edge. Without slowing stride, they leapt off the ledge and slammed against bamboo scaffolding surrounding a Roman Catholic church under renovation. Emma climbed up to an open window and pulled herself through, then helped Amina inside and caught her breath.

Across from the church was a gaping hole in the marketplace wall where the two men stood glaring in her direction. Emma stepped back a split second before a supernatural percussive force ripped through the side of the church. With the floor crumbling beneath her, she chased Amina across the room before bursting into an empty corridor. The force hunted after them as they bounded down the stairs and darted into a main sanctuary that had been totally gutted.

"We are powerless to fight back," Emma said.

"A day will come," Amina replied. "But it is not today."

Exiting through a side door, they found themselves standing in a vacant parking lot. They headed down the street, racing between bulldozers and cranes—as if they were leading Rowell and Crozier in a dance at the Sword and Fan. Traffic flowed steadily across five lanes while Emma flagged down a chingchi—an auto-rickshaw.

"Seven Tides Hostel near Rojhan Street," Amina instructed the driver as she and Emma slipped into a passenger seat. "Five hundred rupees if you get us there in the next twenty minutes."

Emma glanced back through a glassless window of the passenger carriage as the chingchi revved and whined through traffic. She watched the men enter the church, knowing she and Amina would never be able to return to Empress Market again.

"At least we have a name," she whispered.

Amina turned toward her. "Hopefully Faizan Khalid is a true healer."

Dark clouds loomed over the city as a torrential downpour washed away clues of where they'd been and where they were going. A war waged in the shadows for centuries now left the fate of all who believed in the beating heart of an outlier.

2

NEAR KARACHI HARBOUR, across from Shaheed Benazir Bhutto Park, Emma and Amina stepped out from Pranzo Restaurant with their hoodies pulled over their heads. They moved north along Rojhan Street while a deluge of a storm flooded the sidewalk. Streaks of rain crept down their cheeks and dripped off the bridges of their noses. Amina gripped a plastic bag as they escaped into the stale lobby of their hostel while the downpour intensified.

They greeted a young man working behind the counter, then took a stairwell to the second floor and knocked on a door. A moment passed before the door cracked open. Vince peered out cautiously before he pulled the door wide enough for them to slip inside.

The simple living area was sparsely furnished with a cheap

lacquered coffee table, wooden chairs, a sofa, and a small flat-screen TV. It opened onto a kitchenette and two bedrooms, but there was only one bathroom—which had proven to be the greatest challenge while Emma, Amina, Vince, Tim, and Jack remained holed up in the hostel for weeks. Their backpacks were lined up near the door beside a garbage bag overflowing with Styrofoam take-out boxes.

"Any luck?" Vince asked, skeptical.

Amina set the plastic bag on the coffee table. "We have the name of a healer."

"That's good news." Vince nodded toward the bedroom. "He's getting worse."

Amina grabbed paper plates from a countertop. "We are being hunted."

"Merikh or Cherub?"

"We do not know who they are or how they found us." Emma removed her soaked hoodie and laid it over the back of a chair. "But they are closer than we imagined."

Vince glanced at the plates on the coffee table. "How much cash is left?"

"If we tighten our belts another notch," Amina quipped, "enough for a fortnight or three."

Tim looked up from the sofa and turned his tablet around. "Mum and Dad say hello."

On the screen, Elis and Beca Lloyd smiled warmly. In the bottom right corner of the screen was a Messagezilla icon confirming a secured untraceable connection. Emma, Amina, and Vince huddled around the tablet, peering over Tim's shoulder.

"It is so good to see you," Amina said. "Tim has missed you terribly."

"We have missed him very much, especially today," Mrs. Lloyd replied. "Of course, each one of you are missed and have remained unceasingly in our prayers."

"Heard you talking about money," Mr. Lloyd interrupted. "We can wire if needed."

"Mr. Lloyd, you are so thoughtful," Amina answered. "But it is too dangerous."

"Have you heard from my parents?" Emma chimed in. "Are they alive?"

"The highest Cherub are still searching, dear," Mrs. Lloyd replied. "Many have gone underground, so it is quite possible your mum and dad have done the same."

"Have you seen Will?" Vince asked. "Has he asked about us?"

"Elis?" Mrs. Lloyd glanced toward Mr. Lloyd, then back to the screen. "Amina, we visited with your parents earlier this morning, and they are remaining strong."

"Thank you." Amina's eyes grew glossy. "Please tell them I love them."

"Mum, you never said anything to me about going underground," Tim cut in.

"Much has changed since you have been gone," Mr. Lloyd answered. "But we are safe."

"And where are you, exactly?"

A long pause lingered before Mrs. Lloyd replied, "Beacon Hill."

Her words sucked the oxygen from the room and left everyone speechless until Amina broke the silence. "We thought the school was closed."

"What has been broken with the Mercy Covenant cannot be undone." Mr. Lloyd's brows furrowed. "Frankly, no one seems to know the exact moment when the covenant was broken. Rumors are spreading that it was undone by the Elders many years ago. Regardless, now the highest Cherub are demanding a new circle of Elders be formed. Bickering and arguing among ourselves, seeking vengeance against the one who murdered Peter Leung, and searching for those responsible for the massacre at the Sanctuary of Prayer on Mount Hareh. We were once united; however, these events have caused some to choose the faction as a place to hide."

Emma's gaze shifted between the screen and Amina. "Do they know it is Jack?"

"Secrets are never buried deep enough." Mrs. Lloyd's gaze turned solemn. "The highest Cherub were given his name by someone within the Merikh. We do not know who that might be, so we are keeping to ourselves for now."

"He will be proven justified," Amina reassured. "Truth is on his side."

"We can only pray the highest Cherub choose to accept it," Mr. Lloyd warned.

"Since the Mercy Covenant is broken," Vince said, "why return to Beacon Hill?"

"Exactly what I was going to ask," Tim blurted. "Mum . . . Dad . . . are you *mad*?"

"Merikh hunt those believed to be hiding your whereabouts," Mr. Lloyd answered. "If we remained in Singapore, they would have found us. In these days the world around us is darker, but we are convinced there is a light at Beacon Hill that will protect us."

"We are grateful to be among those who have found refuge here as we prepare for what lies ahead . . ." Mrs. Lloyd's voice trailed off.

Vince asked, "Have you seen my mom and dad at Beacon Hill?"

"We know they are staying on their yacht in Repulse Bay," Mr. Lloyd noted. "Both have questioned the resolve of the HKPF investigation, and they have publicly accused Headmaster Fargher of lying about your disappearance. Understandable, of course."

"Please don't tell them anything," Vince begged. "Less they know, the better."

"There may come a time when they will need to know, no matter the risk."

"Have you made any progress?" Mrs. Lloyd asked.

"We are still alive, talking to you." Tim smirked. "That is progress, I guess."

Emma glanced toward the bedroom. "Sharing too much creates a greater danger."

"Well, it is good you are together," Mrs. Lloyd said warmly. "Watch out for each other."

"That is the plan." Tim blinked several times, catching the tears welling up. "Mum and Dad, we have to go, but I will message you in a few days."

"May your search for answers be greater than your fear," Mr. Lloyd said. "We love you, Timothy. Your mum and I have never been more proud of you."

Emma slipped into the bedroom while Tim said goodbye and disconnected Messagezilla. She left the door open as Amina and Vince gathered around the coffee table.

Inside the bedroom, a soft glow illuminated stained paint peeling from a ceiling directly above a curled-up body on the bed. Seated on the edge of the mattress, Emma watched Jack's shallow breathing then reached out and touched his forehead, which was blazing hot. She ran her fingers across a scar on his brow and continued her touch over deep scars on his forearms from the Temple of the Nephilim. Even though he was drenched in sweat, his body was shivering. Her heartbeat quickened when his pale-blue eyes opened and gazed up at her.

"How are you feeling, Jack?"

"Like I've been run over by a train," he groaned. "A thousand times."

"Better than yesterday, then," she mused sadly. "Are you hungry?"

"Let me guess, my favorite . . . catfish and rice."

Emma helped him out of bed and shouldered his weight. Spread across his bare chest was a crude reminder of Eden's Star living within him. She helped slip a shirt over his bony body, then supported his weight as he shuffled gingerly toward the living room.

"We need to leave in the morning," she whispered. "It is no longer safe here."

"I know," he grunted.

3

Jack slumped onto the sofa as the others scooted chairs closer and gathered around the coffee table, where two take-out boxes awaited them. Emma dished up catfish and rice on paper plates. Two orders stretched to five with leftovers. While it was miraculous, it was a far cry from the delicacies they'd enjoyed at Beacon Hill or the handmade dumplings from Olivia Fargher. Emma handed Jack a plate and fork, which he gripped with trembling hands. He avoided locking eyes with Vince or Tim, ashamed he had failed to become the hero everyone expected.

I've never been more determined, but my body's never felt more broken.

When the others closed their eyes during Emma's prayer, his gaze shifted between them as he listened to Dabria's voice echo in his foggy mind.

"Dreams are reflections of our imagination, but visions from Elyon are rooted and inspired in truth."

The nightmares had faded, but the visions continued, and they seemed to be happening closer to real time. He had woken earlier that afternoon to flashes from Empress Market through Emma's eyes. He had seen the men chasing Emma and Amina—neither of them were Michael Chung. It would be simpler to believe they were Merikh, but he knew more than anyone that others were hunting him too.

Never thought I'd be a fugitive—and I never thought I'd be an enemy of others who believe in Elyon. Everyone I can trust is in this room.

Setting his fork on the plate, he clenched his fist and tried to control a tremor in his hand. As his index finger twitched, he grew even more convinced that killing left scars so deep in one's soul it was impossible for those wounds to fully heal. Ending a life revered by millions of Cherub around the world meant harsh consequences—for all of them.

Who will kill me first for my sin? Cherub? Merikh? Elyon?

"Beacon Hill is a refuge," Tim said in disbelief. "You were right, mate."

Jack snapped out of his thoughts and mumbled, "Did you ask about Will?"

"I tried, but neither of them answered," Vince replied. "Fargher is probably keeping him safe under lock and key. And I'll bet Natalie is guarding his every move."

"We have the name of a healer," Amina chimed in. "Faizan Khalid."

"Before sunrise, we will leave for Kati Pahari," Emma added.

"Finally," Tim exhaled, "we are paroled from solitary confinement."

Amina reached over and squeezed Tim's thigh. "Show everyone what you found."

"Right." Tim popped up, nearly knocking over the coffee table. He retrieved his tablet and slipped back onto his chair. Pushing his black-framed glasses up the bridge of his nose, he swiped across the screen before flipping the tablet around. "So we know about Nightingale's sketches, but it dawned on me that in all of Rachel's journals there is only one page with a drawing—and it's quite incredible."

On the screen was displayed a king cypress tree. A thick trunk jutted from the ground with giant horizontal branches casting a massive crown over vibrant crimson plants and lush emerald grass. Copper-colored dirt faded at the edges of the page.

Jack noticed the intricate detail in every stroke. He had never known Rachel to be a skilled artist—a poet, yes, but never one to create a work of art so masterful. He stared hard at the drawing before his gaze shifted to words scribbled across the bottom.

"Elyon's Vine," he read aloud. "What does it mean?"

"In the ancient Cherub writings, trees are symbols of life." Amina pointed at the screen. "Elyon is the true vine from the first Garden that never withers, only bears fruit for those branches that remain rooted to the vine."

Emma grabbed a napkin and wiped a trickle of blood from Jack's nose. "We are called to bring healing, but apart from Elyon we can do nothing to reach the lost."

"If we remain rooted to the vine," Amina interjected, "we will be protected in the hottest fires."

"Even when the darkest forces stand against us."

"The hottest fires," Jack mumbled. "Sounds familiar." He

remembered Xui Li's words as if he were still walking next to her in Metro Manila:

"After the first sin in the Garden, Elyon crafted Eden's Star in the hottest fires to remove all impurity from the gold. From the beginning of time, Cherub were chosen by Elyon as protectors of the artifacts—when Eden's Star was created as a compass. Its true powers have never been revealed—which is why the artifacts have remained hidden for thousands of years."

She'd told him that a lifetime ago, it seemed.

Amina got up from her chair, retrieved a small box from the refrigerator, and set it on the coffee table. Holding a plastic knife and a candle in one hand, she opened the box with the other.

"Speaking of fire," she began, "we only have one candle—"

"No way," Tim blurted. "You remembered."

"Sorry it's not dim sum this year," Vince said.

Inside the box was a fresh kalakand—Pakistani cheesecake—with chopped nuts sprinkled over the top. It was Tim's favorite kind of dessert, and Jack guessed neither Amina nor Emma second-guessed spending the extra money.

"Happy birthday, Tim!" Amina announced. "You are *finally* eighteen."

Vince pulled a lighter from his pocket and lit the candle. "Better use of this than normal."

"I'm not the only one," Tim bantered. "You know fish messes with my digestion."

"That's one way to explain it."

"In the Keepers' present paradise," Emma sang with a smile, "this flame is a light to remember dinnas of catfish and rice." Her voice crescendoed as if she were singing in the Sydney Opera

House. "From new friends to old, may you never change with your heart of gold."

"Paradise," Vince chuckled. "Heart of gold?"

"Only words I could think of that rhymed," Emma laughed. "'Room of mice' didn't seem appropriate, even though it is likely more true."

"You are loved by all of us." Amina kissed Tim on the cheek. "Especially—me."

"Well, this is a birthday I won't soon forget."

"My dad once told me that wealth comes and goes." Vince squeezed Tim's shoulder and grinned. "And you are only guaranteed the richness of friendships for today."

"Right . . ." Tim wiped his eyes with his sleeve. "That's a good one to remember."

Jack remained quiet while Tim's face turned beet red as he leaned forward and blew out the candle. Breathing in deep, Jack allowed himself a brief escape from the torment that ravaged every second of every day. Leaning back, he eyed the tablet where the king cypress tree seemed to flicker with glints of violet and aurum.

What else did you see before you died, Rachel?

4

GALE-FORCE WINDS WHIPPED around Jack while he crawled through thick grass one agonizing inch at a time. The king cypress with its massive crown swayed violently as blistering ice whisked through the frigid air. *CRACK!* Branches ripped from the thick trunk, launching like spears in battle. A sharp-edged branch pierced the copper dirt beside him as he rolled onto his side. Thunder rumbled through the heavens, and he dug his fingers into the earth. He pressed his elbows deeper into the soil, desperate to move forward.

From clustered vines, a shadow emerged carrying a gold chest carved with intricate figures. *The Testimony*. Two gigantic flaming swords swooped down from the heavens and swung side to side in front of Elyon's Vine, as if protecting the king cypress from further intrusion. Royal blues morphed with reddish oranges in the fire that surged from the blades, leaving flickers of gold floating in the air.

Lightning bolts streaked across gunmetal skies with a brilliant white light, striking the ground with a resounding earthquake. An ominous silence deafened Jack as he stared beyond the flaming swords. A vibrant world shifted to black and white with shades of dull grays. The king cypress was left a charred, disfigured trunk with withered branches. Elyon's Vine was dead. The shadowy figure and the Testimony were gone. All that was left of the magnificent color palette were swords of fire sweeping around the king cypress.

"I am looking for two teenage girls," a voice said. "Asian and African tourists."

Breathing in deep, Jack blinked several times as the voice faded. Many seconds passed before he realized he'd been left on the sofa. *Must've fallen asleep after Tim and Vince finished off my piece of kalakand. I was having another vision, but the voice isn't part of it.* Jack struggled to sit upright.

"What's wrong?" Vince whispered in the dark. "You're wrestling the blanket."

"I heard a voice," Jack mumbled.

Footsteps pattered across the room, and a light switched on. Vince wasted no time as he darted into one of the bedrooms, then reappeared and knocked on the second door. Jack lay back helpless while the others gathered in the living room, barely awake but fully dressed.

"Someone is looking for Emma and Amina," Jack said in a hushed voice.

"Do you know where they are?" Emma asked.

"I think they're downstairs in the hostel."

"That's just great," Tim grumbled. "I have officially celebrated my last birthday."

Amina grabbed a backpack near the door. "We need to leave."

"All we have done for weeks is hide." Vince snatched two

backpacks from the floor and slipped one over each shoulder. "There has to be a better way to find the artifacts than waiting to get caught."

"If they do not find us tonight," Tim added, "then it will be another."

Jack noticed all eyes were glued on him. He was their way to disappear. The last time he used Eden's Star, he nearly died on Karābu Island. Ever since then, the uncontrollable power of the compass crippled his body with each passing hour. He waved Vince over to help him to his feet, then slipped into his boots.

"We can give it a try," he suggested. "See where it takes us."

Emma stepped forward. "You will not survive, Jack."

"If we're caught, then we're dead for sure." Jack's legs were shaky as he wrapped one arm over Vince's shoulder and the other over Emma's. The whole group formed a tight, interlocked circle. "Time we stop hiding from whatever is ahead."

"You cannot control the compass," Tim warned. "We all remember last time."

"No matter where we end up, we're out of choices." With a clenched jaw, Jack mustered up another ounce of strength. "I made a promise—until the very end."

"Let me be on the record—this is a bad idea."

"Noted." Vince squeezed Jack's shoulder. "Let's get on with it."

"Faizan Khalid in Kati Pahari," Emma said. "That is where we need to go."

Jack exhaled long and coughed. "Right—the healer."

Spending his days mostly bedridden had forced Jack to try and turn his focus toward Elyon faster than he would've if he'd been strong enough to choose on his own. He was ready to see what was ahead, because looking back had only left him weaker. Closing his eyes, he attempted to surrender his spirit—most of it anyway. A piece of his soul remained pierced by the dark silhouette inside the Pyramid of Stars, and that piece wanted revenge.

The glorious encounter inside the chapel on Karābu flashed in his mind. A warmth had spread across his chest and raged into an inferno surging through his veins. Purity had reflected the heart of Elyon, so powerful that it created a blinding wave of energy. Squeezing his eyelids tight, Jack tried to muster up the same experience.

A knock at the door left them frozen. Rattled, Jack opened his eyes and glanced at the others, knowing he was useless in a fight. Silence lingered until the lock clicked. Vince let go of Jack and moved with purpose toward the door as it cracked open. Ready to pounce, everyone stood stunned when a young Pakistani slipped inside. He was no older than they were. His wild black hair and dark-olive skin were contrasted by a light-blue salwar kameez—an extra-long shirt over wide-leg trousers cuffed at the bottom—and a black cotton vest.

The Pakistani raised both hands. "I am Faizan."

"How do we know you're telling the truth?" Vince asked point-blank.

"You approached my uncle at the market." He pointed toward Emma and Amina. "One of you showed him a silver coin carried only by the chosen."

"That does not answer how you found us," Tim said.

"All day I searched the hostels around Karachi," he replied calmly. "I am here to help, not harm."

"Which means others will do the same," Amina said. "Do you know who the men were at the market who tried to capture us?"

"My uncle said they were Merikh—but they displayed gifts of the Cherub." Faizan glanced over his shoulder as he pushed the door shut, then turned and eyed them closely. "One of you is sick, yes?"

"That would be me." Jack raised his arm halfway. "You are a healer?"

"A gift granted to me from Elyon since I was a young boy."

"Can you do it here?" Vince asked.

"Not possible." Faizan shook his head. "You must come with me to Kati Pahari."

"I for one am exhausted from being locked up," Tim said, a bit relieved. "Jack?"

"Faizan, we'll introduce ourselves on the way," Jack answered. "We'll follow you."

With backpacks slung over their shoulders, they left the cramped room and moved quietly down the corridor. Vince carried Jack in his arms as Faizan led them down a flight of stairs. Exiting the rear of the hostel, they arrived at a minibus parked in the alley. Faizan unlocked the doors, and everyone piled inside while he slipped behind the wheel.

In most cities, the abstract psychedelic patterns swirling on the outside of the minibus would have garnered everyone's attention. But here in Karachi, the minibus rolled out from the alley onto city streets and blended in with early morning traffic.

"Which one of you is the chosen?" Faizan asked, curious.

Jack nearly answered before he realized Faizan's attention was on Emma, who was seated in the front passenger seat. Emma retrieved a silver coin and held it between her fingers.

"There is also one other," she said in a lowered voice. "He is not here with us."

"I have dreamed of seeing one of the chosen with my own eyes." Faizan glanced in the rearview mirror, and his eyes locked in on Jack. "I am sure you have much wisdom to share with us from the great Elder, may his soul rest in Elyon's arms."

5

OUTSKIRTS OF KARACHI

ON A ONE-LANE HIGHWAY cutting through the center of a mountain range, the minibus sped alongside an overstuffed diesel truck spewing fumes of heavy exhaust. Chingchis whined up the mountain toward the peak before coasting downhill into the city center. Jack counted dozens of forest-green flags waving from power poles—each one bearing a tilted white crescent moon and a star, with a vertical stripe at the hoist end.

One symbol meant to unite an entire country.

Before reaching the next flag, Faizan steered off the main highway and looped around onto a narrow winding road. Trash was scattered on both sides as they drove through an outdoor market beneath a long stretch of palm trees. Iron gates to local district shops were bolted shut. Stacks of rubber tires appeared regularly. Power lines crisscrossed above concrete buildings in a maze connecting to a single electrical tower.

"Elyon's light shines bright this day," Faizan said. "You bring new hope."

"Thank you for helping us," Emma replied.

"When my uncle told us what happened at the market, we were shocked you have been in Karachi for so long. He said he watched you for weeks but was not sure who you were until you showed him the coin. We have heard stories of the great powers given to the chosen. I am honored to be in your presence."

"We each serve a greater purpose, but we must be careful who we reveal ourselves to, as the Merikh are searching for us." Emma glanced over her shoulder. "Faizan, it is extremely important that you help our friend."

"Merikh attacked in Karachi, and they are searching for Cherub in Kati Pahari." Faizan kept his gaze straight ahead. "Those who believe are forced to hide."

"Maybe she should tell him we have no clue what we are doing," Tim mumbled.

Jack listened quietly to the conversation and the grumbling. He knew Emma was building a connection with Faizan because they needed him. And he recognized Tim had been growing increasingly agitated, especially in recent days. Patience wasn't his strongest trait, and he was spending his birthday on the run from the Merikh.

He's not wrong. Elyon, we need a sign, please.

"You doing okay?" Vince whispered.

"Better than earlier." Jack breathed easier the farther they traveled from the hostel, which had ended up being more like house arrest than a hideout. *So much time wasted curled up in the dark—too much time.* "I'm hopeful, I guess."

"Can you heal him?" Amina asked from the back seat.

Faizan glanced in the rearview. "I am not the one who heals."

"Then where are we going?" Tim countered. "Your uncle said you are the bloke."

"I bring those who seek renewal of their mind, body, and spirit closer to the great healer. Healing will only come if it is Elyon's will—but there is something you must see first."

"That explains everything, then." Tim rolled his eyes. "We are on an endless roundabout."

Amina nudged Tim sharply. "Would you rather have been left behind at the hostel?"

"Of course not," Tim bantered. "I'm just saying . . . uh . . . forget it."

At the base of the mountain, their tires skidded through mud while Faizan navigated the road as if he'd driven it thousands of times. Turning a corner, the minibus started up the mountainside, lost in a sea of buildings. Pale greens. Canary yellows. Stark whites. Desert browns. The steep climb and grinding gears left each of them holding on tight. Near the top of the mountain, the minibus stopped outside a solid iron gate. Faizan honked the horn, and a few seconds passed before the gate opened and they were greeted by armed men.

"What's going on?" Vince asked.

"Do not fear," Faizan reassured. "You are among friends."

On the grounds of the hillside property, hundreds of people were crowded together with all eyes fixed on the minibus. Jack stared at their faces as the bus rolled past.

"So much for keeping this on the down-low," Vince said.

Faizan turned toward Emma. "You will bring encouragement to the faithful."

Jack waved off Vince's help as he struggled to slide off the seat and plant his boots on the dirt outside. Leaning against the minibus, he watched the crowd swarming Emma while the guards tried to keep them back. Wide smiles. Tears welling up and streaming down cheeks. An outbreak of emotion swept over the crowd as if they were seeing Elyon with their own eyes.

A young girl grabbed Emma by the hand and led her deeper into the crowd until she was completely surrounded. Jack noticed how Emma moved with ease while showing compassion for each person she touched, never glancing back to see whether he was behind her.

"An outlier guarded by one of the chosen." Faizan turned and faced Jack as they stood near the minibus. "She carries a great responsibility, and you carry a heavy burden."

"You know who I am?" A chill shot down his spine. "What I've done?"

"Cherub and Merikh call you the Executioner's spawn, and an assassin of the great Elder." Faizan paused as if weighing his words. "I have sensed an awakening stirring within the Cherub. It is why I searched the city for Emma and Amina. But this morning, Elyon whispered in my soul: *The outlier is not who they believe him to be.* I know better than to question Elyon's voice. But if my brothers and sisters become aware of who you are, it will be impossible to protect any of you."

"I've been more afraid of dying than living," Jack confessed. "What will you tell them?"

"She is chosen to lead the Cherub." Faizan nodded toward Emma. "And she needs you."

"Look at me." Jack swallowed a lump in his throat. "I'm wrecked."

"Now you have seen the lives that rest in all of your hands."

"You don't know what's inside of me—what's killing me."

"Healing comes when freedom reigns." Faizan hesitated. "There is a place filled with Elyon's mercy that will save you."

"And where might that be?" Vince chimed in, eavesdropping.

"In the Eternal it is known as the Garden—Charis, in the Valley of Grace."

Jack exhaled. "Will you lead us to where we should go?"

"I will take you as far as a gateway." Faizan waved Emma, Amina, and Tim over to the minibus. "But not all may be permitted to enter."

"Wait until you tell Tim," Vince replied. "His eighteenth birthday is going downhill."

"It is his birthday?" Faizan's eyes lit up. "We must celebrate before we leave."

6

CYMBALS CLANGED AND TAMBOURINES chimed while children sang at the top of their lungs. Tim's cheeks were rosy as he was surrounded by strangers from Kati Pahari. Jack, Vince, Amina, and Emma joined in the celebration as they sang the last note with a huge crescendo. Applause was followed by children tossing neon chalk dust into the air before the colors landed on Tim.

"Make one wish!" Vince shouted. "And you better make it a good one."

"He's loving every moment," Jack mused. "He deserves it."

"A real beaut bonza," Emma added. "You would say 'beautifully awesome.'"

"Beaut bonza," Vince said with broad smile. "I'm using that one for sure."

Amina raised her hand, attempting to get the crowd's attention. "We are so grateful for your hospitality." She paused while Faizan interpreted. "You have welcomed us on a special day and offered a precious gift to celebrate Timothy. No matter where we might be tomorrow, you have given of yourselves to help us celebrate him today. He is special—to many of us."

"May I offer Elyon's blessing?" Faizan asked Amina, who nodded her approval. He turned toward Tim, who looked as if he were caught in McDougall's crosshairs during world history. Faizan grabbed Tim by the shoulder and squeezed. "May Elyon bless you beyond your expectations, so in times of shifting shadows you will see his light guiding your path. May you go deeper in your faith and closer in community to all who believe. Elyon created you for a purpose, so may your purpose be celebrated today, and for the rest of your days."

"I'm not great at speeches." Tim cleared his throat, clearly choked up. "Thank you."

Faizan shook his hand. "You are welcome."

Several children approached and offered laddus—ball-shaped ghee-and-sugar desserts—to Jack, Vince, and Emma. Without blinking, Vince accepted three of them while Tim strutted over covered in a myriad of colors. Amina walked by his side along with a dozen more children. Jack's heart warmed as he noticed Tim's sheepish grin spread into a full-blown smile—a flicker of light amid weeks of frustration and disappointment.

"You look like a walking rainbow," Vince chuckled. "Better hope that washes off."

"Oh, we're not done celebrating," Tim replied. "Game time, superstar."

"The children are asking if we will play kabaddi," Amina said.

"Rules are very simple. You must tag as many of the opposing team on their side of the line as you can and return to your side before being tackled."

"You had me until you said *tackle*," Jack bantered. "Count me out."

"No more time for games," Emma said solemnly. "Faizan needs to heal Jack."

Jack breathed in the crisp air and exhaled slowly. "My heart is still beating, Emma."

"One game," Vince interrupted. "Then we get Faizan to follow through."

"No supernatural cheating either," Tim said to Emma. "If you're up for the challenge."

Emma smiled. "I am a kabaddi expert."

Tim's brows raised. "Seriously?"

"I do not think that was part of her training on Karābu," Amina laughed.

Vince stretched his muscles. "Who wants to be on the winning team?"

"Look at him," Tim answered. "We don't have a chance."

"We will see about that," Emma mused. "I do not like to lose."

"Whoa . . ." Tim exhaled with excitement. "Battle of the Keepers."

Emma leaned in close to Jack. "Are you sure you are okay?"

"Never better," Jack whispered. "Go easy on them."

Jack slowly shuffled over to the gathered crowd and considered the fact he didn't collapse an accomplishment. Far too many days left him struggling to get out of bed. He didn't want to bring the celebration to a halt since it might be Tim's only eighteenth birthday party. He knew all the attention lately had been centered on keeping him safe and alive. But the moment wasn't about him, and he wanted to keep it that way.

Children separated Emma and Tim on one side from Vince and Amina on the other. One of the older men selected five children to be on each team, then dropped a line of bright-red chalk dust down the center of an improvised field. Emma glanced over at Jack, who waved back, knowing she hadn't stopped keeping an eye on him for a second.

Faizan stepped alongside Jack. "Those who are on offense are known as raiders, and of course those who are on the opposite side are defenders. Points are scored for each person tagged or stopped. If they are touched or tackled, they are out of the game. But if their team scores a point, then they are back in the game."

For the next hour, the crowd cheered and laughed as the teams competed. Vince was a stellar athlete compared to the rest, but even he found himself tackled more than once by the children, who pounced aggressively and without fear. One of the highlight-reel tackles was from Emma, who lowered her shoulder and caught Vince squarely in the chest, sending him tumbling across the ground. Amina subbed herself out of the game while Tim shouted his play-by-play, which only added to the excitement. Before long, the point spread didn't matter, and the game ended with both sides exhausted.

Jack thought about what Faizan had told them earlier. *"I will take you as far as a gateway. But not all may be permitted to enter."*

He felt a twinge of pain ripple down his spine. "Raiders and defenders, huh?"

"I have always been more of a defender," Faizan admitted. "You?"

"Raider—definitely a raider."

7

AFTER THE IMPROMPTU EIGHTEENTH BIRTHDAY celebration, Jack sat on the edge of the minibus bumper and watched the crowd gravitate again toward Emma. He noticed Amina shadowing Emma with a cell phone in one hand. *Why is she filming Emma? Hope she's not going to post on the* Beacon. *That'd be crazy.* Gazing upon the faces of those he'd never met until hours earlier, the weight of what they were attempting to find pressed down on his shoulders. He snapped out of his thoughts as Tim approached, covered in more neon chalk dust and sweat.

"So what was your wish?" Jack asked.

"That we'll make it out of this alive." Tim grew quiet for a moment. "You know, Faizan is an old soul, but he's just a bloke like us."

Jack nodded slowly. "He definitely talks like he's been born and bred in the Cherub."

"I was raised in the Cherub, but I don't speak that way, do I?"

"You're too busy snoring louder than a T10 typhoon." Jack smiled half-heartedly. "Don't worry, I'm sure you'll be quoting the Eternal in your sleep before this is over."

Tim chuckled. "Mum and Dad would lose their minds."

"I know it hasn't been easy, and none of this has worked out how we hoped."

"Even though I get a bit grumpy—okay, a ton grumpy—we are all doing our best."

"It still seems so impossible."

Jack's mind flashed to the Temple of the Nephilim. He allowed the memory to flow through his veins. At first, he'd been shadowed by the deadliest of sins, and he had failed until he stood side by side with Rachel, Areum, and his mom. *Hard to believe it happened, but it did.* He'd never forget how each woman was poised for battle in their angelic armor. *The prophecy is yours to fulfill.* Bloodied, desperate, and pained by a pierced soul, he'd made a promise before he escaped the temple with Eden's Star. *"I will not let your sacrifices be for nothing."* A promise he refused to break—but so far one he had failed to keep.

Let go of doubt, hold on to truth, and mountains will be moved.

Elyon's voice snapped him out of his thoughts and echoed in his soul. Weeks had passed since he'd heard anything from Elyon. Plenty of nights he wondered if all he'd seen and encountered was simply his imagination. *Maybe I haven't been listening, but I know what I've seen since Rachel died.*

Jack had been consumed with a fear that Eden's Star would explode in his chest and leave him dead in an alley somewhere in

Karachi. He wrestled within as if he were wrestling Elyon himself, which only left him filled with more dread about the days ahead. Bitter from the pain rifling through his body, he'd allowed his heart to harden as the desire for vengeance seeped deeper into his bones.

"If he's not going to heal you," Tim said, "how long do we stay?"

"Faizan brought us here to remind us who we are fighting to protect." Jack white-knuckled the bumper. "And he wanted to show them hope."

"Do you really think Emma will become the next Cherub leader?" Tim pushed his thick black frames up the bridge of his nose. "I heard her talking with Amina a few nights ago, and my parents said something yesterday. The highest Cherub are searching for a new leader, but it doesn't sound like they are looking for Emma. If they find out she's been hanging out with you, then she'll be an outcast. Sorry, mate. But it's true."

"She's the only one I'd trust." Jack eyed several of the armed men as they walked toward the iron gate. "Faizan is going to take us to a gateway that leads to the Valley of Grace."

"Sounds peaceful—but why are we going there?"

"He said it's known in the Eternal as Charis."

Tim's blank stare was evident. "I haven't read it since I was like seven or eight."

"Charis is a place filled with Elyon's mercy that will save me."

"You mean, like heal you completely?"

"I wish I could say I believe Faizan, but I won't know until I'm there." Jack shrugged. "When we get to the gateway, there's something I'll need you to do."

The iron gate swung open, and a caravan of pickup trucks rolled into the compound. Armed men jumped from vehicles, weapons raised. Faizan rushed toward them, waving his arms frantically while shouting in Urdu. Jack couldn't understand a single word, but the weapons aimed at him sent a clear message.

"Step back," Jack whispered to Tim. "Right now."

"No way." Tim stood an inch taller. "I am not going anywhere."

Faizan shoved his way through the crowd and stood between Jack and the armed men. With weapons pointed toward his chest, Jack knew every heartbeat might be his last. His pulse raced like a Formula One car, but he was too weak to run. A woman climbed out of one of the trucks and walked briskly toward them as the crowd stepped back.

"Khala," Faizan called with hands raised. "I beg you."

"You have brought wolves into our home, Nephew."

Out of the corner of his eye, Jack caught sight of Vince charging through the crowd with Emma and Amina right behind. Outnumbered, they were forced back while Faizan was pushed aside. Jack swallowed hard, expecting the worst.

"My name is Salomeh Gashkori," the woman announced as she stepped closer. "I am the highest Cherub shepherd in all of Pakistan." Dressed in a royal blue and gold-embroidered collarless tunic, flat slippers, and a pair of jhumkas in her ears, her dark-brown eyes flickered with confidence and authority. "You are Addison's son."

Jack clenched his fists to stop them from shaking. "I am."

"Many of my dearest brothers and sisters were murdered on Mount Hareh."

"Peter Leung was a traitor to the Cherub."

"Anyone who takes the life of the innocent must be sentenced to death." Salomeh motioned to her men, who stepped forward and forced Jack to his knees. A hush swept over the crowd. "You killed the greatest among us."

"You are mistaken." Faizan pleaded. "Khala, he is protected by one of the chosen."

Salomeh stopped cold and glared at Jack. "You are a liar too?"

"Your nephew doesn't know what he's talking about. No one is protecting me."

Her eyes narrowed and her lips pursed. "Bring the others forward."

The men brought Emma, Amina, and Vince through the crowd until all five stood face-to-face with Salomeh. Reaching out her hand, Emma revealed a pile of silver coins.

"We bring an offering," she said. "Each one given by the great Elder."

Salomeh studied the coins intently. "What is your name?"

"Emma Bennett. My parents are—"

"Oliver and Winnie."

8

BEACON HILL

BENEATH GUNMETAL CLOUDS, a heavily padlocked gate blocked outsiders from entering a winding road leading to the Main Hall. Perched atop the two-story building, the clock tower's hands remained frozen at 11:47. A worn Union Jack whipped in a brisk wind, as if pointing toward a pile of rubble left in the quad. Nightingale, Rowell, Crozier, and Upsdell houses remained abandoned.

Emerging from the Chinese elm hedges in the Oasis of Remembrance, Natalie McNaughton flipped her collar up, a holstered weapon visible beneath her unbuttoned coat. Natalie moved quickly through the memorial garden. Once-blooming plum blossoms were dead vines, and the flower beds were starved of life. Her weathered boots kicked up dirt amid patches of withered grass. She glanced briefly toward the ginkgo tree and concrete stone.

IN LOVING MEMORY OF OLIVIA FARGHER
THE LIGHT OF HER SOUL REMAINS
FOREVER IN THE VINE

Natalie climbed the steps toward a back entrance to the Main Hall. As she slipped inside, her footsteps echoed off the stone walls. Inch-thick dust covered the marble floors in the atrium, and an eerie silence filled the hallways and classrooms.

From the shadows, Bau Hu emerged. "The headmaster is waiting for you."

"Good. I have news from Ming." Natalie continued past the display case, where her reflection was dulled by a cobwebbed House Champions trophy. The engraved crest of a golden lion grew more faded with each passing day. Even the Battle of the Bashers, Bowlers, and Boundaries trophy seemed to have lost its shine. "Heard you were summoned."

"I was chosen by the great Elder on Karābu." Bau walked alongside her. "No matter my age, it is my duty to accept."

"From what I understand, a final decision has not been made." Natalie reached the second floor before entering Rowell Library. "You are one of several under consideration."

"Since Emma chose to leave, I am the only one here with gifts strong enough."

"You may have saved Beacon Hill, but that does not make you a leader."

"No one has heard from Emma since she left. She is the one

who told me to take her place." Bau kept stride but turned quiet for a moment. "Jack killed the great Elder, and he will be held accountable for his sins. No one will be able to protect him, not even Emma."

"We are all sinners." Natalie continued through the library, crunching over shattered glass beneath boarded-up windows. "No sin is greater than another."

She couldn't stop herself from the last jab, knowing Bau's intent. *Sin is relentless when someone is tempted enough to make the wrong choice. How could what Jack did be a sin?* In the dim light, she headed down an aisle where thousands of books gathered dust. She ignored the cobwebbed bronze statues of humanity's icons including Sir James Nightingale, and dozens of black-and-white photos depicting the essence of Hong Kong over the centuries.

Bau pressed his finger against the clock tower on a muted oil painting of Beacon Hill, and a tide rolled across the canvas as shades of gray rippled into three-dimensional art. Natalie led the way through to the other side and headed down a narrow spiral staircase illuminated by an incandescent light bulb. She heard Bau's footsteps behind her but refrained from further conversation.

"You were supposed to be back hours ago." Headmaster Fargher sauntered over with Professor McDougall and Professor Windsor on each side. "We were worried."

"I had to hike up Mount Austin from Central." She reached beneath her coat and removed a folder. "But it was worth it."

Natalie and the others now stood in Nightingale's vault—an enormous space lined with rows of incandescent lamps casting a soft glow. Within the vault, people milled about between makeshift stations. One area was lined with dozens of cots, while another was sectioned off with folding tables and chairs. Laundry hung on ropes tied to WWII-era military vehicles, while children pretended to drive the 1940 Delahaye 135 convertible. Yellow tape blocked the center aisle toward the back of the vault—off-limits to everyone.

"Detective Ming has not been helpful as of late," McDougall cautioned.

"She found a reeducation camp where Merikh are holding Cherub." Natalie motioned them over to an empty table, removed surveillance photos from the folder, then laid them out side by side. Each snapshot showed groups of people gathered along a fence line. Some were barely clothed, while others were clearly beaten. She had seen the photos earlier, and still her stomach twisted into knots the longer she stared at them.

"Do you think Will, Tim, and Amina are there?" Bau asked.

"It is possible, I suppose." Headmaster Fargher scratched his thick beard, which covered his gaunt face. His wrinkled shirt and jeans hung loosely over his bony body. "And it seems there are many others who have been captured."

Professor Windsor nodded toward several photos. "Clear signs of malnutrition."

"What are we supposed to do with this, Freddie?" Professor McDougall waved his crooked finger at the people around them. "We can barely take care of ourselves, let alone launch a hail Crozier rescue mission."

"HKPF determined these camps to be under the PRC's rule, which means there is no chance they will enter," Natalie replied. "Ming believes there are moles within the department who are operating alongside Merikh and the PRC." She noticed that Fargher's grayish pupils had grown paler than ever. "If there is a chance, we have to try."

9

KATI PAHARI, PAKISTAN

SHUFFLING ACROSS A DIRT FLOOR, Jack reached a bunk bed and gripped the metal tight. His head spun and his legs shook as he lowered himself onto the bottom bunk. Dozens of other bunks were lined in rows, each with a pillow and folded blanket. His gaze shifted between Emma and Salomeh while he listened with great intent.

"You know the names of my parents," Emma said.

"We have been friends for many years, since long before you were dedicated in the Sanctuary of Prayer. Your amber eyes were fiery then as they are now."

"Are they alive?" Emma asked point-blank. "Have you seen them?"

"I am afraid no one has heard from them. But we remain hopeful."

"Did Faizan tell you we would be here today?"

"Word of what occurred at Empress Market reached me in Bahria Town. My brother was worried when you were given his son's name as a healer by our eldest brother. Faizan is pure in his soul, and he is blessed with wonderful gifts. However, I have warned my family many times that Faizan's innocence in the Cherub faith will get him killed if we do not watch over him."

Jack noticed how Salomeh never broke eye contact with Emma, as if she were being interrogated by one of her peers and not a teenager. He mumbled, "You traveled here with armed guards, and there are even more within the gates. Why?"

"Do you think all we do is read the Eternal and pray?" Salomeh locked her icy glare on him. "Elyon calls us to protect the light when we are surrounded by darkness. But you have chosen justice by your own hands."

"At the market," Emma interrupted, "were those men Cherub or Merikh?"

"Surely the great Elder taught that only Cherub possess such gifts."

"But we've seen Merikh with superpowers." Jack recognized Salomeh's veiled stare. *She's not surprised.* "Are you saying Michael Chung is a Cherub?"

"Many years ago, he was. However, he is now the Elders' greatest disappointment." Salomeh paused. "Since the Garden, many have questioned whether those who turn from Elyon lose their gifts entirely. Perhaps if one is lured by the Merikh, those gifts remain. Not even the Elders or the highest Cherub can answer this question for certain."

Words from Rachel's diary echoed within.

There are those who have turned from the Cherub, yet their gifts have remained powerful. Peter held back the truth—which haunts me now that I know.

"So there could be more like him," Emma said. "Those who have left the Cherub way."

"He's a killer, and you're blind," Jack blurted. "Cherub with gifts have crossed over."

"Do not be quick to throw stones," Salomeh warned. "Or else a boulder will flatten you."

"Jack fought in another realm to protect the Cherub," Emma defended. "And he continues to fight alongside us to protect all who believe."

"And yet he remains an outlier." Salomeh stepped forward and eyed him closely. "His pain is his greatest strength, but also your weakness, Emma. Guard your heart."

"I've been with the Elders of old—Dabria, Xui Li . . ." Jack was too weak to stand, but he was on the verge of unleashing the rage burning in his soul. "I fought alongside my mom, Rachel, and Areum in the City of Gods."

"Jack is not our enemy," Emma pressed. "We need him in this war."

"Then he is more dangerous than anyone suspects." Salomeh's eyes narrowed. "Gabriella was a mighty warrior, but she was not perfect. She is the one who trained Michael in the Cherub way when he was a young boy, and she went against the Eternal when she married Addison, knowing he was not fully committed to the Cherub."

"She did what she needed to do to protect the Cherub," Jack argued. "She chose not to search for Rachel and me because of the

Mercy Covenant. She loved us both and gave her life to stop the Merikh."

"Love without Elyon's guidance blinds us from the dangers of our choices. Gabriella's death was devastating for all, but equally devastating was the massacre on Mount Hareh. There is no denying she is the reason why we now face our most dangerous enemy."

"My mom sacrificed herself to save everyone. Rachel and Areum did the same." Tears welled up in his eyes as he refused to accept what she said. "All of you should remember them as heroes of the Cherub, not the reason why the Merikh and my father are waging this war."

"Who are Rachel and Areum?" Salomeh asked, curious.

"Rachel is my sister," Jack answered, a bit taken aback. "Areum is our friend. Both are dead."

"They were chosen too," Emma added. "Two of us remain, but only one will lead."

Salomeh turned toward Emma. "You are making the same mistake as the Elders."

"We reached Mount Hareh shortly before the attack," Emma retorted. "The great Elder is not who we believed him to be—he betrayed us. And he lied about the Elders long before."

"If what you say is true, why did you choose to disappear?"

"I was captured by the Merikh." Emma nodded toward Jack. "He risked his life to rescue me and protect what must remain hidden."

"Then we are rudderless in a raging storm," Salomeh admitted reluctantly. "Divided."

"Faizan offered to take us to a gateway," Jack said, matter-of-fact. "The sooner we leave, the better it is for everyone."

Salomeh slipped a bangle from her wrist and gave it to Emma, as if she was handing over a lost treasure from the beginning of time. "Written thousands of years ago in the Eternal, the inscription in Aramaic reads, 'In raging seas and surging tides, Elyon draws close to all who call upon eternity's glory.' Emma, since you were born, your destiny has been determined. Now is the time to step deeper into your calling and encounter all that awaits you."

"If it is Elyon's will," Emma replied as she held the bangle, "it will be so."

"I dare not ask what you found in the City of Gods." Salomeh paused. "Faizan will take you to the gateway, but he will go no further."

Laughter burst into the room as the doors flung open. Vince, Tim, Amina, and a dozen children barged in, carrying plates of biryani with naan, an oven-baked bread. Jack took a plate piled high from Vince, inhaling the scent of pungent spices, steamed rice, tender meat, and potatoes. Even though he was weak, hunger brought an extra ounce of energy.

"I told them you sing like Selena Vice," Amina said to Emma.

Enthusiastic cheers erupted from the children. Jack eyed Salomeh, who smiled cordially when several of the children hugged her tight. His gaze shifted toward the bangle around Emma's wrist. *Raging seas and surging tides—I've been there already and survived.* Emma's voice resonated and captured the full attention of the children. Jack pushed aside the impossible choices ahead, stabbed a potato, and lost himself in her enchanting melody.

10

Opening his eyes, Jack stared at the top bunk, a bit disoriented. Despite his hunger, he'd only picked at half of his plate before lying down while his stomach churned. From the pitch-blackness closing in on all sides, he guessed hours had passed since sunset. He rolled over, and a sharp pain ripped down his spine. Wincing, he struggled to sit upright before running his aching fingers through his mop of chestnut hair—more scraggly than normal. Salomeh's words rang in his ears while he itched the raised scars on his forearms.

"I dare not ask what you found in the City of Gods."

Jack sensed a presence. "Why are you standing in the dark?"

"I was praying," Emma replied. "For all of us, Jack."

"Salomeh is right—you are the one to lead the Cherub. You're wasting your time watching over me. All I'm trying to do is end a nightmare, not spark a revolution."

"Elyon brought us together for a purpose—to bring hope and a future."

"If by some insane miracle we survive whatever deathly realm is on the other side of the gateway, we both know the clock is ticking before I'm pulverized to dust."

"Elyon's timing is perfect. We do not know how this will end—not yet, anyway." Stepping out from her dark corner, Emma sat beside him and grabbed his hand. With their fingers intertwined, she pressed her cheek against his shoulder. "We must stay together. Promise me, Jack."

"You keep praying." He exhaled long. "And I'll keep breathing."

Minutes passed in silence as he found himself more at ease. She was a safe place, one of the few he had left. Even after all they'd survived and the weeks hiding out in Karachi, he'd yet to breathe a word about how hard he'd fallen for her. Without a doubt, the vengeance flowing through his veins was tamed whenever they were together.

Emma reached under his arm and helped him to his feet. When their eyes met, he gazed into her tender soul, then leaned in and kissed her gently on the lips. He stepped back, cheeks flushed and heart pounding. Even though the room was dark, he knew he'd caught her off guard. She squeezed his hand gently but didn't kiss him back.

She's one of the chosen, and you're the Cherub sacrifice—it'll never work.

Stepping outside, they found themselves at the back of a large crowd encircling an enormous bonfire. A splendid emerald flame whipped toward a starry sky while Salomeh reached out and touched man, woman, and child. In the stillness of the night, each one followed the next and moved closer to the fire.

"You're awake." Tim nudged Jack from behind. "Wait 'til you see this, mate."

Without hesitation, each person stepped bravely into the bonfire. Jack's legs buckled for a second until Tim grabbed his shoulders and steadied him. Wide-eyed, Jack realized those who stood in the blaze weren't burning to a crisp. When each vanished, the vibrant emerald flame shot skyward, leaving two angelic silhouettes steadfast amid the flames.

Awestruck, Jack stood as still as a statue. "Where are they going?"

"She knows Merikh are in Karachi." Emma's gaze remained fixed on Salomeh. "Wherever it is will be safer than staying behind in Kati Pahari."

"A righteous rescue," Tim surmised. "Say, maybe we should take a dip in the fire."

"When faith is present," Amina chimed in, "healing is one prayer away."

Vince strolled briskly toward them. "Faizan's got the engine running."

"Jack, what's the plan?" Tim asked. "Leaving or staying?"

Snapping out of his thoughts, he answered, "We're going to Charis, in the Valley of Grace."

Slipping away from the crowd, they piled into the back seats of the minibus while Amina climbed into the front passenger side. Faizan gripped the steering wheel and shifted into gear. Jack leaned back in his seat, remaining quiet as armed guards unlocked and opened the gates.

Staring out a side window at murals passing by along a narrow alley, Jack kept a sinking feeling in his stomach to himself. *What matters right now is staying alive long enough to reach Charis so I can be healed. It's the only way to stop the visions taunting my mind.* Faizan turned a corner and accelerated onto a highway.

Why didn't she kiss me back?

A voice in his head cut off his train of thought: *Better grow a stiff spine, or I'll snap you in two.*

Jack's bones shivered. He knew that voice was not his own, and it wasn't Elyon either. Love of a father for a son was never in the cards for him—only pain and nightmares. While Addison's voice lingered, Jack wondered whether Rachel had protected him longer than he ever realized.

Now that she's gone, I'm ashamed of being so afraid. Everyone believes I'm more than who I am. Maybe that's why Emma didn't kiss me back. She knows I'll fail in the end.

Words his father had spoken to him as a child rooted themselves in deep crevices and chipped away at what mustard seed of courage remained. Beacon Hill and his friends had been a refuge. But neither the school nor the others—not even Emma—were able to rescue him. He already carried the burden of Eden's Star. Hearing Addison's voice seething with hatred made the nightmare even worse.

I'm not even eighteen, and I've lost so much already.

Dizziness swarmed his mind like a horde of killer bees. Out of the corner of his eye, he caught a glimpse of a dusty and muddied Land Cruiser pulling alongside the minibus. Glancing across to the opposite window, he noticed a similar vehicle boxing them in on that side. He gripped the sides of his seat as both vehicles slammed into them with a thunderous explosion. Windows shattered, glass spewing into a million pieces. Tires screeched and smoke billowed from the hood as the minibus swerved violently before Faizan regained control.

Jack heard his own voice call out, "How much farther?"

"We are hours away." Faizan glanced in the rearview. "We cannot outrun them."

A rush of wind forced Jack back against the seat. He heard Tim's voice next. "That's just great—we're gonna be Merikh sandwiches in a minute."

Faizan steered hard to the left, sideswiping one of the Land Cruisers. It skidded and crashed into oncoming traffic. The second cruiser closed in at a high speed and slammed into the side of the minibus again. The front bumper of the cruiser forced the minibus to flip over, rolling end over end across the highway. Grinding metal squealed, sparks sprayed, and a strong aroma of burnt rubber filled Jack's nostrils.

As quickly as it began, it was over. But none of it had happened, at least not yet.

Jack shook off the dizzying sensation and whispered to Emma, "They've found us."

With a quick glance out both windows, Emma turned to him with brows furrowed. "What are you seeing, Jack?"

He knew the visions were close to real time. "Take the next exit."

"Many hours' drive ahead," Faizan replied. "Much better on the highway."

Emma eyed Jack closely. "Faizan, can you find an alternate route?"

With a nod in the rearview, Faizan changed lanes and took the next exit. Heading north, the minibus climbed a winding mountainous road. Vince, Tim, and Amina exchanged curious glances but said nothing. Jack didn't need to look back to know that behind them, somewhere along the highway, Merikh assassins were searching for Eden's Star.

11

VIGAN, MOUNT CODIAPI

PURPLE-AND-RED HORNBILLS chirped nonstop, drowned out by a dull thumping of rotors from a matte-black Eurocopter hovering stealthily in the night. No blinking lights. Hundreds of feet above the camouflaged bridges and tree houses hidden amid giant rosewoods, Will Fargher stepped out onto the skids. With a mask covering his sunken freckled cheeks and a hood pulled over his brown hair, he gazed down on the soft golden glow of tree houses scattered across the mountainside. Beside him on the skids stood the Merikh's most lethal assassin.

"Fast-rope down." Michael Chung grabbed a thick rope secured to the side of the Eurocopter and tossed one end into the dark. "Just like we practiced."

Will wrapped his arms around the rope, then stepped off the skids. As he slid down, his gloves took most of the burn before he landed on a bamboo bridge, which swayed back and forth from his disturbance. He waited a few seconds before Chung dropped down beside him. The jungle turned eerily quiet as they moved silently from one bridge to the next until they reached a large tree house overlooking the valley below.

A voice called out from behind. "Do you plan on burning Vigan the same as Sitio?"

Will and Chung spun around and eyed a white-haired woman with weathered and wrinkled skin standing in the middle of the last bridge they'd crossed.

"Michael, you betrayed the Cherub after we raised you as our own." Moonlight reflected off her piercing grayish eyes. "And you have turned your soul against Elyon."

"You will not be the last to cast the first stone," Chung replied evenly. "You know why we are here, Dabria."

"Seems Peter shared more than his sins with the Merikh. If Addison believes his son found refuge here, then he is mistaken. No one remains in Vigan."

"Do you know where he is?" Will refused to hide his contempt as the wounds in his soul stung deeper. In the desperation of loss, he'd chosen his destiny—revenge for his mum's death along a path he believed would protect his father from the vengeance of Addison and the Merikh. He refused to allow anyone to stand in his way—anyone. "Where is Jack?"

Dabria's gaze shifted toward him, and her stare hardened. "Your mask covers your face, but there is darkness in your eyes." She paused. "Michael brought you here to do what he cannot. You see, he swore on the Eternal to never harm a Cherub Elder. If he breaks his oath, then he will face eternal torment beyond this world and the other realms."

Will reached over his shoulder and grabbed Dragon Soul from its leather scabbard. The sword reflected fire-breathing dragons etched along both sides. Pointing the pure silver razor-sharp blade toward Dabria, he stood his ground. The hair on the back of his neck stood straight up once he realized her hands were hidden behind her back and a smirk pursed her lips.

"Do not wait for her to attack," Chung ordered. "Be the aggressor."

Stepping forward, Will swung Dragon Soul side to side as the adrenaline pumped through his veins. From behind her back, Dabria whipped out two dretium war fans and flipped them open, displaying a feverish red phoenix engraved on both. Moving effortlessly toward Will, crisscrossing one fan in front of the other, she raised her arms and stretched them out with the fans held close together as if protecting her body. Swinging down on the aged woman, sparks flared as Dragon Soul clashed with the dretium war fans. Showing no mercy, Will struck again and again with a relentless vengeance.

Dabria glanced between the war fans before aiming both toward Will's throat. He ducked as she leapt above the blade and landed on the other side of him. Spinning around, he kept a firm grip on the sword as if his next breath depended on it. Dabria sliced the fans round and round until their sparks turned into a spinning reddish-orange glow. Her wide, sweeping movements left Will guessing where she was going to strike next. When she lunged toward him, he backpedaled, keeping Dragon Soul in front of his body to block her attack. He lost his line of sight for a split second, long enough for one of the fans to rip into his flesh.

Will held the sword out in front of him, and the fire-breathing dragons etched on both sides came alive. As he whipped the blade back and forth, a flaming two-headed dragon sprang to life at the point of the sword and unleashed a vile shriek. Fire flowed from the sword, clashing against the dretium war fans before knocking them from Dabria's grasp. Standing defenseless in front of Will, she lowered her hands to her sides.

"The one who holds Dragon Soul protects life and ushers in death," Chung seethed.

"Elyon forgives all who ask," Dabria said. "It is never too late."

"Finish her," Chung growled. "It is your destiny."

With clenched teeth and a heart as dark as death, Will thrust the sword toward her. The flaming dragon attacked with a bursting inferno that raged against the old woman until all that was left of the Cherub Elder was ash. After an unforgivable act of the purest evil, the fiery dragon returned to its lair within the etchings of Dragon Soul. Will slipped the sword over his shoulder and into the scabbard without a shred of remorse.

Chung picked up the dretium war fans. "Windstrikers."

Racing across the bamboo bridges, a rushing wind whipped through the giant rosewoods as growls and roars echoed across the valley. Reaching the thick rope, Chung climbed first as Will glanced around, unnerved by the dangers lurking in the jungle. As soon as he grabbed hold of the rope, the Eurocopter began to fly through the valley. Branches struck his body as he gripped the rope tight. Even though the deep gash on his side bled through his clothes, he felt no pain, no regret, only rage. He'd executed two of the Elders and murdered the highest Cherub on Mount Hareh, but he was no closer to evening the score.

12

HYDERABAD, PAKISTAN

SHORTLY BEFORE DAYBREAK, the psychedelic minibus descended a treacherous mountain road barely wide enough for one vehicle. Staying off the main highway turned a 150-kilometer drive inland from Kati Pahari into an all-night death-defying white-knuckle adventure, most of which occurred in pitch-blackness. Jack dozed off for only minutes at a time, awakened often when bright headlights approached head-on. Faizan navigated the rocky road with Amina in the front passenger seat leaning out the window and relaying how many inches were left to the edge. Vince and Tim crashed in the back row shortly after leaving Kati Pahari. For hours, their rumbling snores dueled to new heights, which left everyone else exhausted.

A fully loaded flatbed truck approached as Faizan steered to the right. Skirting the cliffside yet again left Jack certain this was the one that would send them tumbling down the mountain to their death. He was too weak to protest or do anything to help. Grimacing in pain, he stared out the window as the minibus rolled closer to a thousand-foot drop. His gaze shifted toward a reddish glow in the distance spread across the outskirts of a desert city.

"You look pale," Emma whispered. "How are you feeling?"

"Something's wrong." Jack leaned in closer. "And it's not Eden's Star."

Another hour passed as the minibus descended the mountain before turning onto a paved highway that stretched for miles. Jack's chest tightened, but somehow he forcefully exhaled each breath. In the distance, a burnt-sienna pillared roundabout to a city grew larger as they approached. They drove through it onto streets packed with early morning traffic.

"Hyderabad was once the center of the diamond trade." Faizan pointed out a dozen signs of global tech companies. "Now it is known as Cyberabad—like Silicon Valley."

"How much farther until we reach the gateway to Charis?" Jack asked.

"We have a long journey ahead, my friend." Faizan glanced in the rearview mirror. "Where we are traveling, it is best not to mention Cherub or Merikh."

Jack didn't like that answer, and he couldn't read the street signs, so he leaned back in his seat and tried to take in their surroundings. Temples and mosques appeared on every other block. Iconic global brands were plastered on the sides of buildings. Side streets were busy with merchants displaying vibrant roses, orchids, carnations, and a long list of spectacular flowers he was certain he couldn't pronounce. He remembered finding the stall with the mustard seeds alongside Areum in the City of Gods.

If Areum were here, she'd know what to do—Xui Li and Dabria too.

Faizan slowed the minibus and pulled into a parking lot beside a run-down white building with navy blue trim and hand-painted lettering above the entrance: *Hyderabad Junction.*

"Remember," Faizan told them, "you are foreign exchange students, and I am your guide." He parked the minibus at the far end of the lot and climbed out. Emma reached over the seat and nudged Tim and Vince awake. For a moment, they rubbed sleep from their eyes before helping Jack out of the minibus. Gathering in a circle, they glanced at each other.

"Last chance to turn back," Jack said. "I totally get it if you want to. No hard feelings."

Vince crossed his arms. "None of us are turning back, Jack."

"This is way better than being stuck in the hostel," Tim chimed in. "I say we keep going."

"We made it this far by sticking together," Amina added. "I agree."

Emma asked, "Jack, are you strong enough?"

"I survived Vince and Tim's torture last night," he mused before his smirk disappeared. "Honestly, I don't know what else I'm supposed to do."

"If we are to catch the train," Faizan interrupted, "we must leave now."

Shuffling his feet, Jack gritted his teeth and fought through the pain. Vince and Tim each grabbed one of his arms to hold him steady as they walked across the parking lot. He felt as if he were trudging through wet cement. His muscles ached, and his body was wrecked. By the time they reached the train station entrance, he was winded. Faizan and Amina went ahead across aged tile floors to the ticket counter. A few minutes passed before the group followed other travelers toward the green-and-yellow trains.

"When do you think was the last time someone safety-checked one of these?" Tim asked.

"Probably not since they were built," Vince guessed. "Like a hundred years ago."

"Smashing," Tim replied with a heavy dose of sarcasm. "What could possibly go wrong?"

Faizan motioned for them to follow as they boarded one of the trains and found a six-person compartment one step up from economy class. Three metal bunks were bolted on both sides, but there was no door for privacy. Directly outside the glassless windows, carts rolled past, stacked high with cardboard shipping boxes. Jack slumped onto the bottom bunk, trying to catch his breath and stop his hands from shaking. Closing his eyes, he was too embarrassed to look at the others, knowing the walk from the minibus to the train had been a test of his endurance. He sensed Elyon's presence pushing him beyond his limits.

If I'm going to die, let it be because I never gave up.

Another forty minutes passed before the locomotive pulled away from the station, crossing over rusted, grass-covered tracks heading deeper into an endless desert.

13

HYDERABAD HAD DISAPPEARED hours earlier behind shifting sand dunes as the locomotive rumbled along the tracks beneath cloudless blue skies. Vince grabbed Jack's hand and pulled him up onto the roof through an opening in the passenger car. Jack crawled along the roof until he reached Tim, Amina, Emma, and dozens of other passengers escaping the sweltering interior of the train. He'd seen videos of people riding on top of trains before but never imagined he'd be one of them.

"Pretty incredible, right?" Tim asked. "An epic adventure, mate."

Jack glanced around as he inched close to Emma. "Looks like it goes on forever."

"From the northern Aravalli hills and Punjab region," Amina

explained, "to the great Rann of Kutch along the seas, to the open plains of the Indus River to the west, the Thar Desert spreads across the border between Pakistan and India."

"How do you know all of this?" Vince asked.

"When I was growing up, my mother spoke often about a woman admired by the highest Cherub. She was raised with her family in India before moving to Pakistan, even spending several years secluded here in the desert." Amina paused. "Many believed there was a time when Salomeh Gashkori was asked to join the Elders, but she declined. She chose to remain in Pakistan as a shepherd to all who believe in Elyon—and she remains a legend to many of us."

"You met your hero," Tim surmised. "No wonder she's miffed her nephew is with us lot."

"Did Faizan say how much farther we have to travel?" Jack asked.

"After we left the station, he brought us up here," Emma answered. "You were asleep."

"I didn't see him when I went to wake Jack," Vince said. "Want me to find him?"

"He knows where we are," Tim answered. "Not like we're going to jump off the train."

Grayish smoke billowed from the locomotive while buzzards flew overhead and a herd of gazelles raced across the desert. Jack noticed there were nomadic huts in the distance, surrounded by acacia trees. *If you live out here, you're hiding from something or someone.* A dry heat warmed his chest and soothed the ache in his bones. Still, he couldn't shake the uneasiness that had started inside the minibus as they drove to the train station and only grown stronger since.

Emma leaned in close and whispered, "About yesterday—I was not expecting—"

"Don't worry about it," he interrupted. "Won't happen again."

Faizan's head popped up through the opening. "Ready to get off the train?"

"We are in the middle of nowhere." Tim waved his arms around. "Jack, seriously?"

"You heard him," Jack replied. "Time to get off."

Vince helped lower Jack into the passenger car as wheels screeched against iron rails while the locomotive slowed. Gathering their backpacks, Jack noticed curious stares from passengers who seemed more suspicious than when he first boarded. All eyes were on him as he shuffled down the aisle before stepping off the train. Standing in the sand beneath an umbrella of shade from the acacia trees, he watched as the locomotive rolled forward before picking up speed and disappearing like a mirage.

A thick-bearded elderly man wrapped in a cotton robe approached from one of the huts, carrying an armful of earth-toned clothing. He greeted Faizan as if they were friends, then proceeded to size the others up. Handing over a loose-fitting robe to each, he waited until they slipped the robes over their shoulders.

"Layering more clothes in this heat?" Tim grumbled. "I've got heatstroke already."

"Makes me like the house unis even better," Vince mused.

"These will help prevent dehydration," Faizan reassured. "We have miles more to travel, and there is limited water until we reach Sakkhela."

"I thought we were going to Charis," Jack said. "Valley of Grace, remember?"

"Sakkhela is on the way, and it will be a good place to rest."

Tim studied his robe and shrugged. "We've been transported to the set of *Dune*."

The bearded nomad stepped forward and wrapped another piece of cloth around Jack's head, then stepped back to admire his work. Jack wiped a trickle of blood from his nostril and eyed the rest of them. He noticed that the robe hung loosely on everyone except for Vince with his broad shoulders. A rush of lightheadedness washed over him, but he managed to keep his balance.

"Where's our ride?" Tim asked.

"We're probably going on some tricked-out semitruck." Vince tugged on his robe, which nearly tore at the seams. "With massive speakers blaring music along Fury Road."

"Better not be—a Jeep with air-conditioning would be perfect."

"Keep on dreaming, love." Amina grinned and pointed toward a second nomad who appeared pulling four camels by their reins. "This will not be like riding a horse."

"Approach the camels from the side, *confidently*," Faizan instructed. "Do not look them in the eyes, especially if you are nervous. Put your foot in the stirrup, throw your leg between the humps, and climb on quickly."

"Approach from the side," Vince repeated. "And don't look them in the eyes."

All four camels moaned and groaned as the nomads held them steady before leading them down onto their knees.

"Who will go first?" Faizan asked with a wide grin. "The chosen or the outlier?"

"Good call," Tim agreed. "Lead the way, one of you."

Jack shuffled forward and approached the first camel. He stopped cold when the camel turned its head, stared directly at him, then unleashed a rumbling roar. Emma stepped past, dug her boot into the stirrup, and threw her leg between the humps as if she'd done it a thousand times. Exhaling long, Jack took another step closer and followed her lead. Before he had a chance to throw his leg over, the camel rose up on all fours. Vince grabbed him and lifted him onto the camel behind Emma.

"That was way more difficult than it looked," Jack said. "Giddyup."

Tim and Amina climbed onto one of the camels while Vince straddled the third for himself. Faizan saddled the last one before taking the lead. The bearded nomads watched as the caravan headed away from their huts and the train tracks. Jack held Emma's waist while the camel's odd side-to-side gait left him swaying awkwardly. A twinge struck, then shot down his spine to his tailbone. His grip tightened around Emma as the camel's herky-jerky stride continued. Ahead of their makeshift caravan was nothing except sand dunes.

14

THE SWELTERING HEAT COOLED by late afternoon as the caravan traveled across an endless desert while the sun sank below the horizon. Vibrant oranges, brilliant reds, and intense blues spread across the skies as if Elyon painted a canvas before their eyes. Jack drank from a canteen, then offered it to Emma, who drank too. He felt as if they'd been traveling for days, even though it had only been a matter of hours since stepping off the train.

Since leaving Karachi, he'd pushed his body to the limit just keeping up with everyone. He couldn't deny there were moments in the hostel when he'd wanted to lock himself in his room and lose himself in a six-pack of liquid courage. While the temptation lingered, he'd fought the battles in his mind and believed Elyon's presence helped keep him from surrendering to his old life. He was relieved to leave the hostel behind, even though the physical suffering had been nearly unbearable. Another sharp pain ripped down his spine. Every ounce of his being wanted to scream in agony, but that wouldn't change anything except freak everyone else out.

"When I get off this animal, I won't be able to sit or walk for a month." Tim's camel reared its head back and tried to bite his leg. "Blasted beast! How much longer before we get off this merry-go-round?"

"A city on a hill bringing light to the world cannot be hidden," Faizan said.

"What riddle are you spewing now?" Tim shouted in frustration. "Seriously, mate."

"He means you'll know we're there when you see it," Vince replied.

A migraine pulsed behind Jack's eyes. "We've come this far . . ."

"I'm just saying," Tim interrupted angrily, "there has to be an easier way."

"Breathe," Amina suggested. "I am sure we are not too far."

Jack leaned forward and rested his head against Emma's shoulder, too weak to sit upright any longer. He remembered standing in the rain and dropping a white rose on Rachel's grave in Sitio Veterans. *Prayers are wishes that never come true.* On that day he believed those words without apology, but that was before he'd stood side by side with Rachel, Areum, and his mom inside the Temple of the Nephilim. *In that moment everything changed.* Sure, he had doubts, but with each passing day in his weakness, he grew more certain Elyon heard his prayers.

No matter how it ends, prayer is the only way to get through this.

Emma asked over her shoulder, "Are you doing okay?"

"Stomach is queasy, and my head is pounding." Jack paused. "I don't regret it, you know."

He waited for a response, but instead she stayed quiet. For a while he kept his cheek pressed against her back and tried to keep himself from passing out. He expected the camels to get spooked once the sunlight disappeared, but their stride labored on as if they'd traveled the route many times before. He raised his head and gazed up at a full moon and a sea of twinkling stars scattered across the heavens. One of the stars shone brighter than millions of others—breathtaking.

The caravan headed toward the brightest star, which seemed to point to one place—an oasis. Jack grabbed Emma's waist tighter when the camel dropped slowly to its knees without a command. Vince hopped from his camel and hurried to help Jack down off the beast. Everyone stretched sore muscles and aching bones as the four camels stood and sauntered over to a natural spring where the starry night reflected off still waters.

"We fried ourselves like bacon all afternoon, and now we're going to freeze to death," Tim complained. "My eighteenth year is off to a horrible start."

"Faizan, is this the gateway to Charis?" Jack asked, shivering.

"Sakkhela is a city hidden in plain sight between this world and the other realms. We must pass through this gateway, and then we will rest in Sakkhela before traveling through a second gateway to the Valley of Grace."

"Now you're talking about an invisible city," Vince said, skeptically. "And we have to go through more than one gateway? That's not what you said when we asked you the first time."

"We should've stayed at the hostel," Tim sighed. "This is another dead end."

Jack was weak, yet his anger boiled over. "Lately, all you've done is complain."

"We've been waiting on you for weeks to do something—anything." Tim pointed at the others one at a time. "Our families are hiding in Nightingale's vault, missing since Mount Hareh, or equally as twisted, believe their son simply vanished into thin air. And so far, Eden's—"

"Enough bickering, you two," Emma interrupted. "Faizan, what is required to enter the gateway to Sakkhela?"

"An offering," Faizan replied. "The gateway to Charis will require more."

"And that gateway is the same as the one which leads to the Valley of Grace?" Amina asked.

Faizan nodded slowly. "One gateway leads to both places."

"Another cursed riddle," Tim mumbled. "Might as well curl up and die."

"Timothy," Amina chastised. "Stop being impossible."

"Are you mad?" Tim's brows raised. "*I'm* the impossible one?"

Emma retrieved silver coins from beneath the loose-fitting robe and handed one to each of them. While Faizan stared at the coins in amazement and reverence, Emma gave a coin engraved with the moon to Jack and leaned in close.

"Did you know there was more than one gateway to Charis?"

"I thought it was only one. Emma, what's more than an offering?"

"An offering is a pure gift to Elyon," she replied. "I am not sure what is more."

A warmth spread across Jack's chest as he stepped away and walked gingerly over to the camels, who drank from the natural spring. He closed his eyes as the heat inside his body intensified until it seared his soul as if sealing an open wound. *Eden's Star is alive, and the compass is still guiding us.* When he opened his eyes, the others stood beside him, including Tim—all united as one. Jack was first to toss his coin into the natural spring, and the others followed.

In the skies above, a swirling wave of bluish-green light collided with a river of stars. At first Jack thought he was having another vision. Then he guessed he might be hallucinating. Blinking several times, he realized the aurora was real. The wave of light crashed down onto the oasis, splashing into the natural springs. Water gushed toward the skies as if a giant geyser erupted, splitting in half before leaving an opening guarded by a majestic rose gold gate.

Wide-eyed, Jack slipped the loose-fitting robe off his shoulders and dropped it to the sand. Stepping forward into the natural spring, he removed the material wrapped around his head and left it floating in the water. Wading toward the rose gold gate, he heard the others behind as the searing heat within his body cooled. Glancing down at his chest, he noticed the stark-white glow beneath his shirt. *No pain, only peacefulness and calm.* Reaching the opened gate, he turned back toward the others, who were already waist-deep in the water.

"Healing comes when freedom reigns," he whispered.

15

HONG KONG

PERCHED ON A ROCKY CLIFF, Natalie peered through infrared binoculars across dark waters toward Shelter Island. In the early seventies, a drug lord had hidden shipments of fentanyl on the island before smuggling them aboard ships headed west—a story Natalie had heard from one of her previous clients whose daughter attended Beacon Hill. She hadn't thought much of it at the time, or even after she accepted an offer to work for Addison Reynolds—a decision she'd regretted ever since the bombing in Osaka. Flashes from the attack at Beacon Hill struck her. It had been a chaotic night when she turned her back on Jack and Vince for a split second before they vanished.

I was supposed to protect him. Jack, where are you?

An hour earlier, she and Bau had slipped out of Nightingale's vault and driven across Kowloon while avoiding HKPF checkpoints. One month had passed since a swift government crackdown, when thousands of protesters across Kowloon and Wan Chai were arrested. Millions of Hong Kongers chose self-imposed lockdowns to avoid being questioned by the PRC. And all the while, the Merikh scoured the districts for Cherub.

Even though it was late at night, she recognized the iconic green-and-white ferries sailing across the bay. Star Ferry had closed immediately after anarchists destroyed The Peninsula and left Kowloon—a city known across Asia as Nine Dragons—on the brink. Still, she was surprised to see the ferries in operation so far from Victoria Harbour. The longer she watched, the more she wondered how long the Merikh had controlled Shelter Island. Zooming in with the binoculars, her gaze locked in on armed men patrolling the shores while passengers from the ferries were lined up against barbed wire fencing that stretched the length of the island.

"Impossible to get any closer," she said in a lowered voice. "There are too many."

"How did Detective Ming get the photos?" Bau asked.

"She has an informant on the island." Natalie kept her eyes on the dozens of Hong Kongers being forced through the entrance of a heavily guarded fortress. "Merikh hide their Cherub prisoners in these reeducation camps. No one knows how many are missing, but from the looks of it, there are more than anyone expected."

"Is her informant one of the Merikh?"

"I am not certain." Natalie shook her head. "Everyone is keeping their secrets close."

"We cannot wait for Emma to return to rescue those who are imprisoned."

"I have given Detective Ming photos of Tim, Amina, and Will. She promised to find out whether they are being held on the island or somewhere else. You are right, we cannot wait much longer or else it will be too late."

Bau checked his phone. "The Council is meeting in thirty minutes."

"It will be up to you to convince the Cherub." Natalie lowered the binoculars and tucked them inside her jacket. "Not one word about Jack, Emma, or Vince."

"I will not stop them from searching for him," Bau answered. "He is a danger to us all."

Natalie held her tongue, knowing she needed Bau on her side if there was any chance of surviving and fighting back. He was only a teenager, but she'd witnessed how he fought during the attack on Beacon Hill. No doubt he was gifted. Leaving the cliffside, they hurried down a winding path until they reached a cul-de-sac where a rusted Mazda sedan was parked—a far cry from the Mercedes and Range Rover she'd driven as head of security for Addison. Slipping behind the wheel, Natalie pumped the pedal several times and turned the ignition. At first the engine struggled to start before sputtering to life.

A twenty-minute drive from Clear Water Bay along Hiram's Highway ended in Sai Kung, on the eastern edge of the New Territories. Parking along the road, they crossed the street and headed into the dense hillside of Ma On Sham Country Park. Natalie followed Bau as they hiked a half mile until they reached an opening to a cave. Glancing around, she realized there were shadows hiding in the brush surrounding them.

"Watchmen." Bau motioned for Natalie to enter the cave. "We are safe here."

Torches lined the sides of the cave and cast a soft glow ahead. Natalie fought to keep her wits about her, as her instincts were on overdrive. She stayed on Bau's shoulder as if she were guarding one of her clients or precious cargo. Reaching the epicenter of the cave, she noticed a group gathered in red-and-white hooded robes.

"You are right on time." A snowy-haired woman with pearl skin and a rigid jaw stepped forward and embraced Bau. Her gaze shifted toward Natalie. "I am Fang Xue, leader of the Cherub—for now, at least. The rest of my brothers and sisters are the Council chosen to decide our future leader. Everyone here this evening is aware of who you are, Natalie."

A bright ocean glow appeared in one corner of the cave. A woman dressed in a royal blue and gold-embroidered tunic stepped forward out of thin air. Her dark-brown eyes flickered, reflecting the torches mounted on the rock walls.

"Salomeh," Fang Xue said, surprised. "We worried you might not come."

"Merikh hunt for the outlier in Karachi," she replied. "Very dangerous times."

"Have any of the Cherub seen him?" Bau asked.

Natalie clenched her teeth and fought the urge to defend Jack. Instead, she remained silent and listened, even though her blood boiled beneath the surface. *I thought we had a deal not to mention Jack, Emma, or Vince.* Even at his young age the ambition was crystal clear.

"What do you know about the massacre on Mount Hareh?" Salomeh asked Fang Xue.

"The outlier murdered the great Elder," Fang Xue answered. "And we lost those we love."

"We have no witnesses to testify to such an occurrence involving the outlier."

"When I confronted him with Emma, he did not deny it," Bau pressed. "He is guilty."

"Salomeh, it is true." Fang Xue exhaled long. "He must be held accountable."

"What if Jack is innocent?" Natalie asked. "You do not know him."

"If he is proven innocent, then he will walk free," Fang Xue replied pointedly. "Until then, he remains an enemy to the Cherub, and he must be brought to justice."

Natalie's ears perked up as she spun around and, on reflex, retrieved a Glock from her back holster. On the opposite side from where she'd seen the glow and Salomeh's entrance, two women emerged from the tunnel she'd walked through only moments earlier. The dim light cast a shadow across Professor Burwick's gruesomely disfigured face as she leaned heavily on a cane. Beside her stood Eliška, whose blonde hair was braided over one shoulder.

"You should not be here," Fang Xue scolded. "Either of you."

"There was a time when you welcomed me to the inner circle of the Council," Burwick replied, stone-faced. "My daughter was raped and murdered by the Merikh. I have as much of a right to stand here as anyone else present."

"You chose to separate yourself from the Council—and the Cherub."

"We are deeply sorry for your loss," Salomeh said. "Your anger is justified, Harley."

"But your faction remains divisive," Fang Xue insisted.

"Those who believe in Elyon, yet refuse to blindly follow your commands, are seen as less than worthy." Burwick glanced briefly at Bau and Natalie. "That changes tonight."

Natalie lowered her weapon and slipped it back into the holster, intrigued by the stalemate. She listened intently while remaining invisible—she'd mastered the art of fading into the background when she guarded the wealthiest and most powerful in society. One look at Professor Burwick and it was clear whatever history she had with the others left them on opposing sides.

"Our differences must not divide us," Salomeh warned. "Common ground is the only way to defeat the Merikh."

"While the Elders failed to protect those who believe, the highest Cherub did nothing." Burwick shifted her weight and winced as she put her hand on Eliška's shoulder. "You know who stands beside me, and what she has sacrificed in the name of Elyon."

"I am one of the chosen," Bau challenged. "I will lead a new generation."

Salomeh's brows furrowed. "You are not the only one."

"Who else is there?" Natalie asked.

Salomeh retrieved her cell phone and swiped across the screen. While the others inside the cave gathered around, she played a video and held it up for all to see. A lump lodged in Natalie's throat when she recognized Emma staring back at them—and in the background, seated on the bumper of a vehicle, was Jack. She swallowed hard when she noticed how frail he looked, while Emma stood surrounded by dozens of children who gazed at the camera.

"I was taken by the Merikh from Mount Hareh and was tortured. I am alive only because of the outlier you are hunting to avenge the great Elder's death. Those who lost their lives in the Sanctuary of Prayer were murdered because of a betrayal from one of our own. There is much you do not know, but there is no time to convince you of the truth." With a clear edit, the day disappeared and night cut in to a large crowd encircling an emerald bonfire. Natalie's eyes widened as she watched men and women step into a whirling flame. Then Emma's voice continued. "It is true, the Mercy Covenant is broken. But the words of the Eternal remain. All who believe are worthy to shine a light against the dark. War is not coming—it is already here."

Salomeh stopped the video and slipped the cell phone back into her pocket. Natalie's stare shifted around the Cherub who stood like statues in their customary robes. No one said a word. No one moved an inch. In that moment, she knew she was witnessing the most powerful women of all the Cherub—and two teenage girls she knew very little about. And seeing Jack alive, well, that ignited a determination that had faded in recent days.

"The Eternal is clear," Salomeh said sternly. "All are deemed worthy."

"It is settled, then," Burwick replied. "Let the will of Elyon be done—whether it be Emma, Bau, or Eliška."

16

THE HIGHLANDS

JACK STEPPED OUT FROM THE WATER onto a stone path as Eden's Star faded beneath his scars. Glancing down, he noticed his clothes and boots were bone dry. Relieved, he waited while the others followed him before the rose gold gate slammed shut. *We all made it through, so this isn't the gateway Faizan warned me about.* He turned back and stared at steely gray skies above rolling hills of lush green. Lavender flowers and evergreen shrubs blanketed the steep terrain.

"We have entered through one edge of the Highlands." Faizan pointed at a stone-walled city in the distance. "Sakkhela is where the Silk Road once began—where your journey continues to Charis in the Valley of Grace."

"Along a silk road this secret will one day return," Jack recited under his breath. "To a story of mercy and love evil attempted to burn."

"Once the Silk Road was filled with legends of freedom for the Cherub," Emma said. "Now there are those who believe the Merikh are able to cross through the gateways to these places."

"I am afraid it is true," Faizan replied. "Peace has abandoned the Silk Road."

Emma stepped alongside, her gaze locked straight ahead. "That is why you said not to speak of Merikh or Cherub."

"There was a time when Sakkhela was beyond the Merikh—when the Mercy Covenant offered protection. For those places once known to be a refuge, much has changed."

Xui Li's voice was crystal clear in his memory. *"Gabriella believed the artifacts were hidden in other realms within the Golden Triangle along the Silk Road. Remember, your purpose is to protect Eden's Star, but it is far too dangerous to discover what it guards."*

He knew that what he was doing was the exact opposite of Xui Li's wisdom, but he sensed the Merikh were closer than ever. "How do we get to Sakkhela?"

"Don't tell us we have to walk or ride a blasted camel," Tim retorted.

"Cardio is a great way to relieve stress," Vince quipped with a wide grin. "Maybe you'll get another game ball from Bashers, Bowlers, and Boundaries."

"Now you're tempting me." Tim relaxed a bit. "Faizan, what's the plan, my man?"

Faizan turned toward the rolling hills, then let out a high-pitched whistle. Jack's jaw dropped at the sight of a colossal pure-white eagle soaring between the hills before diving low, straight toward the ledge they were standing on. Rocks tumbled down the cliffside as the majestic creature planted its claws and towered over them with golden eyes peering steadfastly at each one.

"Blimey," Tim said, awestruck. "It won't eat us, will it?"

"Sahil is very gentle," Faizan replied. "But she is also very powerful."

"I've never seen an eagle that size," Vince said. "How is it possible?"

"The Eternal speaks of angelic beings who protect Elyon's creation," Amina answered. "Faizan, is Sahil a pentaloon written about in the text?"

He nodded. "Since I was a young boy, she has watched over me when I visit Sakkhela."

"She is quite a stunning creature."

"Pentaloons are believed to have healing powers," Emma explained. "They are able to take sickness into themselves and release it to the heavens."

Jack remembered the words Rachel had written in her diary. *A storm wind carrying a soaring eagle south with wings spread wide, as if protecting the outlier.* Even though his mind drifted for a moment, he caught what Emma said—healing powers. Stepping forward, he reached out his shaky hand. Sahil turned her beak toward him and gazed deep into his soul. He was drawn close as his fingers touched her velvety feathers. As he pressed his hand against Sahil's muscular body, the pentaloon wrapped her wing over his shoulder.

"I think she's fond of you." Amina turned toward Faizan. "Can she heal him?"

"The burden he carries can only be lifted in Charis—there is no other place."

"Then why is the giant bird here?" Tim asked. "Are we riding her into town?"

"Faizan brought us this way for a reason," Jack said. "Emma needs healing too."

An intense stare from Sahil shifted toward Emma, as if the ancient creature understood what he was saying. Those few seconds under Sahil's wing left him feeling safer than he had ever been, but it was only for a brief moment. He slipped out from beneath her wing and stepped aside. Emma walked slowly toward him while the others grew quiet.

"Will you go with me?" Emma asked.

"Sure." Jack grabbed her hand gently. "You won't be alone."

"Wait," Tim protested. "Are you coming back?"

"I hope so," Jack confessed.

Sahil's beak lowered again as Emma and Jack climbed onto her broad back. From behind, Emma wrapped her arms around Jack's waist as he gripped a handful of feathers. Sahil jumped from the ledge and with her wings tucked against her body dove straight downward. Jack's adrenaline surged as a rushing wind pierced his cheeks. Jutting rocks flew past at breakneck speeds. Only feet from the ground, Sahil spread her wings and then flapped them with great force and swooped across the lush Highlands, soaring as if she were boosted by a rocket.

A high-pitched whistle mimicked Faizan's earlier call and echoed across the valleys. Exhilaration flooded Jack's veins as he white-knuckled the feathers while Emma's grip tightened around his waist. A smile broke through the corners of his lips, as he could no longer contain the rush of energy bursting from within.

"Woo-hoo! "

Jack laughed aloud when he heard Emma whoop too. It was a

sound of purest joy. Sahil changed directions and pointed her beak toward the sky. Flapping her wings in a strong, steady rhythm, she bolted upward. Bursting through steely gray clouds, Jack felt his body press harder against the pentaloon. There was no time to think about what was happening as he held on with every muscle in his body.

From the bluish-violet sky, a deep-scarlet lightning bolt struck and paralyzed them in midair. A wave of energy encircled them before lifting Emma from Sahil. Jack spun around and watched as she floated toward the heavens.

"Emma!"

For a split second he feared she was going to die, but then she opened her eyes and stared back at him with a fiery glare. A ball of pure white light formed in the palm of her hands—the same light he'd seen her control at Star Ferry when Michael Chung and the Merikh unleashed their fury. Emma's amber eyes glowed stark white as the scarlet wave of miraculous energy guided her back to Sahil, who wasted no time carrying them back through the skies toward the far edge of the Highlands.

17

SAHIL TUCKED HER WINGS and landed gently on the edge of the rocky cliffside where Tim, Amina, Vince, and Faizan waited. Slipping off the pentaloon, Jack wanted to believe he was stronger than he'd been in weeks, but he sensed healing from Elyon was not yet granted to him—at least not fully. Running his palm over Sahil's soft feathers was the only way he could show his gratitude as Emma dropped to the ground and walked toward the others.

"Your eyes are glowing," Vince said in disbelief.

"It's kinda freaking me out," Tim added. "In a good way."

"Elyon restored my gifts," she answered. "My soul is thankful."

Tears welled up in Amina's eyes, spilling onto her cheeks as she rushed forward and hugged Emma tight. Tim and Vince shot curious stares at Jack. He shrugged with a slight grin. Picking up his backpack, which Vince had carried since Eden's Star brought them to Karachi, he slipped it over his shoulder with clenched teeth. *I'm not going to show them the pain, not any longer. I've got to keep my eyes on reaching Charis—and hope I'll live long enough to experience healing. Until then, Elyon, thank you for what you have done for Emma.*

He caught a glimpse of everyone's surprise as he headed up the stone path and called over his shoulder, "C'mon, we've got a world to save."

"He's feeling better all of a sudden," Vince said. "Is he healed or has he gone crazy?"

"Whatever just happened up there must've been cracking," Tim replied.

"It is a miracle." Amina grabbed Tim's hand and pulled him along. "Elyon is with us."

Faizan whistled as he had done before, and Sahil mimicked the call. Flapping her wings, she rose into the air, hovered over them, then flew in the direction of Sakkhela.

Jack glanced over at Emma and felt an overwhelming sense of gratefulness. He witnessed Elyon's power flowing through Emma once again, which brought a sense of joy that had been missing for far too long. For a while they walked in silence, traveling the stone path bordered by lush greenery.

Is there such a thing as partial healing? I'm feeling a bit stronger, but I'm definitely far from normal.

"That was quite a ride," he said. "Crazier than the Hair Raiser at Ocean Park."

"Definitely crazier." Emma smiled. "I do miss Beacon Hill, though."

"Me too. Makes me wonder if it'll ever be the same."

"One day the Cherub will know what you have done." Emma paused. "Thank you for going with me, Jack."

"All of you have stuck by my side." A lump lodged in his throat. "It was my turn."

"Did you feel anything? I mean, do you . . . ?"

"I don't know how long it will last, but something changed when your powers were restored." Jack knew he was holding back the whole truth—he was still dying from Eden's Star. He stared into her eyes. "There's only one way to know for sure."

"Once we reach Charis, you will find . . ."

"Believe me, I don't want to die—but I'm ready for whatever is next."

The stone path ascended gradually, and Jack realized the agony that had been hijacking his body eased a bit more with each step. While the pain in his spine remained constant, the piercing in his soul from the Temple of the Nephilim seemed less haunting.

Elyon, give me strength until the end—to die with Eden's Star if that's what I must do.

Faizan was first to reach the top of the hill, where the path ended in the courtyard of a stone castle overlooking Sakkhela and an endless countryside. Sahil flew over a smaller village below on the outskirts of the walled city, repeating a high-pitched whistle until she returned to them and landed on top of a castle tower. Jack took in his surroundings and noticed Sakkhela looked to be a deserted city in partial ruin.

"Seems a bit creepy," Amina said as she looked around. "Is anyone else here?"

"We should keep going to Charis—this doesn't feel right," Vince suggested.

"Do we still need to go to Charis if Jack's been healed?" Tim asked.

Jack hesitated, unsure of how to answer. "I'm not totally healed."

"Oh . . ." Tim's cheeks flushed. "Sorry, mate."

Jack stepped over to the edge of the courtyard and eyed a narrow stone road that led from the castle down into the city wrapped around the hillside. Turning back, he walked straight toward Faizan.

"Why did you bring us here instead of the gateway to Charis?" Jack asked.

"I do not understand what you mean." Faizan's brows furrowed. "We traveled through a gateway to Sakkhela, but we must continue farther in the Highlands to a second gateway that leads to the Valley of Grace. It is there you will find Charis."

"If the gateways require an offering, how have you traveled to Sakkhela before?"

"Khala Salomeh is selective over who is given a coin to travel through the gateway, and she trusts me to be a guide," Faizan replied.

"How did you know Emma needed her powers back?" Jack watched Faizan pace back and forth as if deciding how to respond. He nodded at Vince, who stepped closer, ready to tackle Faizan. "Tell us the truth, or we're not going any farther."

"I am a healer." Faizan held up his hand and stepped back. "Khala Salomeh asked me to bring you to Sakkhela because Emma is one of the chosen, and she needed Elyon to restore what was taken from her—Sahil was the only way."

Tim started pacing as he scratched his head. "This is seriously twisted."

"How long has everyone in Sakkhela been missing?" Jack asked point-blank.

"An old friend of Khala Salomeh arrived in Karachi before you." Faizan pointed at the large oak doors of the castle. "She wished to come to Slybourne Castle, where the greatest Cherub warriors once guarded the Silk Road. When we arrived, we discovered the castle, the city, and the village were abandoned. She stayed behind while I returned to Kati Pahari to let Khala Salomeh know what we discovered. We do not know where the people have gone."

"So you were lying to us this whole time?" Tim argued. "You said Jack could be healed if we traveled to Charis. Then it was a pit stop in Sakkhela after a most uncomfortable camel ride in the desert—I still can't feel my legs. And you knew Emma needed to be healed—*Khala Salomeh* told you so—but you acted like you were doing all of this as a *healer* for Jack. We cannot trust another word that comes out of your mouth."

"I am not a liar," Faizan retorted. "You are not the only ones searching for answers."

Jack stepped closer, and Vince did the same. "Describe the woman."

"Chinese. Straight black hair. Pale skin. Ageless. And eyes of fire."

"Did Sahil take her above the clouds too?"

"She was not permitted. Khala Salomeh made her promise on the Eternal." Faizan's gaze darted between them. "I do not know her name—I swear this to you."

"Jack, what now?" Vince asked. "He said we can't make it to the gateway before dark."

"We'll stay here until the morning. Then all of us will go to Charis."

"Stay in an abandoned castle—which looks haunted, by the way—in a place where everyone vanished out of thin air. Are you mental?" Tim looked to the others for backup, and when no one joined in, he continued. "We are in one of those movies where a group of teenagers go out for a stroll, poke their noses where they don't belong, then run for their lives when an insane bloke chases them through a forest with a chainsaw."

"You wanted an adventure—well now you've got one," Jack quipped as he took another step toward Faizan. "Any other secrets you're holding back from us?"

"I swear to you there are no other secrets." Faizan motioned for them to follow as he headed for the oak doors. "Sahil will guard the castle and warn us if we are not alone."

"It's like an episode of Cherub Cribs." Vince smirked. "Might as well look around."

Jack's mind flashed to the destruction in Sitio Veterans at the hands of Michael Chung and the Merikh assassins. He stayed back along with Emma, whose eyes locked in on his.

"Do you know who the woman is?" she asked.

He nodded slowly. "I think so."

18

THE GROUP ENTERED THROUGH the solid oak doors, and a grand entryway welcomed them into the castle. Jack was immediately reminded of the Main Hall at Beacon Hill. Instead of a glass case holding the House Champions trophy and the Battle of the Bashers, Bowlers, and Boundaries trophy, though, centuries-old marble statues surrounded them. A hooded man walking hunched over with a staff. A woman wrestling a lion. A muscular man holding up two pillars. Another on a horse wielding a sword. A queen kneeling in prayer beside a throne. And a boy grasping a chalice with both hands. Jack couldn't help but wonder if a statue of his mom was somewhere within the castle.

You are part of a house of heroes, Jack.

"Ryder Slybourne was the greatest swordsman of the Cherub."

Faizan's voice echoed off the vaulted ceilings as he pointed at the center statue. "Traveling through many gateways, he battled enemies of Elyon and led the Cherub to victory. At the end of the First Great War, he returned to Sakkhela during a century of peace to watch over others who fought for the Cherub—until he was called by Elyon to command the armies of the Seven Tribes in the Battle of Everest."

"I'm guessing no internet or cell service then?" Tim asked with a tinge of sarcasm.

Amina nudged his shoulder and said in a hushed tone, "Enough, Timothy."

"Memories of the great warrior faded after the swordsman crossed into eternity and the Seven Tribes scattered during the Age of Trepidation." Faizan pushed another set of oak doors open and led them into a larger room at the heart of the castle. "When the Mercy Covenant was broken, a bridge between our world and the other realms opened for Cherub and Merikh through Sakkhela."

"What is this room?" Vince asked, intrigued.

"Chamber of Shadowlight." Faizan paused. "Elyon is Light, and Cherub are shadows of his glory. Great warriors who fought along Slybourne once stood in this place."

Along stone walls aged for centuries, stained glass windows depicted angels in the Garden, the Testimony being carried into battle, and an image of Elyon's Vine, which was remarkably similar to Rachel's drawing. Jack stared intently at the king cypress and its massive crown, surrounded by crimson plants and lush emerald grass. A dull light from the overcast skies broke through the stained glass, casting faded rays of color across rows of flags hanging directly overhead. A bronze lion, a violet temple, an emerald tree, a chestnut deer, a silver serpent, a crimson wolf, and a turquoise ship—the Seven Tribes of Cherub—and a crimson dragon, symbolizing the Merikh. He remembered seeing those same emblems on the scroll inside the House of Luminescence.

"With the Mercy Covenant broken," Emma said, "could there be a reason besides the Merikh why everyone is gone from Sakkhela?"

Faizan nodded. "It is possible."

"Definitely throws a wrench into this place being neutral ground," Vince pointed out.

"How did Slybourne die?" Jack asked, matter-of-fact.

"He commanded the Seven Tribes in the Battle of Everest."

"Hold on," Tim interrupted. "Wouldn't Slybourne have been more than a century old when the Battle of Everest occurred?"

"In the age of the Great War, those who were called by Elyon lived for hundreds of years." Faizan stopped in front of a row of medieval swords hanging on the stone walls. "He was the last one standing on Everest, and with Dragon Soul he fought against an army of Nephilim and their king who stood alongside betrayers of Elyon. None believed there was a more powerful sword than Dragon Soul, but the great warrior was killed by an even greater weapon. Khala Salomeh believes Elyon welcomed Ryder Slybourne into eternity with the words 'My good and faithful servant.' My prayer is one day I will hear those same words."

"Upsdell found Dragon Soul on Everest," Amina noted. "What was the weapon that killed Slybourne?"

"Lost for centuries, it is believed to be an artifact once guarded within the Testimony." Faizan eyed them carefully, then continued. "The highest Cherub taught that Ryder Slybourne was the greatest warrior, equal to any written about in the Eternal. Before the Battle of Everest, he fell in love with a beautiful woman—

a bladesmith and outlier who forged Dragon Soul from the purest of metals."

"Sounds like big trouble was about to happen in Sakkhela," Vince chuckled.

"When Florence Upsdell was told of Slybourne's death, she went insane."

"Upsdell?" Tim's brows raised. "Whoa . . ."

"Headmaster Upsdell must have been a direct descendant," Jack surmised.

"Sounds more like a fairy tale gone happily never after," Vince mused.

"Once the headmaster found Dragon Soul on Everest, he must have brought the sword back to Beacon Hill," Emma said. "With the Mercy Covenant as protection, the school would have been the safest place to keep it close and hidden."

"Since he found Dragon Soul the first time," Tim chimed in again, "why go back to Everest?"

"He was searching for the artifact that killed Slybourne." Jack turned around and faced Faizan. "The woman you brought here was following Upsdell's trail?"

"There are no secrets," Emma said to Faizan. "You must tell us the truth."

"Many years ago, when Khala Salomeh was a young girl, she remembered two men from Beacon Hill who searched for the same artifact." Faizan hesitated. "She said one of them was a direct descendant of Florence Upsdell, and the other—"

"Sir James Nightingale," Jack guessed. "He would've been much older by then."

Faizan nodded, a bit surprised. "Nightingale was the only one who returned."

"So the million-dollar question remains." Tim pushed his glasses up the bridge of his nose. "Whatever artifact killed Slybourne is either still lost on Everest or is somewhere else on the planet or in one of a thousand other realms. Our search has gone from excessively unattainable to remarkably impossible. Thank you, Faizan."

"Always the optimist." Vince smirked. "Listen, we're still after the artifacts, and Jack still needs to be healed, right? If this artifact is being hidden on Everest, and that helps bring Jack back to a hundred percent, then we go find it. If not, let's give up and head home."

"Are you hearing yourself?" Tim argued. "Climb Everest? Be real, Vince."

"Faizan, does Salomeh believe the artifact is still on Everest?" Jack waited for an answer, but when there was none, he continued. "That's why we're traveling the Silk Road to Charis—not for me to be healed, but so Emma with her gifts restored can find the artifact somewhere there."

Vince pounced and pinned Faizan up against a wall. "Have you told us everything?"

"I followed Khala's instructions," Faizan replied with fear in his eyes. "That is all."

"Let him down." Jack crossed his arms. "Can Dragon Soul be used against Cherub?"

"Dragon Soul can only be mastered by Cherub or Merikh with gifts strong enough to control the sword's deadly power." Faizan landed on his feet, visibly shaken once he was free from Vince's iron grip. "Never by an outlier—but yes, it can be used against Cherub."

"Nightingale and Upsdell were decades ahead of us." Jack tried to stop his hands from shaking by shoving them into his pockets.

"We'll leave in the morning and travel the Silk Road to Charis. Maybe there we'll find what they couldn't."

"And you will find healing," Emma said softly.

"I am sorry," Faizan said solemnly. "You must understand—"

"We should stay together in this room," Tim interrupted. "Just in case there are visitors."

"Help me find some blankets," Amina said to Tim. "It will be cold tonight."

"You guys go." Vince glared at Faizan. "I'll keep an eye on our friend."

Leaving Faizan in the crosshairs of Vince, Amina and Tim exited through one of the doors while Jack and Emma stepped back into the entryway. Jack stared at the statues, guessing Emma knew the history of each one. He found himself drawn in not by the great Ryder Slybourne, but by the unnamed man hunched over with a staff.

"My parents told me stories passed down through generations about the courage and faith of the heroes who served Elyon." Emma pointed to the statue that captured Jack's attention. "I do not recognize this one."

"Looks familiar though, right? From Nightingale's drawing."

"And the gold sketch on the bell inside the Clock Tower at Star Ferry." Emma paused. "Jack, you know the woman Faizan brought here."

"I'd bet Eden's Star it's Xui Li."

19

SHADOW HILLS, CALIFORNIA

BEYOND THE GATES CLOSING OFF a dead-end road, lights from a long driveway appeared between the hedges and wrapped along a hillside leading to a ranch house. A matte-black Mercedes rolled slowly toward the house, its tires crunching over gravel. With its headlights off, the Mercedes idled near the gates. Will leaned back in the passenger seat and rubbed the sleep from his eyes.

"How long have you known Addison?" Will asked.

"Our paths crossed years ago when I was around your age," Chung replied flatly. "In the end, we made the same choice."

"You mean when you left the Cherub." Will paused. "Does he possess gifts too?"

"Those were stripped away when he nearly killed Gabriella—"

"Jack's mum," Will interrupted. "How did he climb the ranks of the Merikh?"

"Addison is more dangerous than anyone anticipated, including the Cherub and the Merikh. However, I was certain of his intentions long before he betrayed Charlotte Taylor."

"Do you think he killed Rachel—and my mum?"

"I would think twice before asking such questions. If Addison senses you do not trust him, then he will not restrain himself from harming you and your father." Chung's eyes narrowed. "How are your stitches?"

"The blasted Elder tried to slice me in half, but it's healing quite nicely." Will stared at the gates of the property while flashes of memory from Vigan pushed him deeper into the abyss. "Who are we hunting tonight?"

"High-value targets who escaped from the Sanctuary of Prayer."

Chung shut off the engine and climbed out. Will did the same, then slipped the scabbard over his shoulder. Together, they disappeared into the darkness along the fence line. From beneath his jacket, Chung retrieved the Windstrikers and grasped one in each hand. With a flick of the wrist, the Windstrikers tore through the iron fence as if it were paper. "Be on guard for lightforcers or benders."

Will retrieved Dragon Soul from its scabbard. "Lead the way."

In the stillness of the night, Chung pushed against the severed fence rods and let them drop to the ground with a thud. A strong odor of manure filled Will's nostrils as he moved stealthily across the property in tandem with Chung. Moonlight cast shadows across the driveway, and within minutes they reached the side of a Craftsman house. Will inched forward and peered through a window, noticing an empty kitchen and a dining room with plates left on the table. Adrenaline surged through his veins when he realized Chung was more on edge than he'd been in Vigan.

Will steadied himself and whispered, "Who did Addison send us to capture?"

Without answering, Chung showed Will surveillance photos on his cell phone. One was of a man in his early forties, medium build, dark-brown eyes, and wavy hair. The next was of a Chinese woman around the same age, slender, long jet-black hair, and a penetrating stare. Both were standing on the steps of the very same Craftsman, unaware of the lens that captured them.

Across the property, a horse neighed and startled them both. Will spun around with Dragon Soul pointed ahead as his eyes darted in all directions. His heartbeat quickened when shadows appeared from a barn and scrambled across the grass, away from them. Chung unleashed the Windstrikers, the feverish red phoenix glowing on both. The sharp-edged dretium fans whipped through the air with fire sparks flying. Will stood stunned as the Windstrikers cut down one shadow after another before being lured back to Chung's grasp.

Will kept Dragon Soul raised as he stepped across the grass, then knelt beside the first shadow and turned the body over. Lifeless eyes stared back at him. He moved on to the next, and the next. The Windstrikers had killed with lethal swiftness. Will counted eight bodies, but none of them were the man or woman from the photos.

"They aren't here," he said. "How long ago were the photos taken?"

"Yesterday," Chung replied. "Search the barn carefully."

A white light streaked across the skies, exploding against the Craftsman and leaving a crater where the house had been a split second earlier. Chung reacted first and moved toward a second ball of light, knocking it away with one of the Windstrikers. His palms glowed as he unleashed an inferno, leaving the barn raging with flames. Two more shadows appeared from the barn, but they were not running for their lives. Instead, they moved quickly toward Will and Chung, shooting bursts of energy one pulse after another.

Will swung Dragon Soul with ease and deflected their lightforce. Then he counterattacked with a vengeance. The fire-breathing dragons etched on the sword resurrected as a two-headed beast, unleashing a vile shriek that echoed across the hills. Will's stride accelerated as the blade grew even more alive in his grasp. He wasn't a master swordsman yet—but he was already a murderer. He pounced on the first shadow and edged the blade against the man's neck, itching to allow the beast to swarm another Cherub.

A woman's voice stopped him cold. "Wait!"

Will glanced up briefly at the Chinese woman, who stood only a few feet away. He recognized them both from the photos. Moonlight reflected off her eyes, and for a brief moment the darkness pushing him to be an executioner eased. Still, he kept Dragon Soul pressed against the man's throat, deciding whether to listen. Chung stepped forward with the Windstrikers pointed at the woman, even more on edge than earlier.

"You know why we are here," Chung said coldly. "We only need one of you."

The woman slowly lowered onto her knees, and Chung moved in quick. From his jacket, he retrieved a hood that he slipped over her head, and then he grabbed her wrists. An orange glow wrapped around her wrists and covered her hands. Will removed the blade from the man's throat while Chung pulled a black hood over his head and handcuffed him with the same lightforce. Will waited while Chung dialed on his cell phone.

"We have found them," Chung said in a lowered voice. "Both of them."

20

SAKKHELA

VINCE FLICKED A LIGHTER AND lit the torches on the wall. Flames filled the Chamber of Shadowlight with an enchanting glow. Jack slipped out of the chamber and walked the corridors for a while, relieved the excruciating pain that had kept him bedridden for weeks was now bearable. His hands continued to shake—a reminder that he wasn't healed completely. If Faizan was right, total healing would be found in Charis.

Was I only healed enough to keep going? How long will it last? Maybe I can't be healed as long as Eden's Star is inside of me. Is something else killing me because of what I've done? Elyon, only you can answer the unanswered. All I can do is hold on to the faith of a mustard seed and not let go.

"Jack, wait up." Tim hurried down the hallway. "We weren't sure where you disappeared off to."

"Needed a few minutes to clear my head."

"Listen, I wanted to apologize for earlier—and for the last few weeks."

"We're all on edge and beyond tired. Don't worry about it. It's all good."

"Amina said I've been insufferable lately."

"Trouble in paradise?" Jack teased. "She's been right a lot so far."

"Can't deny that one, mate."

"We should know better by now—Amina and Emma are way smarter than either of us." Jack continued down the corridor with Tim alongside. "I thought Vince was going to snap Faizan in half. Haven't seen him that amped up in a while."

"Makes two of us," Tim chuckled. "Got Faizan to spill the beans, though."

"If Will were here, he would've been right there with Vince, no doubt."

"Between you and me, I miss him." Tim paused. "It's like we're missing a piece of us."

"Yeah . . ." Jack's voice trailed off as he stopped in front of a window without glass and peered down on the deserted city and village beyond the walls. "I'd imagine the headmaster has Will somewhere safe until this is over. Everyone is doing what they think is right, but it makes me wonder if everyone has stopped listening for Elyon's voice—including me. I'm a sinner, not a saint. But I gotta admit, when Elyon's voice breaks through the silence, it leaves me more at peace."

"Mum said she doesn't hear a voice, but she senses Elyon's presence—and when we're too busy trying to fix our own problems, it's hard to listen or feel him close."

"A good reminder for all of us, I guess."

Tim pointed at Jack's chest. "Are you strong enough to use Eden's Star?"

"If I tried, I'm not sure where it would take us." Jack caught a glimpse of a reflective blink from a cottage in the village. At first he thought his eyes were playing tricks, but then the reflection appeared again. Adrenaline surged as he pointed toward the village. "Look, something's down there."

Tim was on his tiptoes, peering over Jack's shoulder. "What'd I miss now?"

"Wait a minute." A few seconds passed before the reflection blinked a third time. "See?"

"I just got chills," Tim exclaimed. "What do you think it is?"

"Only one way to find out." Jack hustled down the corridor. "Let's get the others."

Ten minutes later, Jack led the way down the hillside from Slybourne Castle with Emma, Amina, Tim, Vince, and Faizan on his heels. Reaching the main road, he picked up the pace, passing a dozen cottages before he reached the one.

"Should've brought a sword from the castle," Vince said. "We're out in the open."

"We don't need no stinking swords." Tim offered a lame impersonation. "We've got the chosen one right here, and I'm not talking about Jack either."

"Are you sure you saw the light coming from this house?" Emma asked.

"Positive," Jack answered. "Do you know who lives here, Faizan?"

"I have only stayed in the castle when visiting Sakkhela."

"Never slummed it down here with the little people," Tim chastised. "Not surprised."

Jack ignored him. "We need to look inside."

"I'll go with you," Emma said. "Everyone else, wait out here."

"Perfect," Tim replied. "We'll guard the empty streets."

"I don't like this," Vince warned. "Doesn't feel right."

Jack pushed the door open and slipped inside. For a moment, he stood in one corner of a living room furnished with handmade wooden sofas and chairs. His boots creaked across the floor as he approached the staircase.

"Upstairs window," he whispered.

Climbing the steps, Jack realized he wasn't afraid as long as Emma was right behind him. They reached the second floor and approached a corner bedroom at the end of a narrow hallway. He stopped abruptly as the walls seemed to close in on him. Paralyzed by dread, he clenched his fists. His wide-eyed stare remained fixed on the door, and for a moment he was petrified of what awaited him on the other side. His mind flashed to the cage home on Castle Peak Road in Sham Shui Po. He'd buried most of the nightmares deep down, forcing himself to forget those nights, but one raged to the surface the longer he stared at the door.

He remembered being five or six years old, curled up in the corner of a closet-sized room barely wide enough for a single mattress. He was terrified. Rachel hovered over him as a dark shadow moved closer with a belt wrapped around his fist. With his hands over his ears, Jack screamed as the shadow struck. *"If you tell anyone, you are dead."*

Snapping out of the horrific flashback of his father—the man he referred to now as Addison—he steadied himself. *C'mon, Jack. Keep it together.* Entering the bedroom, he glanced around and noticed a shard of a mirror left on a windowsill. Pointing it out to Emma, he lowered himself onto all fours and peered beneath the bed. He flinched when he realized someone was staring back at him. Reaching out his hand, he held it there for a few seconds until the child grabbed hold. Jack helped the boy out from under the bed, then pulled himself to his feet. Staring at the child, whose clothes were stained and covered in filth, Jack tried to make sense of it all.

"Do not be afraid." Emma knelt and added reassuringly, "We are here to help you."

The boy's bloodshot eyes shifted between them, then he darted from the room. Jack chased him down the stairs, burst through the front door, and stopped cold. While the boy raced across the road, other women and children appeared from between the cottages as if they were seeing daylight for the first time in weeks.

"What is going on?" Jack said in a hushed voice.

Faizan stepped away and walked toward the growing crowd of villagers. Jack and his friends followed but kept their distance. A young woman held the little boy's hand as she greeted Faizan with tears in her eyes. Faizan motioned Jack and the others closer until the villagers gathered around them with haunting gazes.

Faizan interpreted the young woman's words. "Weeks ago, the Merikh attacked the city and captured the Chinese woman," he relayed. "They swore to return and take the women and children of Sakkhela too."

The young woman beckoned for them to follow. Jack was reeling from the thought that Xui Li was in the hands of the Merikh. *They will show her no mercy.* The woman led them around the back of the cottages, then stepped aside. Jack's eyes widened at the sight of fresh mounds of dirt scattered across the Highlands beyond the stone-walled city.

"All of the men and boys were killed." Faizan nodded toward the young woman. "She kept the boy hidden underground. He is the only one left alive."

"If the Merikh are coming back . . ." Jack swallowed hard as a righteous anger boiled and vengeance etched deeper into his soul. "We can't leave these people here to die."

21

PERCHED ATOP A TOWER, Sahil guarded the castle as a curtain of darkness closed over the sun. The oak doors flew open as dozens of women and children were ushered into the Chamber of Shadowlight. Amina and Tim grabbed the blankets they'd found earlier and wrapped them around the villagers' shoulders. Vince and Emma handed out whatever food was left in their backpacks.

"They have not eaten in ten days," Faizan said. "Too afraid to be seen."

"Merikh killed the men and boys," Jack said in disbelief, nodding to the child he'd found in the cottage. "He's the bravest one out of all of us." He eyed Emma, who moved among the villagers as if she were one of them. "We can't go back, and we can't leave them here."

"I should have told you about the Chinese woman," Faizan admitted. "Khala Salomeh believes you are an outlier with darkness in your soul and will never fully surrender yourself to the Cherub. Her instructions were clear to keep this from you. She also sensed Emma's gifts were weak. Sahil was the only way for Emma's gifts to be restored by Elyon. No other in this realm could have touched the heavens. You are also right—I brought you to the Silk Road so Emma could find the artifact. But I did tell you the truth, Jack. Healing awaits you in Charis—it is the only place that will restore you."

"It was worth the risk. Believe me, I wouldn't bet on me either. And I believe you about Charis—which is why there is no other choice for me but to keep going."

"You witnessed a miracle, one that will breathe life into the fight." Faizan hesitated. "Cherub search for you, and so do the Merikh. Each will use the many gateways along the Silk Road to find you. If that occurs, then Emma will be their greater prize."

"She won't be able to save everyone at once, and the Merikh will use her as a warning to all Cherub. You said that when we reach the gateway to Charis, not all will be able to enter. You brought the woman here to the castle and left before she was captured. If she was still here when the Merikh arrived, maybe she wasn't able to enter through the gateway either."

Faizan's eyes narrowed. "Khala Salomeh warned her of the possibility."

"So the gateway is here—in the castle." Jack noticed Faizan hesitate again. "Look, whatever you're keeping from us needs to be explained right now."

"Two gateways are hidden," Faizan confessed. "One leads to

a place known only by the Cherub—where those in Kati Pahari have escaped to—and the other is believed to lead deeper into the Highlands to Charis in the Valley of Grace. She must have been captured by the Merikh before she found the gateway to Charis."

"And she was caught before she reached the first gateway too." Jack had one more burning question. "Why would the woman go to Charis? Did she say what she was searching for?"

If the woman is Xui Li, why was she traveling to Charis? Was it to restore her gifts since Sahil wasn't an option? Was she searching for one of the artifacts, even though she warned me not to? Where did the Merikh take her? Is she still alive? He shivered at the thought of what Addison might do to her to get to him.

"Khala Salomeh and the woman believed the weapon that killed Ryder Slybourne centuries ago is hidden there—one of the artifacts once protected inside the Testimony."

"So Tim was right—sort of." A chill shot down his spine as the words sank in. "The artifact wasn't lost on Everest after all. It's hidden in another realm."

"Tonight I will take the women and children through the castle gateway," Faizan said, solemnly. "It will be up to you whether you will leave with us."

A rescue mission or a suicide mission—that's a tough choice.

"You have done all you can do," Jack said, reassuringly. "The rest is in Elyon's hands."

Leaving Faizan in a corner of the chamber, Jack crossed the room and waved for his friends to follow him into the grand entryway. Surrounded by the statues, he waited until they were alone, then tried to camouflage the edge in his voice.

"There are two gateways," he said pointedly. "One is here in the castle. Faizan plans to take the women and children through it to a safe place. The other gateway is believed to lead to Charis—and, well, it doesn't sound like anyone is sure where that one is."

"I'm sticking with you," Vince said. "I'm not bailing, Jack."

"Something else you should know—even if we find the other gateway, there's no guarantee we'll all make it through."

"Well, that's a twist I didn't see coming in this Rubik's Cube," Tim replied. "So some of us might be left behind?"

"It is a risk worth taking," Emma chimed in. "Whoever is left behind can use one of the silver coins to travel through the gateway here in the castle."

"That's what I was thinking," Jack agreed. "But it's a choice you each have to make."

"The Merikh might return to Sakkhela," Tim said. "What do we do if they show up before we've found the gateway to Charis?"

"Like I said, we all must decide for ourselves." Jack's gaze shifted between each one. "If you leave with the women and children, there's no hard feelings."

Jack didn't want to force anyone into anything, even though he'd made his decision. He remembered the night he met Peter Leung with Areum by his side, and the attack at Beacon Hill that sparked his journey to Karābu Island. He'd been tricked by the Cherub, and that fact still stung.

For a while, he kept to himself and watched the women and children, some wrapped in blankets while others finished off the Heavenly Fuel bars and cans of Spitfire Jolt. Seeing their reaction to the meal brought a smile, which quickly faded as he wondered about the devastation that had occurred in Sakkhela before they arrived. The fresh graves were a reminder of the survivors' pain—a pain he knew all too well. Emma, Vince, Tim, and Amina stood quietly on the other side of the room while Faizan stepped into the center and spoke in the survivors' native tongue. Jack noticed their eyes widen as they all turned their attention toward Emma.

"You are the chosen," Faizan said to Emma. "All are honored to serve you."

Emma stepped forward and began singing softly. Jack guessed it was an old Cherub hymn. As her voice echoed off the stone walls, the women and children joined in. Jack stayed quiet as he listened to the haunting melody, which grew stronger with every word. Amina slipped among the crowd, handing a silver coin to each one including Faizan. When she placed a coin in Jack's palm, the weight of the silver pressed down. Vince and Tim wandered over, and Amina gave them coins as well.

"Feels like we're about to get on a ride at Ocean Park," Vince whispered.

"Wait until you meet a Nephilim face-to-face," Jack replied. "Now that's a ride."

"Please tell me that's not going to happen," Tim chimed in.

"Anything's possible," Jack mused darkly. "The Mental Disruptor is child's play, Tim."

"I'm about to throw a wobbly—my birthday is officially gutted."

Faizan stepped beneath the flags hanging overhead, then dropped his coin to the floor. A deep emerald glow spread across the stone floor and up the walls. The women and children stood and dropped their coins within the circle. One by one, each vanished until only Faizan remained. Jack glanced around him, waiting for one of them to step forward. He swallowed a lump in his throat when none of them moved.

"Where does the gateway lead?" Amina asked.

"The House of Luminescence," Faizan answered, "within Beacon Hill."

"What?" Jack shouted. "You can't take them there!"

Before he could lunge forward, Faizan vanished and so did the emerald glow. All of them were stunned by Faizan's words. For a moment, the silence was deafening. The ringing in Jack's ears intensified.

"Why take them to Beacon Hill?" Tim asked, bewildered. "Everyone there is hiding out."

"Nothing we can do about it," Vince answered. "We've got our own treasure hunt, and the clock is ticking."

22

BEACON HILL

NATALIE DARTED DOWN THE STEPS with her Glock raised. She moved with purpose toward an open door leading to the House of Luminescence. A turquoise glow emanated from the room into the corridor. She'd placed a sensor on the door, and when the alarm buzzed on her cell phone, she'd raced from Nightingale's vault through Rowell Library before bounding down the stairs of the Main Hall in Olympic time.

Cautiously, she peered inside at the vaulted wood beams and thick vines creeping down the walls onto the copper-colored stone floor. Her index finger squeezed lightly against the trigger, but then she exhaled and lowered her weapon. Standing in front of her were dozens of women and children wearing oddly fashioned clothes. She thought she was hallucinating until a teenager stepped forward.

"My name is Faizan," he said. "I have brought Cherub exiled from Sakkhela."

Natalie holstered her weapon. "How did you get inside this room?"

"We traveled through a gateway," he replied calmly. "Salomeh Gashkori is my aunt."

Natalie remembered the woman dressed in royal blue and gold who entered the cave through a glowing light. *"Salomeh,"* Fang Xue had said. *"We worried you might not come."* Natalie turned away from the House of Luminescence as Headmaster Fargher appeared on the staircase. Scratching his thick beard, he eyed them closely, then approached and shook Faizan's hand with a half-hearted smile.

"You are not the first," Fargher said cordially. "I assume you will not be the last."

"We need to get them into the vault," Natalie pressed.

Natalie stayed at the back of the crowd and tried to help the children hurry through the empty corridors. Headmaster Fargher led the way through the library, then pressed his finger against the painting of Beacon Hill. Fargher casually stepped through the painting as if he were merely entering another room. The women and children followed him in amazement. Natalie glanced over her shoulder to be sure no one was behind her, then stepped through before the opening sealed itself.

In the depths of Nightingale's vault, Professor Windsor hurried over and escorted the women and children into one line. Without so much as introducing herself, she grabbed a CT wand and waved it over each of them to be sure they were in good health—and to identify whether any of them brought viruses into such close quarters.

"Third group to arrive in the last twenty-four hours," Natalie said. "So far, all of them have entered through the House of Luminescence. Are they all from the same place?"

"Jack told me a day was coming when the lost and hurting would find refuge at Beacon Hill," Fargher replied. "Seems that day is upon us, no matter where they are coming from."

"Freddie, I warned you, but you refused to listen to reason." Professor McDougall sauntered over with his tattered and stained Burberry coat hanging loosely over his shoulders. He waved his arms around in frustration. "There is only so much oxygen in this blasted dungeon."

"We cannot turn anyone away, Mac," Fargher answered coolly.

Knowing the same argument had gone on for days, Natalie tuned out the bickering. Her gaze shifted toward Faizan as he stepped away from being poked and prodded by Professor Windsor. She watched him closely as he walked toward a large group of Pakistanis with his arms wide—the same group who said they were from Kati Pahari.

Natalie found Bau seated on the edge of a cot. "They traveled through a gateway."

"I do not know why they are coming to Beacon Hill," he replied.

Natalie pointed toward Faizan. "Says he's Salomeh Gashkori's nephew."

"She is the one who arrived in the cave—the highest Cherub in all of Pakistan."

"And she's also someone who has seen Emma and Jack. Since you are the resident Cherub expert at Beacon Hill—and, it seems, the golden child of the highest Cherub—I thought you might lend me a hand."

"Cherub can only travel through gateways with an offering." Bau bounced to his feet and followed Natalie toward the group from Kati Pahari. "But Merikh travel through gateways with a blood sacrifice, defying the commands of Elyon."

"If Merikh are killing Cherub, is it possible for them to use the same gateway to get here?"

"The Mercy Covenant was our only protection. If Merikh find the gateway, it is possible."

"Excuse me," Natalie said as they approached Faizan. "Sorry to interrupt. We have not officially met."

Faizan turned around and smiled warmly. "Yes, I am Faizan Khalid."

"I am Natalie McNaughton." She nodded toward Bau. "And this is Bau Hu."

"Thank you for helping us," Faizan said. "I cannot believe I am here."

"In an underground vault?" Bau asked, on edge. "Where did you come from, exactly?"

"The gateway brought us here from Sakkhela."

"No way." Bau stepped back, surprised. "Where Dragon Soul was forged?"

"Yes." Faizan grinned wide. "You know of the place."

"I was the keeper of the sword in Upsdell House."

Faizan's brows raised as he shook Bau's hand vigorously. "I am honored."

"We have met your aunt Salomeh," Natalie interrupted. "She showed us a video of some friends of ours we have been trying to find. Jack Reynolds, Emma Bennett, and Vince Tobias. Do you know who they are?"

"I have met them," Faizan replied. "Amina and Tim as well."

"Amina and Tim?" Bau turned toward Natalie. "The whole lot is together."

"Answers a few of our questions," she admitted. "Were they in Kati Pahari?"

"I brought them there from Karachi." Faizan nodded. "Then we traveled to Sakkhela."

"What are they doing there?" Bau asked.

Faizan's grin faded as he returned a blank stare. Natalie knew there was more, but she didn't want to push too hard. She was surprised when she realized Headmaster Fargher had been standing behind her the whole time.

"Was William with them? William Fargher?"

Faizan shook his head. "I do not know a William."

23

SOUTH CHINA SEA

IN A VAST OCEAN, the Spratly Islands were a blink on the radar in a hotly disputed region. A Gulfstream broke through thick clouds and descended rapidly before landing on a military base with anti-ship, anti-aircraft missile systems, laser-jamming equipment, and fighter jets. After taxiing along the runway, the pilot stopped the aircraft outside of a hangar.

Will glanced over his shoulder at the two hooded prisoners who were bound by Chung's lightforce. Neither had breathed a word since they were captured in Shadow Hills and transported to a private airfield in Van Nuys, where they bypassed security at the hands of a PRC operative. Hours had passed since takeoff, leaving Will even more impressed by how Chung's lightforce remained strong enough to keep them secured. He unbuckled his seat belt and headed toward the exit, then stepped down onto the tarmac.

"You continue to surprise me." Addison smiled. "A great strike against our enemy."

"Michael kept them bound—which is remarkable," Will replied. "Who are they?"

"Our paramount capture of the highest Cherub." Addison paused as Chung emerged from the Gulfstream. "Michael, we have prepared transport for our stellar prize."

Will looked past Addison and noticed a large square metal box inside the hangar. "Are you sure that will stop them from breaking free? One of them is definitely a lightforcer."

"It is made of pure breilium," Addison replied. "Nearly as strong as dretium."

"A lightforcer cannot penetrate dretium, but is that true for breilium?"

"It is the strongest metal made by man—virtually indestructible—and dretium has not been unearthed in centuries. Both will be sedated before takeoff and secured within the chamber. You and Michael will travel with the transport to ensure they arrive safely without incident."

Will nodded as Chung reappeared and pushed the prisoners down the stairs until they stood on the tarmac. Addison sauntered over, a smirk pursing his lips. He walked around the two prisoners, and his sadistic eyes lingered on each one.

"Where are your Elders now?" Addison taunted. "You will be the ones to return what once belonged to me—and then you will die in the same way as the others."

Will followed Chung's cue as they grabbed the prisoners and dragged them toward the breilium box. Both prisoners fought blindly, until Chung stabbed each with a syringe. Will watched as they slumped to the concrete, his curiosity piqued as to what made them so valuable. He helped drag them inside the container, then waited while Chung secured the door and punched in a code that locked them inside.

"We are behind schedule," a soldier in military fatigues called out. "Are you ready?"

"I have been ready for a long time," Addison replied darkly. "Wheels up."

A Xi'an Y-20 Kunpeng wide-fuselage transport aircraft rolled down the tarmac, stopping outside of the hangar. A large aft ramp opened automatically as the soldier climbed onto a forklift and maneuvered the forks beneath the breilium box. With the box lifted off the ground, the forklift spun around and drove up the ramp, disappearing inside the aircraft. Addison was already headed for the Gulfstream, but he stopped midstride.

He turned slowly. "Michael . . ."

Chung approached cautiously. "What is it?"

"Jack has traveled to Sakkhela." Addison grabbed the side of his head and closed his eyes, clearly struggling to keep a connection to the vision of Jack's whereabouts. "He is with the others, including the girl."

"If they are together, I will need the protégé." Chung waved Will over. "His ability to jump the gateway will get us there quicker. Once they are captured, he has the power to move them through a gateway without traveling with them. We may not get another opportunity."

Addison gathered himself and waved off the soldier who waited on the aft ramp of the transport aircraft. He waited until the ramp closed. "It is worth the risk."

"We will return through the Po Lin Monastery gateway," Chung confirmed.

"They took the prisoners without us." Will stepped over, confused. "Aren't we going with them?"

"Change of plans," Addison replied. "I will follow the transport in the Gulfstream."

"Wait for me before opening the box," Chung warned. "Sedation will wear off within twelve hours."

Addison grabbed Will by the shoulders. "Your day is here—revenge is now."

"We must go to the Thar Desert," Chung said. "Gateway to Sakkhela."

"Are you sure you can jump the gateway?" Addison asked Will.

"Yeah." Will's gaze hardened. "I can jump the gateway."

24

SAKKHELA

SEVERAL HOURS HAD PASSED since Faizan and the refugees from Sakkhela stepped through the gateway to the House of Luminescence. In the quietness of the night, Jack couldn't deny the temptation to drop a silver coin and follow them. Searching the endless rooms of the vast castle left them no closer to finding the gateway to Charis. Returning to the Chamber of Shadowlight, he found Vince and Tim already there.

"We are searching for a single ant named George in the Amazon jungle," Tim complained. "It's maddening."

"We should call it a night and start fresh in the morning," Vince suggested. "It's totally possible the gateway isn't inside the castle but somewhere else, maybe in the city."

"That's what I was thinking—tomorrow's another day." Jack glanced toward the grand entryway. "Where's—"

A high-pitched whistle startled them, and all three jumped. Panic struck when Emma and Amina burst into the chamber. Another second passed before Jack and the others realized what was wrong.

"Merikh are here," Amina said in a hushed tone. "Move quickly."

"Better to remain a ghost than show ourselves," Emma urged. "Stay together."

As they were sneaking out of the chamber, beams of light cut across the stained glass windows. Hurrying down the corridor, they reached stone steps leading to the second floor. While the others took the stairs two at a time, Jack stopped for a moment. *I have to know if Xui Li is with them.* Turning back, he raced down the corridor, only slowing his pace when he neared the doorway. As he peered around the corner, his heart pounded through his chest. Inside the chamber, wearing all black, stood Michael Chung, six Merikh assassins, and a masked shadow gripping Dragon Soul. He'd seen the masked shadow before, and the deadliness of Dragon Soul was undeniable.

"Search the castle," Chung ordered. "They were seen crossing the desert to the gateway."

While the assassins split up, Chung and the masked shadow stayed behind. Jack wished he could explode with Eden's Star to end the life of Michael Chung. Being so close to the one who murdered Rachel was almost too much to bear as he surrendered to the temptation of retribution.

It's how this all began—standing over Rachel's grave vowing revenge.

Emma squeezed his shoulder as she whispered, "Jack, we need to go."

"Kill him, Emma." Jack knew it was a twisted request. "Please, end his life."

"Then we will be no better." Emma pulled him gently away from the doorway. "A day will come when they will be held accountable for their sins and judged at the throne of Elyon."

"But I want judgment now," he replied. Tears welled up in his eyes as he gritted his teeth, desperate to hold on to his sanity. Moving down the corridor, they reached the stairs without being noticed. Gunfire erupted on the floor above. Jack glanced back and realized the masked shadow and Chung were in the corridor.

Flames burst from Chung's outstretched hands, exploding against the stone walls. Emma stepped in front of Jack and unleashed a ball of stark-white lightforce, creating a wall between them. He'd seen Wilson face off against Chung in Sitio Veterans with the same magnificent power. He expected the pursuers to back off, but instead the masked shadow sliced through the energy wall with Dragon Soul while unleashing violet bursts, which exploded within inches of Jack and Emma.

"Tonight, Eden's Star will be torn from your flesh," Chung seethed.

As the masked shadow darted toward them, Jack retreated with Emma upstairs to the second floor. More gunfire echoed. Emma led the way down a hallway and up another flight of stairs. *I hope she knows where she's going.* When they reached the last step, Jack realized they were on the roof, where Vince, Tim, and Amina crouched behind a stone tower.

"We're trapped up here," Vince said, "unless we're ready to jump."

Tim urged, "Now would be a good time for Eden's Star, mate."

Jack tried to settle the adrenaline flowing through his veins as he searched for a moment of peace so he could surrender his spirit. Red laser beams streaked across the opposite side of the roof. Out of the corner of his eye, Jack realized Chung and the masked shadow had appeared. Emma stood and held her arms out wide, creating a whirlwind around them. Her eyes turned bone white as centuries-old stones shook and rumbled before breaking free. With a sweeping of her arms, the stones floated in midair before screaming across the roof in both directions.

Rapid fire erupted, bullets ricocheting off the stones. Chung unleashed bursts of fire in a relentless attack. Purple sonic pulses followed from the shadow, who moved forward, unafraid of Emma's powerful defenses.

In the skies above, a high-pitched whistle added to the chaos. Sahil swooped down with her colossal wings tucked in close, attracting the attention of the Merikh. Her claws gripped the edge of the rooftop as she lowered her beak. Bullets ricocheted and pierced the stone all around.

"Don't wait for an invitation," Jack shouted. "Get on."

Vince grabbed Amina and tossed her onto Sahil's broad back, then did the same to Tim before climbing on himself. Jack scrambled across the rooftop and pulled Emma back toward him. *I'm not leaving her behind.* She never released her control of the chunks of stone floating between them and the Merikh assassin squad.

Flapping her wings, Sahil lifted off the roof and hovered over them. The colossal white eagle lowered herself enough to clasp her claws around Jack's and Emma's shoulders. Jack held on for his life while Emma shifted the stones one last time, slamming them into the rooftop. Slybourne Castle buckled under the weight, and the roof imploded. Sahil turned from the castle and flew like a rocket toward the south with the wind rushing against them.

With his feet dangling, Jack shouted at Emma, "Are you okay?"

Her eyes turned from stark white to amber. "That was too close."

From above they heard Tim scream, "Doesn't this blasted bird have a seat belt?"

25

SAHIL FLAPPED HER WINGS and bolted through the thick clouds of a thundering storm. Drenched to their bones, Jack and Emma remained in Sahil's gentle clawed grasp. Butterflies fluttered in Jack's stomach as Sahil descended rapidly in the darkness, then turned and swooped in a giant circle.

Glancing down, he realized they were soaring above a vast ocean and crashing waves exploding against sheer cliffs hundreds of feet tall. Closing his eyes, he tried to calm a queasiness that reminded him he was deathly afraid of heights. Squeezing his eyelids tighter, he was struck with piercing flashes amid the rushing wind.

Buildings burned across Hong Kong. People beaten and tortured. Eden's Star ripped from his bloodied hands. Blurred sketches across weathered papers. Rolling highlands. White-capped mountains. Barren deserts. In rapid succession, the faces of Emma, Vince, Tim, Amina, Will, then a sea of thousands desperate to enter through the gates of Beacon Hill. Dark silhouettes whipped across the skies, unleashing vile squeals and sending shivers down Jack's spine, even though he knew it was only in his mind.

The visions are closer to real time—but Emma, Vince, Tim, and Amina are with me.

Sahil slowed her flight and released her claws from Jack's shoulders. He opened his eyes once he felt his boots touch the ground. While the others climbed off Sahil, he glanced around, expecting the dark silhouettes to appear from nowhere. Strong gusts of wind swirled as they stood in a torrential downpour only a few steps from the edge of the cliffs.

"This doesn't look like the Valley of Grace—more like the Cliffs of No Escape." Tim tried to wipe water spots from his lenses, which was an impossible task as rain pelted him faster than he could clean. "Our only options are to plunge to our death or be found a century from now frozen in the ground. We've got no food, no clothes, and no cash. A total failure."

Vince pointed toward the raging ocean. "We've got plenty of water."

"No one takes me seriously," Tim groaned. "Why am I even talking?"

"We're out of time," Jack replied. "There's only one way forward."

"You may not survive," Emma warned. "Where will Eden's Star take us?"

"Emma, there is no other logical choice," Amina argued. "We cannot stay in Sakkhela any longer—or wherever we are right now."

"For the record," Tim interrupted, "I wasn't serious about plunging or freezing to death."

Jack stepped away and walked over to Sahil. Her golden eyes peered deep into his soul, as if she knew the reason why she'd brought them to the cliff's edge. As thunder rumbled and lightning flashed against the darkened skies, he leaned into the magnificent creature and touched her velvety feathers.

"You were the one to bring us this far," he whispered. "Well done, Sahil."

Jack stepped back as Sahil spread her wings and lifted off the ground. He stayed where he was until he could no longer see the pentaloon. *If Eden's Star is a compass, then it'll need to show us the way from here.* He exhaled long, turned around, and walked back to the others, who were drenched to the bone.

Tim broke the awkward silence. "So, we're giving up on finding Charis."

"Nothing has gone to plan." Jack shivered. "But we're not giving up."

"Sahil brought us here on purpose," Emma surmised. "We must be standing at the gateway that leads to the Valley of Grace and Charis."

"Which requires more than an offering—Faizan was talking about Eden's Star."

"Jack, you haven't been able to get Eden's Star to work since Karābu," Vince said.

"We're at the end of the road if we don't give it a shot."

Jack tried to settle his spirit, which seemed impossible. He breathed in deep and exhaled slowly, blocking out all distractions. *Blind faith is what is required.* Ignoring the storm, he walked back toward the edge of the cliff. *Elyon, guide our steps into the unknown—allow Eden's Star to take us where you need us to be.* He felt a searing heat within him, but instead of being afraid, he welcomed it as an old friend knocking at the door.

Within seconds, a raging inferno spread across his chest as a white light glowed beneath his shirt. *I'll never get used to this.* Emma grabbed his hand, and their fingers interlaced. Gripping her hand tight, he reached out and grabbed Vince's hand next to him. Looking down the line, he realized Tim and Amina were alongside them.

Vince grabbed Tim's hand. "Don't make it weird."

"What are we supposed to do?" Tim asked. "Flap our arms?"

"Take a step of faith," Jack replied. "That's what Elyon requires."

"This is totally insane. Take a step where? I mean, you can't be serious."

"We have to believe," Amina said. "Stay beside me, Timothy."

Jack stared out into blackness as light exploded. "One . . . two . . ."

On three, they stepped off the cliff and vanished.

26

KYOTO, JAPAN

JACK STUMBLED OUT OF A BATHROOM, knocking into several people who were lip-locked in a corner of a narrow hallway. Still dazed, he staggered toward bright flashing lights and a thumping beat. For a moment, he braced himself against the wall, desperate to shake off the fog drifting through his mind. He entered a packed dance floor, where a DJ was whipping the crowd into a frenzy with another techno beat blasting from a stage stacked with speakers. Asians and expats around his age mingled with one common purpose—to lose themselves partying with their drugs of choice.

How many nights was I lost at the Shack? Where did it get me?

A searing pain tore at Jack's skin as he gripped his chest and tried to catch his breath. He pushed his way through the crowd, rainbow lights streaking across the nightclub to the beat of the music. He reached a bar where alcohol flowed freely, then glanced over his shoulder searching for Emma, Vince, Tim, and Amina. *This isn't like the last time.* A scantily dressed bartender slammed an empty glass in front of him and offered a flirtatious smile.

She asked, "Sake or beer?"

"Where am I?" Jack asked, confused. "What city?"

Clearly caught off guard, she replied, "Butterfly World in Kyoto."

"Kyoto, Japan?"

"You drink too much already." She swiped the glass from the bar, then nodded to a security guard who lingered near the dance floor. "We will call you a taxi, *gaijin*." *Outsider.*

Jack knew better than to resist, so he followed the guard outside. Instead of climbing into a waiting taxi at the curb, he headed down the sidewalk. Breathing in the brisk air, he reached a street corner and stared aimlessly across at a pagoda. He leaned his head back, staring up at the sky, and fought an urge to empty his stomach until the agony subsided. Wiping a trickle of blood from his nostrils onto the back of his hand, he replayed what he remembered.

I couldn't hold on to Vince or Emma.

He panicked, realizing they had been separated before reaching their destination. A group of teens headed toward him from the direction of the nightclub. He ignored their stares, knowing he looked like he'd been dragged through a desert and dumped by a tornado. As they approached, he shoved his bloodied hands deep into his pockets and kept his head low.

"Jack!"

Spinning around, he exhaled at the sight of Emma hurrying down the sidewalk. The group of teens brushed past while he looked beyond Emma, expecting Vince, Tim, or Amina to appear at any second.

"You are alive." Emma hugged him tight. "I have been searching for nearly an hour."

He wrapped his arms around her waist and leaned in. "I couldn't hold on to you."

"It was not like the first time, on Karābu." Emma pushed back gently and wiped a tear from her eye. "Do you know where we are?"

"Kyoto, Japan." Jack nodded toward Butterfly World. "Somehow I ended up in there."

"So we are no longer in the Highlands," she said. "We need to search—"

A black van with tinted windows screeched around the corner and accelerated toward them. Instinctively, Jack and Emma darted away from the vehicle. Emma was quicker than Jack, but he did his best to keep up. As the van gained ground, a glowing white light balled between Emma's palms. Jack nearly knocked her over as she stopped on a dime and faced the van. The pavement ripped tread from the tires as the van stopped abruptly, leaving Jack and Emma caught in the headlights. A sliding door opened and a head poked out.

"Get in," Eliška ordered. "Both of you."

Emma lowered her hands and the ball of light evaporated. She hurried over while Jack stood shocked. A moment passed before he followed and climbed into the van. Eliška slammed the door shut once he was inside, and the driver punched the accelerator.

"What are you doing here?" Jack asked Eliška, dumbstruck.

"Tim and Amina are safe." Eliška texted on her cell phone. As she glanced over at Jack, her deep-brown eyes softened. "Vince was found a mile from here—he is injured." She fired off another text, then slipped her phone into her pocket. "We are meeting them in Ine Town."

Jack swallowed hard as he asked shakily, "He's not going to die, is he?"

"He is being cared for on the way." Eliška shot a quick look at Emma. "Faizan and those from Sakkhela arrived at Beacon Hill. Faizan would not say much to anyone about either of you."

"The Merikh found us in Sakkhela," Emma replied, stone-cold. "Michael Chung and the assassins—including the one who stole Dragon Soul."

Jack tried hard to keep himself calm. "Eliška, how did you know where to find us?"

"Salomeh Gashkori confirmed you were searching for the Valley of Grace deeper in the Highlands." Eliška glanced back through the rear window. "The faction has been searching for Charis for many years, and we have narrowed our search to the regions of Kyoto and Osaka. Since Faizan arrived with the others at Beacon Hill, we mobilized hundreds of the faction who have been looking for you in both cities. The fact you are here means we are searching in the right place." Eliška eyed them steadily. "How did you find the gateway?"

"Sahil brought us here," Emma answered. "A pentaloon."

"How do you know about all of this?" Jack interrupted, increasingly more confused. "Have you been one of the Cherub this entire time?"

He couldn't help himself from wanting to ask more questions. *Who are the faction?* He never imagined Eliška being any part of this. He remembered the first time he laid eyes on her when she was escorted onto the *Eastern Dragon*, bound and blindfolded. He had questioned why Xui Li put him on the freighter, which was owned by Charlotte Taylor and the Merikh. Even though Eliška didn't answer, the longer he stared into her fiery eyes, the more certain he was that none of it was a coincidence. Xui Li knew exactly what she was doing, but the question remained: Why?

"I am a follower of Elyon," Eliška finally answered.

"She is part of a faction who challenge the Cherub," Emma added.

"And you were once destined to lead the Cherub," Eliška replied flatly.

Jack sensed the edge sharpen between them. His mind flashed to the Oasis of Remembrance when he introduced them to each other, and the coldness was even more frigid this time around. He was caught in the middle, and he knew better than to light a match and try to melt the tension.

"How long until we get to Ine Town?" Jack asked Eliška.

"We will arrive in two hours."

27

THE BLACK VAN NAVIGATED THE STREETS, traveling out of the main city surrounded by the mountains of Higashiyama, Kitayama, and Nishiyama. Jack clenched his jaw and balled his hands into fists as he counted the minutes. *I never should've used Eden's Star until I knew how to control it. I trusted it to guide us, and now look what's happened. More than anyone, I know how dangerous it is. I'm reckless, and all of this is my fault.* He wanted to say something to Emma and Eliška to knock down the wall between them, but the words refused to leave his lips.

Forty minutes later, the van entered a neighborhood where dozens of boathouses on stilts seemed to hover over the surface of the water. The driver slowed and parked in front of one. Jack grabbed a handle on the side door, yanked it open, and hopped out. He was met by Amina.

"Where is Vince?" Jack asked.

"He is inside." Amina's eyes were puffy. "Timothy is with him."

Jack entered around the side near a boat shed where a group of men and women were huddled together, each one armed with a semiautomatic weapon. Inside, he climbed the steps of the two-story boathouse, ignoring others who were seated in the living room—who looked to be no older than early twenties. He searched until he found Tim standing in a doorway, teary eyed. A chill shot down his spine when he heard Vince screaming and groaning in agony. Jack's legs weakened as he peered over Tim's shoulder, watching Beacon Hill's strongest athlete sprawled out on a blood-soaked mattress, flailing his arms as a woman hovered over him.

Professor Burwick glanced up as she ripped a sheet into shreds. Jack nearly fell over, stunned not only by her presence but her appearance. Reddish scarred skin covered her face, and her frizzy ginger hair was matted in patches against her skull.

"Fetch Amina," Burwick instructed. "I need her right away."

Tim bolted and ran down the hallway, leaving Jack alone. "Professor—"

"There will be time to explain later. Right now, we must stop the bleeding." She waved Jack into the room. "Give me a hand and pull this tight."

Jack stepped forward, and Vince's wide eyes locked in on him. Standing alongside Professor Burwick, he grabbed hold of the tourniquet she offered. He realized Vince's femur was poking out from a deep gash along his right leg. He swallowed puke in his throat, hands shaking as his gaze shifted away, too ashamed to look at his friend.

Amina entered the bedroom. "Professor, what can I do?"

"Salomeh said you are the only healer here," Burwick answered. "Come closer."

"I have never used my gifts." Amina took another step. "I am not certain I can do it."

"There is no time to wait. He will die, Amina."

"Do something," Jack said softly. "Please."

Vince was barely conscious when Emma and Eliška entered and waited near the foot of the bed. Jack kept his grip on the tourniquet, willing his friend to fight through. Amina grabbed hold of Vince's hand and squeezed. From over his shoulder, Jack noticed Tim hadn't moved from the doorway as voices from the living room grew louder—intense prayers echoed throughout the boathouse. Vince's pupils rolled back in his head, leaving only the whites of his eyes.

"He's stopped breathing," Burwick said urgently. "Amina, only you can save him."

"Elyon, you are the great healer and physician." Amina prayed with one hand on Vince's chest and the other on the bloodied wound. Jack was shaken to his core. "The heavens and earth surrender to your power as you promised to make all things new." Amina's hand was covered in blood as she moved her fingers across the deep gash. "We ask you to restore life and bring healing now."

Jack stood helpless, willing Vince to breathe again. Seconds passed, but Vince remained lifeless. Burwick stepped forward and placed her hand on top of Amina's, then Eliška and Emma did the same. With their hands stacked on top of each other, a white-and-violet glow spread across Vince's chest.

Without thinking about what he was doing, Jack reached out and placed one hand on top of Emma's while holding the tourniquet tight with the other. Energy surged through his body, as if

Amina's healing gift flowed from one person to the next. Purest power. An unexplainable presence greater than anything he'd ever experienced before entered the room. He kept his hand on top of Emma's as the walls and floors of the boathouse shook hard until it seemed as if the whole place might explode.

Everyone flinched when Vince sat straight up with a giant gasp, as if inhaling all the oxygen in the room. Immediately, Amina turned her attention to the femur and the pool of blood soaking through the mattress. Grabbing hold of the femur, she shifted the bone back where it belonged, Vince wailing in agony until the gash sealed against his skin. A few seconds passed before the presence in the room lifted and the boathouse settled in peace. Voices from the living room ceased, and there was a moment when the beating in Jack's chest was all he heard.

"We were not the only ones praying," Emma said quietly.

Vince said in a weakened voice, "That was a rush."

"Rest now," Amina replied. "Elyon has healed you."

Vince's eyes closed while his chest rose and fell. Amina dropped to her knees, beyond drained. Emma and Eliška helped Amina to her feet and ushered her out of the room. Jack pulled the bloodied sheet from the bed and held it in his hands. He wasn't sure how to explain it in words, but it was clear Amina had used her gift of healing at a cost to herself. When he glanced over his shoulder, he noticed Tim was gone too.

Burwick grabbed a cane leaning against a wall. "Amina said the Merikh found you."

"I nearly got my best friend killed." Disgusted with himself, Jack balled up the sheet and tossed it on the floor. He didn't worry about weighing his words, not caring how the professor might react. "I can't be trusted to protect Eden's Star any longer."

"So it is true." Burwick's eyes narrowed. "You are the outlier."

"Professor, I'm not who everyone thinks I am."

"You are an unexpected choice," she admitted. "But Rachel picked you for a reason."

"What do you know about Rachel?"

"I helped her disappear without the Cherub knowing where she had gone." Burwick stabbed her cane into the floor. "A secret discovered by the Merikh—and your father."

"Ever since Rachel was murdered, all I have left are more questions."

"I assure you, you are not the only one."

28

STANDING OUTSIDE WITH EMMA on the balcony the next morning, Jack gazed across the river where a haunting fog drifted. Floating in the middle of the river were round net pens to capture yellowtail and red sea bream. Wearing a fresh hoodie and jeans—courtesy of Eliška, who found clothes hanging in a bedroom closet—his hands dug into the hoodie pocket as he breathed in the brisk air.

"Why didn't you tell me you knew each other?" Jack asked.

"I have only seen her twice," Emma replied. "Star Ferry and Oasis of Remembrance."

"But you know who she is—you said she's part of a faction."

"Professor Burwick is known to lead a faction of those who

do not believe in all the Cherub ways—Eliška is one of Burwick's most loyal." Emma brushed her hair away from her face. "Many of the highest Cherub do not trust them, even though they are followers of Elyon."

"Did you know she was smuggled aboard the *Eastern Dragon*?"

Emma shook her head. "Not until I saw her with my own eyes at Star Ferry."

"Xui Li put me on that ship because she must've known about Eliška and the others. But how could she be sure that I'd find them or that you'd be at Victoria Harbour to rescue all of us? I can't answer those questions, but I'm positive she brought us together for a reason."

"Jack, just be careful trusting Eliška or Professor Burwick."

A sliding-glass door opened, and Burwick stepped onto the balcony, leaning heavily on her cane. "Thought I might find you two out here on this beautiful morning."

"Is Vince going to be okay, Professor?" Jack asked.

"Amina's gifts saved his life, but he needs rest. He will have a long road ahead."

"She never told me she is a healer," Emma said. "Why was she so sick afterward?"

"I believe this was her first time using her gifts in such a way, which takes its toll. As she grows stronger in her gifts, her healing power will not deplete as quickly. Tim and Eliška are keeping an eye on both as they rest." Burwick paused. "The gateway in Sakkhela should not have done this to Vince."

"Faizan said going through the gateway to the Valley of Grace would require more than an offering," Emma replied. "We had no other way to keep going except—"

"I chose to use Eden's Star to bring us to where Elyon wanted us," Jack interrupted. "Professor, I can't explain why everything went wrong this time."

"You have used the compass before?"

"One other time, and we all made it through. Are we still in the Highlands?"

Burwick nodded. "You are in the Kansai region."

"So we can still find the Valley of Grace and Charis."

"It seems we are closer than we may have realized." Burwick hesitated. "Rachel confided in me when she knew she could no longer trust Peter Leung. She told me about a key she kept hidden, one she suspected would unlock the whereabouts of Eden's Star. The last time she was in Hong Kong, after she watched you from afar to ensure you were okay, I helped her leave the city without the knowledge of Peter or the Cherub. She never revealed where she hid the key—and I never revealed her whereabouts when she returned to Sitio Veterans and Vigan."

"Do you know about the City of Gods?"

"Rachel traveled there more than once but failed like the others—including your mother. Dabria, Xui Li, and I—in our own ways—did all we could to help Rachel find and recover the compass. Your sister knew she was being hunted, and keeping the key with her had become far too dangerous." Burwick ignored the stunned expression on Jack's face and continued. "Rachel was executed in Sitio Veterans, but she was not killed by a single bullet. Her gifts had grown much too powerful to die so easily. Jack, whatever it was that took her life was beyond this world." Burwick grew quiet for a long moment. "We have all lost someone we love—taken far too soon from this earth. Until one has experienced such loss, one cannot understand how the true love of Elyon keeps us fighting in this war."

Emma broke her silence. "Who did you lose, Professor?"

"My daughter—Darcy." Burwick shifted her weight, and the grooves on her scarred cheeks deepened. Her raspy voice shook slightly. "Eliška and Darcy were in Ho Chi Minh searching for Merikh traffickers. Near a hostel where they stayed, they found a nightclub known as a place where expats and other female tourists were often abducted. Merikh were there waiting and captured them." Burwick's eyes grew glossy. "Eliška would have died too if it had not been for you, Jack."

He swallowed hard as he searched for words. "I am sorry, Professor."

"Charlotte Taylor and Michael Chung tortured me for the truth about Rachel, the artifacts, and your whereabouts. I am ashamed to admit I was not as strong as Darcy or Eliška. Both Cherub and Merikh now know you are the outlier who searches for the artifacts—but I will do whatever is in my power to help you, no matter the cost."

Jack looked back and forth between Burwick and Emma. "I used the key that Rachel kept hidden and found Eden's Star in the City of Gods—but obviously we don't know how to control it. Do you know, Professor?"

"Many have searched for Eden's Star." Burwick's eyes narrowed. "No one has ever found it."

"Jack is telling the truth," Emma reassured. "I have seen it with my own eyes."

"If that is so, then there is an explanation for what occurred last night." Burwick leaned against the balcony railing, as if to take some weight off her feet. "Eden's Star is a compass formed by Elyon to guard the artifacts once kept within the Testimony. The compass leads the Protector to these artifacts, but it hides them from everyone else—including the Elders and Cherub. From the ancient writings, it is believed the Protector of Eden's Star must never use the compass with more than two or three others. Beyond that, it can be deadly—as we have witnessed."

Jack leaned his head back. "That's why Vince nearly died."

"Too many of us at one time," Emma added. "Jack, you didn't know."

"Maybe that's why we couldn't hold on to each other." Jack hesitated. "Professor, Eden's Star transported us from Karābu Island—all of us at once."

"Then you are lucky to be alive." Burwick's gaze hardened. "As the Protector, you are being forced into a war you are clearly unprepared to fight. Within the Cherub there exists a division, as those who refuse to follow the rules of the highest Cherub are seen as outcasts. If we are to defeat the Merikh, it is time for all of Elyon's followers to put their differences aside and unite to protect the light."

"Have you told the Cherub what you know about the Highlands?" Jack asked. "And how you've narrowed down your search for Charis?"

She turned her attention directly toward him. "Perhaps you should consider lightening your burden by passing Eden's Star to another—to someone who is more prepared."

"You're talking about Eliška. She's one of the faction, right?"

"Emma should be the one who protects Eden's Star." Salomeh Gashkori stepped out from the boathouse onto the balcony, startling Jack and Emma. "She has been chosen and possesses the gifts necessary to defend us from the Merikh."

"From my perspective, it does not seem that way," Burwick replied. "Eliška is willing to go straight into the darkness without fear of the Merikh, while Emma hides in the shadows."

"I am willing to do the same," Emma corrected. "You do not know me well, Professor."

Salomeh held up her hand with a grin. "Before we start a debate that could last for eternity, perhaps we should see Eden's Star for ourselves."

Jack was caught in the middle with all eyes on him. He knew Salomeh had deceived them to go to Sakkhela for Emma to be healed, and Professor Burwick's intentions were clearly to disrupt the Cherub in order to destroy the Merikh. *It's not like I can just pull the compass out of my chest.* "Who is the shadow who stole Dragon Soul?" A bewildered expression washed over Salomeh and Burwick. "Find out who it is, and I'll hand you Eden's Star. Until then, I'm the Protector."

29

LANTAU ISLAND

SHEK PIK PRISON, a high-tech maximum security facility surrounded by razor-wire fencing and infrared perimeter alarms, remained under twenty-four-hour surveillance. The prison locked away the most notorious criminals in the Orient. Serial killers. Political activists. Terrorists. White-collar criminals tied to Asia's most lethal crime syndicates. Lately, a steady stream of new inmates—the highest Cherub—had entered through the solid iron gate surrounded by lush greenery.

An armored truck made of pure breilium stopped at the iron gate while heavily armed security and highly trained German shepherds searched the vehicle. Seated behind bulletproof glass in the front seat, Michael Chung kept his eyes glued to his cell phone. On the screen was a video feed of the chained cargo in the back.

Once the iron gate opened, the armored truck rolled through and stopped in the center of the prison yard. Chung climbed out and rounded the back of the vehicle, then punched in a code on his phone to unlock the rear door. Pulling the door wide, he stared at the two hooded prisoners, whose wrists and ankles were chained through fiery looped hooks bolted to the metal. He climbed inside and released the chains, leaving the prisoners handcuffed in his lightforce around their wrists and ankles. Leading the prisoners to the edge, he pushed them out of the armored truck. Each fell forward, slamming face-first against the concrete with a heavy thud.

"On your feet," Chung ordered.

The male prisoner crawled on all fours and blindly searched the ground until his hand touched the woman prisoner's thigh. He helped her to her feet, and they stood surrounded by guards aiming semiautomatic weapons at each of them. Chung pushed both forward while security circled. He prodded them into the main building, where a maze of locked doors automatically opened, leading deeper into Shek Pik Prison.

Entering a secured hospital wing, both prisoners were pushed past rows of inmates handcuffed to beds and hooked up to blood transfusion machines. They were forced onto empty beds, where they were handcuffed like the others. Chung watched as a medical team approached and immediately started transfusions on each one—exchanging their blood for another's. He waited until a sedative was administered that left both unconscious, and then he released his lightforce from securing them.

One of the doctors asked, "Names?"

"High-priority targets," Chung replied. "Solitary confinement."

"Procedure will be finished within a few hours."

"Text me when the transfer is complete. Their blood must be examined."

"Understood."

Chung left the hospital wing, and the doctors continued drawing blood from the Cherub prisoners and replacing it with the most evil of humanity. None manifested gifts as powerful as the ones he'd seen in Emma, but stripping them of their abilities was a safeguard to be sure the Cherub were unable to mount an attack from within the prison. Wickedness injected into their veins would leave the Cherub fractured for generations, and for those who were lost without their gifts, death was inevitable. Chung walked the corridors until he reached the solitary wing. A door buzzed and he entered, knowing his every move was monitored. He stepped up to one of the cells and nodded toward a guard to unlock it.

Inside, he found Xui Li seated on the edge of a single mattress beside an open toilet. He inhaled the putrid stench, which was now suffocating the room since he'd ordered the ventilation to be limited a bit more each day. It was one way to wear her down and get her to talk.

"I may not be able to kill you"—he crossed his arms while she ignored him—"but I will bring you to your knees one way or another."

Xui Li stared at a graffitied wall depicting the vilest of sins. Chung had chosen this particular cell because he knew it once belonged to a man who murdered a dozen women in Wan Chai. He thought he was immune to the darkness that surrounded him, yet the longer he stood in the cell, the more on edge he became.

"There is still time." Xui Li turned her intense dark-brown

eyes toward him. "Turn from your wicked ways before you spend eternity separated from Elyon."

"You speak to me as if I am your student." Chung harnessed his disgust. "I will not be caught on the wrong side of history." He stepped forward and tossed two passports on the bed. "Oliver and Winnie Bennett were found in Los Angeles."

Xui Li shifted methodically. "You cannot control Emma."

"Love is her downfall." Chung smirked. "It is the same for you."

"I will never reveal what I know about the artifacts."

"Why were you in Sakkhela?" Chung pressed a bit harder. "What were you looking for?"

"Whatever it was, it seems you have failed to find it too."

"Jack, Emma, and the others from Beacon Hill were in Sakkhela as well. How do you know we haven't killed them already?" Chung balled his hand into a fist, tempted to strike her. "The Elders brought this upon themselves. You have failed, again."

"All have fallen short of Elyon's perfection, but deep down in my soul there is no doubt they are very much alive." Xui Li paused. "Forgiveness is available for each of us, Michael."

"Your need to seek forgiveness from Elyon shows how weak you are—and how weak the Cherub faith remains. We have captured dozens of the highest Cherub without a fight. There is no courage left to defend Elyon." He noticed her eyes flared for a split second. "You are the only Elder left alive. Dabria is dead. Vigan is abandoned. None of it was done by my hands—I was simply a teacher."

"You are one of the few with gifts powerful enough to defend the Cherub." Xui Li narrowed her eyes at him. "Yet you allow yourself to be controlled by Addison and the Merikh."

"Once you are dead, then I will be free."

"He will betray you as he has done to everyone else."

"Betrayal is the name of the game," Chung snapped. "It is how this world survives."

Xui Li turned her face away and stared at the concrete wall. Chung stepped out of the cell, and the door slammed shut. He stood in the corridor for a moment, knowing he had delivered the message in the exact way Addison requested. Soon, the Cherub would know who had been captured, and no doubt the news would reach Jack and Emma—wherever they might be.

He returned to the hospital wing and waited until he was given an insulated carrier that contained a dozen blood samples of the highest Cherub held in solitary, including the Bennetts'. Reaching the outside, he carried the insulated box toward the armored vehicle while inmates loaded black body bags into the back of another truck.

30

INE TOWN, KYOTO, JAPAN

JACK GLANCED OVER HIS SHOULDER as the armed guards from the boat shed shadowed them along the banks of the river. Professor Burwick's steps were slow but deliberate. Jack didn't know whether she trusted him, but he was certain she wanted what he kept hidden—and she had secrets of her own from the Cherub.

"Did you know the Wishing Tree at Beacon Hill was planted by the Cherub?" Burwick asked. "Many believe it began as a branch from Elyon's Vine, which was discovered deep in the Highlands—somewhere in the Valley of Grace, where Charis has remained lost to this world."

"Is that why the tree is able to determine someone's destiny?"

"Elyon determines our path." Burwick paused. "It is our choice whether to follow."

"Eden's Star brought us here within the Highlands," Jack noted. "It could have taken us anywhere else, but it kept us on this path for a reason."

"Salomeh wants Eden's Star to be returned to the highest Cherub. However, my belief is it must be kept from the highest Cherub *and* Merikh—protected by those who believe in Elyon's commands, not the commands or will of man." Burwick dug her cane into the soft dirt and stopped. "Will you show it to me, Jack?"

"I'm an outlier so I'm who you're describing, but I'm not part of your faction. I'm the Protector, so I can't show the compass to anyone." Jack's gaze shifted. "Professor, how do the Cherub gifts work?"

"You mean why do some have supernatural powers to move ships and throw balls of fire, while the rest of us have gifts that seem less dynamic?" Burwick smiled. "There was a time, centuries ago, when the gifts you have seen from Emma were common among the Cherub. Since the defeat in the Battle of Everest, and the sin of the Elders, those gifts have become increasingly rare. For most of Elyon's followers, the gifts granted to us are less outwardly dynamic and more inwardly powerful."

"You mean like Amina," Jack guessed. "Elyon used her to heal Vince."

"Without a doubt." Burwick nodded. "Power through faith does not always need to be a light show with fireworks."

"I guess I was wondering why Rachel was given gifts but I wasn't." Jack shoved his hands deep into his pockets, weighing whether to tell Burwick about his visions. "Even though I'm the Protector of Eden's Star, there hasn't been any change when it comes to those kinds of gifts—but I get what you mean, because my faith in Elyon is growing stronger in other ways."

"I am sure Emma will tell you that her gifts are both a blessing and a curse—a great responsibility with even greater consequences." Burwick's stare softened. "Cherub who have lost their gifts believe those abilities will return if there is one chosen who finds what has remained hidden—what Eden's Star has protected from Cherub and Merikh. Unfortunately, your generation is being forced to fight a war that mothers and fathers are too afraid to lose. I fear in the end, we will be no closer to peace than when the first battle was waged in the Valley of Grace many ages ago."

"I'm not sure what I'm supposed to do next." Jack glanced over his shoulder again, realizing their shadows lingered nearby. "I can't just wait here until the Merikh find me."

"Faith rooted in Elyon requires one to travel a narrow road—there's not much room on either side for a misstep. Salomeh and the highest Cherub believe the faction is a threat because we have chosen a path that places Elyon's commands written in the Eternal above all others. For too long, the Cherub followed the great Elder, and his word was final. Now he is gone, and they are uncertain how to keep their followers united. If you ask me, they have lost what first began in each of their souls—a relationship with Elyon. To answer your question, if you are prepared to go deeper in your faith, then there is no way forward other than a narrow road."

"You know I'm protecting Eden's Star, but do you know what is hidden in Charis?"

"Remember, Salomeh also knows that you're the Protector." Burwick paused. "As far as what is hidden in Charis, I suppose one will know when one finds it."

"So that's what's keeping you both on the same side."

"For now, we have placed our personal feelings aside to keep everyone alive."

"Rachel trusted Headmaster Fargher and you with her secrets—with what she discovered about Eden's Star and the artifacts. I've read her diaries, so I know there was a time when Dabria and Xui Li kept the truth from her about being Elders." Rachel's cursive writings flashed in his mind. "Dabria encouraged her to demand a meeting from Peter Leung *with* the Elders—a meeting that never happened. Maybe Rachel found out the Elders were history after her diary entries—I don't know—but she trusted all of you. She knew she was following in my mom's footsteps searching for Eden's Star, and she kept this from me to keep me safe." Jack swallowed hard. "You're right, she was being hunted by the Merikh, and they're the ones who murdered her in Sitio. None of us were able to protect her and stop others from being killed too. How do I keep going without risking everyone else getting hurt?"

"The only certainty in a fallen world is that a deeper faith in Elyon brings freedom," Burwick said, matter-of-fact. "Vince, Tim, and Amina will not survive what you will face on your journey through the Highlands. So I will watch over them until you return."

Jack glanced around. "Is this a safe place, Professor?"

"As safe as one can be during these unsettling times."

"So I should take Emma and Eliška with me." Jack exhaled. "That's like adding ice to your fire mood experiment."

Burwick smiled slightly. "Each is gifted in her own way."

"They can't stand each other."

"Emma's calling is to unite the Cherub, while Eliška leads the faction to action."

"Taking them both will keep you and Salomeh in check and on the same side."

"We want what is best to defeat the Merikh, and in this moment you are our best hope."

"Okay, I'll ask them—separately." Jack expected a response from Burwick, but when she remained quiet he switched subjects. "Rachel drew an illustration of Elyon's Vine."

Burwick's brows raised. "I'd like to see it."

"After last night, I'm not sure we still have it—but I'll check with the others."

Returning along the riverbank, they grew quiet, as if they were on a Sunday stroll. Jack was surprised by how easy it was to talk to Burwick, since his only previous interaction with her was in the classroom—in a subject he was failing for the second time. He couldn't help but stare at the burn scars on her face and arms, knowing that beneath the sleeves of his hoodie were wounds caused by dark forces fueled by the Merikh.

When they entered the boathouse, he found Emma, Amina, and Tim seated around a wooden table. Eliška was nowhere to be seen. He was relieved that Amina looked to be back to her normal self. He walked down the hallway to check on Vince but stopped in the doorway when he realized Eliška was at the foot of the bed with her arms crossed. Jack stepped into the room and stared at Vince, who seemed to be asleep. The sheets had been changed, and the tourniquet around Vince's leg showed no crimson stain.

"The story you told me about Vietnam," Jack said. "Was it true?"

"I did not know who you were on the *Eastern Dragon*."

"So you lied about which part?"

"Professor Burwick is the closest thing I will ever have to a mother," Eliška admitted. "She sent her daughter, Darcy, and me to Ho Chi Minh to find where the Merikh were kidnapping and trafficking expats and local girls. We found ourselves at the backpacker hostel, which led us to the nightclub. We were drugged and taken—weeks later Darcy was killed."

She told me the truth—mostly.

"The professor wants you to go with me to find the Valley of Grace and Charis."

"Salomeh will never allow this without . . ." Eliška's voice trailed off.

"Tim, Amina, and Vince will stay behind and be protected by the faction." Jack eyed Vince as the guilt lingered and swelled. "There's something I want to show you."

He stepped out of the room with Eliška on his heels. She found a seat at the table while Burwick and Salomeh stood back. "Tim, was everything left behind in Sakkhela?"

"All of our backpacks, yes . . ." Tim's brows raised. "But not everything."

"Okay, then show everyone."

Unzipping his hoodie, Tim reached inside and retrieved a tablet. Amina's lips pursed as if she were going to lean over and kiss him. Jack waited until Tim powered on the device and brought Rachel's drawing onto the screen. He grabbed the tablet from Tim and showed it to Salomeh, Eliška, and Burwick.

"Elyon's Vine," Salomeh whispered, awestruck. "In all its glory."

Burwick held the tablet for a moment. "Is this from one of her visions?"

"How do you know she was having visions?" Jack asked.

Salomeh nodded as if to approve Burwick's answer. "Dabria told us, separately."

"Xui Li knew of the same when she came to me for help," Salomeh added coolly. "It is one of the reasons why I instructed Faizan to take her to Sakkhela to find a gateway to the Valley of Grace."

"Months have passed since either of us have heard from Dabria." Professor Burwick paused. "She shared about Rachel's visions, in hopes we might be able to translate what she was experiencing. After Rachel's death, Xui Li reappeared from the City of Gods and was our strongest opportunity to uncover the gateway."

"And now she's been captured by the Merikh," Emma said.

"I traveled to Vigan to see Dabria after Kati Pahari," Salomeh admitted. "However . . ."

A chill shot down Jack's spine. "What happened in Vigan?"

"We do not know exactly, but Vigan is abandoned and Dabria is missing."

31

Jack stood in a corner of Vince's room, unable to move any closer. An hour earlier, he'd left everyone in the dining room entranced by Rachel's drawing while eating lunch boxes of udon, gyudon beef, and steamed white rice. Bodyguards remained stationed outside the boathouse while Salomeh met with Burwick behind closed doors in another room. Jack watched Vince's chest rise and fall, and he questioned whether he'd made the right decision bringing his friends with him. So far, none of their plans had worked out how anyone expected. Now they were holed up in a boathouse without a clue of the next step, while somewhere out there, the Merikh hunted. His shoulders slouched as the room closed in on him.

Elyon, please heal Vince so he can play in the next Bashers, Bowlers, and Boundaries. I pray he forgives me for what's happened. Protect Xui Li and Dabria from the Merikh, and keep them alive until I can find them. And be with Tim, Amina, Emma, and Eliška in the days ahead. My faith in you is deeper than when this first began, but will it be enough?

"That was a brutal ride, bro." Vince's weakened voice was barely above a whisper. "Definitely wasn't like our first time on Karābu, which was epic in its own way. Everyone else come through okay?"

"Everyone else is fine." Jack cleared his throat. "You got the worst of it."

"Do I look as bad as you've looked with Eden's Star shooting around in your body?" Vince's brows furrowed as he stared intently at his leg, which was heavily wrapped in gauze. "It's not amputated, is it? Don't tell me what I'm feeling is phantom pain."

"Leg is still attached," Jack replied. "Your heart stopped, though."

"That explains the white light—thought I was heading toward a train in the Thar Desert."

"Elyon used Amina to bring you back." Jack weighed his words, knowing an apology would never be enough, but it was all he could offer. "Vince, I'm so sorry."

"Eden's Star didn't come with an owner's manual."

"I didn't know the compass should only be used with two or three people at a time."

Vince offered a bit of dark humor. "Well, then just call me a crash test dummy."

"If it was any one of us but you, I'm not sure we would've made it. Listen—"

"I don't want to hear it. I've never quit on anyone or anything."

"No one's quitting." Jack smiled half-heartedly. "You're just on the injured reserve."

"Don't leave me on the sidelines. My half speed is still better than Tim on his best day."

"You're preaching to the choir." Jack chuckled. "You'll be back cracking sixers soon."

Vince's curiosity spread across his face. "What's the next move then, Jack?"

"Professor Burwick is going to watch over you, Tim, and Amina until you're on your feet. She said this place is one of the best safe houses for the faction. She also thinks she can get a message to your mom and dad to let them know you're alive."

"I'm not sure how I feel with all that's gone on. Better they don't know, or else they'll be put in more danger. Maybe once you're totally healed and we take the fight to the Merikh."

"That decision is up to you. If you want them to know, she can make it happen."

Vince nodded slightly. "Did you figure out why Eden's Star brought us here?"

"We're still in the Highlands," Jack explained. "Which I think means the compass is leading us closer to the Valley of Grace and Charis. Hopefully whatever is there will be worth it—and Elyon will heal me completely so I can put an end to the Merikh."

"You're not alone on this journey," Vince reminded him. "We're all by your side."

Jack nodded slowly. "I've never doubted it."

"Who's going with you then?"

"Emma and Eliška."

"Trading us in for the dynamic duo." Vince's lips pursed. "When is this going down?"

"We're leaving as soon as possible, since now we know for sure Rachel's drawing is Elyon's Vine. That's what we're going to be searching for in the Highlands." Jack ran his fingers through his hair. "This would be so much easier if I knew how to control Eden's Star."

"For the record, I'm not a fan of the plan." Vince's gaze shifted toward the door as Tim appeared. "What's going on, Romeo?"

"If I weren't such a catch, Amina may not have been here to save you," Tim teased. "Glad you're awake."

"Were you able to figure anything out about the drawing?" Jack asked.

"Spent the last hour messing with the colors to see if anything stood out." Tim handed Jack the tablet and waited while he stared at the digitized rendition of Elyon's Vine. "When I started to strip colors away from the trunk, it began to look different from the normal king cypress."

Jack stared hard at the trunk for a moment until it hit him like a sledgehammer. "Can you invert the image and get rid of all the color?"

With a stylus in one hand, Tim grabbed the tablet and sat on the edge of the bed. Vince and Jack watched quietly as Tim went to work as if he were restoring a Van Gogh. Minutes passed before Tim flipped the tablet around and showed them a heavily inked black-and-white image that barely resembled the original Elyon's Vine drawn by Rachel. With all the colors stripped away, it looked more like an abstract piece of art where the muted background came alive with bamboo. He pointed at the screen and waited for them to see it too.

"Never would've noticed it was part of the background without removing the color."

"Definitely looks like bamboo," Jack agreed.

"There are millions of bamboo trees in Asia," Vince pointed out. "Just sayin'."

"What if Rachel knew where to start in the Highlands?" Jack suggested. "She tried to get to Eden's Star in the City of Gods more than once. Maybe she also searched the Highlands for the Valley of Grace using the drawing as her guide."

"I thought I would find you two back here." Amina stood in the doorway with Emma peering over her shoulder. "Professor Burwick and Salomeh left, but they will return before dark."

"The look on your face is a dead giveaway," Emma said to Jack. "Spill it."

Jack handed the tablet over and stepped back. "Might be nothing."

Seconds passed as Emma and Amina stared at the screen. "How did she do this?"

"Crazy, right?" Tim agreed. "She must've sketched it out and placed an inverted image beneath the page where she colored in the drawing. Clever, really."

Everyone stopped talking when Eliška appeared in the doorway. She paused before entering, as if waiting for someone to invite her in. Vince waved her closer.

"Full house," he mused. "Hope we're not all sleeping in the same room."

Emma handed the tablet to Eliška. "Does it mean anything to you?"

"Umm . . ." Eliška took a moment before glancing up at the rest of them. "Arishiyama."

"Say what?" Vince asked. "Arishi . . ."

"Arishiyama." Eliška handed the tablet back. "A bamboo forest with giant twisted vines like in the drawing."

"Holy shenanigans," Tim blurted. "I'd say pack our bags, but we don't have any."

Whether from relief or sheer tiredness, all of them burst out laughing.

32

HONG KONG

BAU HURRIED THROUGH A WOODED AREA near King's Park Villa with a large box in his grasp. He reached an iron door hidden in the brush and pounded twice. The door creaked open and Faizan poked his head out, cautiously glancing around. Handing off the box filled with cans of spiced pork cubes, condensed milk, fried dace, Spam, and corned beef, Bau darted back the same way he'd come until he reappeared on a street where a ParkNShop truck idled.

While the driver remained in the cab, Bau grabbed another box from the rear and headed back into the wooded area. His pace was quick, and he kept his head on a swivel for the slightest movement. He slipped through the iron door, which Faizan closed behind him, and pulled a heavy lever down to lock the entrance. Bau set the box on a four-wheel dolly stacked with even more boxes and pushed the dolly down a long tunnel lit with orange glow sticks.

"We have enough food for a fortnight." Bau pushed the dolly a bit faster. "We cannot continue to hide in Nightingale's vault. It is only a matter of time before we are discovered."

"More people have arrived from Shanghai and Guangzhou." Faizan stepped to one side and helped Bau push the dolly. "Many have seen the Merikh kill their loved ones before their eyes."

"I have told Headmaster Fargher that we need to be prepared to fight back."

"You are the keeper of Dragon Soul. Are you also one of the chosen?"

"Yes. Emma is the only other," he admitted. "She left me behind to watch over everyone."

"Seems like an impossible task." Faizan's words radiated sincerity. "However, with Elyon all things are possible."

"That's what the Eternal says," Bau replied. "We will find out soon enough."

For a while they pushed the dolly in silence until they reached an iron ladder leading to an open hole in the ceiling of the tunnel. Headmaster Fargher poked his head through the hole, then summoned others to help. Twenty boxes were hoisted up the ladder into Nightingale's vault. Bau waited until the last box was passed up before pushing the dolly off to one side. He followed Faizan as they climbed the ladder and pulled themselves through the hole.

"Any issues?" Fargher asked.

"We will not receive another delivery until the end of next week."

Bau and Fargher watched while Faizan organized a team of men to carry the boxes toward a storage area. Professor McDougall had gathered a large group of young children and teenagers for an impromptu Hong Kong history lesson with the help of several interpreters. In another sectioned-off area near the rows of cots, adults busied themselves washing laundry in plastic buckets and hanging it on rope lines to drip-dry.

"We have counted nearly five hundred who have arrived so far," Fargher said.

"Headmaster, we cannot feed more than those who are already here."

"Bau, there is no controlling who comes through the gateway." Fargher scratched his scraggly beard. "For now, we will trust Elyon one day at a time."

At the end of the aisle, Natalie McNaughton appeared and waved Bau over. He'd been through this routine a dozen times, so he knew she needed him to go with her upstairs. Following the usual route, they moved quickly through Rowell Library, then headed down to the basement. They approached the House of Luminescence, and Bau noticed the door was open. He kept to one side of the corridor while McNaughton moved along the other with her Glock raised.

Bau wished Dragon Soul was in his grasp, regretting that he'd allowed the ancient sword to be taken from him and wondering who could've stolen it. Knowing those not yet surrendered to the Cherub were forbidden from entering the House of Luminescence, Bau held up his hand to stop McNaughton from going farther than the doorway.

"Stay here," he whispered. "If there is no one inside, we will need to search the grounds for whoever came through the door."

Bau's heartbeat quickened as he slipped inside the House of Luminescence. He walked quietly beneath the high-vaulted wood beams and stepped over the thick vines creeping down the walls onto the floor. His eyes darted from one corner to the next, searching for anyone who might be hiding. He stopped cold as he spotted Salomeh Gashkori and Professor Burwick standing within a turquoise glow near the Mercy Covenant.

"Do not be afraid," Salomeh said in a hushed voice.

"We are here to speak with you," Professor Burwick added. "And only you."

"Why is Fang Xue not present?" Bau asked. "She is the Cherub leader, not me."

"To keep Emma and the others safe"—Salomeh nodded toward Burwick—"no one must know we are acting together. Understood?"

"You have seen them recently?" Bau asked. "They are still alive?"

Burwick nodded slowly. "Vince is hurt quite badly, but the others are in good health."

"Are they any closer to finding the artifacts?"

"We believe they are on the right path," Salomeh answered. "You are the keeper of Dragon Soul, correct?"

"Yes." Bau shifted uncomfortably. "I am the keeper."

"Do you have it here at the school?" Burwick pressed. "Can we see it, Bau?"

He hesitated, unsure of how to answer. "Emma may have told you—"

"Not Emma, but Jack believes someone stole Dragon Soul from you."

"During the attack at Beacon Hill, there was a shadowy figure fighting alongside the Merikh assassins." Bau paused, reluctant to admit Jack was correct. "The shadow took Dragon Soul from my grasp that night, and I have not seen the sword since."

"I have always believed that only uniquely gifted Cherub—or

Merikh with powerful gifts of their own—were strong enough to wield the sword," Salomeh explained. "Are you certain whoever took Dragon Soul from you is Merikh?"

Bau grew more ashamed with each question. "I do not know."

"We are not here to scold you, Bau." Burwick's gaze softened against her scarred skin. "Emma and Eliška will not return unless the artifacts are found, which means they may be gone far longer than we hoped. After much discussion between us, we have realized we cannot leave our fate in the hands of an outlier, especially if he fails in his quest. We must ready ourselves to fight, and we must do it now."

"Do you understand what we are saying?" Salomeh asked. "What we are asking of you?"

Bau searched for the right words. "Emma and Eliška have agreed?"

"We have spoken to both," Burwick replied. "Each has made their choice."

"You will be a mighty commander," Salomeh reassured.

"If I am to be anointed the next Cherub leader," Bau stated, "then I will lead the war."

"Separate the Cherub who have taken refuge here into those who have gifts to defend against the Merikh, and those who must be protected. Merikh wage war against all who believe—against Elyon—and we are defenseless until we have built an army of our own."

"The moment is upon us," Burwick added. "We must stand united."

Salomeh and Burwick stepped back toward the Mercy Covenant. The turquoise glow enveloped them, and they disappeared into thin air. Bau stood perfectly still in the presence of Elyon while the House of Luminescence embraced him in a deeper way.

33

REPULSE BAY, HONG KONG ISLAND

SHUFFLING HIS FEET DOWN A HALLWAY, Will passed the glass-walled lab where secrets found in the Treaty of Nanjing were revealed with each drop of blood spilled. His mind flashed to the black flame he'd seen when he was left alone, then to the night he found his mum dead.

Will strode down white marble steps into the opulent living area. He didn't care for this room. He'd much rather be back in Nightingale's dorm in front of the fire with his mates—at least most of them. But he'd chosen his path—a path of vengeance that left him guarded in a penthouse fortress, haunted by the evils he'd inflicted in the months since Rachel died.

I had nothing to do with her death, but Jack had everything to do with tearing my family apart.

Glancing through the bulletproof glass, he noticed Chung and Addison huddled together near a brightly lit infinity pool surrounded by a perfectly manicured yard. He stopped beside the painting of a pirate ship floating in Repulse Bay with red dragons stitched into waving black flags. It was the only piece of art or furniture he liked in the whole place.

Addison entered the penthouse. "Michael tells me training is going well."

"I have done everything he asked, and more. We should've caught them in Sakkhela."

"Another opportunity will come."

Addison nodded to a glass case, where the Windstrikers were displayed. "And you will be armed with even greater weapons."

"How many artifacts are there?" Will pressed. "Does anyone know?"

"Cherub blood has revealed another clue to the whereabouts of more artifacts." Addison held a piece of paper between his fingers. "A treasure greater than you ever imagined."

"That piece of paper is going to lead to a treasure? Sounds too easy."

"Michael has interrogated dozens of the highest Cherub. A story is emerging about Peter Leung, which we will discover together. We leave for Karnataka tonight."

"A video is trending on Messagezilla." Will glanced at the piece of paper, growing more curious about what they might find. "Emma called out the Merikh, and she is defending the outlier."

"Hard for you to say his name." Addison smirked. "He is the reason for your pain."

"*Jack* hates you more than anyone—but not as much as I hate him." Will allowed his own rage to course through him. "Why did you order me to return when Michael is still hunting?"

"Your ego is your greatest strength, but you are not invincible—not yet, anyway. The Highlands are far riskier than what you have encountered so far. Michael is fully aware, and he is well-equipped to finish the hunt."

Addison grabbed the cell phone from Will and tapped on the screen where Emma appeared within a crowd he didn't recognize.

"I was taken by the Merikh from Mount Hareh and was tortured. But I am alive only because of the outlier you are hunting to avenge the great Elder's death. Those who lost their lives in the Sanctuary of Prayer were murdered because of a betrayal from one of our own. There is much you do not know, but there is no time to convince you of the truth. It is true, the Mercy Covenant is broken. But the words of the Eternal remain. All who believe are worthy to shine a light against the dark. War is not coming—it is already here."

"Will they fight—the Cherub?" Will asked.

"We have imprisoned thousands already, and there will come a day when their deaths will be shown for all the world to see. You have killed two of the greatest Elders in Cherub history and exterminated many of the highest Cherub on Mount Hareh. There will be no uprising, only a slaughter of the weak." Addison stared at Emma's face on the screen. "But she brings them hope—which makes her even more dangerous than her gifts."

"After all the places we have searched, we still do not know where they are hiding. We missed them in Karachi and Kati Pahari, and they escaped from us in Sakkhela."

"The key to hunting Cherub is to expose their love for one

another." Addison slipped the paper inside his suit coat. "Cherub turned my wife and child into fanatics and freaks."

Will noticed how Addison referred to only one child. *Is that because Jack isn't a lightforcer, bender, or healer? He has Eden's Star, but that doesn't make him as powerful as me.* Will bit his lip, tempted to challenge the Merikh leader to do more to find them. For weeks he'd traveled with Michael hunting, and in Sakkhela they were so close, but Emma had stood in his way.

Since his first kill, guilt had weighed on him. At first he'd convinced himself his desire for revenge against Jack wasn't doing the Merikh's bidding—it was to save himself and his father. But as the months passed, his reasons blurred while his anger sharpened. *I'm more of a Merikh now than I've ever been.* When he swung Dragon Soul, ending Charlotte Taylor's and Dabria's lives, he realized his sins were beyond redemption. *Why beg forgiveness when your soul is as black as coal?* As if reading his mind, Addison broke the silence.

"Peter kept you a secret from the Cherub because he knew the power of your gifts is unlimited—and it threatened him. Those who thirst for greater power are always motivated by fear that another will expose their weakness. Peter planned to use you to keep his lies buried, which is why it was so easy for him to betray the Cherub."

"Jack is the one who killed the Elder," Will said. "No one knows the truth but us."

"You are wrong, Will. I have made sure the highest Cherub are aware of Jack's transgressions against them—which is why the Cherub are searching for him, to hold him to account. We will allow them to believe the truth within our lies and wait for the right moment to shatter their faith into a trillion pieces." Addison checked his watch. "But tonight, we fly to Karnataka to see if the great Elder's deception will lead us to a greater treasure. Pack your bags and bring Dragon Soul."

Will realized he never unpacked from the last hunt, and now they were headed to India. He hesitated, unsure of whether it was the right time to ask. "The Elder in Vigan said Michael cannot harm a Cherub Elder, and if he breaks this oath, he will face eternal torment. Is this true?"

"Dabria always prided herself on being smarter than the rest." Addison smirked. "She is correct, which is why one day you will become more powerful than Michael has ever been. When the time comes, you will fulfill your destiny and silence the Elders forever—but that time must be chosen carefully. You will be rewarded for your loyalty with the blood of your enemies. Never turn your back on what you desire most. Ever."

Will headed down the hallway into one of the bedrooms. He grabbed his backpack off the floor, then punched in a code to a wall safe. Opening the safe, he grabbed the leather scabbard protecting Dragon Soul and slung it over his shoulder. As he closed the safe, he was struck by how he was helping a man he hated while betraying the father he loved—all to even the score.

34

INE TOWN, KYOTO, JAPAN

PROFESSOR BURWICK SPLASHED through puddles as a downpour blew across the river town. Stabbing her cane into the mud, she struggled to keep her balance while carrying two backpacks in her other hand. Several bodyguards kept their positions around the boathouse, while others remained camouflaged. Eliška stepped out from the boathouse and grabbed the backpacks, then helped the professor inside. Burwick slumped onto a bamboo chair as if she'd hiked the Great Wall.

Jack eyed her curiously. "Where is Salomeh?"

"She remained in Kowloon." Burwick wrestled out of the hooded raincoat, revealing matted ginger hair against cauliflower ears. "Cherub business of some sort, I suppose."

"Why did you both go to Hong Kong? Did you see Headmaster Fargher?"

"You have asked more questions in the last day than you ever did in one of my classes." Burwick chuckled to herself. "Frankly, I am too exhausted to explain our visit."

"We might have figured out Rachel's drawing of Elyon's Vine." Eliška showed Burwick the rendering Tim manipulated on his tablet. "Looks like the forest in Arishiyama."

"Similar styling," Burwick agreed. "Inverting is a smart way to hide a clue."

"Rachel might have uncovered more than Eden's Star in the City of Gods."

"The visions she was having may have revealed Arishiyama." Burwick stared at the drawing for a moment longer. "Arishiyama has been revered by Cherub throughout the centuries as a holy place. Quite possibly it is within the Highlands and will lead to the Valley of Grace."

"And if we find the Valley of Grace," Jack interrupted, "we find Charis too."

"The Eternal speaks of the Garden hidden in a valley, awaiting all who surrender themselves to Elyon." Burwick glanced past Eliška. "You should know, the faction and the highest Cherub have agreed to Bau Hu becoming the next Cherub leader."

"Emma should be the one," Jack argued. "Professor—"

"One might debate the mantle should be passed down to Eliška." Burwick shifted her weight and winced in pain. "Titles do not build a strong community—unity does."

"If Bau becomes the next leader, then the Cherub will unite against me."

"Jack, I am afraid that ship has already sailed," Burwick replied.

"To defeat the darkness unleashed by the Merikh, one must choose to live in the shadows, not the spotlight."

"Who will tell Emma?"

"Cherub are fleeing to Beacon Hill to escape the Merikh. Thousands more have been captured and are imprisoned in Hong Kong. Emma cannot build an army to protect the Cherub *and* search for the artifacts. A choice had to be made, and it is done. Besides, Salomeh and I have spoken with Emma and Eliška. Both agreed."

"Professor Burwick is right," Eliška confirmed.

Jack spun around, sensing someone behind him. He locked eyes on Emma and remembered what she'd said the afternoon in Admiralty when they met up with Bau. *"You two can barely stay in the same room, but you both are needed."* She predicted the outcome, but it didn't mean he trusted Bau.

I'm still an outlier—a target of Cherub and Merikh—Addison's bloodline.

"I have chosen the narrow path," Emma said. "For Cherub to survive while we search for the artifacts, there is no one stronger to build an army than Bau."

"He's fought in a war before? I must've missed that one." Jack waited for a response, and when no one spoke, he continued his rant. "Bau is the same person who lost Dragon Soul—and he hates me, Emma. Isn't that enough to disqualify him?"

"All are deemed worthy." Burwick poked her cane at the two backpacks. "Fresh clothes for the three of you. Supplies will arrive in the morning before you leave for Arishiyama."

"We should tell the others," Emma said. "It is only fair."

Jack realized all eyes were turned toward him. "Right, I'll do it."

Shuffling down the hallway, he searched for the words, knowing there was a good reason why he never tried out for the Rebuttal Society's debate team at Beacon Hill. He found Tim and Amina seated on the bed talking with Vince, but once they noticed he was there, they stopped.

"Are you trying to decide whether to vote me off the island?" Jack mused.

"Vince was telling us you are planning to leave us behind," Amina answered.

"I'm not calling the shots in this whole deal. Right now, thousands of Cherub are being held by the Merikh in Hong Kong. If everyone waits for us to find the artifacts, they will die."

"We heard Professor Burwick," Tim replied. "No secrets in this shack, Jack."

"Doesn't Emma have pull with the highest Cherub?" Vince asked. "She's one of the chosen, if not *the* chosen. I thought she was raised to take over one day."

"C'mon, Jack. You gotta stand up and make some demands," Tim cut in. "Bau is going to be the new leader. How is that right?"

"Burwick made it clear we are fighting a war against the Merikh from two sides. One is building an army to protect the Cherub, while the other searches for the artifacts."

"So, who are we?" Vince asked, on edge. "Cherub? Faction? Outliers?"

Jack shook his head. "I can't answer that for anyone."

"We followed you for months searching for these blasted artifacts," Tim railed. "Which, by the way, we still have no idea where or what they are, or even how many we're supposed to find. Now, after all of this, you are ditching us and disappearing with the dynamic duo?"

"Gotta admit," Vince chuckled, "that was one of your best lines in recent memory."

"Eden's Star is only safe with three," Jack countered. "Vince is proof."

"All of us made it from Karābu to Karachi in one piece."

Jack pointed at Vince's heavily bandaged leg. "Are you forgetting about last night?"

"Everyone take a breather," Amina suggested. "We are still the Keepers."

"Stupid name," Tim grumbled. "You know what—I just want to go home."

Jack accepted that there was nothing he could say to make the situation better. With his head lowered, he left the room and stormed out of the boathouse. Ignoring the bodyguards who watched his movements, he walked briskly along the riverbank until he reached a columned shrine jutting out on the edge of the water. While the rain pelted him in the face, he looked up toward the cloudy skies and yelled at the top of his lungs.

"Elyon, where are you?"

35

SUNLIGHT PEEKED BETWEEN pillowy white clouds while Jack loaded a duffel bag filled with dried food, bottled water, and other gear onto a sampan docked beneath the boathouse. He'd been awake since daybreak, eager to leave. Stepping off the sampan onto the lower dock, he noticed that the pain in his spine seemed less than the days before. Rounding the corner, he came face-to-face with Professor Burwick.

"Good morning, Jack."

"Morning," he replied. "We're loaded up."

"Strange to be here a world away from Beacon Hill, isn't it?"

"Never thought I'd be standing in a place like this." Jack glanced around at the early morning beauty and serenity of the river. "Professor, how long have you led the faction?"

"Long enough to know walking out my faith in Elyon is not rooted in belonging to the Cherub." Burwick motioned for him to follow. "There is freedom in a relationship with Elyon, but I have found that the Cherub often create too many rules and regulations. And I am not blind to the sin that exists in the Cherub either. In days like these, my hope remains centered on the words of the Eternal, not the plans of man."

Jack walked alongside at a slow pace, attempting to follow the conversation as they headed down the road. He wasn't sure what Burwick wanted, but it was clear something was on her mind. She stopped at another boathouse and unlocked the door. Jack was surprised to see a nicely furnished home, a stark contrast to the sparse boathouse they'd stayed in.

"During the summer breaks from Beacon Hill, this is where I spend my time between my efforts with the faction." Burwick leaned her cane up against the wall and hobbled over to a bookshelf filled with hardcovers. "Sir James Nightingale was a strong believer in Elyon—but not much of a fan of the Cherub."

"Have you ever been inside his vault, Professor?"

"Headmaster Fargher kept it a closely guarded secret, much like the House of Luminescence. But there are other ways to uncover what motivated Nightingale on his expeditions." Burwick removed a leather-bound book from the shelf. "The highest Cherub believe Nightingale spent many years searching for Elyon's Vine—and some are convinced he reached the Valley of Grace and Charis before finding the root of our existence."

Jack's mind flashed to his vision from the hostel. "He found the Testimony."

"You have seen it then." Burwick lowered herself onto a chair and set the leather book on her lap. "Within the pages of the

Eternal it is revealed the Testimony must never be touched—otherwise it will take one's life. While most Cherub know this as truth, Dabria and Xui Li were convinced the Testimony could be carried if it was empty. However, once the artifacts are returned to the acacia box, then the Testimony must not be touched by anyone from this world. Honestly, I do not know if it is true."

"I touched the Testimony inside Nightingale's vault."

Burwick's brows raised. "And you are still very much alive."

"I looked inside, and it was empty."

Burwick's bottom lip twitched. "Maybe they are right."

"Why is that important now?"

"If you are to find the artifacts, the Testimony is where you should return them to contain their powers. And for the rest of eternity, the Testimony must be guarded at all times. It is one reason why I have agreed to support Bau as the new Cherub leader. While he is quite ambitious, and at times his ego gains the upper hand, I believe he will commit to protecting the Testimony until he passes his oath to the next generation."

"Professor, we haven't even found the first artifact yet." Jack stared at the leather book, growing more curious about what she held in her hands. "I guess at least we know where the Testimony is if we are lucky enough to find one."

"Somewhere on Nightingale's expeditions he came across this book." Burwick held up the leather-bound volume. "Perhaps it was when he found the Testimony, or possibly on another adventure. Within these pages are the original writings from the Elders of old and the heroes who have gone before. Throughout the centuries, it has been known as the Eternal."

Jack's eyes widened. "An original copy?"

"I am giving this to you as a sign of my commitment to stand with you, no matter who stands against you." Burwick held the Eternal out, but Jack hesitated to reach for it. "In this war against the Merikh, we have been called for a purpose. I believe in your purpose, Jack, whether anyone else sees it or not."

"Dabria told me the Elders believe only I can fulfill the prophecy sworn to Rachel because we share a deep connection that can't be broken even in death. I'm not worthy to take her place, especially since I don't even know what the prophecy means."

"Many of the highest Cherub have offered their interpretation," Burwick admitted. "Rachel was called to be the Protector of Eden's Star to fulfill the prophecy." She set the Eternal on her lap and tapped on the cover. "There is one phrase in particular that has caused much debate: *Along a silk road this secret will one day return, to a story of mercy and love evil attempted to burn.*"

"Isn't the *secret* about Eden's Star and the hidden artifacts from the Testimony?"

"Perhaps it is not the whole secret." Burwick offered the Eternal to Jack a second time. "If you want to find the answers and go deeper in your relationship with Elyon, the only way is to discover the truth within the pages of this book."

His hands shook as he carefully grasped the Eternal, his fingers moving gently across the worn leather embossed with ancient characters. He slowly flipped through the pages, noticing among the text there were familiar illustrations depicting light, skies, seas, trees, sun, moon, birds, creatures of the ocean, and humanity. He was reminded of the silver coins Emma kept close. "Thank you, Professor."

"I planned on giving it to Rachel when she returned from the

City of Gods." Burwick's eyes grew teary. "When we were together the last time, I asked her for a favor. Darcy and Eliška were missing, and Rachel agreed to search for them after she attempted to enter the City of Gods and the Temple of the Nephilim once more. In return, she asked for my help to find out the truth. She shared her suspicions about the great Elder, and her beliefs about the Elders as a whole."

"You mean the fact they didn't exist anymore, except for Peter Leung?"

Burwick nodded slowly. "She was not certain, but she was on to the greatest lie."

"Sounds like Rachel trusted you—along with Dabria, Xui Li, and Headmaster Fargher."

"She earned trust from each one of us as well," Burwick replied. "We each played a role to help her on her quest to search for Eden's Star and the hidden artifacts. Losing her has been difficult on all of us, but it does not compare to the loss you have endured."

"You have experienced loss too, Professor." Jack glanced down at the leather book, still amazed he held an original copy of the Eternal in his hands. His cheeks flushed as he clenched his teeth to stop himself from breaking down. "Why are you telling me all of this?"

"My upbringing was, shall we say, difficult." Burwick wiped a tear from her cheek. "My father was very abusive to me and my two sisters. When you are young, you do all you can to survive and block those moments out of your mind. However, when you get older, those memories surface without warning and drown you in a life you desperately wanted to escape."

Jack swallowed hard. "Rachel told you about our childhood in Sham Shui Po."

"Enough for me to know what you both endured." Burwick hesitated. "As I have shared with you, I was captured by the Merikh after you first disappeared, and without mercy Charlotte Taylor had me tortured by Michael Chung."

"Chung murdered Rachel." Jack nodded. "And Olivia Fargher too."

"He is powerful, yet he is not the most dangerous of the Merikh." Burwick touched the scars on her face. "I thought courage would protect me, as I have seen darkness up close. When my body burned, however, fear took control and I was powerless. I am ashamed for not being stronger—for admitting Rachel passed on her secrets to an outlier. I am sorry, Jack."

"Professor, we are all trying our best to protect those we love." Jack placed the Eternal on a side table, then pulled up his sleeves far enough for Burwick to see the deep scars on both of his arms. "Scars are a reminder of why we are here."

36

Professor Burwick and Jack returned to the other boathouse and were greeted by Emma, Tim, and Amina, who gathered outside. Everyone turned their attention to the sound of footsteps as Vince hobbled around the corner, favoring his injured leg.

"What?" Vince asked with a smile. "I'm not going to stay in bed all day."

"You should be resting," Amina said. "No pressure on your leg for another week."

"The reigning Triple B champion cannot be kept down," Tim mused. "I mean, look at him—he's a specimen."

"I couldn't have said it better," Jack chimed in. "All of you are champions."

"Normally one of Tim's cheesier lines," Vince laughed. "But we'll take it from you."

Eliška appeared from below the boathouse. "We are ready."

"I'm not good at long speeches," Jack began. "I'm not really sure what I'm supposed to say, but our lives will never be the same after today. I want each of you to know that you have done what many have not—you stood by each other's sides when it mattered most."

"Jack, this isn't a funeral, mate." Tim crossed his arms. "You are coming back."

"Timothy . . ." Amina rolled her eyes. "Read the room—right, Vince?"

Vince laughed. "He'd interrupt a boxing match by climbing into the ring."

"I would not," Tim blurted. "I'm just saying . . ."

Jack retrieved a burner phone from his pocket and handed it to Tim. "Keep this with you, and when we return, you'll be the first to know."

"You don't happen to have Natalie's number programmed in here, do you?" Tim stared at the phone as if he were being handed the keys to a Lambo. "She'd be useful right about now to talk you out of what you three are planning."

Jack smirked half-heartedly. "Only Messagezilla like you've suggested all along."

Emma grabbed Jack's hand, and he did the same with Amina. Each one grabbed a hand on their right and left, forming a tight circle. A moment passed as they stared at one another.

Jack glanced over his shoulder. "Professor, please join us."

Vince let go of Eliška's hand, allowing Burwick to step into the circle. She held her cane under her arm and gripped their hands tight. Bowing her head, she waited until everyone within the circle closed their eyes before she prayed.

"In the fiery battles of this world, Elyon promises strength with a righteous hand and courage poured out upon our bravery. We will not fear—and we will not be dismayed—for we are chosen to glorify Elyon and defend the light, in this realm and beyond. For us to live is Elyon, and to die is a gateway to eternal glory. Amidst the darkness unchained through flames and strife lies a hope our souls may be reborn from death to life. Elyon, we stand before you as one. Amen."

Everyone opened their eyes and looked at each other.

"Professor, what a powerful prayer," Vince said solemnly. "Thank you."

"In the Eternal it is written as the warrior's prayer."

"Rachel used one of those lines in her poem," Jack pointed out. "She was a warrior."

Tim was ready to kneel. "Is this the moment when we're knighted or something?"

"No knighthood required," Burwick replied. "Perhaps one day, Mr. Lloyd."

"Righteous. I'd like to have a shiny sword like Dragon Soul too, please."

Jack fist-bumped Vince and Tim, then offered Amina a quick embrace. It was an awkward moment as each said goodbye—for now. Emma and Amina hugged one another while Eliška disappeared beneath the boathouse.

"Jack, promise"—Tim wiped a sniffle with his sleeve—"you'll bring us some souvenirs."

He smiled sadly. "As many as I can carry."

With that, Jack and Emma turned from the others and walked side by side until they boarded the sampan roped to a stilt of the boathouse. A few moments later the sampan drifted out on the water with Eliška manning the helm. Emma's angelic voice echoed across the waters with a haunting melody. Jack waved toward shore as the motor whined and the sampan headed downriver until it was out of sight.

"Very well," Burwick announced. "Are you three packed and ready to go?"

"Uh . . . I thought we were staying here." Vince's brows raised. "Where are we going?"

Burwick winked. "Home, of course."

37

BEACON HILL

FOR MOST OF THE MORNING a group of men helped move stacked crates filled with Nightingale's discoveries, leaving a large open space in one corner of the enormous vault. Faizan and Bau spoke with nearly all five hundred of the refugees who'd arrived from Kati Pahari, Sakkhela, Shanghai, and Guangzhou before separating selected ones into three groups.

"I do not understand what you are doing." Professor McDougall shoved his pudgy hands into his worn Burberry coat pockets. "Adults, children, and teenagers in the same group?"

"The Wishing Tree separates students based on gifting," Headmaster Fargher explained.

"I do not need a history lesson about Beacon Hill. I am the

history professor, Freddie." McDougall pointed toward a bronze statue of a Greek god with a sword in one hand and a decapitated head in the other. "Does that look anything like the Wishing Tree? This is a far cry from sorting students into houses."

"Professor McDougall," Bau called out as he approached. "You look confused."

"What are you up to, Bau?"

"The houses of Beacon Hill were established to identify students' gifts through the Wishing Tree—and for the Cherub those gifts guarded times of peace since the Mercy Covenant existed." Bau pointed toward the three groups. "In times of war between Cherub and Merikh, those who must be identified have more unique and rare gifts: lightforcers, benders, and healers."

"Times of war?" McDougall turned toward Fargher. "You cannot be serious."

"These are uncertain times," Fargher replied. "Bau, try not to burn the vault down."

"Yes, Headmaster." Bau motioned for Faizan to begin. "The first group is lightforcers."

Faizan gathered the group of twenty-three into a single line and walked them to within ten feet of the bronze statue. At the front of the line was a young Pakistani teen. She stepped up to where Faizan stood and waited. He nudged her forward as everyone in the vault gathered around with their attention focused on her.

Without saying a word, she held her arms out with palms up. A faded pink glow appeared in both palms and formed into whirling balls of vibrant light. She brought her hands together, and the two lights became one. She aimed the light toward the statue and unleashed its power. An intense pink streak shot across the vault before exploding against the bronze statue, ripping one of the arms from the Greek god and sending it bouncing across the concrete floor.

"She is a lightforcer," Bau confirmed. "Her gift will grow brighter as she gets older."

McDougall's jaw dropped. "Remarkable."

Instead of applause from the gathered refugees, there was silence as Faizan led the next one in line to the same starting point. Out of the twenty-three, only one failed to produce the lightforce when requested. By the time they were finished, the Greek god was shattered in pieces on the ground. Faizan gathered the next group and prepared them to begin.

"Benders?" Fargher asked. "Seems to be a larger group."

"Lightforcers are the rarest," Bau replied. "Benders are discovered more frequently."

Faizan led the first one in the group—a young boy dressed in clothing which appeared to be from another age—up to the front. Again, everyone within the vault watched in silence as the boy held up his tiny hands toward the destroyed statue. A gust of wind blew through the vault as the boy's hands outstretched. One of the bronze pieces began to levitate. A few seconds passed before the piece dropped to the ground with a clanging thud. One by one, each person in the group stepped up and lifted the bronze pieces without touching them.

Lightforcers and benders stepped back from center stage but remained huddled together. Bau waved Professor Windsor over.

"Professor, I will need your help."

"We have limited medical supplies, Bau."

"Hopefully you will not be needed since Faizan is a healer. But it is better to be safe. Please stand beside Faizan." Bau glanced toward those who were left, then approached the girl with charcoal hair and bronze skin—the first in line for the lightforcers. "What is your name?"

"Navi," she said shyly. "Navi Singh."

"Come with me, Navi."

Bau led Navi over to Faizan, then kept walking until he stood in the midst of the shattered statue fragments. Professor Windsor stepped closer, clearly unaware of what he had in mind—as were Fargher and McDougall. He braced himself and stood with his hands by his sides.

"Navi," he called out. "Release your force directly at me."

"Hold on a minute," McDougall objected. "I will not stand by and allow this insanity."

Fargher grabbed McDougall by the shoulder. "Bite your tongue for a change."

"Prepare the healers to respond, Faizan." Bau tensed his muscles, knowing the pain he was about to endure—the same pain he experienced on Karābu Island when the great Elder tested each of them to their limits. "Let me know when you are ready."

Faizan gave him a thumbs-up, then instructed Navi to continue. She held out her arms, and the same vivid pink glow reappeared. Bau's breathing sped up until he was on the verge of hyperventilating. Navi held out her hands, and in an instant the pink streak shot across the vault and slammed into Bau's chest, sending him flying backward ten feet. Faizan and Professor Windsor raced toward him alongside the healers. Fargher and McDougall were last to stand over Bau's lifeless body. Faizan knelt and held out his hand toward Bau while the other healers did the same. Windsor pressed her fingers against his neck, then glanced up at Fargher and McDougall with a concerned stare.

"He is not breathing," Windsor said. "I do not feel a pulse."

Faizan continued to mumble under his breath, and the other healers joined in. It was a language unlike any other spoken on earth. Faizan placed his hand on Bau's chest and motioned for the others to do the same. Their voices grew louder.

"Open his airway and start compressions," Windsor said urgently. "Please, move aside."

With an enormous gasp of air, Bau sat straight up, wide-eyed. The healers pulled back and watched him quietly. Windsor snatched her inch-thick glasses off her nose and placed her fingers against Bau's neck to be certain.

"Bau, are you okay?" Windsor asked, concerned yet relieved.

"She packs quite a punch," Bau said as he tried to catch his breath. "We will need more with the spirit of Navi, but it is a start."

"You do realize, if the Merikh catch wind of this," McDougall whispered to Fargher, "we will end up like that blasted statue."

38

KARNATAKA, INDIA

A CARAVAN OF EARTH-TONED, mud-covered Land Rovers sped down an express highway, switching lanes in unison. From the back seat of the middle Land Rover, Will stared out the window at the open road and endless desert. He'd slept most of the flight before the Gulfstream touched down at Bangalore International. The hunt for the highest Cherub had left him exhausted and in a fog. He struggled to distinguish reality from nightmares.

"Peter used Eden's Star to bring me here once," Addison stated. "He needed my gifts to unseal what remained hidden. I have searched for this place many times in the years since, but I was never able to pinpoint the exact location."

"What is the treasure we are searching for?" Will asked.

"Several days ago we struck pay dirt in our interrogations at Shek Pik Prison," Addison replied. "Another one of Peter's secrets has been uncovered by Xui Li."

"The woman we captured in Sakkhela—the Elder."

"Centuries ago, Ryder Slybourne and Florence Upsdell were the most powerful among the Cherub. They used their powers not only to defend the Cherub but to gain greater influence and wealth." Addison nodded toward the scabbard across Will's lap. "Upsdell forged Dragon Soul, and Slybourne was the only swordsman strong enough to wield its power, all in the name of Elyon—but ultimately for their own glory."

"Do you believe that to be true?"

"Most of it is folklore; however, the lineage of the Cherub is stained with their names. Even in the archives of Merikh history, Slybourne and Upsdell are deemed to be great warriors and even greater enemies." Addison retrieved his cell phone and swiped across the screen. "See for yourself, then decide how much of it you believe."

On the screen a video played, showing Xui Li beaten and bloodied. Will noticed she was handcuffed to a metal chair with restraints glowing a fiery orange.

"What do you know of the artifacts Eden's Star protects?" Chung's words cut through the phone speakers, even though he couldn't be seen. "Begin with why you were in Sakkhela."

"I do not know what the artifacts are that remain hidden, but in Sakkhela I was searching as you are doing now." Xui Li's weakened and frail words were barely above a whisper. "Ryder Slybourne is one of our greatest heroes in the faith who led the Cherub warriors during the First Great War and in the Battle of Everest against the legion, the Nephilim, and their king. He was invincible. On the mountain, thousands were slaughtered, but Slybourne fought valiantly against the darkness with Dragon Soul until he was the last one standing."

"He was defeated," Chung interrupted. "What weapon killed him?"

Xui Li shook her head. "That remains a mystery."

"You are forbidden to lie, Xui Li."

She raised her head and stared into the camera. "I have spoken the truth."

A chill shot down Will's spine.

"What do you know about Eden's Star?" Chung pressed.

"After the battle was lost on Everest, the Nephilim searched the mountain for Dragon Soul, but the sword had vanished." Xui Li paused. "For centuries, Slybourne and Upsdell's riches—once kept in Sakkhela—were lost, while the Nephilim enslaved Cherub across the earth. I searched Sakkhela for any clue to Slybourne's treasure, hoping a discovery would lead to the artifacts."

"You did find something in Sakkhela before we caught you," Chung suggested.

"Throughout the years, Cherub and Merikh have attempted to find the gateway to the Valley of Grace and Charis for the same purpose—to search for the artifacts and to find Slybourne's riches. Sir James Nightingale was the first to discover Eden's Star along his journey to find the Testimony. He returned to Beacon Hill, where he trusted the Elders to keep it safe."

"The Elders possessed Eden's Star?" Chung asked, a tinge of surprise in his voice. "What did the Elders do with the compass?"

Will's gaze shifted toward Addison, who remained stone-cold. Will said in a lowered voice, "The Testimony could still be at Beacon Hill."

"We argued over what to do with Eden's Star, knowing what was written in the Eternal—Eden's Star was created to protect the artifacts, never to seek them out." Xui Li lowered her head, her eyes focused on the floor. "When we uncovered hand-drawn maps in Slybourne Castle, we believed they revealed clues to the artifacts. But we knew searching for the artifacts went against the Mercy Covenant and Elyon's commands—and we were uncertain of how many maps were hidden elsewhere. Before he could be stopped, Peter took Eden's Star and one of the ancient maps, then vanished for many years, leaving the Elders fractured. Each one of us chose our own paths to find him and reclaim what was stolen. When he returned years later, he was more powerful, even though his gifts were stripped in the same way as ours. Gabriella was the last to lose her gifts when she attempted to find Eden's Star."

"Did Peter have the compass with him when he returned?"

Xui Li shook her head. "He claimed to have lost Eden's Star in another realm."

"What else did the great Elder discover?"

"After Slybourne was killed on Mount Everest, Florence Upsdell went insane and swore to avenge his death by waging war against Cherub and Merikh." Xui Li lifted her head a second time. "Before she died, what remained of their riches once kept within Slybourne Castle were taken from Sakkhela. Many of the highest Cherub are convinced that within those treasures are some of the artifacts hidden by Eden's Star—once protected within the Testimony."

"Where were these treasures hidden, Xui Li?"

"In Sakkhela, the truth revealed itself to me within the Chamber of Shadowlight." Xui Li's body tensed as she pulled at the restraints. As an Elder she swore an oath to Elyon that forbid her to lie. Even though the Elders were no more, she fought against revealing the truth. "Slybourne and Upsdell hid the treasure in Karnataka—in the Exodus Mines."

"What about the outlier—has he found the Exodus Mines?"

"You know my gifts are no more." Xui Li shook her head slowly. "I cannot sense his whereabouts, Michael."

"But he does have Eden's Star, correct? Where did he find it?"

"The outlier is one with Eden's Star." Xui Li clenched her jaw and attempted to speak no more, but it was impossible. "He found the compass in the Temple of the Nephilim in the City of Gods—*and* he survived, even though he is not gifted as a lightforcer, bender, or healer. Addison knows what it is like to be an outlier, to choose his own way. Jack has chosen the narrow path, while his father has chosen one of destruction."

Will listened intently, learning far more than he'd been told by Peter Leung.

"She has always been so dramatic." Addison stopped the video and slipped his phone back into his pocket. "If Xui Li is telling the truth, we will uncover Slybourne's spoils of war *and* leave with one or more of the artifacts from the Exodus Mines."

"If we had Eden's Star, the search would go much faster." Will knew finding the compass meant a chance for him to settle the score. "You gave me your word."

Will waited for Addison to respond, but the leader of the Merikh remained silent. After three hours on the road, the Land Rovers exited the highway. Following a twisting and winding mountainous route, they pulled off near a serene lake. Close to shore, a dozen armed men surrounded two semitrucks backed up to the edge of the water.

Addison climbed out of the Land Rover and walked toward the

lake. Will slipped off the seat but stayed near the vehicle. From where he stood, sunlight reflected off the glassy waters like stars twinkling in a night sky.

Addison called back, "Bring Dragon Soul."

Will grabbed the scabbard and slipped it over his shoulder. As he approached, he noticed how the deep-blue water was so dark he couldn't see beneath the surface. Addison stared across the lake, then glanced briefly toward Will, who stood beside him.

"The power of your gifts was denied by the Cherub," Addison said, "even though Peter recognized your strength to wield Dragon Soul. A mistake you must make them regret."

"Bau has the same strength, and he will want the sword back."

"You took what was rightfully yours—sometimes that is the only way." Addison knelt down and dipped his fingers into the water. "Eden's Star lives within my bloodline, and the only way to retrieve it is for Dragon Soul to pierce the heart. When you have succeeded, you will be worshiped by the Merikh, and you will stand at my right hand as I rule over this world."

"I will not stop until it is done—no matter how many Cherub must die."

"Place the tip of the sword into the water."

Removing Dragon Soul from its scabbard, Will dipped the point into the lake. A ripple spread out from the sword across the water. Toward the center, the water bubbled as if being boiled. Will kept his grip tight on the sword and watched in amazement as the water parted to the left and right. A rocky path across the lake was revealed.

Will pushed Dragon Soul deeper into the mud until it stood on its own, keeping the lake divided into two sections. He followed Addison down the path while the armed men remained on shore. Anticipation peaked as he looked to his left and right where walls of water grew taller the farther they descended. When they reached the center, Addison and Will stopped in front of a flat granite stone on the bottom of the lake etched with a fire-breathing dragon.

"Slybourne's crest," Addison said in a lowered voice. "I have finally returned."

Will took a closer look and noticed a gap in the crest. "Same carving is on Dragon Soul."

"I remember the moment you are now experiencing." A sly grin lifted the corners of Addison's lips. "And I know all too well how to get inside—but we will need a helicopter."

39

NANIMI, JAPAN

THE SAMPAN DRIFTED DOWNRIVER. Sheer granite mountains with wooded areas scattered across the rocks loomed on both sides. Hours had passed since Jack, Eliška, and Emma left the others at the boathouse. Jack had dozed off while Eliška navigated the route and Emma watched their surroundings. He jerked awake and pulled himself onto his feet, stretching his aching muscles as he shook off his grogginess while realizing how much easier his muscles moved now.

"I'm guessing you know how to get to Arishiyama," Jack said to Eliška.

"Professor Burwick told me to follow the river for two days."

"We're not going to sleep on the river—right?"

"Nanimi should be close, so we will stay there for the night."

"Have you been to Arishiyama before?" Emma asked. "Or the Valley of Grace?"

"I have only been as far as Ine Town," Eliška admitted. "Never farther."

"So we're like three blind mice," Jack mused, "trying to find a piece of cheese."

As they rounded a bend in the river, cherry blossom trees created a stunning backdrop to a rural village. Eliška slowed the sampan and steered toward a dilapidated dock. Nearing the shore, Jack noticed a temple with bright-red pillars and a black tiled roof. A crowd gathered near the temple where incense burned, leaving a subtle woody aroma drifting toward the shoreline. Emma grabbed a rope from the deck and jumped onto the dock, then wrapped the rope around a wood post jutting out of the calm waters.

"Wonder if they have a Maxim's here?" Jack asked. "I could go for a mooncake."

Emma mused, "Maybe a Starbucks."

"One on every corner of the planet—who knows, probably in the other realms too."

Grabbing their backpacks and duffel bag, they left the sampan and walked down the center of the dock toward the crowd. Jack remembered stepping foot in the City of Gods, a mash-up of modern and ancient times. Nanimi shared a similar feeling, except they weren't in another realm where spirits waged war for lost souls. A strange thought struck him. *We might be in this world, but that doesn't mean the supernatural isn't around the next corner. Cherub and Merikh are fighting for the souls of everyone—in this world and the others.* Jack breathed in the simplicity surrounding him, far from the fast-paced, tech-driven culture they'd left only a day earlier. At the back of the crowd, he eyed both locals and fellow expats.

"I thought we'd be the only foreigners," he said under his breath.

Emma's gaze shifted from one person to the next. "Better not to draw attention."

"Who could possibly know we are all the way out here?"

"The Merikh found us in Sakkhela—their reach is far and wide."

"I guess I'll keep sleeping with one eye open, then."

Eliška turned toward them with her cell phone in one hand. "There is a place to stay."

Leaving the crowd at the temple, Eliška led Jack and Emma down a dirt road where two-story homes were stacked one next to the other, their ceramic roofs poking out over the road. Eliška kept checking the map on her phone until they stopped at the entrance of one of the weathered wood homes. She knocked and waited. A moment passed before an elderly man opened the door and tilted his head curiously.

"From here to there," Eliška said.

Jack reacted when he heard Eliška's words, remembering Areum saying that exact thing when they found Xui Li at the mustard seed stall in the City of Gods. Instinctively, he added, "Mountains will move. Pyramids will crumble."

"Justice flows like a raging river." The edges of the elderly man's lips curled as he opened the door wider. "I have been expecting you."

The elderly man motioned for them to remove their shoes on the *agarikamachi*—a step before the no-shoe zone. Jack slipped out of his boots and followed the others into the *ima*, a sparsely furnished living room, where the floor was made of pounded dirt and lime.

"My name is Aki Katsuo." The elderly man's dark eyes and the pronounced scar along the side of his bald head were signs of someone with stories to tell. He bowed slightly. "Welcome."

Emma introduced herself and Eliška but did not introduce Jack. He'd grown used to being the one whose name was never mentioned to anyone outside of their circle. Reaching out, Jack shook hands with Aki Katsuo, feeling the sandpaper of the man's bony palm and fingers.

"You are the outlier," Katsuo said casually. "Harley has told me much about you."

He hesitated. "Just call me Jack."

In the center of the room was a *shabudai*—another reminder of Vigan. On top of the low round table were bowls of steaming rice, udon noodles, miso soup, pickled vegetables, and white fish. Jack inhaled the aroma and was suddenly starving. Katsuo grabbed their backpacks and duffel bag before disappearing into another room.

"Smells good," Jack noted. "Burwick must've told him we were coming."

"She didn't say anything to me," Emma shrugged. "He must be a Cherub, or—"

"Professor Burwick said to find this place as soon as we arrived," Eliška interrupted. "And to trust whoever answered the door as a friend of the faction."

"Well, at least we know we won't starve," Jack said.

Katsuo returned to the living room barefoot in black hakama pants and a loose white shirt. He knelt down on a large mat with his feet beneath him and motioned for them to do the same. They followed his lead, and Jack found himself seated between Emma and Eliška. *Perfect.* A fresh scent wafting through the air filled his nostrils. It seemed to calm the edge on both sides.

"We will give thanks to Elyon," Katsuo said. "Then you will eat and rest."

All heads bowed as Katsuo prayed, and then each one dug into their meal. Jack scarfed down the food in front of him before anyone else.

"If you don't mind me asking," Jack said with a mouthful, "are you faction?"

"I am a follower of Elyon," Katsuo replied. "That is most important."

"Do you know why we are here? Why Professor Burwick asked you to help us?"

"Yes." Katsuo nodded slowly. "You search for what remains hidden."

"Right, the artifacts." Jack hesitated. "If we find them, will the war between Cherub and Merikh be over?"

"There are those who believe if the artifacts are returned to the Testimony, there will be lasting peace." Katsuo eyed Emma and Eliška closely. "But truth is guarded by Eden's Star."

"Do you know what the artifacts are?" Emma asked. "And how many we need to find?"

"Elyon created the universe with the touch of his hand, yet he chose to keep the artifacts hidden from man within the Testimony to be guarded by Eden's Star. One must wonder why this is so." Katsuo's gaze shifted between them. "It is unknown how many artifacts have remained untouched. Going against Elyon's commands in the Eternal to search for the artifacts in the name of light could bring consequences beyond our war against the Merikh."

"But if the artifacts are found," Eliška chimed in, "will the Merikh's sins be judged?"

"Only Elyon judges the sins of man," Katsuo replied somberly. "A day will come when each will stand before him."

After they finished lunch, Katsuo led them into one of the other rooms, where he had left their backpacks and duffel bag. Sliding open a closet door, he reached farther inside and slid the back wall to one side, revealing a hidden room within the closet where two folding cots filled most of the space.

"If there is a knock at the door," Katsuo said, "you must hide in here."

Jack picked up the duffel bag and set it inside the hidden room, then did the same with the two backpacks. "What happens if they don't knock?"

"You will run."

40

KARNATAKA, INDIA

A HELICOPTER LANDED NEAR THE SEMITRUCKS, and Will stepped onto the skids. Gripping the side of the aircraft, he held on as the pilot lifted off and flew low toward the center of the lake. With Dragon Soul secured in the scabbard over his shoulder, he waited until the helicopter hovered over where the water had parted earlier and revealed Slybourne's crest. Rotor wash whipped across the lake as he let go and jumped into the water. As soon as he swam to the surface, he breathed in deep, then dove straight down, kicking his legs and pulling at the water until he reached the flat granite stone.

Slipping Dragon Soul from the scabbard, he felt for the gap in Slybourne's crest, then plunged the sword inside. Grabbing hold with both hands, he braced his feet against the granite stone and with great effort turned the sword counterclockwise. Water formed into a mini tornado, then whirled into a column shooting straight to the surface. With the underwater force tugging at him, he knew he wouldn't be able to hold his breath much longer. He let go of Dragon Soul and kept himself in the center of the tornado, which propelled him upward. When his head popped above the surface, he gasped for air and looked around.

He fought to tread water as the tornado circled rapidly and pulled at him hard. The helicopter returned and hovered overhead, causing wave after wave of rotor wash. Addison stepped onto the skids and dropped a rope down into an open hole in the center of the tornado created by the release of the granite stone's seal. Will knew the burning in his muscles meant he couldn't tread water forever. Swimming toward the center of the whirling column, he found himself sliding down the tornado's inner wall before slamming onto the rocky bottom of the lake.

Rolling onto his knees, Will glared at Addison, who touched down near Slybourne's crest. Will winced as he scrambled over, glancing up from the bottom of Sagara Lake at the starry skies. Standing over the opened seal, he expected a thundering boom from the current, but instead he heard only the swirling of water. Dragon Soul remained speared into Slybourne's crest, and the opened seal led deeper beneath the lake bed. Addison and Will watched as the underwater tornado eased and shifted directions until the water created the same rocky path they'd walked earlier.

"Leave the sword in place," Addison ordered. "We need to be able to return."

Staring down into the black hole, Will clenched his fist until a pale glow wrapped around his hand, casting a dim light by which he illuminated narrow stone steps descending into the earth. Taking the first steps, he cautiously disappeared into the hole. He breathed easier when the steps widened until he reached the bottom. Addison was at his right shoulder with a flashlight.

"We need to see more," Addison said. "Do it."

Will threw the pale glow from his hand ahead of them, and a royal-purple light shot across an enormous cavern. A mountain of gold coins, necklaces, bracelets, brooches, crowns, statues, and brilliant reflections of sapphires, rubies, and silver radiated from the extravagant wealth left behind centuries ago.

"Slybourne's bounty," Addison said, awestruck. "His spoils of war now belong to me."

Will stood wide-eyed. "Why is it called the Exodus Mines?"

"The Cherub name everything, as if their history is greater than all others."

"She said the highest Cherub believe there might be artifacts here."

"Artifacts are relics until they are placed in the right hands. We are looking at one of the greatest weapons in history—hundreds of millions, maybe even billions in fact, to uphold the Merikh's rule *and* my reign." Addison stepped closer, entranced by the riches surrounding them. "Power and wealth by any blood necessary."

"But are there artifacts protected by Eden's Star being kept in the Exodus Mines?"

Addison smirked. "Now that the mines belong to me, we will find out together."

"Do you think Peter Leung and the Cherub took treasure from here?"

"The only way to get inside was for someone gifted like you

and me to use Dragon Soul." Addison's eyes narrowed. "Peter used me to gain entrance once before—but only once."

"Bau Hu is one of the chosen," Will replied. "He's also the last one to guard Dragon Soul, before I took it from him. The great Elder might've used him to come back here again."

"Then you have answered your own question." Addison picked up a handful of gold coins and smiled. "Now the next question is, how do we haul all of this out of here?"

"You are going to need more than two trucks."

"We will take what we can for now. Wait here."

Addison turned and left Will standing alone in the cavern. He stepped forward and climbed onto the mountain of gold. Slumping down on the riches, he sat quietly, struck by the magnitude of their discovery. He reached down and grabbed a handful of coins in the same way as Addison. Running his thumb over the intricately detailed engravings, he wondered how much of the Exodus Mines would one day belong to him.

41

NANIMI, JAPAN

JACK CRACKED THE DOOR OPEN and stared into a bare room where Emma was shadowboxing. He nearly shut the door when he realized her eyes were closed. She moved effortlessly with balance and fluidity flowing through every muscle and limb. Her auburn highlights, which were so pronounced the first time he laid eyes on her, seemed faded, leaving her long jet-black hair even more striking.

Perched on one leg, Emma reached her arm toward the ceiling, stretching her fingers for every inch. Jack had never seen her wearing short sleeves—a strange realization, considering they'd been together for weeks. He was shocked when he eyed a collage of tattooed blackwork sleeved on both arms—more than the characters he'd seen before. 勇氣. *Courage.* Her amber eyes opened and stared back at him, causing his cheeks to flush.

"Sorry—it's just your tattoos remind me of Areum's."

Emma lowered her leg and arm. "We were given our first ones when we were young."

"I don't think Rachel had any tattoos, did she?"

"She chose not to have them," Emma replied. "I was never offered a choice."

Jack's brows raised as he stepped closer. "Looks painful."

"Extremely." Emma smiled as she held out her arms. "But it is my story."

"It does look epic." Jack wanted to know more about each tattoo, but he was too embarrassed to ask. "I've never learned how to shadowbox."

"We were trained on Karābu to control our gifts through focusing our mind, soul, and body." Jack's heartbeat quickened as Emma grabbed his hands and pulled him close, then pushed him back one step. "When you search inwardly for Elyon's power, the flow of your body will move through your hips, shoulders, and into every strike."

"Whoa . . ." Jack exhaled. "You're like Mr. Miyagi."

"Stand strong and follow."

Emma moved her arms effortlessly, and her hands flowed as if she held the paper fans with Tibetan rosefinch feathers from the Sword and Fan. Jack tried to stay focused, but he was distracted by her beauty and strength. He was falling even harder, and he wasn't sure how to deal with it. Snapping himself back, he mimicked her as best he could, imagining he was looking into a mirror.

"Precision in movement," she instructed. "And do not rush."

Jack felt his muscles repeat what she was doing. Emma stepped back and lowered her body. He jumped awkwardly as her leg swept beneath him.

"Remember, I'm a rookie." His muscles tensed, anticipating her next move. "I thought we were shadowboxing, not entering the Octagon."

"The Protector of Eden's Star," Emma said, smiling, "will need to learn both."

"Hold on a second," Jack protested with a sheepish grin. "Maybe this isn't such a good idea."

Emma punched forward, and Jack ducked, barely escaping her strike. Without hesitation, she struck with a low kick, which snapped against his thigh.

"Ouch!" Jack hopped on one leg, knowing she'd held back. "End of round one?"

When she tried to kick him again, Jack dodged her strike and pushed her leg away. It wasn't pretty, but it stopped her from nailing the same spot twice.

"We've gone from shadowboxing to full contact, huh?"

Emma grinned. "I would say we are sparring, not fighting."

"Well, that's one way to put it."

Inhaling deep, he realized what she'd said moments earlier. *"When you search inwardly for Elyon's power, the flow of your body will move through your hips, shoulders, and into every strike."* With his instincts in overdrive, he raised his fists in front of him and planted his feet solidly on the floor. Settling his adrenaline, he tried to surrender to Elyon—something he'd struggled to do since the beginning of this nightmare. A fiery tingling sensation spread across his chest, but it wasn't painful like before, when Eden's Star erupted into an inferno.

He knew Emma had waited until she'd seen his eyes flare. When she attacked again, his body moved without his mind. He blocked two leg strikes and defended himself from her fist combinations, but he hesitated to retaliate. He was too afraid to strike back, as it went against everything he'd been taught—to never hit a girl—and he was sure she'd ramp up his next lesson. Emma stopped for a moment and waited, which made him feel like she was just getting started. Again, she moved with grace and purpose. He attempted a leg sweep, but she leapt over his awkward move and responded by shoving him dead in the chest with the palms of her hands. He stumbled and fell on his backside. Emma pounced and pushed him to his back. His eyes were wide as saucers as her fist swung down at him, stopping just an inch from his nose.

Eliška appeared in the doorway and cleared her throat. "Not to interrupt . . ."

"Uh . . . we were just . . ." Jack stumbled for the words as Emma pulled him to his feet, both a bit embarrassed. "What's wrong?"

"Katsuo is gone, and I do not think he is coming back."

"What makes you say that?" Emma asked.

Eliška held up a piece of paper with scribbled handwriting. "He wrote, 'Elyon will fight for you. You need only to be still and trust.' I want to take a look in the village to be certain."

Jack's blank stare camouflaged a vision rifling through his mind and a voice that sent a shiver down his spine. *"Slybourne's bounty—his spoils of war now belong to me."* Tunnel vision offered a glimpse of mountains piled high with gold. Jack sensed Addison was not alone, but he couldn't see who else was there. As quickly as the vision appeared, it was gone like all the others before. He realized Emma and Eliška were staring at him.

Emma grabbed his arm. "What did you see?"

"I think Addison found where one of the artifacts is hidden—maybe more—but it's not where we've been searching. Slybourne's bounty is hidden underground far from the Highlands, and now it belongs to him."

"And one or more of the artifacts too," Eliška said. "What kind of bounty?"

"Gold—and I mean tons of it."

42

When Jack and Eliška stepped out of the house, the night air was brisk and the starry skies were crystal clear. Eliška's sandy-blonde hair was unbraided and loosely draped over her shoulders. The soft yellow glow of candle lanterns attached to the homes guided their path down the center of the village. Jack had known better than to push Emma to join them. She'd offered to stay behind and dig into the Eternal in search of any clues to what Addison might have found in Slybourne's bounty.

"Do you have gifts like Emma?" Jack asked.

"Not everyone who believes are lightforcers, benders, or healers."

"Huh?" Jack said, dumbfounded. "I'm not sure what you're talking about."

"The three rarest gifts of a Cherub. I have never met anyone with more than one, except for Emma." Eliška seemed to be more at ease since they'd left the house. "She is a lightforcer *and* a bender—someone who possesses the ability to harness a power source and move physical objects in remarkable ways."

"Victoria Harbour . . ." Jack's voice trailed off.

"It took great faith to sink the *Eastern Dragon*." Eliška paused. "But she is not a healer."

"Looks like that gift's been given to Amina." Jack couldn't help but wonder how the others were doing in the boathouse along the river. "If Emma were a healer, she would've healed me from Eden's Star. Come to think of it—I should've asked Amina to give it a shot."

Eliška cocked her head to one side. "What does Eden's Star have to do with healing?"

"Hard to explain." Jack knew he'd slipped up. Fearing she might ask to see the compass, he shifted the conversation. "How did you meet Professor Burwick?"

"A few years ago, she visited Silverleaf and spoke at the school assembly. I do not remember all she said, but the way she said it stuck with me. She spoke with conviction and passion. Her daughter, Darcy, was my best friend. At the end of the assembly, I met the professor for the first time."

"Did you know she was the leader of the Cherub faction?"

"Darcy didn't tell me," Eliška admitted. "But she knew I believed in Elyon, so I guess she would have told the professor."

"Is Silverleaf a training ground for the Cherub like Beacon Hill?"

"There were only a few believers at Silverleaf. Darcy was one, and I was another."

"So that's when Burwick recruited you to the faction," Jack guessed.

"She encouraged me to pursue the calling Elyon had for me. Most of us in the faction do not have gifts like the lightforcers, benders, or healers—but it does not mean we are not equipped to defend the light against darkness."

"The Cherub don't respect the professor or the faction because of the supernatural stuff?"

"We believe in Elyon and his miraculous powers, but we also use other means."

"Were you telling the truth about when you were abducted?"

"As I have said, I did not know who you were when we first met." Eliška stopped walking and faced him. "We were searching for traffickers and knew they were spotted at the nightclub. Merikh caught us and held us for many months. When you appeared on the ship, I was as shocked as anyone else when we were rescued."

"Eliška, you were both teenagers," Jack replied. "Going against the Merikh."

"They captured us, drugged us, and the nightmares are ones I will never forget. I cannot forgive myself for failing to protect Darcy or rescuing the others who died before we were taken to the *Eastern Dragon*." Eliška started walking again, and Jack followed. "Professor Burwick believes you are the one to bring the faction and the Cherub together—like your sister. However, Salomeh is not yet convinced."

"Burwick might be wrong about that one," Jack answered. "I'm stuck in the crosshairs."

"That may not be forever. An outlier can create a bridge."

Jack wasn't sure he agreed with Burwick or Eliška, but he

understood the weight they both carried. He had more questions but knew those answers would have to wait.

"If I had listened to Rachel maybe she'd still be alive," Jack said. "She tried convincing me to surrender to Elyon, but I wasn't ready to leave my old vices behind." A rush of guilt washed over him. "I owed the wrong people, and she died paying my debt. I'll never forgive myself for it."

"On the *Eastern Dragon*, you saved us." Eliška slowed her pace as they reached the temple entrance where villagers and expats gathered. "You were a light from Elyon."

"You and Emma are the light. I'm just a shadow."

Standing off to one side of the crowd, Jack eyed the faces and searched for Aki Katsuo. *Why would he let us in and then just disappear? Maybe because it's not his home.* In that moment it dawned on him that they were staying in another safe house for the faction, or maybe the Cherub.

"I don't see him anywhere," Jack said under his breath. "He's like a ghost."

A steady drumbeat interrupted their search as the crowd parted, creating a walkway down the center of the dirt road. Men marched toward them carrying massive fiery torches. Instead of an orange-and-red hue, the flames were ebony. With each emphatic beat of the drum, the bystanders chanted louder as the procession approached. Jack couldn't understand what they were saying, but the tingling in his fingers left him tiptoeing on the edge of the crowd. He counted eight men, each carrying one of the massive sooty torches.

"Looks like one of Burwick's fire mood experiments in chem lab—the Jurassic edition."

"Demon fire." Eliška nodded toward crimson-robed men and women standing near the temple entrance, where an eight-foot-tall hooded figure waited. "Each one has been chosen for purification—an offering to the legions of darkness."

"I got a bad feeling about this," Jack mumbled.

The villagers chanted while the last torch was speared into the ground and those in the crimson robes stepped forward until all eight were in front of the flaming torches. A shiver rattled Jack's bones when a bloodcurdling shriek pierced through the chants and drumbeats. Silence paralyzed everyone while he stared at the hooded figure, certain of where the sound came from. He realized those in the crimson robes were terrified as tears streaked down their cheeks. The men who carried the torches forced those in the robes closer to the ebony flames.

"Eliška, we can't just stand here and watch them die."

Another shriek from the hooded shadow sent Jack's adrenaline spiking. He pushed his way through the crowd until he stood alongside the robed sacrifices, who were outnumbered. Fear rushed through his veins as he braced for an onslaught, knowing he had zero plan of attack or defense.

Search inwardly for Elyon's power.

A brilliant white light streaked across the village and exploded against the nearest torch, extinguishing the ebony flame. Emma stood in the middle of the road, her palms filled with a swirling light. The hooded figure held up a rod resembling a twisted vine, which drew the ebony flames from the other torches. The charcoal flames engulfed the twisted vine, and the hooded figure pointed the rod toward Emma, unleashing a cyclone of fire.

Memories of the dark silhouettes inside the Chamber of Gods flashed in Jack's mind, a reminder of Areum's final seconds. He fought to free himself from those thoughts as Emma released streaks of light, exploding against the fire tornado. Villagers scrambled out of the way while Eliška moved swiftly through the chaos, reaching those in the crimson robes.

When the men who had carried the torches attacked, Eliška struck with precision and beauty. Emma knocked others over with the swipe of her hand. Jack spun around and stopped cold as the ebony flames encircled the hooded figure, who slammed the vine rod against the steps. As the figure's robe dropped to the ground, the vine rod morphed into black flaming chains wrapped around the neck of a skeletal beast. Charcoal wings partially spread out from the beast's back were fractured and ripped. His dark eyes stared with vengeance toward them, and then his shriek pierced every soul in Nanimi.

Jack stood wide-eyed. "What . . . is . . . that?"

"Asiklua." Eliška stepped beside him, awestruck. "Fallen from the legions of Elyon's warriors, expelled from Charis, and bound for a thousand years."

"A thousand-year-old demon," Jack said, panicked. "He looks a little bitter about it."

"You have no power over those who believe!" Emma headed straight for the demon, fearless. "The chain around your neck binds you to Elyon's command."

Asiklua flapped his broken wings and tried to fly but struggled to lift off the ground. Swinging the chain off his neck, Asiklua whipped the black flames forward with a sudden force. Emma shielded herself with her lightforce, but the impact sent her sliding backward. Ebony flames disappeared as the chain wrapped around Emma's body and pulled her toward the demon.

A raging inferno punched Jack in the chest, and he knew right away what he must do. Darting forward, he grabbed hold of the chain and tugged hard. Eliška was right behind, and she grabbed the chain too. Jack dug in his heels as he skidded across the dirt. Asiklua opened his bony jaw, revealing sharp fangs covered in crystallized lava, then unleashed another bone-chilling shriek. Eden's Star glowed beneath Jack's skin as Asiklua fought against the chain before dropping to his knees. Bowing against his will, Asiklua hunched over while the thick chain faded back into the vine rod and dropped to the ground. Jack braced himself as Eden's Star pushed him forward. He stood over Asiklua, who cowered, still desperate to devour but unable to attack. Eliška and Emma approached cautiously as the fallen angel hissed and growled.

"Asiklua once guarded the gates to Charis," Emma explained. "But after the first sin, Elyon formed Eden's Star in the hottest fires and expelled the legions under Asiklua's command from the Garden. The Eternal describes the beast Asiklua became during the Great Wars and beyond."

Jack glanced down at his chest. "Let's hope Eden's Star doesn't short-circuit."

"We cannot stand here all night." Eliška turned and picked up the vine rod from the ground. "Jack . . . Emma . . ."

Glancing over his shoulder, Jack stared at the villagers as they reappeared on the dirt road. When he turned his attention back toward Asiklua, the demon was scurrying up the temple steps before disappearing into the jungle. Turning around, Jack, Emma, and Eliška stood in front of the villagers, who dropped to their knees and bowed.

"This is awkward," Jack whispered. "What do we do now?"

Eliška handed the vine rod to Jack. "You can hold on to this."

"We need to leave," Emma said. "Right away."

43

BEACON HILL

NATALIE WAITED WHILE BAU APPROACHED the door cautiously. Navi Singh stood beside her, along with a dozen other lightforcers who guarded the corridor. Thirty more Cherub had arrived through the gateway a few hours earlier. When her cell phone buzzed, she figured it was another group from who knows where. Stationing lightforcers throughout the grounds had changed the dynamic and brought an extra sense of security.

From inside the House of Luminescence, she heard a muffled voice. "That was bonkers!"

Seconds later the door creaked open, and Timothy Lloyd poked his head into the corridor. Pushing the door open wide, he stepped forward and was followed by Vince Tobias, Amina Okonkwo, and

Professor Burwick. With her instincts on alert, Natalie anticipated Jack and Emma would be next—but there was no one else.

"You're a sight for sore eyes." Vince clenched his teeth as he limped over and fist-bumped Bau. "Wasn't sure I'd make it back to defend our title in the Bashers, Bowlers, and Boundaries. I might be a step slower, but we'll still win the crown."

"We thought you were caught by the Merikh," Bau said to Tim and Amina. "Until Faizan arrived and told us otherwise. Fargher hoped Will might have been with you somehow."

"Do your parents know you were with Jack and Emma?" When neither answered, Natalie turned her attention toward Professor Burwick. "Did you know where they were the entire time?"

"First, never underestimate the bookworms," Tim replied. "Second, we thought Will was with the headmaster. But you lot sound like you haven't seen him." He shifted his gaze toward Natalie. "And third, I plead temporary madness—or whatever it is that stops me from getting in any more trouble than I already am."

"Will is the only one of you missing, then," Natalie concluded.

Bau turned toward Vince. "Your parents will be glad to see you."

"Get moving." Burwick struck the marble floor with her cane. "And stay out of sight."

"We have identified lightforcers, benders, and healers." Bau waved over several lightforcers who helped support Vince's broad shoulders as he shuffled down the corridor. "This is our first night patrolling the grounds."

"You are well on your way," Burwick replied, pleased. "It is only the beginning."

Amina stepped forward and hugged Burwick. "Thank you, Professor."

Leaving Burwick in the doorway, Tim and Amina followed Vince and Bau. As they passed Natalie, each offered a slight nod, which left her wondering whether something horrible had happened. With so many questions flying through her mind, she counted the seconds until they were alone, ready to pounce on the professor for intel.

"Where are Jack and Emma?" Natalie asked as soon as she could.

"Not to worry," Burwick replied. "They are alive and well."

"But they are not with you, which means this was not planned."

"We each have our own path—including you, Natalie." Burwick started to turn around. "I must be going, I'm afraid."

"Wait, you aren't staying?"

"There is somewhere else I need to be—even though I would rather have tea and visit."

Natalie was dumbstruck as the professor disappeared inside the House of Luminescence and the door closed. Shaking her head, she turned toward Navi, who waited beside her quietly.

"Am I the only one with no clue what is happening?" Natalie exhaled.

"Salomeh has done the same." Navi smiled. "Where she goes, I do not know."

"One of these days, we will find out." Natalie paused. "Are you okay for another hour?"

"My parents allow me to stay up late," she said proudly.

"Right . . . good. I will check on you a bit later, then."

Natalie left Navi with the others and returned upstairs to Rowell Library. She'd never seen such a diverse group of people responsible for protecting the lives of those hiding in Nightingale's vault. While she had never been in the military, she'd trained with some of the best and recently guarded one of the worst. Burwick was right—this was only the beginning.

I am not sure they know what they are up against, but there is no denying their powers.

When Natalie entered the library, she found Vince, Tim, and Amina standing in the center of the grand room, which now resembled a dimly lit museum. Beautiful windows shattered during the attack on Beacon Hill had been replaced with large wood boards. Paintings, statues, and thousands of books were covered with inch-thick dust, slumbering from the world.

"Doesn't feel the same," Vince said. "Looks like no one has been in here for years."

"More like a haunted house," Tim agreed. "Maybe Nightingale's spirit is going to appear through the walls and chase us into his vault."

"You have quite an imagination." Amina smiled. "That's why—"

"Don't say it, please." Vince rolled his eyes. "Enough already."

"We should not stay here," Bau warned. "It is safer in the vault."

"Before we go there," Natalie interrupted, "are you going to tell us what is going on?"

"Jack, Emma, and Eliška are still searching," Amina explained. "We returned to help."

"Actually, Professor Burwick insisted," Tim corrected. "But it is good to be back."

Natalie's gaze softened. "Are they okay?"

"As good as can be expected," Amina replied. "Jack has been quite ill, so they are searching for a place to heal him. Hopefully he will get better."

"Everyone else is fine," Tim added. "Except Vince is a little worse for wear."

"Then let us get him into the vault," Bau chided. "You lot never listen."

"Good to see nothing's changed," Tim bantered. "Better yet—no *one's* changed."

Natalie wanted to press the matter, but she sensed Amina's hesitation and Bau's impatience. With her head on a swivel, she headed for the oil painting at the back of the Sir James Nightingale wing. She heard footsteps shuffling behind, so she knew the others were on her heels as Bau walked alongside. *Eliška is with Jack and Emma. Who is she, exactly?* When the painting rippled, she waited until everyone else was through before she stepped to the other side. Vince moved gingerly, so it took a few extra minutes for them to climb down the spiral stairs.

As they entered the vault, the Cherub refugees within were preparing for bed. Most of the younger children were already asleep under the covers on slim mattresses laid atop flimsy folding cots. Teens and adults busied themselves with late-night duties: Drying and stacking dishes. Washing laundry by hand. Tidying up various sectioned-off areas of the vault. At first, no one paid any attention to the new arrivals.

"Incredible," Tim said under his breath.

"We have been living here since you left," Bau said. "That will change soon."

"Mum?" Amina called out. "Dad?"

Maduka and Oni Okonkwo, seemingly in shock, hurried toward them. Amina's parents grabbed her and hugged her tight with wide smiles and plenty of tears.

"You are safe," Maduka cried. "Praise be to Elyon."

"I was worried about you too," Amina replied.

Tim stepped toward his own parents, Elis and Beca Lloyd, who approached as if they were seeing a ghost. Tim's walk turned into a jog right before he grabbed hold of them. The others in Nightingale's vault stopped for a moment and watched quietly. Tears welled up in Natalie's eyes as she stayed back and took it all in.

"We were not expecting you back so soon," Beca said. "What has happened?"

"If I told you," Tim answered, "you wouldn't believe me."

"Professor Burwick brought us through a gateway," Amina explained.

Maduka squeezed his daughter again. "You are the only ones?"

"We left Jack, Emma, and Eliška behind." Vince hobbled over and shook hands with Elis Lloyd and Maduka Okonkwo. "Tim and Amina were very brave. You should be proud."

Fargher appeared from behind. "Welcome home."

Tim, Amina, and Vince spun around and said in unison, "Headmaster!"

Natalie watched him closely, the toll and weight he carried evident in his sunken eyes. She turned her attention back to Tim, Amina, and Vince and recognized that each carried a weight of their own. Months had passed since they disappeared, but it seemed they had lived an entire lifetime.

"We believed you were captured by the Merikh," Fargher said in a hoarse voice.

"Bau told us Will is missing," Vince replied. "We will help you find him, sir."

"I am relieved you are all well." Fargher's eyes were glossy. "Be with your families."

Maduka and Oni Okonkwo, as well as Elis and Beca Lloyd, turned their gazes toward the ground. In that moment, Natalie realized they knew the entire time their children were searching for the artifacts alongside Jack and Emma but had not said a word.

"Vince, I will take you to your parents in the morning," Natalie offered. "As you can imagine, they have been through quite a lot, and they will be thrilled to end their nightmare."

"Thank you." Vince hesitated. "Is it safe for them?"

"It is far more dangerous to be searching for you."

"If you don't mind, let me think it over. After what we've seen, I'm not so sure it's the best idea. If the Merikh know I'm part of this, that'll only make it more dangerous for them. Addison knows who they are—and that they have deep pockets."

Natalie nodded. "You let me know when you are ready."

"Hungry?" Oni's smile was pearly white. "We have leftover curry."

"Curry?" Tim's ears perked up. "Lead the way to the Promised Land, Mrs. Okonkwo."

Natalie noticed Fargher and Bau had slipped away from the tearful reunion. She spotted them in a corner, but as she approached, they stopped whispering.

"What we thought was true is not to be," Fargher said solemnly.

"We stick to the plan," Natalie replied. "Will is still out there, and so are the others."

"Cherub gifts remain at Beacon Hill." Bau glanced over his shoulder. "So there is hope."

Fargher scratched his scraggly beard. "Perhaps it is time to return to the light."

44

NANIMI, JAPAN

JACK HURRIED THROUGH THE SAFE HOUSE into the empty bedroom. He leaned into the closet and opened the hidden back wall. He grabbed both backpacks, then handed them over his shoulder to Emma and Eliška. Once more, he reached into the secret room and snatched the duffel bag. With the twisted vine rod in one hand, he slipped the duffel over his other shoulder. He was surprised to discover that his fingers wrapped around the vine rod naturally. He expected black flames to erupt as his mind flashed to Asiklua bowing at his feet—surrendering to Eden's Star.

"That was crazy," he said under his breath. "And this is even crazier."

"Eden's Star controlled the flames," Emma said. "It has powers we did not even know about."

"Sounds logical when you say it." Jack held the vine rod up. "Maybe you should take this."

"We can search the Eternal for answers about Eden's Star later," Eliška interrupted. "The sooner we disappear, the less of a trail we leave behind."

A low thumping and vibration perked Jack's ears. "Do you hear that?"

Emma and Eliška exchanged glances, but he didn't wait for either to answer. He rushed out of the room and down the hallway with both on his heels. Reaching the living space, he peered between the curtains and eyed the empty streets. Everything seemed quiet—eerily quiet—until a chill shot down his spine.

"Search every home," Michael Chung's voice ordered. "He cannot run forever."

Jack cracked the curtain, leaving enough of a gap to keep one eye on the street. *Elyon, you are in control—help us get out of this in one piece.* A few seconds passed before shadows appeared, moving stealthily along both sides of the street. Red laser sights reflected off the windows. Jack pulled the curtain closed and glanced over his shoulder.

"Chung found us," he whispered. "And he's brought the Merikh assassin squad."

"We need to find a way out," Eliška replied calmly. "Without being seen."

Emma nodded. "We cannot return to the dock."

Red laser sights pierced through the curtains before sweeping across the living room. Jack, Emma, and Eliška ducked low and kept themselves pressed against the walls. Jack's heart pounded through his chest as his grip on the vine rod tightened. Shadows approached on the other side of the windows and stopped for what seemed like an eternity.

"You will not live beyond tonight, Jack." Chung's words dripped with contempt. "Your blood belongs to your father—and so does Eden's Star. Surrender yourself and no one else will be harmed. Run from me, and we will burn this village down."

In the pitch-black, Jack flinched when Emma grabbed his shoulder and pulled him back. They crab-walked across the floor into the empty bedroom. Climbing into the closet, Emma slid the secret wall open and stepped into the hidden room. Jack was the last one in before Eliška closed the opening, leaving them in a cramped space barely wide enough for all three.

BAM!

Footsteps echoed on the other side of the wall. Jack was certain the man who'd murdered Rachel was only a few feet away. Even with the powers of Eden's Star flowing through his veins and the twisted vine rod in his grip, he was powerless to even the score.

Emma moved quietly toward one corner, searching for a way out. Eliška was on her knees, feeling the floor for the same. Jack wanted to ask Emma again to unleash her gifts against Chung and the Merikh assassins. *End their lives. It's not vengeance; it's protecting the light.* Exhaling slowly, he knew the voice in his head was not Elyon. *Why can't I just pray for forgiveness after it's done? Isn't that how it works?* He snapped out of a quick argument with himself, knowing his momentary desire came from the darkest corners of his soul.

Eliška tapped his arm and Emma's at the same time. In the darkness, she'd found a latched door in the floor. Sliding the latch to one side, she carefully pulled the door open and revealed a river beneath the house. He knew better than to argue as he slipped the duffel off his shoulder and lowered it through the hole.

"We should ditch this." Jack held out the rod. "We've got enough luggage."

Eliška snatched the vine rod from him. "You go first, and I will carry the stick."

Lowering himself, he allowed his boots and legs to dip into the chilly water before letting go of his grip on the wood floor. With one hand, he gripped one of the stilts beneath the house, and with the other, he hugged the duffel. Eliška was next into the water, then Emma. All three kept close as a white beam of light swept across the river.

Jack ducked beneath the surface and pulled the duffel down with him. He held his breath while the light skimmed back and forth over the river, then disappeared. His head slowly popped up to the surface, where he joined Emma and Eliška. Together, they waded through the water, keeping themselves hidden beneath the houses until they reached the far end of Nanimi.

45

DRENCHED TO THE BONE, Jack shivered from the cold as he hiked up the mountain trying to keep pace with Eliška and Emma. The darkness shifted and the jungle grew more alive as they left the river and village farther behind. Jack couldn't shake the eerie feeling that they were being watched. Knowing Chung and the Merikh assassins were on the hunt meant every snapping twig or rustling bush spiked his senses. Even though his legs ached and his spine tingled, he kept his boots trudging up the mountain.

The overgrown brush made for tedious trekking as the hours passed. With the weight of the duffel growing heavier on his shoulders, he dug the vine rod into the dirt and pushed himself harder than he had in weeks. Branches poked and prodded, leaving stinging scrapes and scratches on his hands. When they reached a plateau, they finally dropped their bags and rested.

"Are you sure we're going in the right direction?" Jack asked.

Eliška pointed her navigation screen toward him. "Two days north is Arishiyama."

"By river," Jack pointed out. "It'll take way longer on foot."

"We are one day on the river." Emma unzipped the duffel bag and removed bottled water and power bars. "We must keep our pace or else Chung will catch up."

"He won't hunt us on foot." Jack remembered how Chung and the assassins had arrived in Sitio Veterans. "They'll be in the air with high-tech gear, searching for heat signatures."

Emma handed each of them water and bars, then zipped the duffel back up and slung it over her shoulders. "Then we should keep going."

Jack unwrapped the power bar and finished it with two bites, then downed a full bottle of water and crumpled the plastic together. He grabbed the backpack Emma carried and stuffed the recycled bottle inside, not wanting to leave any clues behind.

"I wish we knew if Vince, Tim, Amina, and the professor are okay."

"Professor Burwick kept herself unharmed until . . ." Eliška's voice trailed off.

"She told me." Jack clenched his jaw. "I've seen what he's capable of, Eliška."

"We have a long journey ahead," Emma interrupted. "It will be morning soon."

In the pitch-blackness, Jack was grateful not to be stuck in bed dreading the moment Eden's Star might explode. Eliška led the way, and he found himself lingering behind with Emma. She reached over and intertwined her fingers with his. A rush of heat spread across his cheeks as they followed the edge of the plateau and Eliška's footsteps.

"Are you gauging my emotions?" Jack asked, curious. "Or is this something else?"

"Both, I suppose." Emma glanced at him and smiled. "I am stronger when you are too."

"Elyon is keeping us alive by the skin of our teeth." Jack squeezed her hand and stabbed the twisted vine rod into the ground. "You have your gifts back, so . . ."

"I do care for you, Jack. But there is more at stake than just you and me."

"Yeah, the fate of the world is left up to a bunch of teenagers."

"Our generation is not ready for this war—but there is no time left to prepare." Emma paused. "It is impossible to protect everyone at once."

Jack eyed her closely. "You're thinking about him, aren't you?"

"Will needs his friends more than ever."

"I'm sure Headmaster Fargher is keeping a close eye on him."

Emma replied solemnly, "He has lost so much, Jack."

"He's not the only one who lost a mom," Jack snapped as he let go of Emma's hand. "My whole family is gone—and it's my father who is trying to kill me and everyone else. Emma, I'm known to the Merikh as the Executioner's spawn. C'mon, how twisted is that?"

"I do not know what that feels like," she admitted. "But you are stronger than Will."

"I'm not so sure." Jack brushed it off. "At least he's not on the run twenty-four seven."

Darkness faded into daylight as Jack picked up his pace and

stayed between Eliška and Emma. *Why do I keep getting so defensive? Will's my best friend—I want him to be okay. And I want us to go back to the way it was before all of this started.* A heavy fog drifted beneath the mountain peaks across the Highlands. Reaching the edge of the plateau, he stopped next to Eliška, who was on the verge of a thousand-foot drop down a sheer mountain face.

"Dead end," Jack said under his breath. "Now what?"

"We find another way," Eliška replied. "There is always another, Jack."

Emma stood beside them. "Elyon will guide us to the narrow path."

"We're on the edge." Jack pointed straight down. "How much narrower can it get?"

Eliška turned and climbed higher, toward the peak of the mountain. Jack and Emma followed, and when they reached the summit, he stopped for a moment to catch his breath. With the early morning glow burning off the dense fog, a rainbow of gold and emerald green rice paddies rolled along the Highlands as far as the eye could see. Jack gazed out on the enchanted pattern and thought of Nightingale's illustration of rolling hills.

It's missing the stone wall stretching beyond.

"Where do you think we are?" Jack asked.

"Arishiyama is near." Eliška checked the navigation on her cell phone and tapped the screen several times. "No signal. Maybe we have reached the Valley of Grace."

"We are on top of a mountain," Emma pointed out. "Not in a valley."

"Then we need to head down to see if we have arrived."

Jack wasn't sure what he expected—a city sign or a welcome party? He guessed Eliška knew what she was talking about since it was possible Burwick had told her about the rice paddies or some other clue that gave it away. Not wanting to bog her down with more questions, he let it go and absorbed the breathtaking view.

They hiked downward another few miles through the rice paddies before anyone noticed the stone pillars, which were barely visible within the overgrown jungle. *Are we entering the Valley of Grace?* The chill of the morning burned off and the day grew warmer as they continued north—this time beneath the rugged dome-shaped mountains. Heading away from the rice paddies, huge roots appeared like veins pumping life into the jungle. *I've seen roots like these before, in the House of Luminescence and at the Wishing Tree.* He quickened his pace with even greater purpose.

Above their heads loomed orange-and-red-leaved trees. They climbed over another giant vine, deeper into a lush green landscape. They stopped when they reached a bamboo forest, which looked even more like an enchanted world. On both sides of the naturally formed entrance, giant stone pillars carved with ancient figures stood as tall as the highest bamboo.

"Arishiyama," he guessed. "Totally looks like a sacred place, but I'm no Cherub expert."

"We are on the edge of this world within the Highlands," Eliška replied. "We must have faith the Valley of Grace and Charis are beyond."

"Elyon's presence is here with us," Emma said reverently. "Can you sense him?"

"He's not the only one I'm sensing," Jack answered.

Eliška nodded slowly. "We are being watched."

46

NEAR THE NATURAL ENTRANCE to the bamboo forest, Jack sensed Elyon's presence stronger than he'd ever felt it before. It wasn't a resounding voice calling down from on high, but rather a confidence flowing through his veins. Gripping the twisted vine rod tight, he glanced over his shoulder and searched for anyone moving within the forest. In the skies overhead, the low thumping of a helicopter broke the silence, sending Jack, Emma, and Eliška hiding among the trees.

"More will come on foot," Eliška warned. "Especially if they are tracking us."

Emma stepped up to the edge of the bamboo forest, and with one more step she was thrown back by an invisible force. Jack hurried to help her onto her feet. Eliška gazed curiously and approached with greater caution. She followed in Emma's footsteps, and the invisible force punched with a stronger force, propelling Eliška backward into the arms of Jack and Emma. The sound of thumping rotors grew louder. When Jack stepped back and peered between the woody ringed stems growing from the bamboo overhead, he caught sight of two helicopters hovering near the entrance to Arishiyama.

"Third time is not the charm," he mumbled. "Now what're we supposed to do?"

Emma brushed herself off. "Oftentimes, sacred grounds are guarded by Elyon."

"We need to figure out another way through before we are cornered," Eliška warned.

"I thought Professor Burwick would have given you a clue at least," Emma quipped.

Usually, Jack was clueless, but in that moment even he knew the tension was impenetrable. "Faizan said he would take me as far as the gateway, but not all may be permitted to enter—it would require more than an offering."

"A gateway to the Valley of Grace and Charis," Eliška reiterated. "Faizan's warning would have been good to know before we left Ine Town."

"We were going to leave either way," Emma deflected. "Now we find a way forward."

"Why? When we ask Elyon for help," Jack pointed out, "we don't always get an answer."

"Our prayers are always heard, though," Eliška replied. "We need to be still and trust."

"Believe me, I hear what you're saying." Jack glanced up at the sky while both helicopters hovered. "But I'm watching the Merikh getting closer."

The bushes rustled, causing Jack to retreat with the twisted vine rod as his only defense. His eyes narrowed as he stopped cold. Asiklua peered through the bushes with a lifeless onyx stare as Emma and Eliška stood by Jack's side. The leaves separated, and Asiklua limped forward with torn feathers partially spread across a spiny back. His low growl left them standing like statues, yet ready to fight.

"He doesn't look very friendly," Jack whispered. "He probably wants the stick."

Eliška nodded toward the rod. "You must not give it back."

"That's easy for you to say. You're not the one holding it."

"If he gets the rod, he will toast us like marshmallows," Emma warned.

"Let's try not to have any more black fire—we all know what that means."

Asiklua's jaw stretched open, revealing sharp fangs encased in crystallized lava. A long hiss seized the moment. Jack gripped the rod, and his knuckles turned ghostly white. He dug in his boots, centered his stance, and prepared to swing for the fences.

At least I'll get in one shot before it's over.

"Emma, now would be a good time for the light show," Jack whispered.

"Asiklua was expelled from Charis a thousand years ago." Emma stepped forward with an outstretched hand. No ball of pure energy. No eyes of stark white. Instead, she gazed upon the fallen angel with sorrow instead of contempt. "He cannot return to Charis until his sins are forgiven and he repents from leading a fallen legion of Cherub."

"Hold on." Jack pointed at the bamboo forest. "You're saying this creature wants to go with us, even though he tried to kill us in Nanimi."

"If Arishiyama is a gateway to the Valley of Grace, which leads to Charis, perhaps Asiklua wishes to return home." Eliška inched forward, then stopped when the fallen angel warned her with a rumbling growl. "It is what we all wish for in the end."

Jack wasn't sure whether the theory about Arishiyama was right, but he was relieved the tension between Emma and Eliška eased when they spoke of Asiklua, Charis, and Elyon. *Where is home?* Jack's stare locked in on Asiklua, even though his instincts were to escape into the jungle and disappear from both Cherub and Merikh. As Eliška's words resonated, he realized there was no home left for him to return to anyway.

Emma touched Asiklua's shoulder while Jack held his breath. *She's fearless and compassionate, all at the same time.* He stood awe-struck when the fallen angel slowly lowered onto his knees with his beady black eyes staring straight ahead.

"You once served the great Elyon," Emma said boldly. "You have been lost to the darkness for many centuries. We are searching for Charis in the Valley of Grace. You will be set free if you take us to Elyon's Vine."

Asiklua raised a bony finger and pointed a long, razor-sharp nail at Jack.

"Right, go with the lava-breathing demon straight into the forest to find Elyon's Vine." Jack walked toward the edge of the bamboo forest as if he were shuffling down death row. "Totally insane considering a few hours ago we were nearly left in ashes because of the demon angel."

"If he goes alone, we will not be able to protect him," Eliška warned. "Emma . . ."

For a long moment, Emma stared intently into Asiklua's soulless eyes, then let go of the angel's shoulder. "It is up to Eden's Star who will enter through Arishiyama's gateway."

Jack wondered how glorious the angel must've looked a thousand years earlier, before Elyon banned the fallen legion from Charis. *How could you have been so close to Elyon, yet still allowed sin to separate you?*

It was a deep question—one he knew he'd yet to answer. *I'm no better than anyone else, including a demon angel who wants to rip me apart.* Fear morphed into self-pity as Jack listened to Asiklua's labored breathing.

Above the bamboo forest, ropes dropped from both helicopters and the Merikh assassins slid down. Jack's gaze locked in on Chung in the front passenger seat. They were cornered. Asiklua pointed at the twisted vine rod and motioned for Jack to hold it out in front of him. Without thinking, Jack raised the rod, and an inferno swarmed within his chest—a sensation that had grown more powerful each time it occurred. Eden's Star glowed beneath his shirt. He watched in amazement as the glowing energy from the compass flowed visibly through his veins before wrapping around the twisted vine rod.

"What is going on?" Jack blurted.

"Time to go," Eliška ordered. "Now!"

All three scrambled in the same direction as they headed straight for the edge of the bamboo forest on the outskirts of Arishiyama. The twisted vine rod in Jack's grasp pointed ahead as the air rippled, creating a circular bubble at the naturally formed entrance. Jack hurried between the stone pillars into the bamboo forest, and Emma, Eliška, and Asiklua followed close behind.

Once they were through, Jack lowered the twisted vine rod, and the circular bubble sealed. Merikh assassins raced toward them firing rounds, while Chung unleashed bursts of fire. Instinctively, Jack ducked for cover, but the bullets and flames were repelled by a force field surrounding the bamboo forest.

Jack gripped the twisted vine rod tight as Chung approached without any sign of fear. Only a few inches away, almost nose to nose, Jack glared at the assassin who killed Rachel and Olivia Fargher. Seconds passed before he turned and followed Emma, Eliška, and Asiklua deeper into the forest.

47

WITH THE DUFFEL STRAPPED to his back, Jack's heart pounded as he stomped away from the Arishiyama gateway. Once again, he'd failed to get revenge against Michael Chung. He knew better than to pray for that day to come, but he wanted another chance at payback regardless of whether it was Elyon's will.

"He murdered Rachel." Jack swallowed hard. "And all I've done is run from him."

"You are honoring her sacrifice," Emma replied. "Remember, there is more at stake."

"I know—but it doesn't seem like I've done enough."

Thick bamboo trees swallowed them, leaving only a narrow trail. Eliška led the way as they headed deeper into the Valley of Grace and kept a close watch on Asiklua. *Never thought I'd walk through a forest with a demon angel who wants nothing more than to take the rod back and probably pull Eden's Star from beneath my skin along with my beating heart. That's dark, Jack.* He was beyond exhausted, but he wasn't going to complain. If Tim were here, though, he'd definitely have a few choice words.

"Do you think Chung and the others will cross through the gateway?" Jack asked.

"I do not have all the answers," Emma replied. "But we must be prepared if they do."

"Now we have Asiklua to keep an eye on." He paused for a moment and glanced around. "I thought the gateway would take us to Charis, but how are we supposed to find it in this maze? We don't even know how big the Valley of Grace is—it could be endless."

"Some gateways are transporters, and others guard what Elyon keeps hidden."

"Elyon's Vine, for example," Eliška suggested.

"Like I said," Jack added. "Bamboo in a stack of bamboo."

"Not all of us would have made it through with Eden's Star, but now we are here."

"In another realm, and we don't know where to go."

"That is why we have faith," Emma reassured.

"Why does faith have to be so hard? You'd think Elyon would make it a bit easier."

"If we knew our future, or if we just lived stuck in our past, there would be no reason to trust in Elyon."

Another hour passed before they reached three waterfalls cascading over natural rock, creating a white foamy whirlwind of rushing water plunging into a turquoise pool. Jack gazed upon the glow rising up from the depths of the pool, his mind flashing back to the Cave of Prophets. Asiklua knelt near the edge of the water, keeping his dark glare locked on them. Jack stared back at the fallen angel surrounded by orchids, hydrangeas, and overgrown vegetation.

"Indescribable beauty hidden within sacred grounds," Eliška exhaled.

"Charis has remained lost in time," Emma said, wonderstruck. "Untouched by history."

Eliška nodded toward Asiklua. "How do we talk to a fallen angel?"

"Very carefully." Jack smirked at his twisted sense of humor, which normally garnered chuckles and laughter from Will, Tim, and Vince. When neither Emma nor Eliška responded, he tightened his grip on the twisted vine rod. "You'd think it would be written in the Eternal."

Emma approached, but this time she didn't reach out her hand. "Elyon's promise remains."

Asiklua's spiny back twitched as his bony finger pointed toward the waterfalls. Jack walked along the edge of the pond, tempted to dive into the serene water. He stood beneath the waterfalls plunging from above, powerful and soothing. Curious, he stepped toward the rear of the waterfalls and noticed stone steps carved into the rocks. His instinct was to keep going, so he dropped the duffel bag on the ground.

"There's a way to the top," he called. "I'm going to check it out."

Jack stepped behind the thundering falls. Grasping the twisted vine rod, he climbed the stone steps until he reached the top. He looked down on the sparkling turquoise pool, then realized Emma's and Eliška's attention was focused on the overgrown vegetation. He nearly called out to them, then stood stunned when they darted toward the bushes. Seconds later, Chung and the Merikh assassins emerged from the forest with weapons raised, surrounding Asiklua, who towered over them.

How did they get through?

Jack crouched low and eyed the overgrown vegetation for any sign of Emma or Eliška. For a split second he was paralyzed, unsure of whether to keep going or turn back. *"The prophecy is yours to fulfill."* Spinning around at Areum's voice, he crawled away from the edge and sprinted toward a wooden shack with a reddish-brown tiled roof perched along the valley wall. Pumping his arms and legs, he pushed harder as he slid down the other side, boots splashing through oases of lush greenery and rice paddies strung across the valley.

Clear blue skies swarmed with gunmetal clouds as an ominous silence deafened his ears. When he blinked again, the world around him had turned from a magnificent color palette to black and white with shades of dull gray. Slowing his pace, he approached a charred, disfigured king cypress trunk with withered branches and dead vines. He was awestruck by the fiery swords sweeping around the dead tree and realized he was definitely standing on holy ground.

"Elyon's Vine—is real."

48

A POWERFUL WIND WHIPPED around Jack as he gripped the twisted vine rod. Thunder rumbled and cracked across the heavens seconds before lightning struck the dead king cypress, splitting the trunk in half. Royal blue and reddish-orange flames erupted from the circling sword blades. Flickers of gold floated in the air, whisking into a whirlwind around Jack and what remained of Elyon's Vine.

"Trees are a symbol of life," he whispered. "Stay rooted to the vine, Jack."

The golden whirlwind exploded against his chest, dropping him to his knees. Clawing at the dirt, he desperately tried to get closer to the flaming circle. A blazing inferno scorched the earth in front of him. Stabbing the twisted vine rod into the ground, he pulled himself to his feet. Each time the swords circled around him, a deafening whooshing sound created a rhythm. Stepping back, he counted the seconds between the swords swooping past.

One. Two. Three. Go on two—maybe three. Split the difference.

Eden's Star resurrected beneath his skin and blazed, on the verge of bursting through his chest. The compass was drawing him closer to Elyon's Vine, whether he was ready or not.

"One . . . two . . ." Jack lunged forward. "Three!"

For a split second, he closed his eyes as flames from one of the swords singed the back of his hoodie. Tripping over his own feet, he tumbled across the ground and barrel-rolled. Frantic, he ripped off his burning hoodie, checked to make sure he wasn't on fire, then tossed it aside. With the scars visible on his bare arms, he picked up the twisted vine rod and approached the split trunk jutting from the ground.

"Those swords tried to fry me like bacon. Elyon, what's next—fire walking?"

The fragrant aroma of jasmine filled his nostrils. Staring inside the center of the split trunk, he found something unexpected—life. Clustered white bell-shaped flowers grew on one side of a leafless stalk. Eden's Star cast a stark-white glow, illuminating the untouched flowers. Jack felt the twisted vine rod pulling harder toward the discovery. He kept a firm grip but allowed the rod to direct him until the point touched one of the flower petals. Pieces of the weathered vine broke free from the rod, revealing dark, smooth heartwood beneath.

Jack's brows raised as the rest of the twisted vine crumbled away. His fingertips touched the smooth heartwood of the rod as he eyed the white bell-shaped flowers. Thunder rumbled and lightning flashed, releasing a torrential downpour that washed over the charred and disfigured king cypress. Jack took a few steps back, and his eyes widened as the white flowers grew fuller. Withered branches and dead vines scattered on the ground began to rise as if drawn to the life exposed within the trunk.

Pure energy burst from Jack's chest, striking the trunk until all that was left was the white bell-shaped flowers and leafless stalk. *I'm gonna explode like a supernova.* The flowers grew at a miraculous speed while a fresh king cypress trunk emerged from the ground. Droplets of rain breathed life into dead vines and withered branches, casting a massive crown over vibrant crimson plants and lush emerald grass. Jack's jaw dropped as creation unveiled its power, Elyon's Vine reborn to a magnificent splendor.

Soaked to the bone, Jack spun around as gunfire echoed across the valley. While the flaming swords circled around Elyon's Vine, he caught sight of Chung moving swiftly toward him. Gripping the rod with both hands, he inhaled deep and tried to center himself as Emma's voice echoed in his mind. *"When you search inwardly for Elyon's power, the flow of your body will move through your hips, shoulders, and into every strike."* Closing his eyes, he shut off his mind and opened up his soul. His grip tightened around the dark heartwood as if the rod were his lifeline to Elyon.

While he couldn't explain it, Jack knew Eden's Star and the rod were connected. He moved toward the flaming swords, and they slowed enough for him to walk between. Out in the open, his instincts were in overdrive as he moved with purpose toward Chung. Without a second thought, the rod spun between his fingers faster and faster. Chung's palms glowed bright before launching fireballs, which exploded against the heartwood of the rod. Jack double-checked he was still in one piece, unharmed and even more determined.

"You found Soulweaver," Chung shouted with contempt. "But like your sister, you have failed to save anyone—including yourself. You will never be free from Addison until you have surrendered Eden's Star—and Soulweaver will be my bounty. Before this day is over, you will lose your life, and your friends will die."

Jack's fury surged as more gunfire erupted. With two quick breaths, he charged toward Chung, who unleashed an even greater inferno than he had in Sitio Veterans. A raging fire engulfed Jack, and for a few seconds his eyes caught sight of a glowing figure beside him—a being not of this world but from the throne of Elyon.

I will never leave you, Jack. I will stand with you until the end.

Emerging from the onslaught remarkably untouched, the rod spun at lightning speed between Jack's fingers as he launched himself with force and flow. His first strike cracked against Chung's ribs, sending the assassin sliding backward across the ground as if he were hit by a locomotive.

Chung's eyes turned a fiery orange as a stream of hot lava sprayed from his fingertips. Jack slid on his knees and leaned back as the assassin's rage narrowly missed its target. From his knees, he swung Soulweaver without mercy, striking Chung twice in the legs. The snapping of bones echoed in Jack's ears as bursts of fire pulsed from Chung's fingertips. The assassin crumpled to the ground, both legs twisted. Jack ducked and rolled, then landed on his knees. All around him the forest was ablaze from Chung's relentless attack. Miraculously, heavy rains poured from the heavens and doused the flames, leaving thick smoke wafting in the air.

On his back, Chung continued unleashing fireballs, but each time Jack swung Soulweaver and struck them away. The downpour intensified quickly, and the winds howled with greater force. Jack stood over his enemy—the reason for his pain and loss. Chung's fingers and palms were bloodied, and his legs were pretzeled. Jack glared at the man who'd murdered Rachel, Olivia Fargher, and countless other Cherub. Within his soul a battle raged—vengeance versus mercy. Jack tried to strike Chung, but the rod froze in his grasp. He tried again, but he wasn't strong enough to move the rod an inch against the murderer.

"You know what he has done," Jack said under his breath. "If he lives, more will die."

Soulweaver moved on its own, pointing one end closer to Chung. Loosening his grip slightly, Jack watched as the rod touched Chung's chest. A black flame rose from the assassin's body, controlled by the rod. Tears welled up in Jack's eyes as the assassin gasped for one more breath, and then his body froze. Jack's gaze shifted away from the lifeless stare of Michael Chung—a man who was once a believer in the Cherub, but whose hatred and thirst for greater power left him separated from Elyon's Vine in death.

Jack lowered Soulweaver to his side. His hands shook and his bones trembled as he stepped away. A deafening silence rang in his ears. He returned to the stone steps near the waterfalls, expecting the weight he'd carried since Rachel's murder to be lifted—but he was mistaken.

49

RAYS OF SUNLIGHT PIERCED through grayish clouds as the downpour eased to a gentle mist. Flaming swords circling Elyon's Vine lifted into the skies before disappearing toward the heavens. Peace washed over Charis. Mountains and forests brightened with life as Elyon's masterpiece returned to its glory. Emma and Eliška appeared at the top of the stone steps out of breath, carrying their backpacks and the duffel. They trudged alongside Jack through the rice paddies.

"The Merikh are gone," Eliška exhaled. "Emma kept us alive."

"I'm sorry I left you," he replied. "It all happened so fast."

"We took them deeper into the forest before they retreated." Emma glanced past him toward Elyon's Vine before eyeing Chung's lifeless body. "Are you okay?"

Jack held up the smooth heartwood rod. "He called it Soulweaver."

"Was that hidden inside of Elyon's Vine? How did you . . . ?"

"It's the same rod Asiklua carried that created black fire and the crazy death chain." Jack shook his head. "I can't really explain it, but when Elyon's Vine came back to life, the rod shed its twisted vines, and this is what was underneath."

Emma shared a stunned expression with Eliška, as if they were having a conversation Jack couldn't hear. She broke the awkward silence. "There is another name for what you are holding—the Rod of Elyon, carved from heartwood only found in Charis."

"A legend within the faction says it is the same weapon that defeated Ryder Slybourne." Eliška stared intently, awestruck by the discovery. "It revealed itself to you."

"All of it was dead." Jack pointed toward the magnificent king cypress, thick branches, full vines, plants, and lush emerald grass. "The Rod of Elyon—or Soulweaver—brought it back to life and defended me against Chung before it took the life from him."

"In the Eternal, the Rod of Elyon is not a weapon." Emma's brows furrowed. "The rod is a symbol of life, not death. The legend must be mistaken, and yet . . ."

A rumbling from the ground startled them. Spinning around, Jack was ready for demons to appear from the underworld. Instead, the grass and dirt shifted as Chung's flesh and bones were swallowed up by the earth. Emma brushed past and walked toward Elyon's Vine. Eliška followed. Jack wanted to leave, to escape the guilt of choosing vengeance over mercy in such a sacred place. He tried to shake it off and joined them at the foot of Elyon's Vine, knowing he also desired to stay.

"This is where the world began," Emma said reverently. "Charis in the Valley of Grace."

"Elyon breathed life into existence right here," Eliška agreed. "Stunning and humbling."

"If Nightingale's sketches show his memories," Jack noted, "he took the Testimony from Elyon's Vine before it was a dead tree. One day we'll return the Testimony to where it belongs."

"When this is over," Emma said somberly.

"Differences between the highest Cherub and the faction do not matter," Eliška added. "We must protect the Rod of Elyon from the Merikh, and we must find the other artifacts to restore peace."

"We can all agree on that," Emma assured. "The Eternal writes of Slybourne leading his army into battle to defend the light with Dragon Soul in the name of Elyon. He was victorious during the First Great War, yet he was conquered by a more powerful weapon in the Battle of Everest. Eliška, you are saying the faction believes the weapon is the Rod of Elyon?"

"We believe Soulweaver killed Slybourne and defeated the Cherub," Eliška responded, nodding. "After the Battle of Everest, the Cherub endured the Age of Trepidation without Slybourne or Dragon Soul to defend them during the Second Great War. Only by the power of Elyon was the war ended with the Mercy Covenant between the Seven Tribes of Cherub and the Merikh. If we do not defeat the Merikh, followers of Elyon will surrender the rest of their lives."

"Doesn't matter what name you use for the rod." Jack held up Soulweaver. "We were led here by Eden's Star to find this—to use it against the Merikh. I'm sure of it, Emma."

"Then we will have to ask Salomeh and Burwick what it means."

"I could stay here forever," Eliška said, "in the presence of Elyon."

"Me too." Jack exhaled. "This is a place I'd never want to leave."

Grunts and groans interrupted the moment. Asiklua limped

toward them, twitching and laboring with each step. Eyeing the rod, the beast's dark gaze glimmered slightly as mist glistened off his skeletal body. The demon hunched over and let out a low groan as if wanting to say something, but no words were spoken.

"If you believe in Elyon," Emma said calmly, "surrender again."

Asiklua knelt and bowed. Jack glanced at Emma and Eliška before remembering a promise was left to keep. *Emma knows the most about the Eternal and the Cherub, so she better know what she's doing.* A few seconds passed before he realized they were waiting on him.

He stepped forward with Soulweaver pointed toward Asiklua. Only moments earlier he'd witnessed the rod take life from evil. He gripped the rod tight, and an energy pulled him closer. Another step, and he was right in front of Asiklua. The rod slowly lowered until it rested on a bony shoulder. Energy flowed through Soulweaver into Jack's fingertips, as if he'd poked his finger into an electrical current.

"No one is too far from forgiveness," Emma prayed. "Elyon, please restore Asiklua."

The point of Soulweaver touched Asiklua's shoulder. Thick, hardened skin broke open and floated to the ground. More cracks appeared as if layered armor pieces were peeling away. Beneath Asiklua's scaly features, milky skin revealed itself. Jack's gaze shifted over Asiklua's shoulders as the bony and broken wings transformed like the clustered white bell-shaped flowers—reborn into a stunning and muscular feathered wingspan.

As the last of the thick, scaly skin dropped to the ground, Asiklua stood ten feet tall with toned muscles. He stretched his mighty wings, layered in velvety, bone-white feathers. Jack's mind flashed to Sahil, except it was clear that Asiklua was not an eagle but an angel. Eyes as blue as a vast ocean stared back at them while Jack lowered Soulweaver to his side.

Asiklua bowed again, then burst into the air with a sonic boom as one of the flaming swords returned from the heavens. *I swear I hear a thousand voices singing right now.* Catching the sword in midair, the angel landed with a resounding rumble in front of Elyon's Vine and speared the flaming sword into the earth.

Beneath Asiklua's feet, flames from the sword scorched the earth and burned emblems into the perfect blades of grass. Eden's Star reawakened within Jack as he stared intently at each one. A lion, a temple, a tree, a deer, a serpent, a wolf, and a ship. Even without the colors, he recognized them from the House of Luminescence. One glance at Emma and Eliška reassured him that he was staring at the Seven Tribes of Cherub.

"You are Asiklua," Emma said. "The great angel who stood beside Elyon."

"I am." Asiklua glided toward them as a restored being. "Now I am freed from the chains that bound me for a thousand years, forgiven by the grace and mercy of Elyon."

"Forgiveness is offered to all who believe," Eliška said. "We simply need to accept it."

"For centuries I was consumed with darkness—fallen to sin. I am the one who commanded Elyon's legion, and I am the one who caused separation from our Creator."

"Now that you're forgiven . . ." Jack gripped Soulweaver a bit tighter. "What now?"

"I will remain in Charis for eternity." Asiklua wielded the flaming sword majestically. "To guard Elyon's creation against those who wish to bring death and destruction."

Eliška pointed at the ground. "What is the significance of the Seven Tribes of Cherub?"

"One artifact was formed for each tribe, blessed by Elyon, to be kept in the realms of Charis and protected within the Testimony." Asiklua's gaze hardened. "The Seven Tribes argued over which artifact was the most powerful while the legion of angels who fought in the name of Elyon thirsted for greater power."

"That's a bad combination," Jack said under his breath.

"Sin altered this world when the tribes demanded the artifacts for themselves, and I commanded the legion to rebel against Elyon. Eden's Star was formed by Elyon's hands in the purity of Charis to hide the artifacts given to the Seven Tribes of Cherub from this world and the other realms. Only a Protector was entrusted with Eden's Star. I sense one among us now."

"Either the artifacts were stolen from the Testimony," Eliška pointed out, "or the artifacts were hidden by Elyon somewhere in our world or the other realms."

"Charis remained unguarded for ages." Asiklua's eyes shone bright. "Never again."

"Asiklua, we will find the artifacts and return them to the Testimony," Emma promised.

"Then your journey will continue beyond the Valley of Grace. In the fiery battles of this world, Elyon promises strength with a righteous hand and courage poured out upon your bravery. Until you stand in glory."

With his mind blown, Jack recognized the words of the warrior's prayer as he watched Asiklua bow, then step away before wandering across the peaceful serenity and beauty of Charis toward Elyon's Vine.

We know how many artifacts there are now—seven. We've found Soulweaver, and if the Merikh have found one, then that leaves five. And what if they've found more than one?

Jack stood perfectly still as a warmth spread across his chest, certain Eden's Star was on the verge of transporting them somewhere else. With his eyes closed, he breathed in deep as the warmth grew hotter and tingled through his arms, legs, shoulders, and spine.

I am the healer of sickness and pain. In my name all who believe are restored. You are the Protector of Eden's Star, a guardian against the darkness of man in this world and the demons in other realms. I have touched your pain this day, but your full healing will only come when freedom reigns.

Jack remembered saying those same words in Thar Desert. *Healing comes when freedom reigns.* For a moment, he allowed Elyon's voice to resonate in his spirit, realizing in the desert Elyon spoke through him. He wasn't sure how to explain to Emma or Eliška that he was healed, at least more than seconds before, but he was still dying with Eden's Star inside of him.

"No one will believe this if we tell them," Jack whispered. "I don't even believe it."

Emma wiped a tear from her cheek. "Asiklua is redeemed."

"We have a long journey back to Ine Town." Eliška handed Jack the duffel bag. "Or we could trust Eden's Star to take us further into the Highlands."

"The Merikh will be waiting if we return the same way," Emma pointed out.

"There *are* only three of us," Jack replied. "I guess we'll never know unless we try."

As he slipped the duffel over his shoulder, Emma stepped toward him and reached out her hand. His fingers interlaced with hers as seamlessly as the first time. Eliška grabbed hold of his hand and Emma's, forming a tight circle. Before settling his spirit, Jack glanced toward Asiklua as the corners of his mouth rose slightly in a smile. Then Eden's Star awakened within his soul, and in a flash they disappeared.

50

Beneath a mountain peak, a rolling mist cleared enough to reveal Jack, Emma, and Eliška standing on a sheer cliff. Strong winds whipped and whirled, creating a bitter chill in the air. Seconds earlier, they had witnessed the restoration of Charis and Asiklua to Elyon's magnificent beauty—and Jack had experienced a touch from Elyon. Then Eden's Star brought them here, to a sierra of jagged white-capped mountains.

Jack's mind flashed to the vision where buildings had burned across Hong Kong and Eden's Star was ripped from his bloodied hands. He vividly pictured the next flashes of rolling hills dissolving into white-capped mountains, and the reverent moments with Asiklua and Elyon disappeared.

"I've seen this in one of my visions," Jack said loud enough for them to hear, yet partially drowned out by the heavy gusts of wind. "I tried to keep Beacon Hill in the center of my mind, but Eden's Star brought us here instead. I'm sorry."

"If we stay, we will freeze to death," Eliška exclaimed. "We need to find another way."

"We do not know where we are," Emma pointed out. "Or if we are still in the Highlands."

Eliška peered over the edge of the cliff. "Only one way down."

"Before we turn ourselves into markhor goats and risk falling to our death, let's give Eden's Star another shot." Jack kept his grip on Soulweaver. "Maybe it'll be different and we'll end up somewhere warmer."

"Or we might end up somewhere worse," Eliška retorted.

Jack closed his eyes and attempted to surrender his spirit while he fought frostbite. *Elyon, we need to return to Beacon Hill. Make the compass work. I don't know what I'm doing. I need you now to help us, please.* He waited a few seconds for a warming sensation to spread across his chest. But Eden's Star remained dormant, right when he needed the compass most. He opened his eyes and gazed apologetically at Emma and Eliška, knowing he'd failed them again.

I wanted Chung to pay the price for murdering Rachel, and now it's done. Elyon, I feel no remorse. If that's why I'm struggling to fully surrender to Eden's Star, then we'll never return home. I've carried the weight of Rachel's death and being the Protector of Eden's Star, but the weight is only getting heavier. I don't know how much more I can take. I'm not an angel like Asiklua.

Vile squeals resounded across the sierra, sending Jack, Emma, and Eliška diving against the rock ledge. In the far distance, a legion of dark silhouettes streaked across the skies. Flat on his stomach, Jack stared in disbelief. He crawled across the stone until he was in between Emma and Eliška.

"What in the name of Elyon are those?" Jack blurted.

Eliška glanced toward him, wide-eyed. "Demons."

"Do not move," Emma instructed. "There are too many to escape."

Jack's heart pounded through his chest as his fingers gripped the rock and his right hand grasped Soulweaver. He still had his duffel, but he'd nearly forgotten about it. The silhouettes whipped toward them, then hovered in the sky within arm's reach. The skeletal features of the demons emerged more distinctly, paralyzing Jack. Their lifeless onyx stares sent shivers down his spine, in the same way that Asiklua's had done. A low growl followed as one of the silhouettes attacked. Jack braced himself to be ravaged, but as the seconds ticked by, he realized he was still breathing.

He noticed a rippling in the air. "Another force field?"

"We must be at the edge of the Highlands," Emma guessed. "So they cannot cross."

"Do you see the resemblance?" Jack asked urgently. "I mean, they look like—"

"Asiklua," Eliška finished. "Fallen angels who betrayed Elyon."

"And were banned from Charis," Emma agreed. "They are not demons."

"Well, I don't think these ones are looking for forgiveness." The silhouettes continued to glare with a deathly stare. "How many fallen angels are there?"

"The Eternal does not reveal a number," Eliška replied. "Could be a legion, or more."

"We should've asked Asiklua." Jack shivered from the bitter cold. "How many are in a legion?"

"Thousands," Emma answered. "But the force field means we are safe for the moment."

"Do you think Nightingale made it this far?" Jack asked, not breathing any easier.

Emma eyed the silhouettes closely. "I do not believe anyone has made it this far."

"We won't win a staring contest, so what do we do?"

Eliška slowly stood and inched toward the edge of the cliff. The silhouettes shifted formation as if mimicking her movements. She glanced over the edge again, then turned toward Jack and Emma. "We have to go down. Better we do it now before nightfall."

Jack crawled onto his knees as the silhouettes hovered. Eliška pulled the duffel off his shoulder and dropped the bag onto the rock. She unzipped it and dug inside, retrieving a climbing rope, three harnesses, belay devices that served as mechanical friction brakes, and carabiners to clip onto the ropes.

"No wonder it was so heavy," Jack said. "That's been in there the whole time?"

"Professor Burwick thought we might need the gear to reach Charis."

"Little does she know, we're using it to escape Elyon's banned angel army."

Eliška slipped into the first harness. "We better be going."

"Have you climbed a sheer cliff before?" Emma asked.

"You are not the only one trained to serve Elyon."

Jack stood with Soulweaver in his grasp. Eliška helped him step awkwardly into a harness, while Emma handled hers with ease. *Looks like I'm the only one who's never traversed a mountain. But I did do a zip line thanks to Areum. Probably the same thing, right?* He eyed the fallen angels and noticed they gravitated near him. He shifted his weight and stepped closer to the edge. Again, the silhouettes shifted in unison until they were right in front of him. Jack pointed Soulweaver in their direction and stabbed at the force field. Ripples appeared in the barrier, and the silhouettes shrieked and growled, growing even more agitated than when they first appeared.

"Looks like they know what this is." Jack gripped Soulweaver tight. "The Rod of Elyon probably brings back some bad memories for the fallen angels."

Emma grabbed Jack's shoulder. "Do not taunt the darkness."

As swiftly as the silhouettes had crossed the rugged terrain, they streaked away, high above the desolate and barren land. Jack turned toward Emma and Eliška with a twinge of righteous satisfaction.

"Who goes first?"

"I will," Eliška replied. "You will be next, and Emma last."

Eliška secured one end of the rope around a sharp rock, then tossed the rest over the edge. She tugged on the rope several times and clipped her harness to it. Jack watched in amazement as she stepped over to the edge, turned her back to the ground, and leaned back so her body hung over the ledge. With one step, she disappeared over the sheer cliff. Jack stepped to the edge alongside Emma and cautiously peered down. A queasiness rattled his stomach as he watched Eliška rappel down the granite wall as if she were flying.

"She's definitely done this before," Jack said. "Have you?"

"We were trained on Karābu in the basics," Emma replied. "Never this high."

"Any advice to make sure I won't die?"

"Do not look down," Emma replied. "Much easier if you keep your eyes on the rock."

"I guess we'll just leave the duffel here." Emma nodded as Jack kept a firm grip on Soulweaver, begging the rod to strip him of his fear of heights. They'd nearly died to find the artifact, so there was no chance he was going to let it out of his sight. He tucked Soulweaver through a loop in his jeans and made sure it was tight. "Here goes nothing."

51

JACK STRUGGLED TO CONTROL the rope line with the belay device. He squeezed the mechanical friction brake and tried to slow his descent. Halfway down the granite surface, he stopped to catch his breath. A sharp pain tore through his chest, and a burning ignited every fiber of his body. He hadn't experienced anything as intense since using Eden's Star to leave Karābu and arrive in Karachi. With one hand he gripped the rope, and with the other he clenched his chest, hoping Soulweaver would not fall.

"Jack, keep going," Eliška shouted from below. "You are doing good."

"Something isn't right." Jack gritted his teeth and fought through the pain. "Elyon . . ."

His heartbeat became erratic as he broke out into a cold sweat and tried not to panic. The pressure in his chest intensified, leaving him light-headed. From above, the rope tightened, and he glanced up to make sure it was still secure. Emma had clipped onto the rope and pushed off the granite. She dropped through the air, landing a few feet overhead.

"Jack, what is wrong?"

"I can't . . . breathe right." Jack doubled over, still keeping his grip on the rope while checking to be sure he hadn't dropped Soulweaver. "I don't know if it's Eden's Star or what."

Emma unhooked her carabiner from the rope, then gripped a crevice in the granite. She free soloed down the sheer rock one careful move after another until she was right beside Jack, then placed her fingers against his neck. His vision narrowed and stars flickered before his eyes. He felt himself on the edge of consciousness.

"Your heartbeat is skipping," Emma said calmly. "We need to get you down."

"I'm afraid to let go," Jack replied, barely coherent. "Leave me . . ."

"Hang on," she said. "We will go together."

Emma clipped back onto the rope. She pried Jack's fingers loose from the belay device, then grabbed tight around his waist from behind. She pushed off the cliffside and pulled Jack along with her. Weightlessness struck the pit of his stomach as they dropped thirty feet before slamming into the granite with a hard thud. Emma struggled to handle his weight, but she managed to push off again, and the same sensation twisted in his gut. He couldn't help, and he couldn't stop her from forcing him down. Near the bottom, he felt Eliška grab his ankles and Soulweaver slide free before dropping to the ground. His legs crumpled as he collapsed—a softer fall thanks to Emma and Eliška.

With eyes closed, he lay on his back unable to explain why it hadn't happened earlier to him in the Highlands. An answer didn't matter—he knew there wasn't much time left. Emma unclipped them both from the rope and leaned over him.

"Jack, can you hear me?" Emma paused. "Eliška, help me."

They both grabbed under his arms and pulled him up into a sitting position. He lowered his head between his legs and struggled for each breath. *Elyon, I'm not ready to die. Spare me so I can finish what's been started.* He opened his eyes and stared at Emma and Eliška. With a fiery gaze, Emma placed her hand on his chest as her fingers glowed stark white. Eliška squeezed his shoulder, and her tears welled up as he breathed his last breath.

A flash of darkness left Jack surrounded by flames bursting from the rubble and destruction of an abandoned city. He glanced at his scarred arms and bloodied knuckles. Then his gaze locked in on Soulweaver, which was shattered on the ground, its heartwood split into pieces. When he looked up again, a shadow holding Dragon Soul stood before him. Fear rippled through his body as he realized the shadow also held a bloodied Eden's Star in its grasp. He ripped his shirt apart and stared at his bare chest. A deep open wound flowed with crimson, and shattered bone poked through his skin. He was defenseless, knowing he was no longer the Protector. The battle between darkness and light was over—and darkness had won.

A surge of energy shot through his body, as if he'd been shocked by a defibrillator. He gasped and rolled onto his side. Emma and Eliška jumped back, then returned to his side, certain he'd been snatched from death's door.

"Which one of you is a healer?" Emma and Eliška exchanged curious stares. "Maybe it was both of you. Either way, one of you—or both—saved my life."

"Do you know what happened?" Eliška asked.

Jack nodded slowly, then admitted what he had known. "Eden's Star is killing me."

"Get him on his feet," Emma replied. "We need to find a gateway."

"Yes, we have to try," Eliška agreed. "Come on, Jack."

Emma and Eliška pulled him to his feet, supporting him between them. They trudged through a thick forest of dead trees. As they kept their distance from the invisible barrier between the Highlands and the land beyond, Jack's heartbeat slowly returned to a normal rhythm. *Don't get too comfortable. Eden's Star could strike at any minute.* After a while, he was able to walk on his own. He'd been brought back to life, but death lingered on the edge of every breath.

The three reached a clearing in the forest and stopped abruptly. Before their eyes was a burial ground covered with thousands of roughly chiseled headstones. Jack stepped forward and knelt in front of one, sensing he was being drawn there by Eden's Star. His fingers touched the aged engravings. While he couldn't understand the words etched into the stone, he recognized two of the characters.

勇氣. *Courage.*

Was it the fallen legion who did this?

Emma leaned over his shoulder. "Clearly, Cherub were once in this land."

"Could this be from the Second Great War?" Eliška asked.

"The Eternal does not speak of a battle in the Highlands."

"Nothing good will happen if we stay here." Jack stood, attempting to shake off the earlier vision of the shadow who stood victorious. He glanced around at the lifeless forest, which seemed to have given up ages ago. "We gotta give Eden's Star another shot."

Surrounded by the graves of those who had gone before, Emma handed Soulweaver back to him and grabbed his free hand. Eliška reached for his arm and squeezed reassuringly. With all three connected, Jack closed his eyes and attempted to settle his spirit amid the weight of where they stood. Seconds passed, but his mind refused to stop running through scenarios that left them dead.

"Surrender to where the compass will guide us," Emma said. "Not where you want to go."

Her words were true, and they helped him settle.

In a blink, the burial ground turned deathly silent once again.

52

ZURICH, SWITZERLAND

SETTLED OVER TWO THOUSAND YEARS AGO by the Romans, Zurich was now a known safe haven for the wealthiest in society. Millions traveled each year to one of the world's busiest financial centers, which also boasted the largest airport and railway system in Switzerland. Along the Limmat River, between the Münsterbrücke and Quaibrücke bridges, armored trucks rolled through the gates of one of the most secure banks on the planet—Kreidler.

In a private vault large enough to store a shipment of treasures brought from the Exodus Mines, Will stood beside Addison while the president of the bank double-checked a long inventory list. Once the president signed on a tablet, he excused himself and left Addison and Will alone in the vault, surrounded by more wealth than any other client of Kreidler.

"There has been no word from Michael," Addison said. "But that is to be expected."

"I should have been allowed to go with him," Will replied, stone-cold. "It is my right."

"You have made your wishes perfectly clear." Addison's eyes narrowed. "You are too valuable to risk—until you are ready."

"I am ready now," Will argued. "Jack won't know what hit him."

"It is not Jack I am concerned about." Addison gazed upon the riches and smiled. "I will make you an offer—one I have not extended to anyone else."

"All I want is to inflict the same pain Jack has caused me—and to protect my father."

"What I am offering will be your reward when the day arrives." Addison waved at the rows of stacked gold coins, necklaces, crowns, sapphires, and rubies. "When you have spilled his blood, Eden's Star will become mine, and all you see within this chamber will be yours."

"What about my father? What will you do with him?"

"He continues to protect the Cherub—and Jack. If he loved you, he would be searching for you. Instead, he has abandoned you."

"You do not know my father like I do," Will bantered. "He is afraid of you—that is all."

"Fear is the greatest test of one's courage. Your father lacks the resolve to conquer his own fears. What makes you think he loves you more than the Cherub? He has chosen to protect Jack while sacrificing everyone else since you have been gone." Addison exhaled long and hard. "The world will soon see that I am not the enemy. I am a savior to all who have been disillusioned by the Cherub."

Will's gaze hardened as he eyed the vast treasure. "All of this will be mine?"

"Every last ounce."

53

HONG KONG

A HORN BLARED AS HEADLIGHTS from a canary yellow double-decker barreled down the street. Wide-eyed, Jack was yanked off to the side as the bus swerved into another lane, nearly sideswiping a taxi. The bus driver leaned out the window and shouted angrily in Cantonese. Only then did Jack realize Emma was the one who'd grabbed his arm and pulled him to safety. Eliška was right beside them, and they dodged oncoming traffic until they reached the sidewalk.

"That was too close," Jack gasped, catching his breath.

"We are all in one piece." Eliška double-checked herself. "You are getting the hang of it."

"Feels like it's controlling me instead of the other way around."

"Eden's Star *is* a compass." Emma eyed him closely. "Do you know where we are?"

"We're on Castle Peak Road." *Back where the nightmares began.*

"Were you thinking about this district?"

"I'm not sure, exactly." He shook his head, knowing this was the worst place for him to be. *But I'd love an order of lo bak go and a Vitasoy right about now.* "At the last second it crossed my mind, but I tried to surrender to Eden's Star."

"So it did work," Eliška said, surprised. "Way to go, Jack."

A few more seconds passed before Jack's grip tightened on Soulweaver. He tried to decide which direction to go, searching for the quickest way out of Sham Shui Po. Sirens blared as HKPF vehicles flew down Castle Peak with two black SUVs tailing them. In the middle of the street, the vehicles screeched to a halt and HKPF climbed out with weapons raised. Moving in tactical formation, they approached a group of teens lounging near the entrance to the Golden Shopping Centre.

Half a dozen men and several women exited the SUVs. They wore dark clothes and gave no sign of being part of the HKPF. *Definitely Merikh.* They made their way through the bystanders, who watched curiously from the sidewalk, and demanded the teens provide IDs for inspection. Less than ten feet away, Jack stepped back and faded into the crowd alongside Emma and Eliška.

"Are they searching for us?" Jack whispered. "How could they know we'd be here?"

"The sooner we are away from this district the better," Emma answered.

Eliška nodded ahead. "We cannot go much farther."

His chest tightened with an unsettling sense that the city he loved refused to welcome his return. With the crowd growing more on edge, he nudged his way in the direction of the HKPF officers guarding a barricade. He remembered the last time he'd been in Sham Shui Po as he crossed the street while Emma and Eliška shadowed behind. *Don't look back, Jack.* He couldn't help himself. A brief glance over his shoulder caught the attention of those from the SUVs.

"Follow me," Jack said in a hushed voice.

Without missing a step, Emma and Eliška changed direction and all three ducked into a hole-in-the-wall dim sum house—the same place he'd been with Will when he'd returned for the first time since he was young. He walked quickly through the restaurant, passing elderly men huddled around a mah-jongg game. A twinge of temptation raised the hair on his arms, but he kept moving until he exited out a rear door. Stepping into a dingy alley piled with trash, he inhaled a pungent aroma as his stomach twisted into knots.

"Where are we going?" Eliška asked.

Jack pointed to the end of the alley. "I've got an idea."

He walked briskly toward the back alley of the Golden Shopping Centre, Emma and Eliška on his heels until they reached a main street. *Emma could use her power to stop them, no doubt. But what happens if she does? Addison will know we are back, and everyone hiding at Beacon Hill will be at risk—again.* His pace quickened as they headed deeper into the heart of the northwestern district of Kowloon Peninsula.

"We can't go back to Beacon Hill . . ." Jack's voice trailed off as they entered an outdoor market on Ki Lung Street. "Not until we're sure we aren't being followed."

"Right now, we need to find a place to hide." Emma stepped alongside. "Unless—"

"If you face off with them, then we'll put everyone else in danger."

In the distance, more sirens blared. Migrants, working class, and seniors bargained at vendor stalls, ignoring the commotion a few blocks away. Lost among the locals, Jack was the first to reach the opposite end of the market where the neighborhood was more run-down. Thirty-story buildings were crammed side by side in the densest and poorest neighborhood in the city. He slowed his stride as they approached one of the weathered buildings filled with subdivided flats. He stared upward at the barred windows of one of the apartments—his childhood prison.

"What is wrong, Jack?" Emma asked.

"I swore I'd never return to this place—and now I've been back twice." Sweat seeped down the back of his neck as nightmares battled in his mind. He wanted to take another step, but the pounding in his chest left him paralyzed. He peered through the glass doors at the sparse lobby with flickering fluorescents as his fingers clenched into fists. "It's where this all started."

"What do you mean?"

"After Addison nearly killed my mom, this is where he hid Rachel and me."

"I am sorry, Jack." Emma grabbed his hand. "But we should leave."

He swallowed a lump in his throat. "Right."

Without questioning, Eliška hailed a red-and-silver taxi before climbing into the front passenger seat. Jack and Emma slid into the back seat, and the driver pulled away from the curb, speeding down the street as Jack's nightmares faded. He didn't ask Eliška or Emma where they were going. Instead, he gazed out the window as the taxi traveled over the Boundary Street Flyover onto

Waterloo Road. At each government checkpoint, they kept their gaze straight ahead and attempted to avoid any unwanted attention. Reaching Cross-Harbour Tunnel, the taxi continued beneath Victoria Harbour before emerging on Hong Kong Island.

As early evening faded into night, Jack eyed The Peninsula across the harbor in Tsim Sha Tsui. The five-star hotel was being rebuilt—he could see bamboo scaffolding wrapped in green netting. The *Eastern Dragon* was gone from the harbor, leaving no sign of what had occurred months before. The driver exited and turned onto Hoi Yu Street, then took a sharp right onto Hoi Chak Street. He pulled over to the curb and waited for one of them to pay. Emma reached into her pocket and removed a handful of cash. Jack climbed out and waited next to Eliška until Emma joined them and the taxi drove away.

"I've never been to this district," Jack said. "Where are we?"

"Quarry Bay," Emma replied matter-of-factly. "We should not—"

"Follow me," Eliška interrupted. "It is time you were welcomed by the faction."

54

Eighteen-story buildings rose up with multicolored floors stacked one on top of the other as lights illuminated thousands of units. Hong Kongers living in the housing estate were split into five dense blocks surrounding one large square courtyard. Jack stared upward at the darkened skies framed between the buildings. Bright-red lanterns lined the courtyard as the concrete reflected a bluish glow from the flats above.

Professor Burwick appeared from one of the buildings. The burn scars on her face were noticeable, but her arms were covered in long sleeves and her head was wrapped with a scarf. She limped toward them with a half smile. Her gaze softened as she embraced each one. Jack noticed a dozen men and women scattered around the courtyard perimeter with eyes fixed on them.

"We have prayed daily for Elyon's protection over you," Burwick said. "Of course, we remained hopeful your journey would bring you back safe. You have been gone for weeks."

"First six hours, then three days, and now weeks." Jack scratched his head as he took in their surroundings, including the many faces that appeared in the windows of the flats above. "Each time I've used Eden's Star, it feels like a blink—but time passes."

"Much like the Elders, it seems Eden's Star is not confined by the limits of time." Burwick's brows furrowed as she eyed the rod in Jack's hand. "Let's get you settled."

Jack, Emma, and Eliška followed Burwick into the apartment building and were greeted by four armed men guarding the elevator. He recognized several from the boathouse near Ine Town. *Seems like Burwick and the faction are more prepared than the Cherub to fight this war.* The elevator rattled and hummed as they rode in silence to the eighteenth floor.

Burwick limped down a hallway and unlocked a metal door leading to a stairwell that accessed the rooftop. Jack remembered the night he'd gone to Wan Chai to find Areum, and the ease with which she crossed the planks between buildings. On the rooftop, potted plants were lined up against a barbed wire fence that encircled the roof. Beneath a large metal awning covering half of the rooftop were rows of cots, a small outdoor kitchen, and an enclosure that Jack guessed was a bathroom.

"The Merikh and Cherub do not know our whereabouts," Burwick said. "You are safe."

"Where are Tim, Vince, and Amina?" Jack asked. "Did you leave them at the boathouse?"

"I brought them back to Beacon Hill. It is where they belong."

Jack was shocked, but he kept calm. "Do Vince's parents know he's alive?"

"He chose to remain hidden in Nightingale's vault to protect them. He is concerned the Merikh will torture his parents to find out your whereabouts if they know he is alive. Better to be left in the darkness of sorrow than to suffer for the light. I must confess, Joseph and Imani Tobias's wealth would be welcomed by the faction in this fight." Burwick shook her head slowly. "You caused quite a stir on your return to Sham Shui Po."

Jack's brows raised. "How do you know that's where Eden's Star brought us?"

"Since the riots, Merikh have infiltrated most of the districts and corrupted divisions of the HKPF. However, we have our ways of gathering information—which includes hundreds of sightings of you since you disappeared from Beacon Hill. A bounty remains on your head from both Merikh and Cherub."

"The Merikh and HKPF were literally minutes behind us," Jack pointed out. "I nearly got run over by a double-decker too. How could they know if we didn't even know?"

"Our source within HKPF notified us there had been a sighting. Your father has control of the streets in Sham Shui Po, so they must have been patrolling nearby." Burwick glanced between Emma and Eliška. "Are you two getting along better?"

"Splendidly," Emma replied pointedly.

"If we have been gone for weeks," Eliška said, "are things worse than before?"

"Merikh continue capturing Cherub and confining them in reeducation camps." Burwick hesitated. "Headmaster Fargher remains convinced Will is being held in one of the locations.

Addison knows how close the two of you are, Jack, so he won't hesitate to leverage your friendship."

Emma and Eliška set their backpacks on a cot and listened.

"Do you have any idea where they are holding him?" Jack asked.

"We do not know for certain," Burwick admitted. "However, we are searching."

"How many others have been taken?" Emma asked.

"Thousands," Burwick answered flatly. "There has been no news about your parents."

"We cannot leave followers of Elyon as prisoners to the Merikh," Eliška chimed in. "How can we free them?"

"Cherub continue to arrive through the House of Luminescence and have found refuge at Beacon Hill. Salomeh and I have discussed ways to free the innocent without the knowledge of the highest Cherub."

Jack kept his grip on Soulweaver, tempted to test the limits of its power. "Count me in."

"Have the Cherub anointed a new leader?" Emma asked.

"Bau Hu remains the front-runner. Salomeh and I have communicated our support; however, there is division among the highest Cherub since Bau is the one who lost Dragon Soul." Burwick's gaze shifted between them. "Now, tell me what you found."

"We reached Elyon's Vine in Charis," Eliška replied. "Merikh assassins hunted us."

"Michael Chung was one of them." Jack's fingers wrapped tighter around Soulweaver. "He's buried in the soil of Charis—which is far better than where he murdered Rachel."

"Michael's gifts were extremely powerful," Burwick said, curious. "How did you—?"

Jack held the rod out in front of him. "The Rod of Elyon—aka Soulweaver."

"The rod was corrupted by Asiklua before being restored by Elyon's Vine," Emma explained. "Darkness was wrapped around the rod. Now the light has returned. In Charis, it was the weapon that struck down Michael Chung."

"You speak of the commanding angel," Burwick noted, "who betrayed Elyon."

"He's been restored too," Jack clarified. "And now he's guarding Elyon's Vine *and* Charis."

"We believe the Rod of Elyon is one of the artifacts." Eliška glanced briefly between Jack and Emma. "There were seven artifacts formed by Elyon representing each tribe of Cherub."

"Of course." Burwick nodded.

"I'm pretty sure the Merikh have found one of the artifacts too," Jack added. "Maybe more."

"Must all of the artifacts be found to defeat the Merikh?" Emma asked.

"I am not certain," Burwick admitted. "One will know when they are found, I suppose."

Burwick motioned for them to follow her to an oval folding table and chairs. Jack left Soulweaver on one of the cots, then joined the others. He inhaled the aroma of charbroiled burgers and salty fries. Slipping onto one of the chairs, he watched as Eliška passed out wrapped burgers, then piled the fries high onto paper plates. Jack dug into the beef and grabbed a handful of fries, realizing how long it had been since he'd eaten.

For a moment, Burwick eyed each of them. "Which one of you killed Michael?"

"Um . . ." Jack's cheeks flushed as he swallowed hard. "It was me."

"Before Ryder Slybourne was defeated, he wielded Dragon Soul against great armies of Merikh and ushered in a century of peace. After a hundred years, darkness returned and threatened to destroy the Silk Road. Once again, Slybourne was called upon by Elyon to leave Sakkhela and command the Seven Tribes of Cherub in the Battle of Everest. He remained a valiant warrior who battled the fallen legion led by Asiklua under the command of the Nephilim king—but he died by a weapon greater than the legend of Dragon Soul."

"Is that written in the Eternal?" Jack asked.

Burwick shook her head. "Not all Cherub history is written within the pages."

"Nephilim, Merikh, and Asiklua must have corrupted the Rod of Elyon with Cherub blood," Emma suggested. "An artifact created to protect the Cherub became a weapon against Slybourne and Dragon Soul on Everest."

"Which is why in the hands of a Cherub the rod is known as the Rod of Elyon, yet in the hands of darkness it is known as Soulweaver." Burwick leaned back in her chair with arms crossed. "The Rod of Elyon protects life, but Soulweaver takes the darkest souls in death." Her gaze locked in on Jack. "Strange that you referred to the rod as Soulweaver so easily."

55

JACK RETRIEVED THE LEATHER-BOUND ORIGINAL of the Eternal from one of the backpacks. Since Burwick gave it to him, there hadn't been two minutes when he wasn't running or fighting for his life. He'd forgotten it was in the backpack until Burwick requested it. He slid back onto his seat at the oval table and handed her the book.

"During the Roman Empire, those who professed to believe in Elyon were living during a century of peace. However, when a new ruler became emperor, those who professed to believe in Elyon were tortured for their faith." Burwick flipped through the Eternal as if she'd memorized every chapter. "The ancient writings tell us that millions were killed under the command of Emperor Nero." She stopped turning the pages. "A prophet of Roman descent known as Kaeso preached throughout Rome. He spoke out against government corruption and the emperor."

Burwick glanced briefly at Emma and Eliška before she read aloud from the Eternal.

"'Kaeso, the prophet, professed the message of Elyon to all with ears to hear and hearts to receive. He traveled across the great empire of Rome sharing the good news with Romans and those enslaved by the emperor. He prayed to the heavens, asking Elyon to grant him strength and courage against the darkness. Kaeso was guided to a gateway that led to the land of Charis, where he received a wondrous gift—a rod crafted from a single branch of Elyon's Vine. When he returned to Rome, greater numbers accepted the message and were eager to follow him into the presence of Elyon, while those enslaved cried out for mercy.'"

Burwick handed the Eternal over so Jack could pick up where she left off.

"'With the rod in his grasp, Kaeso created water out of stone and stabbed the soil in fields, causing the crops to grow faster and larger. Many Romans followed his teachings, and his miracles reached the ears of Nero, who was threatened by the prophet's miraculous powers. The emperor wanted the rod for himself, so he sent his centurions to find Kaeso and kill him. Kaeso used the rod formed from Elyon's Vine to set the captives free from the brutal empire. Reaching the Tyrrhenian Sea, Kaeso raised the rod and parted the waters. A great multitude walked across the seabed to Tunisia. Emperor Nero ordered his soldiers to hunt after Kaeso, but when the Roman army reached the Tyrrhenian Sea, the passage was no more.'"

He paused for a moment.

"'Kaeso set sail from Tunisia to spread the message far and

wide. Many years passed as he journeyed across the vast oceans before he reached the Orient, where his boat capsized and left him stranded on a remote island. He fell into a deep sleep until Elyon's voice awakened him with a renewed purpose to defend the light.'"

Jack reached the end of the chapter, growing more curious to keep reading. His fingers touched the worn leather as the story resonated in his imagination.

"Kaeso was the one stranded on Karābu Island."

"We will never know for how long," Burwick replied. "The Elders believed when Kaeso left Karābu, there came a time when the Rod of Elyon fell into the possession of the Nephilim king before the great Battle of Everest. After the blood spilled in battle, the rod took on another name—Soulweaver—and remained missing for centuries. It is no coincidence that Headmaster Upsdell found Dragon Soul on the mountain, then returned a second time in search of the rod. As you well know, he failed to make it back alive."

"But Nightingale returned to Sakkhela," Jack pointed out. "He survived."

"In the Battle of Everest, the rod was used against Slybourne under the command of the Nephilim king," Emma reiterated. "So who controlled the Rod of Elyon during the battle?"

"Asiklua," Jack exhaled in disbelief. "He is the one who conquered Slybourne."

"That makes his redemption even more powerful," Emma admitted. "But—"

"It's difficult to accept for all who have served the commands of Elyon," Eliška cut in. "Professor, what are we to learn from the prophet?"

"In the ancient writings, one will discover Kaeso was not a

Cherub—he was a man without any extraordinary or supernatural gifts. However, he was a fully committed believer in Elyon who spoke the truth to all who would listen. For too long the highest Cherub have taught that one must be a Cherub with gifts—a light-forcer, bender, or healer—to be deemed as one of the chosen. But if you were to read the story of Kaeso, you would understand that freedom is only found in Elyon, not in one's own abilities. We have all been given gifts—some supernatural, others not. These gifts will either unite us or divide us, but they can all be used for Elyon's glory."

"Professor, I'm not sure where I belong," Jack confessed. "Cherub? Faction? Outlier?"

"You are an outlier to the Cherub, and a danger to the Merikh." Burwick's brows furrowed. "But there is no denying your faith in Elyon has brought you this far."

"And kept you alive," Emma added. "Jack, you have proven yourself worthy."

"Only you can decide whether you will remain an outlier." Burwick shot a quick glance toward Emma. "Of course, the same is true for any of us. Our gifts should never define who we become unless they are firmly rooted in Elyon's calling for our lives." Burwick pushed her chair back. "I am certain you three are knackered after your great adventure. Eliška, please show Jack and Emma around. Tomorrow is a new day to continue the fight, but tonight allow yourselves time to rest."

Jack watched Burwick limp toward the metal door and disappear into the stairwell. *Burwick said the rod was known as the Rod of Elyon before the Battle of Everest, but afterward it took on the name of Soulweaver. Am I more like Asiklua than Slybourne? Weird to be comparing myself with an angel who led a legion in rebellion against*

Elyon, then most likely used Soulweaver to kill the Cherub's greatest warrior. You've got issues, Jack. He understood what Burwick meant about believing even if you didn't have gifts like the chosen. And he wondered if there would be a freedom in being part of the faction and righting wrongs by any means necessary. But he wasn't sure which choice was right, so until he was certain, he'd remain an outlier who believed in Elyon.

"Any ideas what we should do next?" Jack asked.

"The Merikh will never stop," Emma replied. "I am afraid neither will your father."

"We cannot stand by while more are captured," Eliška added. "We have Emma, Eden's Star, and the Rod of Elyon, and we must ask ourselves if that will be enough to defeat the Merikh."

"Our search for the artifacts shall continue—whether the highest Cherub agree or not."

"No one said this would be easy or even possible. If we can help Asiklua return to the light, then there's still hope, right?" Jack retrieved Soulweaver, then shuffled back over. "Time to welcome you into the Keepers, Eliška. You've earned it." He held out Soulweaver and touched the point to each of Eliška's shoulders. "You're the newest member of our band of misfits."

Eliška's cheeks flushed. "What about the faction?"

"We're nonexclusive," he replied. "You can belong to both."

Emma stood from the table and retrieved her backpack. Quietly she removed a change of clothes, then grabbed a folded towel near the doorway to the restroom. She slipped inside, and the door slammed shut. Jack jumped at the sound. He stood there holding Soulweaver as if the ceremony weren't over yet.

Sometimes these two are almost as icy as me and Bau—almost.

He slipped Soulweaver underneath the cot. When he turned

around, Eliška stood near the fence surrounding the rooftop. He joined her, and they gazed out onto the skyline of Tsim Sha Tsui. It was not as iconic as Hong Kong Island, but still beautiful.

Jack eyed the barbed wire on top of the fence. "All of this is so crazy."

"I know about the fire mood experiment between you and Emma." Eliška grew quiet for a moment. "You two share a strong bond—stronger than the others."

"She is the one who should lead the Cherub, but instead she's stuck with me."

"We have found one of the artifacts, but will that be enough?" Eliška turned and faced Jack, her stare steady as she handed him a burner cell. "We cannot defeat the Merikh if we are on defense. What you said in the Highlands—well, it means the clock is ticking."

"Then it's time to send a message."

56

SHORTLY AFTER 7:15 A.M., Jack and Emma walked through an empty courtyard at Quarry Bay. It had been well after midnight by the time he showered and his head touched the pillow. He'd fallen into a deep sleep until he'd jerked awake thirty minutes ago. He rolled out of bed, well aware it was the first night in weeks without a nightmare. Just another bloody nose. Now he held Soulweaver in one hand and shook off the grogginess as he and Emma waited at the bus stop. *Weird to be holding an ancient artifact formed from Elyon's Vine as if it's just a walking stick.* As soon as the thought struck, the rod vibrated in his grasp and shrunk, then slithered up his wrist before constricting around his forearm.

"Whoa . . ."

"Incredible," Emma whispered. "How did you do that?"

"I'm not sure—but it doesn't hurt. Actually, feels like it fits perfectly."

Emma slipped off her Beacon Hill hoodie and handed it over. "Best to not draw attention."

"Right." Jack tugged it on. "Good idea."

He glanced at Emma's long-sleeved T-shirt, knowing the inked arms beneath told so much more of her story. The moment was interrupted by the N122 double-decker as it stopped in front of them. They found two empty seats on the bottom deck.

"Not sure I'll ever be comfortable riding on a bus again," Jack mumbled. "I nearly left the rod with Eliška. I wonder if it would've done the same thing if she held it."

"Better you keep the rod in your possession, and not trust the faction."

"I trust Eliška." Jack checked his burner for any texts. "You need to trust her too, Emma."

The double-decker sped down King's Road before stopping at Canal Road West, where Jack and Emma switched to the N121 bus. Swerving between lanes, the driver navigated early morning traffic like a pro as the bus headed into Cross-Harbour Tunnel toward Kowloon. Jack flinched when his cell phone buzzed.

WALLED CITY. 8 SHARP.

"We're on," Jack said in a lowered voice. "Hopefully he doesn't change his mind."

"And how do you know him?"

"He used to go to Beacon Hill, until his father was arrested. Big headlines."

"You have quite a variety of friends, Jack."

"Yeah, seems that way."

The double-decker pulled over at Argyle Street Playground, an area Jack knew well. He led the way as they headed north toward Kowloon Walled City Park. They cut through the basketball courts and followed a concrete path beneath dense trees until they reached the Yamen, a building from the Qing Dynasty that dated back to 1847. Jack stood in the center of the square and eyed their surroundings. He knew he was asking a huge favor—monumental—but it was the only way to send a message.

Ren Lai appeared in the doorway of one of the stone buildings. When he didn't step out into the open, Jack took that as a sign and waited. He knew both were checking to see if either had been followed. Once Ren disappeared inside, Jack entered the building with Emma right behind. Inside, the empty space was dim with barely enough light for them to see each other.

"A typhoon follows everywhere you go," Ren warned. "Addison is offering five hundred grand to anyone who brings you to him—dead or alive. He has taken control of the Merikh."

"You know about the Merikh?" Jack asked, surprised.

"How else do you think my father ended up in prison?" Ren shifted his weight, clearly uncomfortable and itching to leave. "If Addison finds out we are breathing the same air, then we both know how this will end."

"Ren, you have my word. Whatever you tell me stays between us."

"Most of what I know are rumors." Ren paused. "You texted me about the reeducation camps, right? Addison and the PRC have strengthened their alliance, to control those who have spoken out against them."

"Headmaster Fargher believes that Will got caught up in one of their arrests."

"He never could keep his nose out of trouble." Ren shook his head. "If the rumors are true, the reeducation camps are actually prisons. And there are only two of them so far—Shelter Island and Shek Pik Prison. Both are heavily guarded."

"Do you know who is being held there?" Emma asked. "Have you heard any names?"

"A few weeks ago, I visited my father at Shek Pik and he told me about experiments being conducted on the inmates. Half of his cell block has disappeared without any explanation. He heard one of the guards complaining about an entire wing of the prison being locked off for refugees who have been transferred in. But I do not know any names."

"What kind of experiments?" Emma asked.

"Not the ethical kind, I am guessing," Ren replied flatly. "My father watched delivery trucks arrive in the loading dock at the prison and haul away dozens of body bags. Whatever you are searching for regarding the Merikh, I would suggest you leave it well enough alone."

"Have you heard anything about Addison finding any artifacts?" Jack asked.

"Artifacts?" Ren's brows raised in confusion. "What does that have to do with anything?"

"He is searching for some extremely valuable and dangerous items. It is possible he is running experiments on those being held as a way to find these artifacts." Jack noticed Ren's gaze shift away from them, a dead giveaway he knew something. "What have you heard?"

"Addison is hosting a dinner tomorrow night for a delegation of Hong Kong officials." Ren reached into his pocket and retrieved a metal card. *Ren is always one step ahead. He just needed a nudge.* "My cousin works at Aqua, so he's been busy putting the details of the event together—including setting up a display for some priceless relics Addison is bringing to the dinner." Ren handed the card over to Jack. "Access to a private elevator is the best I can do."

"Thank you," Jack replied. "I mean it."

Ren brushed past them and said over his shoulder, "Lose my number, Jack."

57

"GUARDIANS LIFE."

The stone wall opened with those two simple words. Jack and Emma headed through the tunnel into the basement of the Main Hall. On the twenty-minute walk from Kowloon Walled City Park, Jack had questioned whether it was a good idea to return. As they stood in the basement, he remembered the night Emma's eyes glowed stark white.

"Doesn't seem like anything has changed."

"Everything has changed," Emma replied. "But not all of it is bad."

Voices echoed off the walls above as they approached the steps. Before either could react, a group of men appeared on the stairwell and surrounded them.

One of the men barked, "Who are you?"

"Jack Reynolds," he blurted, "and Emma Bennett."

The man relayed their names through a walkie-talkie. A familiar voice crackled a response. "Bring them to the quad."

When Jack heard Bau's voice he knew it was better not to ask too many questions. Shadowed by the group of men, Jack and Emma headed for the quad. *I don't recognize any of these guys.* On the ground floor of the Main Hall, Jack noticed a new bronze plaque. He stopped and stared hard at the engraved names, realizing these were the students killed during the attack on Beacon Hill. Emma grabbed his hand and pulled him along.

In the chaos of the night when he'd escaped with Vince, neither one had realized the destruction left by Chung and the Merikh. Jack's jaw dropped as he gazed at the pile of rubble and an entire side of Nightingale House that was still in ruins. Several teens were in the quad, and without touching the debris they were moving large chunks of concrete.

"Benders," Emma whispered. "They are able to shift objects with their mind."

Jack nodded toward the walls of the grounds. Other teens and adults were scattered around the perimeter of the property. "What gifts do they have?"

Bau approached Jack and Emma. "You were seen yesterday in Sham Shui Po."

"Tell us something we don't know," Jack bantered.

"The Merikh and HKPF nearly caught us," Emma admitted.

"Your arrival leaves everyone in danger," Bau said. "We could have helped you, Emma."

"It wasn't like we planned to return to that exact spot." Jack didn't mention that the district had flashed in his mind before they left the Highlands. "But someone from the Merikh knew we were there for sure."

"Headmaster Fargher will want to see the two of you." Bau noticed their gaze was fixed on those in the quad and guarding the grounds. "There has been a steady stream of Cherub arriving through the House of Luminescence. Lightforcers. Benders. Healers. At first they were coming from Pakistan, then the mainland. We have lost count of the countries represented. Nearly six hundred are living in Nightingale's vault."

"Six hundred?" Jack stood dumbstruck. "Underground this whole time?"

"The gateway has been opened, and they have chosen to seek refuge here."

"Do you think it is safe for them to be out in the open—even the lightforcers and benders?" Emma asked. "The Merikh may attack once they realize Beacon Hill is occupied."

"You will have to speak to the headmaster." Bau waved at the men who were gathered nearby. "Make another round through the grounds to be sure they were not followed."

Emma crossed her arms. "We were careful, Bau."

"Have you heard anything about Will?" Jack interrupted, annoyed by Bau's presence.

"We have found no clues to his whereabouts, but there are many stories of families within the Cherub who are missing." Bau turned his attention toward Emma. "I have asked those within the highest Cherub, including Fang Xue, but no one has heard from your parents since Mount Hareh. I am sorry, Emma."

She bit her bottom lip as her eyes grew glossy. "We found one of the artifacts."

"And we think the Merikh have found one too," Jack added. "Maybe more."

Bau shot a quick glance between them. "It must be protected inside the Testimony."

"We are keeping Soulweaver in a safe place for now—we might need it."

"You speak of the Rod of Elyon?" Bau asked, skeptical.

"Jack is telling the truth," Emma replied. "We found Charis, and the Rod of Elyon revealed itself to us—well, to Jack, actually."

"And we're going to use it to help free those who are being held by the Merikh." Jack mustered up another ounce of courage to show Bau he wasn't going to stand down. "We're here to ask for your help—and anyone else who is willing."

"If the Cherub know you have the Rod of Elyon in your possession, they will not allow you to keep it or use it." Bau hesitated. "I am supposed to meet with the highest Cherub this afternoon, and I must inform them of what you have found."

"I'm not handing over Soulweaver to the Cherub," Jack argued. "Not until this is over."

"Emma, you cannot be in agreement."

"I am asking you to keep this a secret for now," Emma replied. "Until we know what the Merikh have in their possession."

Bau returned his attention to Jack. "Which reeducation camp are you going after?"

"Shelter Island," Jack replied. "Shek Pik Prison seems like a long shot."

"What makes you think you will be able to get onto Shelter Island?"

Jack nodded at those near the outer walls. "We could use a few more lightforcers."

"We have worked hard with each one. Their responsibility is to protect Beacon Hill and those who are trusting us in Nightingale's vault."

"C'mon, Bau," Jack protested. "Don't you want to score a few points?"

"I have told you before," Bau said to Emma, "he is reckless."

"I'm not the one who lost Dragon Soul."

"That is enough," Emma chided. "Arguing will get us nowhere."

Bau leaned in close to Jack. "Your actions have not been forgotten."

"Seriously?" Jack scoffed. "Go ahead and try to turn me in."

"We are going to Shelter Island tonight, and we are taking the Rod of Elyon with us." Emma's eyes flared, leaving Bau and Jack quiet for a moment. "Bau, we need your help."

"There are only a few lightforcers who can be spared." Bau glared at Jack, and they were right back to the afternoon when they wrestled during the house match after Bau beaned Will in the head with a cricket ball. "I will go with you as well. That is the best I can do."

"Look forward to it." From deep within envy crept beneath the surface at the thought that Bau would one day become the Cherub leader instead of Emma. Jack glanced over his shoulder as Tim, Vince, and Amina appeared from the Main Hall. He noticed how cautiously they stepped out into the daylight, and he realized he'd forgotten to message Tim when he'd returned. A few seconds passed before the others noticed him and Emma. Jack stepped away from Bau and headed straight in their direction.

"Jack!" Tim hurried over with a wide smile. "You are a sight for sore eyes, mate."

"Rumor was you might be back," Vince said. "But we've had a few false alarms."

Jack fist-bumped Tim and Vince. "It's so good to see you two troublemakers."

Amina looked past him toward Emma. "Are you all . . . ?"

"Don't worry, Eliška and Emma haven't killed each other yet."

"We were worried about that—at least, I was worried."

"Why isn't Eliška with you two?" Vince asked.

"She's staying with Burwick on Hong Kong Island."

"Professor Burwick brought us straight here as soon as you three disappeared down the river." Tim pushed his frames up the bridge of his nose. "Well?"

"We found one of the artifacts," Jack said in a lowered voice. "We're going to use it to help rescue the Cherub who are being held on Shelter Island."

"I'm a step slower." Vince's shoulders broadened a bit. "But I'm in."

"When are you going to tell your parents you're alive?"

"I decided it was better not to for now. Look what's happened to Fargher with Will."

"Word is Shelter Island and Shek Pik Prison are heavily guarded," Jack explained. "It would make sense for Addison to keep Will at either of those places."

"So, what time is this little adventure?" Tim asked.

"Later tonight. Bau is going with us, along with a few handpicked lightforcers."

"He's been running the gifted like a general," Vince pointed out. "He's a natural leader."

"It pains me to admit it," Tim chimed in, "but Vince is right."

"I have been working with the healers," Amina said. "Elyon is growing my gifts too."

"That's incredible, Amina." Jack smiled warmly. "You were the one who saved Vince."

"Healers are as important as any of the others." Tim grabbed a flag draped over his shoulder and pointed toward the clock tower. "When Fargher heard you might be back, he asked us to switch out the flag. Maybe you should do the honors."

"You three go ahead. I will catch up with Emma." Amina smiled at Jack. "We are grateful you have returned safely. Now all of us are together again."

Jack, Tim, and Vince entered the Main Hall and took the stairs to the rooftop. Tim carried the flag as if he were in a processional as they entered the crow's nest. Jack noticed the gaping hole in the floor and the stopped clock where he'd placed Eden's Star months earlier. He was surprised he'd not thought about the compass since he woke up earlier that morning.

Tim held the flag out for Jack. "You should be the one."

"No way." Jack waved him off. "The honor is all yours—you've earned it."

Tim reached out through an open window and snatched a rope securing the Union Jack. He pulled hard until he lowered the flag near the window. Jack and Vince watched quietly as Tim switched out the old with the new. Pulling the rope again, he hoisted the flag that bore the lion crest, signifying the history and legacy of all who had gone before.

Jack, Tim, and Vince left the clock tower and returned to the rooftop. As they glanced up at the Beacon Hill crest, Jack had a sense that the pages were turning once again.

"I'm starving," Tim announced. "Jack, fill us in over lunch."

"You won't believe half of what I'm going to tell you."

"Give us a clue then."

"Michael Chung is dead."

58

REPULSE BAY, HONG KONG ISLAND

ADDISON REMOVED THE IV from his forearm and rolled down his shirtsleeve. He breathed in deep as he clenched his fists, then exhaled and uncurled his fingers. A few seconds passed while he waited impatiently. Slipping off the gurney, he grabbed a glass beaker filled with blood and threw it across the room. Crimson splattered on the walls as the beaker shattered near the scientist who cowered by the glass door of the penthouse lab.

"How many more transfusions until it works?" Addison seethed.

"Rejuvenating the DNA is not a guaranteed process," the scientist replied cautiously.

"There was a time when my power flowed freely through my

veins until it was taken against my will." Addison stepped forward until he was within a few inches of the scientist. "Let's hope for your sake my gifts return to their full strength."

Will watched closely while he waited in the corner, quiet as a ghost. Addison grabbed his suit coat off a hook and brushed past the scientist. Will followed him into the hallway, shadowed by heavy security. They climbed aboard the private elevator and rode down in silence. The bodyguards stepped onto the street first as an SUV that resembled an armored tank pulled up to the curb. Addison slipped into the back seat and Will joined him. Thick glass separated them from the driver.

"You and Michael had gifts like the Cherub," Will said.

"He kept his longer than I did because there was a time when he was fully surrendered to the Cherub." Addison paused. "I have always been an outlier, dipping my soul only for a brief time into the beliefs of Elyon."

"How can I stop my abilities from being taken?"

"There is no good answer." Addison checked his watch. "Charlotte was the first to capture and transfuse Cherub blood to restore her powers—stealing from the most gifted. Many of the Cherub are not strong enough to survive such a procedure when they are transfused with the blood of those deemed as evil. But the girl survived, and based on what you witnessed in Sakkhela, her gifts have returned. Now that Michael is gone, Emma has become a greater threat. You must push your gifts further than you have before."

"Do you know what happened to him?"

"He followed Jack to the Valley of Grace, and the others lost contact with him," Addison replied, shaking his head. "Several were killed at the entrance to Arishiyama to gain access to the gateway. The rest of the team returned but have not spoken much about what took place, except for chasing two girls into the woods. One of them was a lightforcer."

"Must be Emma," Will noted. "I don't know who the other might be. Bau Hu is the only other one left from the chosen, but he has not been seen since the attack at Beacon Hill."

"Peter misguided the chosen for his selfish gain and betrayed the Cherub. He was a pawn in my game, one piece that will never return to the board." Addison paused. "He is also the one who killed your mother as a way to cover up his sins. You were kept a secret so he could secure his reign. Peace and love was a facade. What he was after is what we all desire—power." Addison's lies flowed easily. "You were never going to be one of the chosen—and if you had become one, the Cherub would have done nothing but control your abilities. Your destiny is in your hands, not theirs, and from what I have seen you are a natural."

"Jack was certain you played a role in murdering Rachel *and* my mum."

"There was nothing for me to gain by killing your mother—or killing my own flesh and blood. However, I will admit, to find what needed to be found there were times I pressured your father to cooperate. I warned him about Peter's intentions, yet he chose to place the other students ahead of his own family's safety—above your mother's well-being and your own. Quite a shame considering your father turned his back on you because of his allegiance to the Cherub. Now you are by my side—the son I never had."

Addison isn't wrong. As much as it hurts to admit, Dad chose everyone else over me and Mum. He protected Jack and left the rest of us to fend for ourselves.

The armored vehicle blew through two checkpoints near

Repulse Bay and continued down a winding road toward Admiralty. In front and behind, a fleet of bulletproof SUVs were loaded with Addison's security detail. One could never be too careful, especially when one was responsible for the unrest spreading across the city.

Addison's cell buzzed. "Yes?" His brows furrowed. "When?"

"What is wrong?"

"Beacon Hill is no longer abandoned." Addison stared out the bulletproof glass. "Yesterday I had a vision that Jack returned to the city. When the capture team arrived in Sham Shui Po, they were unable to find him, but I'm certain he was there." Addison set the cell phone on his knee and added under his breath, "Strange he chose that place to return."

Will remembered what Jack had said about Sham Shui Po. *"My father kept us locked up in a cage home, a closet barely wide enough for a single mattress. I remember being left by ourselves for days, and when he would finally show up the nights were hell."*

"Why would Eden's Star take him to that district?" Will asked.

"A question without a clear answer. However, since he has returned from the Valley of Grace, we must assume he has found more of the artifacts." Addison turned toward Will with a hardened glare. "There was a time when I could see where Rachel and Jack were at all times. But as Rachel grew older and was recruited by the Cherub, the connection was lost. I knew where Jack was most of the time until Rachel was murdered in Sitio Veterans. Since then, there have been only brief flashes—such as Sakkhela, as well as yesterday." Addison's jaw clenched. "He betrayed me like his sister—but he cannot run forever."

"What do you want me to do?"

"We need to know who has returned to the school."

"If I reappear out of the blue, there will be questions."

"You must be willing to go deeper into the darkness, but it will bring great pain."

"All I want is for Jack to pay for what he has done. I don't care how much it hurts."

"Trust me, and you will get your revenge."

Forty minutes later, the armored SUV pulled into a shipyard near Aberdeen. Climbing out of the vehicle, the security guards surrounded Addison and Will as they entered a heavily guarded warehouse. Stacked crates filled the space as workers moved piles of golden relics before melting them in a large furnace.

"The Exodus Mines have given us much needed leverage to control the chaos," Addison explained. "To go further along the Silk Road, deeper within the Golden Triangle, we must offer a gift to the PRC. Five hundred million in gold bars should be enough to get their attention—and their cooperation."

"Who would have thought Slybourne's bounty could be used as a weapon?" Will said. "And this barely made a dent in the treasure from the mines."

"Greed is as old as time," Addison mused. "Stay with me and I will show you the riches of the world—and the life you are destined to live."

59

BEACON HILL

CHILDREN DARTED THROUGH the vault chasing after one another while adults and teens busied themselves with their daily chores. A group listened to Professor McDougall carry on about the importance of passing along the world's history in all its glory and failure to the next generation. Jack noticed Elis and Beca Lloyd washing and pinning clothes to lines. He recognized Maduka and Oni Okonkwo, who were sorting through boxes of canned goods and fresh vegetables. Natalie McNaughton and Professor Windsor helped roll up sleeping bags and fold blankets before stacking them onto the cots. Headmaster Fargher sauntered through the vault surrounded by the youngest children.

"Not sure how many more will fit down here," Tim said. "Walls are closing in."

"One of Bau's uncles delivers food every week or so," Vince explained. "We bring the boxes through the tunnel you and I escaped through, Jack. But the supplies aren't lasting as long these days."

"Turns out only a small fraction of the Cherub here are light-forcers, benders, or healers. Amina has been spending most of her time being trained by Salomeh and Faizan."

Jack stood awestruck by the underground community. "Hard to believe this is real."

His voice echoed as all eyes turned toward him. Tim's and Amina's parents hurried over, and not far behind were McNaughton and Professor Windsor. Jack felt as if he were about to be surrounded on all sides as Headmaster Fargher left the children and walked briskly toward him.

"So the rumors around the city are true." Elis smiled wide as he squeezed Jack's shoulders. "You are back."

Beca Lloyd and Oni Okonkwo hugged Jack tight as if he were one of their own children. His cheeks flushed with all the unwanted attention. He noticed Professor McDougall, Professor Windsor, and Headmaster Fargher stayed back from the welcome party.

"Mum, you're going to squeeze the life out of him," Tim said. "Easy."

"Of course." Beca wiped a tear from her cheek as she let go and stepped beside Elis. "We have been praying for a miracle—and here you stand."

"Elyon has answered our prayers," Oni agreed. "Hope remains."

"Was your adventure a success?" Elis asked. "I mean—"

"We found one of the artifacts, which is now safe from the Merikh." Jack shifted his gaze toward Headmaster Fargher. "But they have found at least one of the artifacts too."

"Seems like an impossible task to find *all* of the artifacts,"

Maduka said. "Especially when no one knows how many were once kept inside the Testimony."

Jack stopped himself from answering, guessing it was better not to reveal the number.

"Can you show us what you have found?" Fargher asked.

Jack wasn't expecting the question from the headmaster. "Um . . ."

"If you need to keep it a secret, we understand," McNaughton chimed in. "You are a sight for sore eyes, Jack."

"Probably better no one else knows what it is." Jack felt the awkwardness between them, unsure of what it meant but wanting to get past it. "We are doing our best to find them all."

"Of course you are," Beca answered. "And we are so grateful."

"Right, that's enough interrogation from the adults," Tim interrupted. "C'mon, Jack."

Tim pulled Jack away as they headed down the center aisle of the vault. He wasn't sure what was going on, but something was off-kilter. Vince and Tim exchanged glances but kept quiet until they reached the aisle where they'd found the Testimony.

"Either of you want to explain what that was about?" Jack asked.

"There's been some disagreements," Vince admitted. "We're not sure about what though."

"Mum and Dad said the headmaster has become more isolated and is making decisions without discussing them with anyone else. Perhaps he's realized our parents withheld secrets from him too. Best to keep what you've found to yourself—and us, of course."

Jack approached the smashed crate with an opening large enough to see the acacia box inside—the Testimony.

"No one wants to get too close," Tim said. "Ancient stories have everyone freaked out."

"As long as Eden's Star is inside of me, and the Testimony is empty, it should be safe."

"Famous last words," Vince chuckled. "Give it a shot, Jack."

He reached into the crate and lifted the acacia box out before setting it on the concrete floor. He stared at the etchings in gold and the perfect craftsmanship. *Of course it's perfect—Elyon created it with his own hands.* He lifted his sleeve and revealed Soulweaver wrapped around his arm, ignoring the stares from Tim and Vince. He pointed his fingers toward the acacia box, and the rod released its grip on his arm before straightening into its full length.

"That's some magic trick," Vince said in utter disbelief. "How'd you do that?"

"Kind of does it on its own. Still trying to figure it out."

"Like Eden's Star then." Tim's brows raised. "You have no fear, mate."

With the rod in his grasp, Jack intended to place Soulweaver inside the Testimony where it belonged. He hesitated long enough to leave him questioning his next move. It had always been the plan to return the artifacts to the Testimony, but they'd also considered keeping them out until the Merikh were defeated. He wondered which was the right decision.

"Are you going to put it inside?" Tim asked. "It will have to roll up to fit."

"I was thinking about it . . ." Jack hesitated. "I wanted to test it, I guess."

"What does it do?" Vince asked. "Doesn't look like much."

"The Cherub call it the Rod of Elyon, but it's known to others as Soulweaver. In the Battle of Everest, this was the artifact the Nephilim king used as a weapon to defeat Slybourne and Dragon Soul." Jack watched their reaction, which mirrored his own when he first heard the story. *Wait until I tell them about Asiklua, who is most likely the one who struck down Slybourne on Everest. No way they'll believe me about the legion either.* "I don't know what all it does, but I've got a few ideas already."

"Whoa." Tim swallowed hard. "You are holding the Rod of Elyon."

"Find me something to wrap the Testimony in," Jack said. "I'm taking it with me."

"Are you sure that's a good idea?" Vince asked. "Seems a bit dangerous."

"That's why I'm here—to hide the acacia box in a safe place just in case."

"So you're not staying at Beacon Hill?"

"Until this is over, there's somewhere else for me to stay that is better for everyone."

"What about rescuing the prisoners at the camps?" Vince asked.

"It's game time tonight—and I'm counting on the two of you to be ready."

Tim stepped away and searched the crates until he found a burlap sack filled with an assortment of brass cups. He emptied the burlap sack and held it out in front of him. Jack picked up the acacia box and carefully placed it inside, then pulled the drawstring tight.

"We're not running any longer," he said. "Time we fight back."

"Now you're talking." Vince grinned. "Let's do this."

"Both of you know," Tim said sheepishly, "that I'm a lover, not a—"

"Stop while you're ahead," Vince interrupted. "It's a good thing Amina is the fighter."

"Touché."

60

THE HONG KONG SKYLINE PAINTING rippled seconds before Jack, Tim, and Vince stepped through into Rowell Library. Emma and Amina waited near the boarded-up windows, away from the dust-covered books and cobwebbed statues. Jack set the burlap sack on a table as Emma and Amina gazed past him. He glanced over his shoulder and saw Headmaster Fargher and Natalie McNaughton headed in their direction.

"A moment, please." Fargher itched his stubbly chin. "Jack, it is important."

"Of course, Headmaster." Jack turned toward the others. "Wait for me here."

He followed Fargher and McNaughton as they walked toward the secured elevator. Fargher punched in a code and the doors opened. Jack knew immediately where they were going, but he didn't have a clue why. All three rode the elevator to the secured floor where the Zakhar was locked away.

Stepping into the white-walled room brought back memories of the first time he'd tried the Zakhar and experienced a vision of Nightingale and Crozier during the Battle of Hong Kong. Then there was the second time, when Eden's Star revealed a memory of the Elders before Peter Leung stole the compass and vanished. Neither time had the Zakhar worked properly, yet it revealed so much.

"I am certain you are aware that your father and the Merikh are hunting Cherub." Fargher's voice was hoarse and gravelly. "I suspect you are planning a rescue of those who are imprisoned."

"I'm tired of running. We have to take the fight to them, starting with Shelter Island."

"Why haven't the Cherub fought back?" McNaughton asked. "Lightforcers and benders who are free have not shown themselves, except for the ones who arrived at Beacon Hill."

Jack weighed his words. "Maybe their gifts were taken from them—or maybe they're afraid."

"Does your father have the ability to take another's gift?" Fargher asked.

"I know someone who lost their gifts because of the Merikh." Jack recognized the hesitation between them. "The only Merikh I have seen with supernatural gifts were Charlotte Taylor and Michael Chung—but I watched them both die."

"Jack . . . How . . . ?" McNaughton's voice trailed off.

"Right now it doesn't matter." Jack mustered up enough courage to reveal a deeper truth. "Chung was the one who murdered Rachel—and he's the one who killed Mrs. Fargher. I'm sorry, Headmaster."

Fargher winced as if being punched in the stomach. "Are you certain?"

"I'm positive." Jack realized McNaughton had kept Chung's actions from the headmaster. He pointed toward a solid wall as if a window framed the quad below. "We have lightforcers, benders, and healers on our side. This is our chance to bring everyone home—especially Will, sir."

"There is something you need to see before you go any further," McNaughton said.

"Amina told us about the Zakhar malfunctioning when you used it before." Fargher walked over to a countertop and retrieved a folded silk robe, similar to the ones Jack and Emma wore when they traveled through the gateway to Mount Hareh. "She mentioned the vision of the Elders—and a memory from Eden's Star." Fargher placed the robe inside the glass box and closed it tight. "We have spent many hours sorting through Nightingale's vault, searching for anything to help end this war. We found a Cherub robe belonging to Sir James Nightingale."

Amina told Fargher more than she should, but it's too late now.

"We cross-referenced the Zakhar's media library with DNA found on the robe," McNaughton explained. "And we discovered some footage in the library that only the headmaster can access. It shows Nightingale's travels to Mount Hareh not long before he died. We are unsure how Nightingale captured the footage, but we are certain it was him."

Headmaster Fargher pecked at the virtual keyboard while Jack picked up the VR goggles and slipped them over his head. As he stared into the blackness, he anticipated the worst. His heartbeat quickened, and in a blink he stared down at worn boots trudging up the side of a sand dune. *I know exactly how that feels.* He listened to labored breathing from Nightingale as his muscles tensed with anticipation.

A moment passed before Nightingale reached the stone steps leading up the side of Mount Hareh. A chill shot down Jack's spine as the mountain grew eerily quiet—another time in history. His stomach churned as the camera angle shifted. Nightingale's fingers appeared, and he wiped the lens with a handkerchief, revealing wire-rimmed spectacle frames. *He's filming with his glasses, using tech that wasn't supposed to exist back then. Genius.* Nightingale placed his glasses back on the bridge of his nose and climbed one step at a time.

"Why is he going to the Sanctuary of Prayer?" Jack whispered.

At a slow pace and with great effort, Nightingale reached the top of the mountain. Jack expected to see a gathering of the highest Cherub. Instead, he watched the lone shadow of the aged headmaster appear when he glanced down at weathered boots.

"James, we have been expecting you." Gabriella Reynolds stood at the entrance to the sanctuary. *Mom.* "The others are waiting inside."

"I do not understand why we could not meet somewhere closer," Nightingale grumbled. "I am not as energetic as I once used to be, Gabriella."

"Our apologies. We could not risk being seen."

Jack noticed how his mom looked to be around the same age she was in the photos he and Vince had "borrowed" from Nightingale's mausoleum. Nightingale entered the sanctuary and was greeted by Xui Li, Dabria, and Charlotte Taylor. Jack was just along for the ride as the legendary headmaster shuffled forward to greet old friends. Charlotte's dark eyes unsettled Jack, and the scabbard on her hip was unnerving.

"I have kept these a closely guarded secret for many years." From beneath his coat, Nightingale retrieved two dretium fans with star-shaped projectile blades on each point. "When I found the Testimony, these shurikens were hidden inside."

"Swords in the hand," Xui Li said. "Windstrikers."

"Lost since the Age of Trepidation." Dabria studied the shurikens closely. "The Eternal tells us they were crafted by Elyon himself as a symbol of his magnificent power and elegant beauty."

"Windstrikers may be one of the artifacts," Gabriella said. "And perhaps the only one found and returned to the Testimony."

"After the Fall, the Seven Tribes battled as one without the artifacts during the First Great War," Dabria pointed out. "However, in the ancient writings of the Eternal there is no mention of the artifacts during the century of peace leading to the Battle of Everest. Since the tribes and the legion were banned from Charis, the whereabouts of the artifacts have remained unknown—gifts from Elyon to protect the tribes hidden for centuries because of their sins."

"A thousand years of torment from the Nephilim, Merikh, and legion under Asiklua's command never would have occurred if the Seven Tribes united *with* the artifacts to defend themselves . . ." Jack noticed Charlotte's words dripped with disgust. "The artifacts belong to the Cherub, and as the Elders we must be prepared to use them against our enemies."

"Elyon brought victory and peace in the Mercy Covenant to end the Second Great War," Xui Li protested. "We know the consequences of disobeying Elyon's command and cannot allow our temptation for the artifacts to cause division or distrust."

"We should find Eden's Star *and* use the compass," Charlotte argued. "With our gifts, we shall value the artifacts greater than the Seven Tribes ever did."

Nightingale cleared his throat. "As the Elders, you have agreed to exchange the Windstrikers for Dragon Soul. Upsdell found the sword on Everest, and considering his lineage, it is fitting it be returned to Beacon Hill."

A chill shot down Jack's spine at the thought of Charlotte as a keeper of Dragon Soul.

Gabriella eyed Charlotte closely. "We made promises to search for Eden's Star."

"Perhaps Sir Nightingale will simply gift us the Windstrikers," Charlotte suggested. "Gabriella, the one you love is more than willing to be the next keeper. He is strong enough."

"Dragon Soul does not belong to us or the Cherub," Dabria interrupted. "We must return the sword to its rightful place to honor the sacrifices of Slybourne and Upsdell."

"Nonsense," Charlotte rebuked. "We should keep it for as long as we need."

"The darkness has grown within you since Peter stole Eden's Star." Xui Li stepped between Charlotte and Nightingale. "You will not decide our fate—or the fate of the Cherub."

Fear struck Jack when, out of the corner of his eye, he noticed Charlotte reach for the hilt of Dragon Soul. When she slipped the sword from the scabbard and pointed the edge of the blade toward them, Jack wanted to pounce, but instead he was left clenching his jaw while Nightingale remained steadfast. Gabriella stepped forward, and a ball of light radiated from her palms.

Charlotte charged and swiped the blade across Gabriella's body with precision. As she crumpled to the ground, Gabriella released a lightforce that exploded against Charlotte, sending her sliding backward. Xui Li and Dabria moved swiftly as Gabriella reached for the deep gash across her body. Blood seeped through her clothes and spread across the hallowed stone.

Jack was desperate for Nightingale to be the commander he was during the Battle of Hong Kong, and the headmaster didn't disappoint. Nightingale whipped the Windstrikers in front of him and the fans expanded, garnering Charlotte's attention for a split second. She swung Dragon Soul toward him with such force the walls shook. Xui Li's and Dabria's lightforces joined as one to defend against each strike. *They still had their powers at this point—when did they lose them?* With a swipe of her hand, Xui Li launched granite statues toward Charlotte, knocking Dragon Soul from her grasp. Dabria grabbed the sword, unable to control the power emanating from the blade. Xui Li attacked Charlotte, who defended herself with a brutal assault and a dark fiery vengeance.

"Elyon, take the gifts you have granted Charlotte in your name!" Xui Li shouted.

Dabria speared Dragon Soul into the floor, and a great earthquake erupted, cracking the walls and foundation of the Sanctuary of Prayer. Xui Li unleashed another burst of lightforce, striking Charlotte countless times. Charlotte remained on her feet as she harnessed her own energy. Nightingale released his grip on the Windstrikers, and the shurikens attacked. Wide-eyed, Charlotte stared helplessly at the palms of her hands as if realizing that Elyon had answered Xui Li's prayer. With a tidal wave of violet, Charlotte released a piercing scream and disappeared before the Windstrikers reached their target.

Elyon didn't take all of her gifts in this moment. She was still lethal at Fortress Hill. And Nightingale used the Windstrikers. Even though he wasn't a fan of the Cherub, he was a believer in Elyon, which means my faith is more like Nightingale's than I ever thought possible.

Nightingale stepped forward and knelt beside Gabriella, whose wounds were severe. Jack's chest tightened. He was desperate to reach out and help his mom, though he knew she must've survived beyond this time. Dabria moved her fingers over Gabriella's body, and to Jack's astonishment the wound vanished. *Dabria was a healer, and a powerful one.* He watched as his mom inhaled deep, gasping for more air than was inside the sanctuary.

Xui Li was on her knees beside Gabriella. "Elyon has protected us once more."

"We have lost another to the darkness," Dabria said. "First Peter, now Charlotte."

Nightingale cleared his throat as he grasped the Windstrikers once again. "Excuse me, perhaps I have been a bit too hasty."

"What do you mean, James?" Gabriella slowly pulled herself to her feet, her bloodied clothes the only evidence she had been near death seconds earlier. "We gave you our word."

"Who was it Charlotte spoke of as a possible keeper of Dragon Soul?"

Gabriella glanced at Xui Li, then Dabria. "His name is Addison."

61

JACK YANKED THE VR GOGGLES off his head and spun around toward Fargher and McNaughton. His hands shook as he tried to steady himself, swallowing the vomit in his throat. *What happened after the video cut out? Where did Charlotte disappear to? Did the Elders trust Addison with Dragon Soul? How did the sword end up at Beacon Hill? Was Addison the one who stole the sword back during the attack?* So many questions darted through his mind, leaving him struggling to decide which one to ask.

"My father was strong enough to wield Dragon Soul."

"He is more powerful than anyone anticipated." Fargher's lips pursed. "He will be even more dangerous if he is in possession of the sword or any of the other artifacts."

"Bau told you he lost Dragon Soul?"

Fargher nodded. "So I could hopefully be of some help."

"We searched the vault for the Windstrikers, hoping Nightingale might have kept the artifacts," McNaughton added. "But we have been unable to find them so far."

"You should ask Tim and Amina to help you search. They're actually pretty good at finding hidden clues." Jack weighed his words, unsure of how much Fargher and McNaughton knew about the Elders' history. "Charlotte Taylor's betrayal against the Elders and Cherub explains her rise in the Merikh."

"If your father possesses such gifts," Fargher warned, "you will not stand a chance."

"We found Eden's Star and one of the artifacts—Soulweaver. We have Elyon on our side, Headmaster. Finding courage happens now—if we surrender to fear, we will lose this war."

"Addison's influence is growing significantly," McNaughton said.

"I won't hide the rest of my life in a vault—and neither should anyone else."

Fargher's bloodshot gaze hardened. "You will need a distraction."

"What do you have in mind?" McNaughton asked.

"I will schedule a press conference for tomorrow." Fargher stared at Jack as if considering another alternative. "It is time to reopen the gates of Beacon Hill."

"Headmaster, are you sure?" Jack asked. "The Mercy Covenant can't protect us anymore."

"We have lightforcers, benders, and healers in our midst." Fargher offered a half-hearted smile. "You said it yourself—courage happens now. Your bravery is a valuable lesson to us all."

Jack wiped the sweat from his brow. "I made a promise, and I intend to keep it."

He shook Fargher's hand and gave McNaughton an awkward hug before he rode the elevator down to Rowell Library alone. Stepping out of the elevator, he found the others waiting exactly where they had been twenty minutes earlier.

"So what was all that about?" Tim asked. "Did the Zakhar work this time around?"

"Fargher and Natalie found a video showing another one of the artifacts," Jack replied. "The Elders called them Windstrikers, lost since the Age of Trepidation."

"Now that sounds dark," Vince said. "What did they look like?"

"Fans kind of like the ones Emma and Amina danced with, except they're razor sharp."

"I'll bet that's not all they are," Tim added. "Epic weapons, remember?"

"We'll have to get our hands on them first to find out," Vince said.

"Any idea where we can find them?" Emma asked.

"Nightingale traveled to Mount Hareh and was inside the Sanctuary of Prayer with my mom, Xui Li, Dabria, and Charlotte Taylor. He was there to exchange the Windstrikers for Dragon Soul. Let's just say it didn't go as planned." Jack hesitated. "And I know who might've stolen Dragon Soul the night of the attack on the school—Addison."

"That's just great, isn't it?" Tim waved his arms in frustration. "Your barmy father has Dragon Soul. Was he the shadow who attacked us in Sakkhela?"

"On Fortress Hill, the shadow was there *with* Addison." Jack exhaled. "He might've been the one to steal the sword back, but he's allowing someone else to use it against us."

"What does this mean for tonight?" Vince asked. "Are we going?"

"We're sticking to the plan." Jack glanced toward Amina and Tim. "We'll need to split up. You two should meet up with Natalie and look for anything on the Windstrikers."

"Of course," Amina replied. "We will search the vault and see if we find any items that we can use with the Zakhar."

"What do you want me to do?" Vince asked.

"Make sure Bau is ready for tonight and that he doesn't leave us going solo."

Tim pointed toward the burlap sack. "What about the Testimony?"

"We need to hide it from the Cherub *and* Merikh." Jack slipped the sack over his shoulder. "Emma and I will take care of it, then we'll message you a place to meet up tonight."

"I feel like we should huddle or something," Vince said. "It's like pregame."

"We've been in the game for months." Tim nudged his glasses up the bridge of his nose. "This is way bigger than the Battle of the Bashers, Bowlers, and Boundaries."

"Okay, we know what to do. Use Messagezilla if anything goes wrong or if you find something important." Everyone nodded, then Jack headed for the double doors with Emma by his side. "We will need the faction's help if we're going to survive."

"I understand." Emma leaned in close and gently grabbed his hand as they took the stairs down to the basement. "Eliška told me about your bloody nose."

"I'm feeling better. Nothing to worry about."

"Why do you think the Elders trusted Addison with Dragon Soul?"

Jack stopped in front of the stone wall in the basement. "He was a better man back then."

"Explains why your mum fell in love with him."

"That's the only answer that makes sense, but it doesn't explain what changed."

"Love has a way of bringing light into dark places." Emma stopped abruptly, then pulled Jack near enough to kiss him on the lips. "A great light shines within you, Jack."

His cheeks flushed. "Love makes you do crazy things."

62

A SHORT BRISK WALK FROM Cheung Sha Wan Station brought Jack and Emma to Eagle's Nest. Hidden in the dense trees, they escaped the barricades and patrolling HKPF vehicles. The last time they'd hiked the narrow trail, Jack's body was shredded and his mind was jumbled. As they trekked up the mountain, his muscles were stronger than the weeks before—still, he knew Eden's Star was wearing down whatever time he had left.

"Will you be okay if Bau becomes the next Cherub leader?" Jack asked.

"Ever since I was young, those around me believed it was my destiny." Emma picked up the pace as they neared a lookout point. "But my destiny is wherever Elyon leads me."

On most days, the trails along the ridge were scattered with

Hong Kongers and tourists hiking to the top to enjoy the panoramic views stretching from the New Territories to the Kowloon Peninsula, all the way to Hong Kong Island. Once they reached the lookout point, they paused to take in the views for themselves—as breathtaking during the day as after dark.

"Why did Eden's Star bring us back to Sham Shui Po?" Jack asked. "I know I said it flashed in my mind, but now I'm wondering why the compass guided us there."

"Neither one of us knows how to control it." Emma grew quiet for a moment. "What Elyon created for good is oftentimes used for the wrong reasons. The Elders were warned not to search for Eden's Star or the artifacts—Peter was the first one to disobey, and Charlotte followed not long after. Now we know they were not the last."

"We're disobeying the Cherub too, but how else are we supposed to stop the Merikh?"

"Elyon is keeping us alive for a purpose. Maybe we will find another way forward."

"It would be nice if Eden's Star were easier to understand and control." He stepped back from the granite cliff. "If you ask me, there've been too many secrets and not enough truth."

With the day growing hotter and more humid, they hiked along the northern slope until they reached a landmark known by most Hong Kongers as Amah Rock. Chinese folklore passed down through the generations recounted the legend of a woman whose husband traveled across the seas to provide for his family. Every day the woman climbed to the top of the mountain with her baby strapped to her back and waited for her husband's return, never knowing he'd drowned in the ocean. She waited so long on top of the mountain that she turned to stone with her baby, and their spirits were reunited with her husband in the hereafter.

Jack had heard the story before and thought nothing of it. As he stood in front of Amah Rock now, though, he wondered if there was another side to the fable of the statue. He thought about Rachel, his mom, and Addison—a family torn apart when a father's heart had turned to stone. Since the rainy day when he stood beside Rachel's grave in Sitio Veterans, the miraculous and terrifying had fought against each other within this world and other realms.

Why would he leave the Cherub to inflict such pain on Mom and us? What turned his soul toward such evil? Elyon, I don't understand, but I'm afraid I'll end up like him.

"Tell me we're not going to become statues or be buried six feet under," Jack said.

"Elyon will never leave us or forsake us—above or beneath the ground."

"I guess that'll have to be good enough," Jack mused. "Honestly, it's not totally comforting."

"Far too many followers of Elyon have grown comfortable with certainty."

"Well, at least we know we haven't been guilty of that."

Jack swiveled his head to make sure they were alone, then pulled up his sleeve and watched Soulweaver uncurl from his forearm and stretch to its full length. He stepped around the side of Amah Rock, picked a spot, and dug the point of Soulweaver into the dirt. A surge of energy rushed through his fingers. The earth beneath his boots shifted enough to create a narrow but fairly deep hole. He slipped the burlap sack off his shoulders, then hesitated.

He carefully removed the acacia box from the sack and set the Testimony onto the dirt. With his chest burning, he gently opened the lid and dipped the point of Soulweaver inside. As he touched the bottom of the Testimony, the Rod of Elyon coiled as it had done around his forearm, and lay flat inside the box.

"It shifts shape to fit inside," he whispered. "I wonder if that's the same for the others."

"One of the etchings on the side is moving." Emma pointed. "And glowing."

Jack eyed the waving branches of a tree engraved on the acacia box. It was now glowing emerald. He looked closer and realized there were other emblems he hadn't noticed before—but none of them were moving. *Lion. Temple. Deer. Serpent. Wolf. Ship. And the tree. Each represents one of the Seven Tribes of Cherub. How could I have missed these? I wasn't looking close enough.* He retrieved Soulweaver from the Testimony, and the rod wrapped around his forearm once again.

"It seems when an artifact is placed inside, one of the tribes comes alive," Jack said.

"No others are shifting," Emma agreed. "That will only happen when more artifacts are returned."

Jack slipped the Testimony back inside the burlap sack and pulled the string tight. He gently placed it into the pit. Emma extended her hands, and the mound of dirt shifted, covering the Testimony as if the earth had never been disturbed.

"We are the only ones who know it is here," Emma said.

"In a perfect world, when this is over, the artifacts will be back where they belong, Eden's Star will somehow leave my body, and life will return to normal."

"Is that what you want—to be normal?"

"Not sure I've ever been," he chuckled. "Might be fun to give it a try, though."

Emma smiled warmly. "Okay, normal it is."

On the trail down the mountain, Jack's shoulders were lighter now that he'd unloaded the Testimony. He enjoyed the ease of being with Emma. When they were in Karachi, there were many days he thought his heart was going to stop beating because of Eden's Star. Emma had stayed to watch over him, along with the others. She never complained, and she waited by his side even when it seemed they were going nowhere.

Another thirty minutes and Jack's shirt was drenched in sweat, but he didn't care. When they reached the street, they headed in the opposite direction from where they'd first arrived. They waited at a bus stop until the number 81 double-decker pulled over to the curb. Slipping into a row of seats, they kept their eyes glued to the other passengers as the bus headed toward West Kowloon. Bumper-to-bumper traffic and four additional checkpoints left them arriving in Tsim Sha Tsui later than expected.

Jack and Emma made their way from the bus terminus to H Zentre. They entered the marble-floored lobby without attracting any attention. Instead of heading toward the main elevators, they searched the lobby until they found a private elevator near a stairwell. Jack retrieved the metal card Ren had given them and tapped it against a key card reader. The elevator doors opened, and they wasted no time slipping inside.

"This is definitely easier than walking up seventeen floors." Jack tapped his index finger against his temple. "I've learned a few things since all this hiking, walking, and running started."

"Do you think your father will be here this early?"

"Not a chance. He'll want to make an entrance after all the guests have arrived."

Ding.

Jack and Emma stepped out of the elevator and walked toward Aqua—a five-star restaurant with opulent decor and a floor-to-ceiling glass wall framing a perfect view of Victoria Harbour and the historic skyline of Hong Kong Island. The bar was covered in polished brass, and outside were two expansive terraces where world-class Italian-Japanese fusion cuisine was served to high-profile clientele.

A Chinese man in his early thirties approached in a perfectly tailored black suit. "I am afraid we are closed for a private event."

"Um . . . we're looking for Ren Lai's cousin," Jack said awkwardly.

"And you have found him." He eyed them suspiciously. "Who might you be?"

"We're friends with Ren, that's all." Jack showed him the metal card. "Can you help us?"

"Your father is not one to cross," the man replied in a lowered voice. "As I am sure you are well aware."

"All we need is five minutes to see the relics for the event tonight."

"Ren told me about your sister. He respects you for what you are doing."

The Chinese man turned around and led them between the tables and booths, then cut through a commercial kitchen where a chef barked orders at prep cooks who sliced and diced with their eyes focused on their stations. Behind the kitchen, a hallway led further within the depths of Aqua to a solid steel door.

"You cannot touch." He punched in a security code on a digital panel and the door hissed open. Before he swung the door wider, he glanced over his shoulder. "Do you understand?"

"We just want to take a look," Jack answered. "You have our word."

Lights blinked on as they entered a secured room. A black silky material covered whatever was on top of a rolling display table. Warmth spread across Jack's chest as his fingers tingled. *I know what that means—something big is underneath.*

Ren's cousin removed the black silk and revealed a single relic behind inch-thick glass. "A breilium wall shield used by warriors in battle to protect their entire body."

Jack nodded toward the engraved dragon. "Slybourne's crest."

"Is it one of the artifacts?" Emma asked under her breath.

"My chest is on fire, so I'm betting the answer is yes." Jack turned and faced Ren's cousin. "All we want is to return the shield to its rightful place."

63

ONE BLOCK OVER FROM THE HOLIDAY INN, Jack and Emma emerged from the MTR station tucked away on a narrow street. With both hands, Jack carried a wrapped package the size of a large framed picture. Near the historic Hong Kong Exchange and CMB Wing Lung Bank, they cut down Bristol Avenue, surrounded by high-rise buildings.

"Are you sure the Cherub can help Ren and his cousin?" Sweat dripped down Jack's spine as they stopped outside of Mirador Mansions, directly across from a Starbucks. "They're both taking a huge risk—and their lives will never be the same."

"There is an underground network that helps those needing to disappear." Emma's cell buzzed. She read a message from Faizan. "Patel Custom Tailors."

Jack eyed the signage along the storefronts but didn't see the name. Clothes dried on bamboo poles jutting out of open windows from the apartments above. He guessed the tailor shop was somewhere in the underground shopping center, whose businesses included Kung Fu Garden and Time Travel Agency. The deeper they went into the heart of the building, the tighter the space between stores became. Emma pointed ahead at a plain sign that read, "Patel Custom Tailors—Est. 1928."

A bell chimed as they entered the shop. From behind a curtain, an elderly Indian man appeared with pins sticking out from his vest and a measuring tape draped over his shoulders. Jack set the wrapped package down and leaned it against a row of fabrics. His fingers ached from gripping the package so tight. The tailor shuffled past, locked the door, then pulled the blinds down.

Salomeh Gashkori emerged from behind the curtain and stopped a few feet away. The first time Jack had met Salomeh, she was ready to throw him to the Cherub with no mercy. In Kati Pahari, she'd worn an embroidered tunic and a pair of jhumkas in her ears. He stared at her plain shirt and jeans, which made her seem less regal. But the flicker in her brown eyes was unchanged. Salomeh didn't step any closer. Instead she motioned for the elderly man to leave them.

"Word has traveled of your return," Salomeh said. "Cherub *and* Merikh are aware."

"Made it back yesterday, which was a definite miracle." Jack nodded toward the wrapped package. "We're not the only ones who found one of the artifacts."

Salomeh stepped forward and ripped the packaging away to reveal Slybourne's shield. Her fingers ran over the engraved crest of a fire-breathing dragon. Jack wondered what she was thinking. He had another surprise waiting.

"Addison found the breilium shield," Emma said. "We do not know how or where."

"We stole it," Jack added, a bit proud of himself. "He'll go nuclear when he finds out."

"The shield is not breilium—it is dretium and is in pristine condition, which means it was never in battle. Dretium has not been unearthed for centuries. It is believed to have been created by Elyon at the earth's core." Salomeh lifted the shield and laid it on a glass counter atop a display filled with folded silk ties. "In ancient writings apart from the Testimony, before the Battle of Everest, it is believed Ryder Slybourne and Florence Upsdell took more—but not all—of their treasures from Sakkhela and hid them in the Exodus Mines."

"A dretium shield would definitely count as one of their treasures," Emma added.

"And Headmaster Upsdell didn't find the treasure on Everest when he found Dragon Soul," Jack pointed out. "Do you know where the Exodus Mines are?"

"It has long been rumored one of the Elders discovered their location." Salomeh gripped the shield with both hands. "Dabria confided in me once how she believed Peter found the mines using Eden's Star and gained access with Dragon Soul. Rumors suggest others within the highest Cherub know of its whereabouts."

"Peter took Eden's Star from the Elders," Emma said. "He did not have Dragon Soul."

"The Elders trusted Addison to be keeper of the sword." In utter disbelief, Jack ran his fingers through his hair while his mind spun a thousand miles per second. As his eyes darted between

Emma and Salomeh, he was struck with a revelation. "Peter and Addison found the Exodus Mines together."

"It is possible," Salomeh confessed.

"Another reason why the Mercy Covenant was broken," Emma suggested.

"Addison was never one of the Cherub," Salomeh corrected. "He was an outlier."

"But what if Peter used Eden's Star to find the Exodus Mines for himself?" Jack countered. "The Elders broke the Mercy Covenant, just like we've been trying to tell you. Now Addison has Dragon Soul, and he's returned to the mines."

"Where did Peter hide the treasure he stole?" Emma asked. "I have heard nothing."

"A dangerous question to ask the highest Cherub, including Fang Xue." Salomeh eyed Jack close, and he sensed her curiosity. "Harley said you found something in the Highlands, but she would not say what it was exactly."

"We made it to the Valley of Grace." He pulled up his sleeve, and Soulweaver unwrapped from around his arm. He was growing used to the supernatural movement as it straightened again into a full-length rod. "Elyon's Vine was dead when we reached Charis, but then the tree returned to life when the Rod of Elyon revealed itself—and Asiklua was restored as an angelic being."

"You speak of a fallen warrior from the Nephilim king's army," she said cautiously. "Once a mighty legion were under Asiklua's command. They stood at the right hand of Elyon until their darkened souls left them banished from Charis."

"Asiklua was tormented with Soulweaver, but it was the Rod of Elyon that freed him."

"First Eden's Star, then the Rod of Elyon." Salomeh shook her head slowly. "And you have taken Slybourne's shield from Addison. Remarkable. There is no denying your tenacity."

"We are also searching for the Windstrikers," Emma interrupted. "We believe they are artifacts once kept in the Testimony. We are not sure where to begin the search, though."

"The Highlands reach from Sakkhela to Charis—perhaps beyond—which means there may be other artifacts hidden along the Silk Road within the Golden Triangle. To my knowledge, you have journeyed farther than any Cherub or Elder through the Highlands and survived."

You don't know how right you are, Salomeh. We stood on the very edge.

"We know how many artifacts there are," Jack blurted. "One for each tribe of Cherub."

Salomeh's eyes narrowed as she turned Slybourne's shield over. Jack peered over her shoulder as she pointed to one corner of the dretium where the head of a lion with a great mane was engraved. His heartbeat quickened as he exchanged glances with Emma, knowing they'd now confirmed two of the seven artifacts.

"The question remains," Salomeh said. "How many have the Merikh found already?"

Jack reached into his pocket and retrieved the photo of his mom and Xui Li from Sitio Veterans, hoping Salomeh was warming up to them. *She needs to see we're on the same side and she can trust us.* He handed the photo over and watched as she studied it closely.

"The Nephilim king killed my mom," Jack began. "Charlotte Taylor and Peter Leung are dead. The Merikh have captured Xui Li and possibly Dabria too. If the Elders hold the answers to finding more of the artifacts, then we need to figure out where they are being held and rescue them."

"We have been unable to locate Dabria or Xui Li, and the news I received yesterday confirmed Vigan remains abandoned."

"You may not believe what happened on Mount Hareh, but you can see Elyon is guiding our steps. We're risking our lives to stop this war from killing even more."

"If Addison pillaged the mines, he must keep the treasure in a secure location." Salomeh crossed her arms and shifted her gaze between them. "Which is another reason why you are here, isn't it?"

"Eden's Star is a compass to the artifacts, which means we won't know whether any of the treasure taken or kept in the Exodus Mines can be used as a weapon until we find the treasure and see for ourselves."

"Which makes your quest an impossible one," Salomeh retorted. "Unless you are able to find where it is your father has hidden his bounty, you will continue searching in the dark."

"With any luck, we'll also find where Peter kept his riches." Jack squeezed Soulweaver, and the rod shrank before wrapping around his forearm. "In the Temple of the Nephilim, I made a promise, and I'm not going to stop until it's done. I know you don't trust me—at least not completely—but being here is a way for me to show you we are on the same side."

"Salomeh," Emma chimed in. "You know my parents, and who I am. I would be dead if it were not for Jack, and I would not be standing by his side if I didn't believe what he is saying."

"I have a theory about where Peter kept his riches," Salomeh confessed.

"Does that mean you're going to help us?"

"Harley is right—you are quite unpredictable. So we will see."

Salomeh walked over to the closed curtain and poked her head behind it. A few seconds passed before the elderly Indian man reappeared and went straight to work on Jack.

While the man poked and prodded, Jack stood like a tree with wide branches, afraid to move for fear of being stuck by a pin or stabbed with scissors. He glanced at Emma, unsure why he was being measured. He expected Emma to share his concern, but instead she stood beside Salomeh with a wide grin on the verge of bursting into laughter.

"Boys always have that same look the first time," Salomeh mused.

"He looks like a porcupine," Emma laughed. "So many needles."

"Glad to see the two of you are enjoying the show." He shifted his weight, and the elderly man stuck him with a pin, most likely on purpose. "Ouch!"

64

Jack and Emma returned to the apartment building rooftop by late afternoon and found Eliška busy on her cell phone. He wasn't sure how much to share, but he knew she was taking the same risk. Unzipping his hoodie, he decided she deserved to know as much as possible. He tossed his hoodie over the back of a chair while Soulweaver remained wrapped around his forearm.

"We moved the Testimony from Nightingale's vault," Jack said. "Headmaster Fargher and Natalie showed me proof of another artifact—Windstrikers lost since the Age of Trepidation. Lethal war fans that ended up in Nightingale's possession."

"Slybourne's shield was also found by the Merikh," Emma added. "We nicked it earlier."

"Vince texted about Shelter Island," Eliška replied. "Professor

Burwick knows someone who can help us at Star Ferry, which was reopened a few days ago. We will meet at ten o'clock."

"That's good news," Jack replied, excited. "Tonight we take the fight to them."

"Professor Burwick has decided the faction will not be going with us."

"What?" Jack blurted. "I thought she was all for attacking the Merikh."

"She is concerned you have not proven to the faction you have a thoughtful strategy."

"I'm totally confused." Jack froze. "Even Bau is going to be there, and he hates me."

"Professor Burwick has spoken with Salomeh. A decision was reached to keep the lightforcers and benders at Beacon Hill. With the highest Cherub and Merikh searching for you, neither are willing to take the risk without more planning."

"Last night Burwick said tomorrow is a new day to fight."

Eliška shook her head. "Honestly, I am as shocked as the two of you."

"They don't think we will make it," Emma surmised. "Even after all that has happened."

"If we rescue the Cherub tonight, we will have a better chance to convince those within the faction." Eliška glanced toward Emma. "And possibly the Cherub will change their minds."

Jack harnessed his anger, knowing there was only one decision to be made. A bunch of teenagers attempting to face off with Addison and the Merikh was totally insane. But leaving the Cherub on Shelter Island at the mercy of his father was deranged.

"We're still on our own—and it doesn't sound like that's going to change."

"If we stay together, we have a chance," Emma said. "That is good enough for me."

"We've found Eden's Star, Soulweaver, and Slybourne's shield without their help."

"Where is Slybourne's shield?" Eliška asked. "It is not with you."

"Looks like we're all hedging our bets." Jack was doing exactly the same as Professor Burwick, Salomeh, and the highest Cherub. "We left the shield with someone we hope will be an ally if everything goes south. Hopefully we didn't make a mistake."

Eliška's eyes narrowed. "You do not trust the faction or the Cherub."

"Can you blame me? Look at where they've left us."

"Keeping the artifacts and the Testimony separated protects them from falling into the hands of the Merikh," Emma explained to Eliška. "We will use the artifacts to defend the innocent, and when this war ends, those artifacts will be hidden from the faction and the Cherub as well."

"If Eden's Star helps us find the rest of the artifacts," Jack reiterated, "we'll put the artifacts inside and return the Testimony to Charis." He nodded toward Eliška. "You are part of the faction, Emma is a Cherub, and I'm an outlier. Whichever one of us is left standing must swear to make sure it's done."

"I am with you," Emma reassured. "Until the end."

Eliška replied, "So am I."

"It's a miracle I got the two of you to agree." Jack stepped away, knowing he'd chiseled the ice between Emma and Eliška. He grabbed three Vitasoys from a small refrigerator, then popped the caps and handed one to each of the girls. "Let Elyon's peace rule in our hearts as a lion."

"We will never be alone if we put our trust in him," Emma agreed.

"I never thought this is where he would lead me," Eliška admitted. "But I am ready."

Jack took a swig from the bottle, and instantly his muscles were paralyzed. The bottle slipped from his rigid fingers and shattered against the rooftop. His legs buckled, and his eyes rolled back into his head. A barrage of flashes blinded him, and he struggled to regain control of his limbs. His mind remained sharp as a memory buried deep surfaced in a haunting vision.

Rachel's disheveled hair draped over her slender body as she crawled across a stained mattress inside a dingy and shadowed room. Tears streaked down her cheeks, and her lips quivered as she stared at him.

"He is coming," she whispered.

A chill shot through him and shuddered his bones. Rachel struggled to push the mattress a few inches closer to the wall, then reached her hand underneath. Jack wanted to speak, but the words refused to leave his lips. Instead, he kept his gaze locked on Rachel. He stood and stepped across the mattress so he could look over her shoulder. Her fingers pried a piece of the baseboard loose and exposed a hole in the wall. From beneath the mattress, Rachel retrieved a slim wooden box, and with shaking hands she pushed the box inside the wall and replaced the loose piece of baseboard.

Footsteps echoed in the hallway, sending Rachel scurrying across the mattress. She pushed the edge of the mattress up against the wall to hide the baseboard, then stood between Jack and the door with fists clenched. A lock clicked, and the doorknob turned. Seconds later, the door swung open, and Addison burst into the room with rage burning in his eyes. With a shriek, Rachel lunged at Addison and the world turned dark.

A searing pain ripped down Jack's spine. He was on his back, and his body convulsed as if he'd been electrocuted. Emma and Eliška, on their knees, hovered over him. Emma wasted no time. She placed her hand on him, and a warmth spread through his body. His heartbeat slowed until he was able to catch his breath. Eliška left them and returned a moment later with a towel in her hand. She placed the towel over his nose, and when she pulled it back, he recognized the crimson stain.

Emma leaned in close. "Breathe, Jack."

65

TSIM SHA TSUI

A FLEET OF BLACK SUVs PULLED UP to the entrance of H Zentre. Addison climbed out from the back seat of the armored-tank SUV wearing a thousand-dollar suit and a bright-red silk tie. He was immediately surrounded by his security detail as he walked briskly through the lobby. On the ride up the private elevator, he thought about how quickly Charlotte had been forgotten. For decades she'd ruled the Merikh with an iron fist and a forked tongue. He adjusted his tie and relished the moment until the doors opened on the seventeenth floor.

Addison expected to be greeted, but when he stepped out of the elevator he was surprised to find the hallway empty. He approached the glass doors of the restaurant as his security closed in around him. One of his guards pushed the glass doors open, then stepped back.

"Wait here," Addison ordered. "All of you."

The restaurant was dark. No waiters. No chefs. No one. He had been specific with Aqua's manager down to the last detail and had decided to arrive early to be certain everything was in order. He'd demanded the most expensive wines from Italy and the freshest sushi from Japan. He eyed the empty tables and outdoor patio, attempting to make sense of what was going on. The guests were due to arrive within an hour—top government officials who loved to be wined and dined.

In one corner was the display with the oversize black box. It was his prize to show off to the chief executive of Hong Kong before delivering a stern warning. If she refused to cooperate, she would be deemed unnecessary by the PRC. After months of infiltrating the HKPF, bribing politicians, threatening the one percent, and causing chaos across the city, he was prepared to unleash even more against the only democracy left within China's reign. He lifted the lid of the black box and peered inside. It was empty—Slybourne's shield was missing. Rage flowed through his veins.

"We both have underestimated him, Addison."

He spun around to see the Cherub leader, Fang Xue. "Where is the shield?"

"I do not know, but it is not in our possession." She stepped closer. "You know the sins your son has committed against the Cherub."

"I am the one who told you about Mount Hareh, and in return you confirmed Dragon Soul was the only way to kill an Elder." Addison relished the game, and he lied effortlessly. "I was as shocked as anyone when Jack shot Peter point-blank without mercy. No matter, the results are the same—the great Cherub lie you wished to be rid of is buried."

"My hope was to restore the Cherub and end the Merikh. You were necessary."

"You are a reflection of the great Elder, willing to cross the line in the name of Elyon." Addison chuckled. "And now I sit on the Merikh throne."

"Jack has gone against the Eternal by searching for what Elyon commanded remain hidden. Now he has stolen a prized possession from you, which was never yours to keep."

"Like father, like son," Addison seethed. "Why are you here, Fang?"

"With the Mercy Covenant broken, a truce must be negotiated to protect our interests."

"I hold all the power. Besides, if my sources are worth their price, you are surrendering your role to a boy." Addison's contempt was thick. "Many of the Cherub are imprisoned by the Merikh, and after tonight there will be countless more. You come to me begging for mercy—a weakness of the Cherub."

"Peter once told me there was a time when you faced a choice: surrender yourself to the Cherub or remain an outlier." Fang Xue paused. "You were once strong enough to wield Dragon Soul, to become a great warrior for the Cherub."

"And did he also confess what it was he asked me to do?" Addison's stare hardened. "I have seen more than you realize."

"When you and Gabriella were together, your eyes witnessed at least one of the artifacts she found. Yet you have turned your soul against Elyon, and there will come a day when you will pay for your sins."

Addison's jaw clenched. "Everything was taken from me."

"You asked me where the shield was hidden." Fang Xue's lips pursed. "I have told you the truth; however, I do know who took it from you—your flesh and blood. In fact, I believe he has found several of the artifacts while you have only found one."

"Believe me, more than one is in my possession." Addison deceived with ease as he harnessed his contempt, knowing the truth was never black-and-white. "Your best offer is to prevent mutual destruction, but you will not admit the Cherub have already lost this war."

"Peter shared another part of your story with me." Fang Xue glanced over her shoulder, ensuring the guards remained on the other side of the glass doors. "On the night Gabriella attempted to retrieve Dragon Soul from you, she was left near death from her wounds. Your strength to protect Dragon Soul was weakened, so in order to save yourself you gave the sword to Peter—who then returned Dragon Soul to Beacon Hill. Peter chose someone else to watch over Dragon Soul more than once—and the most recent will one day become our most powerful. However, when Gabriella survived your attack, she was determined to hunt you. Again, to save yourself you agreed to spare your children and keep the Mercy Covenant alive for your own survival."

"Gabriella and the Cherub betrayed me," Addison refuted. "The Mercy Covenant was broken long before Fortress Hill or the great Elder's death, but you refuse to accept it. Are you certain you can believe the tales woven by Peter?" Addison kept his secrets close, including his knowledge of Eden's Star flowing through Jack's veins. "I assure you, when more of the artifacts are in my possession, you will see how dark this world can become."

"Why have you not used the artifact you stole from Gabriella?" Fang Xue's eyes flared. "I see, your gifts are not strong enough, or perhaps the artifact is no longer in your possession. Addison, balance is needed to restore a covenant between Cherub and Merikh. You will not survive if the full power of the artifacts is unleashed against you."

"I will make you an offer: surrender to me and there will be peace."

"You lost Dragon Soul, it seems to me you have lost the artifact Gabriella once discovered, and now Slybourne's shield has vanished." Fang Xue showed no sign of backing down. "Perhaps you are not as dangerous as everyone believes."

"I am neither Cherub nor Merikh, so I am far more lethal than both."

"A war between Cherub and Merikh will destroy this world and unleash the other realms. If you accept a truce, you and I will divide the artifacts between us to ensure there is balance." Fang Xue hesitated. "And if you agree, then when we capture your son, judgment will be yours."

"I will consider it." Addison eyed her closely. "What else, Fang?"

"Tonight, he is going to Shelter Island."

66

TSIM SHA TSUI

DOUBLE-DECKERS AND TAXIS LINED the depot across from the Clock Tower, one block from The Peninsula, which remained under construction after the extensive damage caused during the riots. Some Hong Kongers waited in long lines for buses, while others used their Octopus cards and pushed through turnstiles, heading for the end of the pier. Everyone hurried to get off the streets before the HKPF and Merikh increased the nightly patrols in their districts.

Jack, Emma, and Eliška blended in with locals, expats, and tourists near a twenty-four-hour McDonald's that was shut down. Jack eyed the sidewalk until he caught sight of Vince, Tim, and Amina headed in their direction.

"And then there were six," he whispered.

"I think Bau bailed on us." Tim fist-bumped Jack. "Not surprised—he is a total melt."

"Guarding Beacon Hill is as important as what we are doing," Emma defended. "Especially since more and more Cherub are arriving."

"Hey, Eliška." Vince smiled. "Wasn't sure you'd be here."

"Of course," she answered. "Where else would I be?"

Jack turned toward Amina and Tim. "Your parents are good with all of this?"

"Better to ask forgiveness than permission." Amina held up her phone. "Might be a good opportunity to film another message from Emma."

"If we make it through," Tim replied. "Either way, I guess it will be epic."

"Isn't Emma out of the running for Cherub leader?" Vince asked.

"Until the ceremony, there is a chance to change minds," Amina replied.

"So what's the plan?" Tim asked Jack. "You do have a plan, right?"

"There hasn't been a plan since the clock stopped at Beacon Hill." Jack pointed toward the Clock Tower. "And when the bell rose with Nightingale's drawing glowing in gold."

"The captain is waiting," Eliška reminded them.

"Okay." Jack's muscles tensed as he focused on keeping his wits about him. "We're doing this."

He stayed with Tim and Vince while Emma, Eliška, and Amina walked ahead. There was something encouraging about being together even though no one knew how the night might end. *We're totally outnumbered, but we do have Emma, Eden's Star, and Soulweaver. That has to increase our odds.* Slipping through the turnstiles, Jack felt more determined to preserve his faith in Elyon.

Tim nudged Jack. "Seems like the two of them are getting on better."

"They're from two different worlds, but they're also after the same peace."

"Jack, you do have a plan, right?" Vince asked. "I mean, this is totally insane."

"I'm working on it."

Soulweaver tightened around his forearm, reminding him of the scars on both arms from the City of Gods. He followed Eliška and the others as they headed in the opposite direction from the passengers waiting to board the last ferry to Hong Kong Island. Ducking beneath a chain, they veered down a ramp and boarded another ferry as the only passengers. As soon as Vince pulled the walking plank up and secured the rope, the ferry eased away from the pier.

The ferry navigated east and drifted across Victoria Harbour at a snail's pace. Hong Kong Island's skyline sparkled with bright lights reflecting off calm waters. Jack leaned against the railing and stared at the stunning beauty of the city. *How are we going to get everyone off the island? Think, Jack. And if we do get them onto the ferry by some miracle, then what happens?* He stayed quiet as the ferry passed through Junk Bay and rounded the corner of Tung Lung Island.

In the pitch-black, spotlights surrounded barbed wire fencing on Shelter Island. All the lights on the ferry turned off as water lapped against the hull. Jack played through the scenarios, and each ended with them being caught—except for one.

"Message Bau and tell him we need transportation near Hiu Po Path in Clear Water Bay," Jack said to Emma. "He needs to keep it quiet from the Cherub, but it needs to happen." He turned toward the others. "Tim and Amina will stay aboard and get ready to take care of those we bring back. See if you can find any blankets to use. Vince, Eliška, Emma, and I will take the life raft." He eyed Amina and Tim closely. "If we get caught, tell the captain to leave."

"Sounds simple enough," Vince said. "Let's get going."

While Tim and Amina started their blanket patrol, Vince headed to the back of the ferry and found an inflatable life raft secured inside a compartment. He grabbed the raft and carried it over to the railing. He'd sailed the seas before with his parents, so he was clearly at ease and in his element. Before tossing the flattened watercraft overboard, he pulled the cord. A few seconds passed as the raft inflated fully and rolled with the current. Vince climbed over the railing and down a ladder before stepping on as if he'd done it a thousand times. Emma and Eliška went next, leaving Jack as the last one.

Emma placed her hand into the water, and the raft moved forward without any oars. Silence enveloped them as the life raft headed straight for Shelter Island. Jack glanced over his shoulder, barely able to see the ferry drifting behind. Vince's brows raised as he noticed a glow surrounding Emma's hand beneath the surface of the water. Jack pulled up his sleeve, and Soulweaver unwrapped from around his forearm. He gripped the rod tight, unsure of the magnitude of power it possessed but hoping to put it to the test.

"When we reach the shore, we'll get through the fence and split up to look for those who are able to move," Jack said. "Emma and Eliška, you stay together, and I'll go with Vince. Once we load up the raft, Emma will bring them to the ferry. The three of us will search for more prisoners until she returns."

A few moments later, Emma lifted her hand from the water

and the raft slid onto a rocky beach. Vince jumped out first and pulled the raft further onshore. Jack, Emma, and Eliška helped carry the raft into a cave, then Eliška led the way as they climbed to the top of a rocky hillside. Crouched low in the overgrown brush, Jack watched bright spotlights swoop across barracks in the prison camp and along the fence line. From a distance, he counted half a dozen armed men patrolling.

"Okay," Jack whispered. "Ready?"

67

JACK COUNTED THE SECONDS between the spotlight's beam passing in front of them. *Ten, maybe eleven.* He gripped Soulweaver and motioned to the others. As soon as the spotlight swooped by the next time, all four darted toward the fence line. Emma's palm glowed as she grabbed the fence, allowing the lightforce to melt the metal and leave a hole large enough to climb through. Before the spotlight rounded again, they split up in pairs.

Jack and Vince headed down a row of barracks, keeping to the shadows. Jack remembered how easily Emma had unlocked the Clock Tower, which left him questioning whether splitting up was a good idea. *You're not the strategist, Jack. You're an improviser.* He gripped Soulweaver and pointed the rod toward one of the barracks, touching the tip against the door.

"What're you doing?" Vince asked.

"Thought I'd give it a try. No owner's manual, remember."

"And you picked tonight to test-drive the Rod of Elyon?"

Jack heard voices and ducked with Vince between the barracks. With their backs pressed against the wall, they waited as guards with semiautomatic weapons strolled past.

"This is a bad idea," he whispered. "One of my worst yet."

"We're in it now, Jack. Step it up."

"Right, let's give this another shot." Jack slipped out from the darkness and approached the barracks door for a second time. He whispered, "Elyon, only you can open this door."

He tapped Soulweaver gently against the wood. A clicking noise rang in his ears before the lock shifted and dropped to the ground. He glanced around, expecting to be tackled by an army of Merikh. Vince was right on his shoulder as he pushed the door open and entered. Inside, rows of people lay on the floor with barely enough space to walk between them.

Not wanting to wake the whole room and cause a loud panic, he knelt beside a woman who was asleep. His heart pounded through his chest as he reached out to squeeze her shoulder. Her eyes opened wide, immediately terrified. Jack held his index finger to his lips.

He whispered, "Do you speak English?"

"Yes." She nodded. "I speak."

"We are here to help you. Wake everyone and get ready to leave."

The woman hesitated for a few more seconds before she realized he was serious. Quietly, she rolled onto her knees, then scurried across the floor waking one person after another. Most were confused, but Vince helped her gather everyone into a group.

"Okay, now what?" Vince asked.

"How far under the island do you think the cave we found goes?"

"No idea—that's the plan?"

"I guess we're about to find out."

Jack stabbed Soulweaver into the dirt as the captives watched. The dirt swirled as if being pierced by a drill. He felt the vibration flow from Soulweaver through his fingers and up both arms. He held on tight as the hole grew wider and deeper. Gasps broke the silence as he sank underground. The rod pierced the earth until it broke through the island rock. Jack dropped into darkness and landed on his feet. A strong ocean breeze whistled around him.

"Jack, where are you?" Vince said in a hushed tone from above.

"I'm inside the cave," he answered. "It's the way out."

"Okay, hang on."

Jack took a moment to catch his breath while adrenaline surged through him. Finally, he'd done something right. As he stood beneath the fresh hole, something slapped him in the face. He jumped back, afraid he was being attacked, then grabbed at what was dangling down from the hole. He realized it was a rope made of clothes tied together. *Way to go, Vince. You always find a way to win.* One by one, the captives climbed down into the cave. Jack helped each one land on their feet, and he motioned for them to wait.

Vince whispered loud enough for Jack to hear. "Last one."

"There's too many to take at one time in the life raft," Jack muttered. Then he approached the woman he'd woken minutes earlier. "Take everyone to the entrance of the cave, understand?"

"Yes, I understand."

While she motioned for the rest of the group to follow her, Jack released his tight grip on Soulweaver, and the rod wrapped back around his forearm. He took hold of the homemade rope and pulled himself up. Vince grabbed his hand and yanked him into the barracks.

"That's one down," Vince said. "What about Emma and Eliška?"

"Guard our escape route, and I'll go find them."

Jack slipped out of the barracks and darted across to the opposite side. When he heard voices approaching, he ducked between buildings and held his breath. He was relieved when the guards passed by without noticing the broken lock. With his head on a swivel, he reached the next row. A door opened, and Eliška poked her head out. Jack waved at her until she saw him. She opened the door a bit wider, and more captives emerged on her heels, racing in his direction. Hiding between the buildings, the captives were in shock, but they were aware this was their only chance.

"Where's Emma?" Jack whispered.

"One minute she was next to me." Eliška shook her head. "Then she disappeared."

"Follow me." Jack led everyone between the structures until they were directly across from the original barracks. "Vince is inside. He'll show you what to do."

"There are too many for the life raft," Eliška replied. "You do know, right?"

"I'm working on it. You and Vince take this group and the ones in the cave."

"How will we use the life raft without Emma?"

Jack knew she was right, but he didn't have an answer. "Help Vince, and I'll find Emma."

He waited while Eliška directed the captives toward the barracks, most of them still disoriented. Vince cracked the door open, and the group wasted no time darting over and disappearing inside.

Jack's heart pounded rapidly, and a burning sensation tingled across his chest. *Hopefully I'm not having a heart attack.* He realized the sensation spread down his right side where Soulweaver was wrapped around his forearm.

We're not getting everyone off the island through the cave.

68

VINCE AND ELIŠKA HELPED EACH escapee down into the hole until the two of them were the only ones left. Both stood for a moment, staring at the door. The clock was ticking, and Jack and Emma were nowhere to be seen.

"We have to wait for them," Vince said. "That's what they'd do for us."

"Jack and Emma will find their way off the island." Eliška glanced toward the door again. "We have to save those who are in the cave."

Vince hesitated, torn yet determined. "Okay, let's get them off this rock."

Eliška dropped into the hole first, climbing down the rope of clothes. Vince went next, but the material ripped under his muscular frame. He landed on his feet and moved as if he were chasing down a cricket ball headed for the boundary. Everyone else followed him, including Eliška. When they reached the entrance of the cave, they found the other captives huddled together. Vince counted around fifty, then stared hard at the life raft.

"We need the ferry closer," Vince said. "Give me your cell."

Eliška handed it over, and Vince punched in a number.

On the second ring, Tim answered, "Tasty Lion."

"No time for jokes," Vince chided. "We're in the middle of a rescue."

"And you're taking the time to call me? Seriously—what's up?"

"We need the ferry closer to shore. Can you handle it?"

Tim relayed the message to Amina. "She is going upstairs to tell the captain."

Without saying goodbye, Vince disconnected the call and handed the phone back to Eliška. He grabbed the life raft and, with the help of several others, carried it down to the water's edge. Eliška divided everyone into groups and directed the first dozen toward the raft. Once the raft was packed, Vince and a few of the men pushed it deeper into the water.

"Would've been easier if I had the oars," Vince mumbled to himself.

While the men stepped back toward the shore, Vince kept a vise grip and pushed harder until his feet couldn't touch the bottom. He swam around to the front, then tugged at the raft as he fought the current. Those aboard panicked as the raft tilted, allowing water inside. Vince's breathing was labored and his muscles burned, but he pushed himself even harder. At first he didn't notice anyone swimming toward them, until Eliška emerged from the darkness. She never said a word as she grabbed hold of the raft and pulled alongside Vince. Several captives splashed in the water, attempting to paddle.

"This would be faster . . ." Eliška began.

"I know," Vince barked. "Who takes a life raft when they can't find the oars? Me, apparently."

Eliška's smile broadened. "Race you to the boat."

Waves slapped against the raft as the large shadow of the ferry blocked the moon. Tim and Amina threw a large rope overboard. Vince grabbed hold, pulled the raft toward the ferry, and tied the rope to the side of the raft once they were close. Eliška climbed up a ladder on the side of the ferry.

"Cannot believe you two swam all the way out here," Tim said, impressed.

Eliška gasped for breath. "Hundreds more . . . are waiting."

"Timothy, help Vince get them aboard." Amina wrapped a blanket over Eliška's shoulders. "After you left, we found the oars and some flares down below."

"We will need them this time around," Eliška exhaled.

The freed captives climbed the ladder and stepped onto the ferry. Many shivered from the cold and wiped tears from their eyes. Amina greeted each with a blanket and helped them find a place to rest. Tim rushed across the ferry and returned with four oars and several flares. Vince appeared on deck, soaked to the bone.

"Eliška, I never would have made it without your help," Vince said. "Thank you."

"Are you ready to go back?" she answered. "The night is young."

"Now that's what I'm talking about."

Tim handed over the oars and flares. "You two are bonkers."

"Just getting started." Vince held out his hand as if inviting Eliška to go first. "After you."

Vince and Eliška climbed overboard, disappearing down the ladder, and boarded the raft. Vince untied the rope and left it dangling over the side of the ferry. Eliška secured the oars, and the two of them paddled in unison. The raft glided swiftly through the water. Before they reached land, another group was already darting across the rocky shore. Under the moonlight, several more round trips with Vince and Eliška rowing side by side brought the rest of the captives to the ferry, where they were helped aboard.

Tim assisted Vince and Eliška as they struggled to climb the ladder after the final trip, totally winded and beyond exhausted. Vince dropped to his knees on deck and rolled onto his back. Eliška did the same. After a moment, Vince slowly pulled himself to his feet and walked over to the island side of the ferry. He stared hard as the bright spotlight continued to circle, then glanced over his shoulder at the dozens who'd been rescued. Eliška, Tim, and Amina joined him, and the four stood quiet in the dark.

Eliška was first to break the silence. "We should return to the island."

"First, we get everyone to Hiu Po Path," Vince replied. "Jack and Emma will be okay."

"I am on it." Tim pushed away from the railing and darted upstairs toward the bridge. He called over his shoulder, "Bau better be in Clear Water Bay!"

69

JACK PEERED AROUND A CORNER and caught sight of Emma, who stood outside one of the barracks. He'd searched for nearly thirty minutes—ducking, diving, and crouching behind vehicles and buildings, nearly getting caught a dozen times. On instinct, he wanted to call out her name so he didn't lose her again. She glanced around before opening the door and disappearing inside. A few seconds passed before he made his move, darting along the row of barracks. He reached the same door, turned the knob, and entered.

A white glow illuminated the room where Emma stood over someone curled up on the floor. No bunk beds. No other prisoners. Jack approached cautiously, hoping Emma didn't spin around and pulverize him with a blast of light.

"Help me get him up," she said shakily with her back to him. "Hurry."

Jack rushed over and stared down at a beaten and bloodied best friend. Will's wrists and ankles were zip-tied, and his clothes were soaked in filth. Jack swallowed the puke in his throat and reached down, gently slipping his arms beneath Will's shoulders. He lifted Will into a sitting position, sickened to see his best friend barely conscious and groaning incoherently.

"What did they do to him?" Jack asked, angered.

Emma shook her head. "We can ask these questions later."

Once they got Will on his feet, Jack and Emma carried his weight on each side and headed for the door. Jack couldn't help but imagine the torturous ways Addison had inflicted pain—the depths of evil raging against any hope for light.

"Did you find other prisoners?" Jack asked.

"Yes, they are waiting. And you?"

"Soulweaver dug a hole down to the cave beneath one of the barracks. Vince and Eliška took them to the life raft, and I'm hoping they made it off the island."

"William," Emma said softly, "hold on."

Out in the open they moved slower with a semiconscious Will between them. He stumbled along, and at times his bare feet scraped against the dirt. Emma led the way around a corner, where they saw two guards headed in their direction. A burst of light exploded from her palm, and the guards flew backward. Jack was disoriented for a moment until he realized they were heading in the opposite direction from the cave.

"Wrong way," he said. "Life raft is on the other side."

Emma never slowed until they reached a section of the fence that was torn apart, much like the fence they'd entered using

Emma's lightforce. Jack knew better than to question Emma. He picked up Will, slung him over his shoulder, and grimaced through the pain ripping down his spine. He climbed over steep rocks toward the water's edge while Emma jumped ahead, reaching a larger group who waited for them.

"There are hundreds, with no way off the island."

"Jack, use the power given to you."

At the top of the cliff a siren blared. Jack pulled up his sleeve, and Soulweaver released its coil around his arm before extending into the full rod. He gripped the rod, knowing what he planned to do but unsure whether it would work.

Jack left Will with Emma and jumped down the rocks until he stood at the shore. He dipped the rod into the water's edge. In the pitch-blackness he heard rushing waves before he noticed dry land at his feet. Emma stepped alongside him and, using her lightforce, cast a white glow directly in front of them. The waters had parted enough to reveal a narrow passageway leading to another shore.

"Get everyone moving right now," Jack urged. "You go first to light the way."

Emma hurried and directed the captives toward their freedom. Jack gripped Soulweaver as more and more people passed him in the dark. Several men carried Will through while Jack stayed behind. He waited until the last person had passed before he stepped between the towering walls of water. Gunfire erupted, bullets piercing the waves above him. Water rushed to cover the path behind him, though the passageway ahead remained open.

Chaos erupted at Hiu Po Path when hundreds of people emerged from the water. Locals lounging near the beach late at night were awestruck. At the end of the path, Bau and Amina directed those who were rescued to waiting buses. Soulweaver wrapped around Jack's forearm, and he yanked his sleeve down. He noticed the ferry disappear into the night as he trudged up the sand and climbed the steps before being greeted with fist bumps by Vince and Tim.

"Blimey," Tim said, astonished. "You parted the waters."

Jack nodded at Vince and squeezed Tim's shoulder. "We did it together."

"A beaut bonza," Vince said. "I can't believe you found Will too."

"Emma found him—and I found her." Jack looked around. "Where is he?"

Vince pointed near one of the buses, where Headmaster Fargher's arms were wrapped around his son. A lump lodged in Jack's throat as he watched in silence. *We found him, and he's alive. Thank you, Elyon.* As quickly as his gratefulness struck, rage over Addison's brutality erupted in his soul. His only satisfaction came from knowing that those who stood around him were free—and stealing Slybourne's shield was worth the risk.

"Looks like they're narked at one another," Tim said in a lowered voice.

Jack followed Tim's gaze toward Emma and Eliška, who glared at each other. Buses rolled away from Hiu Po Path until only one remained. Exhausted, they all boarded and found seats near the rear. Jack pulled his hoodie over his head and closed his eyes. Emma slipped into the seat beside him and leaned her head on his shoulder.

The bus driver punched the accelerator, cutting down one narrow street after another while avoiding every checkpoint monitored by the HKPF and Merikh. Tensions remained thick until all the buses drove through the unlocked gates of Beacon Hill.

70

JACK DRAGGED HIMSELF UPSTAIRS to the second floor as Emma led the way to an empty dorm room overlooking the quad. On the bus ride, his adrenaline had subsided, and by the time he walked through the door his muscles ached. Vince was the only one who changed into dry clothes as soon as they returned to Nightingale's vault to retrieve their "ready to run" backpacks—a routine they'd started while hiding out at the hostel in Karachi.

Emma and Jack stopped in a hallway of Rowell House while Tim and Vince shuffled into the room, dropping their backpacks before collapsing on the bottom bunks.

"I am down the hall," Emma said. "Amina is staying with me."

"No more houses, I guess," Jack replied. "At least for now."

"Upsdell and Crozier are already packed with refugees from the vault, and they will most likely exceed capacity with the ones we brought from Shelter Island."

"Nightingale is where I belong." He glanced down the hallway in both directions. "Feels weird. Don't think I've been inside Rowell, ever."

"I offered for Eliška to stay with us, but she decided to return to Quarry Bay."

"You two were starting to get along, so what was with the standoff earlier?"

"On the island, we split up . . . actually, I split away from her, and she was angry." Emma hesitated, then grabbed his arm. "I sensed Will's presence, so I looked for him."

"Are you connected to him like you are to me?"

Emma squeezed his arm and shook her head. "I only felt the connection for a second."

"When you see Eliška next, you need to explain. She'll understand."

"I tried before we boarded the bus, but she refused to listen."

"You know how important it is for us to stick together. We're all we have right now."

"If she is there when we pick up our belongings tomorrow, then I will speak with her." Emma paused. "Jack, you never shared what your vision was in Quarry Bay."

"It's been a long day," he answered. "We'll talk about it tomorrow, I promise."

Emma leaned in and kissed him softly, then headed a few doors down. Jack's cheeks burned as he stepped in to find Tim and Vince sprawled out on the bottom bunks. *I wonder if they'll be rocking the room in another war of the snorers.* He wished he could go back to the days when the four of them lounged in their worn leather chairs, watching highlights from the Bashers, Bowlers, and Boundaries while stuffing their faces with rice boxes filled with barbecue pork. The only colors in this room came from the brown and gold stripes painted on one wall bearing Rowell's mascot—an owl. No leather chairs. No posters of cricket's best. No sense of home. Just a plaid sofa pushed up against one wall across from four empty desks.

Jack shuffled over to a small refrigerator and was pleasantly surprised to find a stash of Heavenly Fuel power bars and cans of Spitfire Jolt.

Maybe we're not so different after all.

"At least we are done sleeping in a dungeon," Tim said. "Even if this isn't Nightingale."

Jack tossed power bars and cans across the room to Tim and Vince, then grabbed several for himself before slumping down onto the sofa.

"Maximum caffeine." Vince downed an entire can in one gulp. "For maximum effort."

Tim shoved one of the power bars into his mouth and chewed loudly. "I wonder if Fargher is going to reopen the Tasty Lion. I've had enough Heavenly Fuel to last a lifetime."

"I can't believe we pulled it off," Vince confessed. "I'll admit, it was a rush."

"Yeah . . ." Jack's voice trailed off as his thoughts turned to the vision that Emma asked about moments earlier—and what it meant. He popped open his Spitfire Jolt and took a long drag. Pushing himself off the sofa, he shuffled over to the window and gazed down on the quad. Professor McDougall was pointing his crooked finger, directing hundreds of Cherub, who were guarded by lightforcers and benders. Another long line waited while

Professor Windsor waved her CT wand over one person at a time. Those who were injured were surrounded by healers, who released their miraculous powers. It was an awe-inspiring sight: Elyon flowed seamlessly through those who believed as one community.

"Wonder how long before we are allowed back in Nightingale?" Tim asked.

"Not sure that's high on Fargher's priority list," Vince answered. "Could be a while."

"Especially after tonight—which was majorly epic, by the way."

From the bottom bunk, Vince tossed the can across the room, where it landed perfectly in the trash. "We did good, fellas."

"Amina, Eliška, and Emma were incredible too." Tim paused. "Bau is still a muppet."

"Bau showed up when he was told not to," Jack admitted. "That's something."

"Wonder how Will is doing?" Vince asked. "He looked in rough shape."

"I can't imagine what he's been through—and it's all my fault."

"What're you talking about, Jack? You didn't do that to him."

"If I hadn't have gone to Sitio Veterans to find Rachel, no one would've gotten hurt."

"You know that's not true." Vince pulled himself up and sat on the edge of the bed. "There was no way for any of us to stop what your father and the Merikh have done."

Jack exhaled. "What if Will doesn't agree, Vince?"

"As soon as he's awake, we'll clear the air."

"Professor Windsor isolated him in Crozier Hospital," Tim noted. "No visitors."

"How do you know?"

Tim held up his cell phone. "Amina's been messaging me."

"Maybe the two of you should do the fire mood experiment again and see if your flames join together like Jack's and Emma's."

Tim smiled sheepishly and tapped on his screen. "Hey, you and Eliška seemed to be . . ."

"She caught me by surprise—and she kept up with me."

"That is no small feat, my friend," Tim laughed. "You better watch out for the arrow."

Even though he was only a few feet away, Jack barely listened. He watched Bau walk across the quad alongside a woman with snow-white hair draped over her shoulders. For a moment he thought she might be Dabria, but the longer he stared the less of a resemblance there was, and his heart sank. Headmaster Fargher greeted them, and the conversation quickly intensified. Salomeh and Faizan joined the circle, and it was clear there was a disagreement between them.

Jack's curiosity was piqued. "I'll be back in a few."

71

QUIETNESS DRIFTED THROUGH a patient wing of Crozier Hospital lined with beds where dozens of injured Cherub refugees and captives rested. *Elyon, why are some healed completely but others are left wounded?* Jack walked past a sterile, white-walled room filled with state-of-the-art equipment. He remembered Professor Windsor restitching the gash over his eyebrow and poking at his crooked nose after his best friend pummeled him in the dining hall. He left the main patient wing and entered a private room. A monitor beeped a steady rhythm as he stopped at the foot of Will's bed. IVs dripped medicine into his veins. Jack's stomach twisted into knots the longer he stared at the bruises and swelling on Will's unconscious body.

Scars are a reminder of why we are here.

Natalie McNaughton stepped out from a corner, surprising Jack. "You should be keeping out of sight."

"Do you know how bad it is?" Jack asked. "Will he be okay?"

"Professor Windsor and several healers were here a bit earlier, before he was sedated. We do not know what he has been through, which can also be said about the others in the patient wing. His mental state is also something Professor Windsor will monitor when he wakes. For now, he is being isolated as a precaution considering he is the headmaster's son *and* your friend."

"Who is the white-haired woman in the quad?"

"Her name is Fang Xue. She is the Cherub leader, at least for now."

"She knows I'm here." Jack kept his gaze fixed on Will. "Bau probably told her."

"Headmaster Fargher will protect you—he promised."

"Since Rachel's murder, every time I've returned to Beacon Hill, I've hoped this would all be over." Jack stepped nearer to Will's bedside. "Cherub and Merikh won't stop hunting me—or the artifacts. And I won't let anyone else be tortured or die because of me."

"I am sorry, Jack." McNaughton stepped next to him. "You are not at fault."

"Everyone keeps telling me the same thing, but that's not how it feels." Jack weighed his words. "I told you that Michael Chung is dead, but the nightmares will never end."

McNaughton's brows raised. "And you are certain he is dead?"

"I held the weapon that killed him—one of the missing artifacts." He lifted his sleeve and held out his arm. "Cherub call it the Rod of Elyon—it's also known as Soulweaver."

"So Eden's Star is working," McNaughton whispered.

Jack tapped his chest. "I don't know for how much longer."

"I noticed the Testimony is gone from the vault."

"We moved it to another hiding place," he replied. "Only Emma and I know where."

For a long moment there was an awkward silence, broken only by the heart monitor's rhythmic beeping. He knew what he needed to do next, but his soul was too crippled to go alone.

"Before going to Shelter Island, we stole an artifact the Merikh had found. A shield that once belonged to a great Cherub warrior known as Ryder Slybourne. I don't have a clue what supernatural power is in the shield, but we took it from Addison and left it with someone we hope we can trust." Tears welled up as he nodded toward the bed. "Will was tortured because of what I've done . . . He's lost his mom . . . I just want it to stop, Natalie."

"Addison is ruthless and vengeful, but he is not immortal."

"We both know with him there are no limits—no boundaries he will not cross."

"Lightforcers, benders, and healers are protecting the school. No further attacks have occurred, so Headmaster Fargher plans to reopen Beacon Hill." McNaughton's gaze hardened. "Perhaps it is time to stop being the hunted, and become the hunter."

"There is somewhere I'll need to go—where the nightmares began."

"And I will go with you, Jack, whenever you are ready."

"Let's do it right now, before I lose my nerve."

Jack pulled his sleeve over Soulweaver and stepped back from Will's bed. He followed McNaughton through the main patient wing out into the corridors. Instead of leaving through the basement tunnel or Nightingale's vault, McNaughton and Jack exited out the back of the Main Hall and took the stone steps down to the patchy grass cricket pitch. He was bone-tired, but the adrenaline kicked in once they entered the Oasis of Remembrance. At this late hour, the ginkgo tree and stone in remembrance of Olivia Fargher were barely noticeable. His boots crunched over dead flowers and plum blossoms as he and McNaughton disappeared into the Chinese elm hedges.

"Headmaster Fargher pointed this way out to me after you left." McNaughton pushed the hedges aside as she went deeper, toward a stone wall. "He did not want to risk exposing the tunnel to Nightingale's vault or the basement tunnel. We never imagined people would arrive through the House of Luminescence, though."

"Have you heard anything from Detective Ming?"

"Since the attack at the school, she has mostly kept her distance. However, she provided proof about Cherub being held on Shelter Island and in Shek Pik Prison."

"Seeing all of the barricades across the city, it seems as if the HKPF has switched sides."

"Ming never struck me as being that way," McNaughton admitted. "She seemed more of a rule breaker than a follower, especially when it came to the Merikh. Remember, Michael Chung killed her partner too. Most likely she is keeping her head down so she does not attract any attention. She has proven she is still an ally."

"You don't think she's told anyone about the Cherub?"

McNaughton shook her head. "If she did, we would all be arrested."

"What do you know about those being held in Shek Pik?"

"Rumors, mostly." McNaughton scanned their surroundings. "The Merikh's detainment facilities—or what the PRC is calling reeducation camps—are so far limited to Shelter Island and Shek Pik. One less prison after tonight." McNaughton stopped in front of a stone wall. "Why do you ask?"

"Only two Elders are left," Jack answered. "I met Dabria when I was with Areum in the Philippines, and there's Xui Li, who was caught by the Merikh when she was searching for artifacts in Pakistan." He knew he was brushing over a ton of details, but he was too drained to become a storyteller. "They are the only ones who once had Eden's Star and the maps together. Addison will want them alive to find out what they know about the compass and how the maps lead to the artifacts."

"If that is the case, he will have them heavily guarded in a place like—"

"Shek Pik."

"Getting into the prison will be much harder than Shelter Island—nearly impossible."

McNaughton pushed against one of the stone blocks in the wall, which released a hidden entrance. She slipped through, and Jack followed. They emerged onto the street, and he realized they were at the far corner of the block from where the basement tunnel opened near the light post. McNaughton picked up the pace with her head on a swivel, and Jack followed her down an alleyway. She turned the dial on a combination lock until it clicked open, then pulled up a narrow garage door. Jack waited until she reappeared from the garage, pushing an orange scooter.

"Now that was unexpected," Jack chuckled. "You don't have a car anymore?"

"Broke down a week ago, so I ditched it." McNaughton slipped onto the seat and pressed the ignition. The engine sputtered with a ticking and rattling. "Easier to avoid the checkpoints on this."

"Are you sure we won't end up pushing it the whole way?" Jack climbed onto the back behind McNaughton, and the scooter sank a few more inches. "Is there a weight limit?"

"Hang on." McNaughton wasted no time as she accelerated out of the alley onto city streets, then asked over her shoulder, "Where are we going?"

Jack held tight onto her waist. "Sham Shui Po."

72

A FEW BLOCKS FROM THE HEART of the northwestern district of Kowloon Peninsula, Jack and McNaughton left the scooter in an alley behind an overflowing dumpster. They kept close to the buildings as they hurried down a sidewalk. At this time of night, the streets were mostly empty except for homeless people sheltered together in makeshift cardboard dwellings. Jack never would have imagined she would be the one to go with him to face the nightmares that had haunted his childhood. He was back in the one place to which he swore he'd never return.

"You kept your word, Natalie." Jack stared across the street at the subdivided flat with blackened walls. "Headmaster Fargher needed you by his side to watch over everyone at Beacon Hill, and you stayed with him." A wave of guilt washed over Jack at the thought of the students who had died. He counted the iron-barred windows of the building until he reached the flats on the twenty-seventh floor. "Eden's Star brought us to Sham Shui Po for a reason—and I need to know why."

"What is this place?"

"My father kept us hidden here after he nearly killed my mom." Years later, Jack still found it hard to believe they'd survived. "I've buried most of the memories—but not all of them. We were locked in a cage home on the twenty-seventh floor, sometimes for days. Whenever he returned, what happened was unimaginable."

"Oh, Jack . . ." McNaughton's voice trailed off.

"Rachel protected me from his rage, and she watched over me after we were abandoned at Fortress Hill." Jack clenched his fists and tried to stop his fingers from twitching. "I was too embarrassed to ask any of the others to come with me. I guess I'm afraid of what they'd think if they knew what happened when I was younger."

"You can trust me, Jack." McNaughton squeezed his shoulder as her gaze hardened. "We both know the evil Addison has inflicted. Maybe Eden's Star brought you here so you can put the past behind and move toward your destiny."

"What if he kept us here because it was protected by the Merikh?"

McNaughton retrieved her Glock from the holster behind her back and kept it lowered by her side. "We will find out together."

Jack shoved his hands into his pockets and stepped off the sidewalk. He second-guessed himself a dozen times before he reached the other side of the street. When they stopped outside the glass doors of the building, his heartbeat quickened and a shiver shuddered down his spine. He was stronger than he'd been in weeks, but on the inside he remained broken with memories.

A metal threshold divided the concrete sidewalk from a weathered tile lobby. *Elyon, give me the strength to take the next step, and the next.* He pulled the glass door open and entered, fully expecting demons to swarm and devour him. A haunting eeriness seeped into his bones, but he breathed in deep, believing Elyon was with him. McNaughton was right behind, her Glock aimed in front of her as she moved ahead and punched a button on a wall.

Ding.

The elevator climbed the building while Jack counted the numbers. On the twenty-seventh floor, he followed McNaughton into a grungy hallway. She kept her index finger along the barrel of her Glock as they kept moving. Jack inhaled the strong aroma of incense sticks burning outside several flats.

His pace slowed as they approached #27D and he noticed something out of the ordinary. "The door is padlocked from the outside, which tells me there's no one living here—or someone's being kept inside."

"You have taken the hardest step," McNaughton said. "It will not get any worse."

"Famous last words," Jack mumbled. "You haven't been around me long enough."

A door creaked open across the hall. An elderly woman in pajamas poked her head out and eyed them curiously. McNaughton shifted her attention and approached the woman with a smile while keeping the Glock behind her back.

"Excuse me." McNaughton pointed over her shoulder. "Do you know who lives in this flat?"

The woman replied, "Why do you ask such question at this hour?"

"I apologize—my friend used to live here many years ago." McNaughton nodded toward Jack. "I know this sounds crazy, but he wants to go inside."

The woman's gaze shifted between them, uncertain. "Are you . . . ?"

"We are not Merikh," McNaughton reassured. "And we are not here to cause trouble."

"No one live there for long time." The woman looked past McNaughton and stared at Jack—which left him more on edge. "No one go inside—no one."

"Thank you for your help," McNaughton replied. "Good night."

Jack watched the woman slip back into her flat and close the door. He grabbed the padlock and tugged hard. It didn't budge. He thought about using Soulweaver, but McNaughton was one step ahead. She checked both ends of the hallway, then slammed the butt of her Glock against the padlock. With one strike, she broke the latch and knocked the lock to the floor. Jack was impressed, but he kept quiet as she turned the knob.

"Do you want me to go first?" she whispered.

"Um . . ." For a moment, Jack struggled to decide. "I'll do it."

He nudged the door open and flipped a light switch. A yellowish bulb blinked on and revealed an empty room, which seemed even smaller than he remembered. Flashes struck him in rapid succession, memories buried so deep he struggled to stop the waves from crashing over him. He imagined the stained mattress on the floor as he stepped over to one corner and knelt. *I don't want to be in here any longer than I need to.* He ran his fingers across the baseboards, looking for a crack in the wood. For a moment, he envisioned himself peering over Rachel's shoulder when she pried the baseboard loose.

"Jack, are you okay?" McNaughton asked.

"Not really." Jack kept searching, convinced he was in the right place. "Hold on."

He dug his fingers into the edge of the baseboard and dislodged a piece. A searing heat spread across his chest as he set a piece of the wooden baseboard aside. He reached inside and wrapped two fingers around an object, pulling it from within the wall. A slim wooden box with a small latch rested in his grasp. He flipped the latch and opened the box. Inside was a rolled-up parchment with worn edges. His heart pounded through his chest as he carefully unrolled the parchment and an ivory figurine dropped to the floor. He picked up the figurine carefully and gazed at the intricate carvings depicting a woman wrapped in serpents. He returned his attention to the parchment and held it out in front of him.

McNaughton peered over his shoulder. "What is it, Jack?"

"It's a map of the Highlands," he whispered, recognizing the names inscribed on the paper. "At Rachel's age, where did she get this from? I thought her diaries and notebooks were the clues to finish what she started."

"What about the carvings on the figurine?"

"A serpent is an emblem for one of the Cherub tribes, but I don't have a clue who the woman is supposed to be." Jack stared hard at the map, realizing McNaughton was wrong—the journey ahead was only going to get harder. "Maybe this is what she was really hiding all along." He turned the parchment over and froze as he stared at scripted pale ink on the back.

I am the vine rooted in soul and spirit. Remain in me, and I will live in you. An everlasting promise for a thousand generations flourishes through the branches of love, joy, peace, grace, and goodness. Depart from my ways and you will wither and die.

A typhoon of flames surged through Jack's chest as he tried to catch his breath. Another scripted line appeared from nowhere. He showed the words to McNaughton and read aloud.

"'I have seen a beast swallowed by darkness, slumbering amidst wild waves of the sea and wandering stars in the skies. Light must never be brought into this realm. —Bella.'"

"Bella means 'beautiful,'" McNaughton said. "And 'devoted to God.'"

Jack ran his fingers over the parchment. "To me it means—Mom."

73

After a late night in Sham Shui Po, Jack and McNaughton returned to the school shortly after 2 a.m. In the quad, McNaughton made Jack promise to tell her what he planned to do next. He knew better than to argue, so he agreed to fill her in before he did anything more. While she headed for the old barracks at the lower end of the grounds, he climbed the steps to Rowell House and slipped inside unnoticed. Most of the night he tossed and turned while Tim and Vince dueled in a snoring battle royale. By daybreak, he was unsure of who the victor might be, as it remained a dead heat.

He climbed down from the top bunk, stretched his aching muscles, and wiped the sleep from his eyes before sniffing beneath both armpits. *Not that bad. I'll shower later.* He slipped into his jeans and grabbed a T-shirt from Vince's backpack. From beneath the covers, he retrieved the tiny wooden box, remembering Rachel's poem, which he'd kept under the pillow when this all began. He slid the wooden box into his front pocket. On his way out of the room, he snatched Vince's Nightingale hoodie and put it on to hide Soulweaver wrapped around his arm.

Emma was waiting in the hallway near her room. "Where did you go last night?"

"Good morning to you too," he replied, a bit defensive.

"I cannot help when I sense your emotions. I have been worried all night."

"Natalie took me to Sham Shui Po," he said in a lowered voice. "You know the vision you asked me about? Well, it wasn't just a vision—it was a memory of me and Rachel when we were young. She kept something hidden in one of the flats. I needed to know if it was still there."

"We made a promise, Jack." Emma stepped closer. "We go together, no matter where."

"Look, I wasn't even planning on going. I ran into Natalie, who was keeping an eye on Will in Crozier Hospital. She offered to go with me—honestly, I was too embarrassed to ask you or anyone else because I wasn't sure what I might find from my past."

"I felt your sorrow." Emma's gaze softened. "All of it."

"I'm sorry, Emma. I didn't mean for you to be freaked out." Jack retrieved the box from his pocket and held it out in front of him. "Inside is a map of the Highlands and a small ivory figurine of a woman wrapped in snakes. I'm betting it's tied to the Seven Tribes."

"How could Rachel have a map of the Highlands when she was young?" Emma asked, confused. "For certain she would have told Peter and the rest of us on Karābu."

"I can't explain why she had the map or why she hid it and left it there. And I've got no idea who the figurine represents. Rachel might've buried it in her memory so she could forget what she'd gone through—or maybe she was like me, too afraid to face the past and what Addison did to us." Jack stuffed the wooden box into his jeans pocket. "I stared at the map for at least an hour, following our route from Sakkhela to the Valley of Grace to Charis—but there is more on the map beyond the edge of the Highlands." Jack swallowed hard. "We found Soulweaver in Charis, but maybe we didn't go far enough."

"You are saying return to the edge of the Highlands," Emma surmised. "And go beyond, into the land the fallen angels protect—the legion that betrayed Elyon."

"Just you and me this time," Jack replied. "No one else."

"C'mon, you two," Amina announced as she walked past, "or else we will miss it."

Jack switched gears and asked, "What're we going to miss?"

"You will see. Take a break from saving the world."

Jack hurried to keep up with Emma and Amina as they walked briskly across the quad before turning the corner around the Main Hall. Beneath gunmetal clouds, all three found a spot on the ledge that surrounded the Main Hall, beside others from Nightingale's vault who looked on with a growing curiosity. His gaze locked in on the young boy who'd helped save the villagers in Sakkhela—and he recognized more of the people in clothing unique from the others.

He's one of the bravest ones here—risking his life to save his village.

Jack's attention shifted to the lightforcers and benders stationed around the grounds. On the steps of the Main Hall, Headmaster Fargher stood behind a cluster of microphones while reporters, camera operators, bloggers, and local officials waited in anticipation. Fargher was clean-shaven, exposing a smooth, gaunt face with a steely jaw. The wrinkled clothes he'd worn over the past months had been replaced with a perfectly pressed suit hanging loose over his bony shoulders. His grayish pupils gazed at those before him. Jack realized the headmaster was far from the charismatic leader he'd been before Olivia Fargher was murdered, Beacon Hill was attacked, students were killed, and Will was taken and tortured by the Merikh.

Fargher's gravelly voice broke the silence.

"Thank you for coming this morning on such short notice. To begin, I would like to take this opportunity to remember those students who were lost during the brazen attack on our school. They and their families will forever remain in our hearts. We have been through a dark time in recent months. Many of us are heartbroken over the losses we have suffered. What occurred on these grounds was beyond a tragedy—it was a hateful act of cowardice."

Fargher waved his arms wide around them.

"From the beginning, Sir James Nightingale had a vision to educate and empower future generations of leaders. What most remember about his legacy began the day he stood on these steps and dedicated the grounds of Beacon Hill. However, Sir Nightingale's vision was birthed on rooftops of districts across this city with those who were forgotten. In the years since, our ambition to educate the next generation led us astray as we found ourselves centered on the elite instead of brilliant students from all walks of life. That changes now. Today, the gates of Beacon Hill are reopened for all who wish to learn."

Fargher started to step away from the microphones, then leaned in once more.

"To those who stormed our school—you will not break our spirit again."

74

TIM CLIMBED OVER DEBRIS INSIDE Nightingale House and ascended the cracked stairwell. From the rooftop, he watched those gathered in front of the Main Hall disperse and the media leave in their vehicles through the gates of Beacon Hill. He'd woken up to the buzzing of his cell phone and a message—which he thought would be from Amina, but he was wrong. Jack was gone and Vince was buried under the covers. Tim had grown used to Jack disappearing, and he noticed Vince had been moving slower than normal, so he didn't want to bother him when he left. As the minutes passed, he waited and wished for everything to be back to the way it was before.

He heard footsteps from behind and turned around. "We're not supposed to be up here."

"That's never stopped us before." Will offered a half-hearted smile. "Good to see you, mate."

"We were worried about you. Now you're back, and it seems your father is too."

"What do you mean?" Will asked, puzzled. "Where has he been?"

"It's an expression—he has been lost without you." Tim paused. "You all right?"

"I feel like I've been dragged through the Mental Disruptor a thousand times." Will limped closer to the edge. "To be honest, I gave up on anyone finding me. I shut myself down and tried to hold on."

"You have Jack and Emma to thank for that one." Tim relaxed a bit. "Last night was mad hatter helping all those people—then there you were at Clear Water Bay."

Will stayed quiet for a moment. "I thought the four of us would conquer the world."

"Definitely not the year we expected. You know, I asked my parents about graduation and college applications—they couldn't answer what all of this means for me. Who knows what the future will hold for any of us after all that's happened."

Will's eyes narrowed. "We have paid a price because of—"

"Addison Reynolds," Tim interrupted. "He is the one to blame—and the Merikh."

"Does anyone know you told me about Eden's Star and the Treaty of Nanjing?"

"I haven't told another soul, not even Amina. Listen, you and Jack need to clear the air. I mean, don't you want to get back at the Merikh for what they've done?"

"More than anyone—but what's stopping them from attacking Beacon Hill again?"

"Lightforcers, benders, and healers." Tim pointed across the grounds at those who were on guard and others who milled about in the quad below. "We are now protected by Cherub from all over the world, not just the chosen like Emma and Bau."

Will nodded slowly. "You have a lot to teach me about the Cherub and Merikh."

"We were in Karachi, Pakistan." Tim's eyes lit up. "Then we were in Kyoto, Japan."

"That sounds barmy. Searching for the artifacts?"

"Jack, Vince, Amina, Emma, *and* Eliška—wait, you haven't met her yet, she's a firecracker. Anyway, we traveled to another realm to this place called Sakkhela where Emma was healed, and Jack might've been partially too—but you'll have to ask him to explain it. At least he's upright now instead of being curled up in a corner. It was totally insane. We found Slybourne Castle—Slybourne is the bloke who actually used Dragon Soul to fight against the Nephilim king and his army. Florence Upsdell, a direct descendant of Headmaster Upsdell, was *the* bladesmith who forged Dragon Soul. And you already know Upsdell found Dragon Soul on Everest." Tim took a deep breath, then rambled on. "The Merikh attacked, and we narrowly escaped. Then Jack used Eden's Star to transport us, and we ended up in this fishing village outside of Kyoto—that's where Eliška comes into the picture. Awesome place, by the way. We should go there—you'd love it. Oh yeah, and Vince nearly lost his leg—it was a total horror show. And Professor Burwick was there, and she helped keep us alive."

"Professor Burwick?" Will asked, surprised. "I thought she was in the hospital."

"She was nearly torched alive by the Merikh." Tim hesitated, sensing an uneasiness between them. "You will not believe who she is. She's the leader of a Cherub faction."

"Cherub faction?" Will's brows furrowed. "What is that all about?"

Tim shook his head. "I haven't fully figured that one out yet."

"Okay, what happened in Kyoto?"

"Right—Jack, Emma, and Eliška separated from us because, well, Vince nearly died, you know, from Jack using Eden's Star in a way he wasn't supposed to. Anyway, Jack, Emma, and Eliška found this place called Charis in the Valley of Grace. In the Eternal, it's the place where Elyon began creation and formed Eden's Star. Now, I wasn't there, but from what Amina told me there was a face-off between Jack and Michael Chung—one of the Merikh assassins, who is also the bloke who murdered Rachel." Tim waved his hands as if his mind was blown. "Jack came out on top—he killed the Merikh's numero uno assassin."

Will's gaze hardened. "How was he able to kill him?"

"Yeah, I left that part out. So, when they got to Charis, guess what was there? Elyon's Vine. You probably don't know all of this, so pay attention because I'm giving you a lightning-speed masterclass. Elyon's Vine is like the Holy Grail for the Cherub, but when Jack found the tree, the branches were withered and the trunk was dead. So he used Eden's Star, and Elyon's Vine came back to life and revealed the Rod of Elyon—which is also called Soulweaver, but only if you've got a bent toward the dark side. It's one of the artifacts with supernatural powers, but I'm not sure how it works. You'll have to ask Jack or Emma. I'm giving you the highlight reel rather than the play-by-play."

"There's something else you're not fessing up," Will probed.

"Umm . . . right . . ." Tim struggled to find the words. "You'll need to ask Jack . . ."

After an awkward silence, Will's eyes narrowed. "Has he found any other artifacts?"

Tim paused, a bit puzzled. "He hasn't mentioned anything to me or Vince, I swear."

"So, you have not heard of any other artifact being found?" Will pressed.

"That's what I just said." Tim eyed him closely. "You're grilling me like I stole something."

"When I was being held on Shelter Island, I overheard guards talking about Jack's twisted father and how he found some ancient treasure from the Exodus Mines."

"Hold on." Tim held up his hand. "*The* Exodus Mines?"

Will nodded. "You have heard of them before?"

"Ryder Slybourne—the Dragon Soul gladiator—hid his treasure there."

"Could the artifacts have been kept there?" Will asked, matter-of-fact.

"Possibly." Tim pushed his frames up his nose. "We should tell Jack."

Will stepped forward and grabbed Tim's shoulders. "You cannot tell anyone, Tim."

"You two have been feuding for months, and where has it gotten any of us?"

"Jack knew the danger he was putting us in when he searched for Rachel's killer, but he didn't care what it meant for the rest of us. After being locked away and shredded by the Merikh, I'm alive to protect all of us before someone else gets hurt or winds up dead." Will glanced briefly over his shoulder, then turned back with a dead stare. "Jack is in way over his head, and he doesn't stand a chance against his father or the Merikh."

"We should be talking with the others." Tim crossed his arms. "I'm not sure I can keep what you know about the Exodus Mines a secret."

"At least find out if he's found any other artifacts before you say anything." Will released his grip on Tim's shoulders. "And tell me where he's keeping Soulweaver."

75

JACK ENTERED THE HOUSE of Luminescence aware that the clock was ticking. Beneath the high-vaulted wood beams, a turquoise glow created a soothing atmosphere. He stepped over thick vines spreading across the stone floor, which had seemingly grown since the last time he snuck inside. He found Salomeh on her knees in front of the Mercy Covenant with her eyes closed. Her lips moved slightly as whispers echoed off the walls. Jack watched quietly before clearing his throat. He stayed on edge as she peered over her shoulder. Her dark-brown eyes flickered with confidence and authority.

"You were supposed to be in our corner," Jack said point-blank. "Professor Burwick too."

"Each of us needed to choose the safety of our people over our own aspirations."

"We managed to pull it off without either of you." Jack paused. "I saw you last night in the quad with Headmaster Fargher. I'm guessing the elderly woman was a Cherub too."

"Fang Xue is our leader, and she is certain you have returned to Beacon Hill." Salomeh slowly stood and adjusted her burgundy-and-silver embroidered tunic. "You remain an enemy to the Cherub, and after last night you pose an even greater threat to the Merikh."

"Bau must've told her I'm here," Jack guessed. "Did he tell her how he helped us?"

"He disobeyed Fang Xue's orders and my wishes, which we neglected to mention when she arrived." Salomeh's fiery gaze left Jack easing off the edge of confronting her further. "Your actions have forced those of us who remain loyal to the Cherub to walk a very fine line to help and protect followers of Elyon, along with an outlier who murdered the great Elder while stirring up a greater hornet's nest. Far too many wish to control the outcome of what is set in motion, but I am afraid the only one who knows for certain whether we will be victorious in the end is Elyon."

"We trusted you with Slybourne's shield because we need you to trust *us.* We need your help to keep Fang Xue and the highest Cherub out of our way. If Bau told Fang Xue we returned, it's possible he's told her what we found, which will only make this worse—not only for me, but for Emma and anyone else who is willing to risk their lives."

"Headmaster Fargher will only be able to keep them away for so long, and the same is true for me. For now, the Merikh will hesitate to test the Cherub power at Beacon Hill. So the grounds will remain a light amid the great darkness that is coming—when Cherub and Merikh lose their patience and the war turns more deadly."

"This is the calm before the storm, then," Jack said. "How can you be so sure?"

"Elyon has shown me a vision—Hong Kong erupting in flames and Eden's Star in the hands of a faceless enemy." Her words stopped Jack cold as he remembered his vision where the city burned and Eden's Star was ripped from his hands. "Harley believes in you, while I have my reservations. However, I have learned to trust her instincts, which is the only reason I was able to convince Fang Xue to leave Beacon Hill alone. Even though you have entrusted me with Slybourne's shield, I must warn you, if you prove to be an even greater threat to the Cherub, then I will bring you before them."

A chill shot down his spine. "You would turn me in, knowing what they would do to me."

"Emma has sacrificed her purpose to stand by you—which no one else understands. She has walked away from her destiny to lead the Cherub, and in her wake she leaves the future in the hands of Fang Xue to anoint Bau Hu—or, if Harley gets her way, possibly Eliška. Neither possess the gifts Elyon granted Emma. You know it to be true, Jack. Until Emma returns to her calling, you grow far more dangerous to the Cherub with each passing day."

"Salomeh, that's why I'm here." Jack lifted his sleeve and showed her Soulweaver again. "I told you we reached the Valley of Grace, found Charis, and Elyon revealed the rod to me. Now Eden's Star and Soulweaver are connected. They are feeding off one another, as if they are synced somehow."

"Yes, you have found one of the artifacts protected by Eden's Star and have trusted me with another." Salomeh studied the rod wrapped around his forearm. "Yet you refuse to return the artifacts to the Cherub or to tell me where you have taken the Testimony."

Jack's forearm tensed, and the rod slipped into his hand until it was once again at its full length and size. He gripped the rod and held it out for Salomeh. "If you think this is the only way to defeat the Merikh, then take it from me."

"I have warned you, Jack." Salomeh didn't reach for Soulweaver. "You must choose to return the Rod of Elyon to the Testimony, as well as Slybourne's shield. It is the only way."

"We need Eden's Star if we are going to find more artifacts, and I need Soulweaver to protect us along the way." His grip instinctively tightened around the carved heartwood. He retrieved the small wooden box from the front pocket of his jeans and handed it over. "We reached the edge of the Highlands, but we need to go farther. So I'm asking for your help. Teach me how to use the power of Soulweaver."

"You mean the Rod of Elyon." Salomeh flipped the latch and opened the box. She carefully unrolled the parchment, set the carved figurine aside, then spread the small map over the top of the Mercy Covenant. She studied the drawings for a long time before picking up the figurine and running her fingers over the ivory. "Did you find this in Charis too?"

"A long time ago Rachel hid the box in a place where no one else would find it—except for me." He stepped closer and hoped Salomeh was slowly beginning to take his side. He pointed at the name: Sakkhela. "You were the one who instructed Faizan to take us to Slybourne Castle, where the Merikh hunted us down. And you helped Xui Li go there too." His index finger crossed over the map toward the east. "Eden's Star took us from Sakkhela to Kyoto—where you were waiting, along with Professor Burwick.

Both of you pointed us to the Valley of Grace to find Charis." He tapped a marking he didn't recognize. "We need to go farther than the Highlands, Salomeh. Whatever lies beyond is greater than any of the artifacts we've found so far. I feel it in the core of my soul."

"How can you be certain?"

Jack turned the parchment over and waited while Salomeh read the text. He noticed the message from his mom was missing. He touched the parchment and watched as Salomeh's eyes widened once the message revealed itself again.

"I don't know how, but Rachel got her hands on this, or it was given to her for a reason." Jack swallowed a lump lodged in his throat. "I think my mom traveled beyond the Highlands, so that's where I need to go too."

"Elyon led you to Eden's Star, the Rod of Elyon, and Slybourne's shield." Salomeh stabbed her finger against the parchment. "However, the highest Cherub view your actions as a threat—a sin against Elyon."

"We've taken the Testimony from Nightingale's vault to keep it safe." Jack refused to back down, even though she intimidated him. "The Cherub don't trust me, but I don't trust them either. Salomeh, my faith in Elyon grows greater each day because of my mom, Rachel, Areum, Emma, Tim, Amina, Vince, Eliška, and so many others. I know Elyon is with me, no matter how this ends. But I need to understand how to use the gifts he's given me."

"You are playing a dangerous game." Her lips curled into a slight smirk. "If Elyon has chosen you, then who am I to question his ways?"

76

BY NOON, Upsdell Dining Hall buzzed with Cherub and a handful of faculty who'd arrived in the hours since Headmaster Fargher made the announcement about reopening the school. His secretary, Ms. Burton, spent the morning on the phone speaking with parents of current Beacon Hillers. Some remained wary, others were eager to return their children to the school, and there was a growing list who did not respond to Burton's inquiry. For the first time in months, an excitement spread across the grounds as the legacy of Sir James Nightingale breathed new life into Beacon Hill.

"Freddie, you are off your blasted rocker." Professor McDougall shuffled alongside him, his weathered Burberry coat replaced with an even older one. "You should have warned us."

"If I told you what I planned to say, you would have cut off all the electricity within a ten-mile radius." Fargher waved at those in line for lunch, then smiled at several others who were seated around the tables. "We cannot hide in Nightingale's vault forever, Mac."

"You have placed a bull's-eye on our foreheads," McDougall retorted. "Again."

Fargher waved Professor Windsor over. "The bull's-eye has always been there."

"Headmaster. Professor." Windsor greeted them both. "Very inspiring speech."

"Please do not encourage him," McDougall chastised. "It will only make it worse."

"How is William doing?" Fargher asked Windsor.

"His injuries were quite severe; however, he is recovering at a remarkable pace." Windsor paused. "Of course, I am not certain whether it is from the medication or from the healers."

Fargher eyed the dining hall, resolute in his decision. "Both will work in tandem."

"We should embrace all of our gifts," Windsor agreed.

Fargher excused himself, leaving Windsor and McDougall behind. He smiled at those who served food and offered encouragement as they worked. Slipping through the swinging doors, he entered the top-of-the-line kitchen and headed toward a long table where Will was seated with Tim, Vince, Amina, and Emma. He clenched his jaw as memories of Olivia's loving presence in the kitchen flooded his mind.

As he approached, his eyes welled up with tears on the verge of spilling over. When he'd first laid eyes on his son in Clear Water Bay, the shock of seeing him alive left him speechless. Anger boiled beneath his skin at the thought of the beating Will had endured.

Still, he was relieved when Professor Windsor confirmed the recovery was going well—at least physically.

"Good afternoon, everyone." Fargher offered another warm smile. "So good to see all of you together. I know the past few months have been difficult, so today is a day to be grateful."

"Headmaster, your speech was extremely motivating," Amina said.

"A real Freddie Fargher Fiver," Tim quipped, then realized he'd given away an inside joke. "It's just a . . . I'm such an idiot."

Fargher smiled wide. "I can guess where you heard that from."

"I will never tell," Tim replied, embarrassed. "Sorry, Headmaster."

"William." Fargher's smile faded. "A moment, please."

Everyone grew quiet as Will slipped gingerly off his chair and shuffled alongside the headmaster out of the kitchen. Fargher led him out of the dining hall, then unlocked a classroom and motioned for Will to go inside. Alone in the room, Fargher locked the door behind them. Without allowing another second to pass, he turned around and embraced his son.

Tears rolled down his cheeks as he hugged him tight. "Elyon answered my prayers."

"I am fine, Dad." Will gently pushed himself away. "Sore, that's all."

"Of course, sorry." Fargher gathered himself and wiped his cheeks with his sleeve. "I never intended for any of this to happen. I am sorry, William."

"Have you told Jack the truth?" Will asked. "About me?"

Fargher shook his head. "I have told no one."

"Addison Reynolds knows about the chosen." Will clenched his teeth. "And he also knows I was removed from Karābu Island to be trained by Peter. While I was being held on Shelter Island, Addison pumped me full of drugs. I could not use my gifts to defend myself. No one was there to stop him—not the Cherub, not Jack, and not even you."

"Allowing Peter to train you in the way of the Cherub was a mistake." A wave of guilt washed over Fargher as he stared into his son's hollow eyes. "He was not who he professed himself to be, and he betrayed those who trusted him the most."

"Jack's father remains deadly against anyone who crosses him," Will said solemnly.

"The Cherub at Beacon Hill will protect us," Fargher reassured, knowing he was holding back the truth about Olivia's killer from his son. The gut-wrenching truth about the Merikh assassin would need to be for another time when Will was stronger. "Lightforcers. Benders. Healers. We have never had so many on the grounds at once. Addison and the Merikh will know better than to attempt another reckless attack. He will pay for what he has done. For now, you must focus on healing."

"Do you believe Jack, Emma, and the others succeeded in rescuing us last night because they outwitted the Merikh? Don't you see? Jack's father allowed it to happen."

Fargher's brows furrowed. "What are you saying, William?"

"He kept me alive because he wanted me to deliver a message." Will's gaze darkened. "Surrender Jack and the artifacts to the Merikh, or more Cherub will be slaughtered."

"I will not bow to fear—not any longer."

"Then we are already dead."

77

JACK ENTERED THROUGH the back door of the Lion's Den. He remembered taking the same route months earlier when he and Will returned from eating lo bak go in Sham Shui Po. Emma, Amina, Tim, and Vince were already waiting inside. No house holograms. No vibrant banners. The gaming room was a black shell on all sides, including center stage.

"Where have you been all morning?" Tim asked.

"I was up early to watch the headmaster's announcement, while you were dreaming in another realm somewhere." Jack smiled at Emma. "I found Salomeh in the House of Luminescence. She should be here shortly."

"Will is back on his feet already," Amina said. "He took off with the headmaster."

"Professor Windsor and the Cherub healers worked their magic," Vince added.

"That's good news," Jack said, relieved. "Not sure whether I should talk to him."

"I would keep your distance," Emma suggested. "Give him time, Jack."

"He's not all there yet," Tim stated. "I mean, who would be after . . ."

"Will needs our patience," Amina suggested. "Healing is a process."

"So what are we doing in the Lion's Den?" Tim asked. "Since Fargher reopened the school, we should be down by the Wishing Tree watching the newbies being separated into their houses. Now that we know where the Wishing Tree came from, I'm intrigued to see which houses the Cherub refugees get separated into—and whether Nightingale will be rebuilt."

"Fargher *just* broke the news," Jack replied. "No other students are back yet, Tim."

"Right . . ." Tim's cheeks flushed. "I guess I'm chuffed to bits—you know, aced."

"Nightingale won't be down for long," Vince reassured. "I gotta admit, I'm *aced* too since we're getting everything back to somewhat normal—as much as possible, I guess."

Salomeh and Faizan arrived, along with a handful of others. *Lightforcers and benders. This isn't my first rodeo. She's going to put Soulweaver to the test. Actually, she's going to put me to the test too. You asked for it, Jack.* He waited while Salomeh took a look around, then turned toward him with her arms crossed.

"I am not certain this room is large enough to test the Rod of Elyon's powers."

Jack stepped over to the wall and pressed a button. The digital wall onstage opened to reveal a larger space and the Mental Disruptor. "Is this large enough?"

"Don't tell me we have to do the Mental Disruptor," Tim sighed. "You do remember what happened the last time."

Salomeh ordered the group to separate, and they headed for the course before splitting up at the different obstacles. "I heard you used the Rod of Elyon to part the waters last night."

"All I did was dip the point in the water and the rod did the rest." *How is the Mental Disruptor going to help me figure out Soulweaver's powers? Maybe this wasn't such a good idea. But I'm the one who asked for her help.* "Okay, tell me what I'm supposed to do."

"Since the artifacts have remained hidden for centuries, no one knows the extent of their true powers. We will need to put the Rod of Elyon to the test, and you with it as well."

"Now this is getting interesting," Tim mused. "Jack, the rod, and the Lion's Den."

"Sounds like a new PlayStation game," Vince chuckled. "Good thing it's him and not us."

"The deeper your faith," Salomeh instructed, "the more powerful the weapon."

"You mean the artifact," Tim corrected. "It's an artifact, right?"

Salomeh shot him a disapproving glare. "Depends who is holding it."

"Right," Tim answered, embarrassed. "Jack, do what she says with the *weapon*."

"Let's get on with it," Jack snapped, growing increasingly impatient. He gripped Soulweaver and stepped off the stage onto the course. He walked toward the first obstacle, which was the rope Tim had struggled to climb during the house competition—a lifetime ago. He jumped back when the other obstacles shifted across the course.

Benders.

"This isn't going to get any easier."

Emma strolled over and joined him. "You are not going to have all the fun."

"At least Emma is brave enough to do the course," he shouted toward the others.

Emma leaned in close. "Actually, I told them to wait there."

"Why would you do that?"

"If it is only you and me going beyond the Highlands, then we need to flow together."

"You mean like in the fire mood experiment when our flames became one? Oh, I get it. You want to be sure we're still connected." He leaned over and kissed her on the cheek. "Are we good?"

Emma's cheeks flushed. "Stronger than ever."

"Whoa!" Tim bellowed. "Now that's a pregame pep talk."

"If you two are finished," Salomeh called out, "we shall begin."

Jack shouted back, "Bring it on, Salomeh."

"That's the spirit," Vince yelled. "You two got this."

With Soulweaver in his grasp and Emma by his side, he felt invincible. As soon as the thought crossed his mind, he was reminded of the temple in the City of Gods. He had stood beside Areum attempting to cross to the other side, and his cockiness nearly ended their quest.

Keep your eyes and your soul on Elyon.

"Ready?" Emma asked.

Jack nodded. "We go together."

Before they could take another step, a barrage of light flashed toward them. Emma was quickest to respond. She held up her hands and deflected the radiant colors of lightforce. Jack pointed Soulweaver in front of him and felt a surge of pure energy flow through his fingers. The lightforcers darted across the course, sending another glowing barrage in their direction. At the same time, the benders shifted the obstacles so they crisscrossed in front of Jack and Emma.

"Mental Disruptor's now a Cherub ninja course," Tim shouted. "Insane *and* addicting!"

"Keep your heads in the game," Vince coached from the stage. "And stay focused."

Another bombardment erupted, and Emma blocked it. With her palms glowing, she unleashed her own stark-white force of light. The lightforcers ducked for cover as one of the obstacles shattered. On instinct, Jack pointed Soulweaver toward the benders, who were controlling another obstacle. As he moved the rod to one side, the obstacle followed. He shifted the rod in the opposite direction—and not only did the obstacle follow, but so did the benders.

Elyon, only you control the power of the rod.

With her arms raised, Emma elevated the obstacle where competitors had to lift the underwater walls before passing through. Jack stood amazed as the giant aquarium ascended even higher. *Still, nothing compared to what she did with the* Eastern Dragon. *She's coasting through the course. I better step it up.* He pressed forward as Emma ran alongside. In a split second, he glanced over and she was gone. He stopped in the middle of the course and spun around to see her standing with a confused expression. He started to run toward her until he slammed into an invisible wall. Salomeh stood on the stage with her arms outstretched in his direction, and that's when he knew she was separating them for a reason.

"You've got to do this on your own," Jack mumbled. "Trust Elyon."

The deeper your faith, the more powerful the weapon.

With Emma stuck behind an invisible force field, the giant aquarium descended and rested gently on the ground. Jack's grip on Soulweaver loosened as he moved toward the finish line. Lightforcers and benders closed in, a full-court press. Light and debris slammed against him as he tumbled backward. He scrambled to his knees, Soulweaver spinning between his fingers. When he blinked again, he was shocked by the speed of the rod as it captured energy from the lightforcers. He struck the rod into the ground, causing a quake strong enough to knock everyone off their feet.

Seizing the opportunity, Jack darted toward the finish line while the others were disoriented. About to cross the line, he stopped on a dime. *Getting to the other side isn't the test.* Even though he was only a few strides away, he turned and darted back across the course in Emma's direction. Spinning the rod between his fingers as if it were a propeller, he never slowed as he launched himself against the force field. Salomeh was pushed back as the invisible barricade shattered. She stayed on her feet only because Tim and Vince caught her before she fell over. Her voice erupted in a language no one else understood. Lightforcers, benders, and Amina dropped to their knees with their eyes raised. Salomeh was next to follow, as were Tim and Vince.

Jack embraced Emma as his eyes darted around them. *We're standing on holy ground right now—connected by Elyon's presence. And Eliška is right, Emma and I share a bond stronger than anyone else.* He lowered Soulweaver by his side, and he and Emma got on their knees with fingers intertwined. Both of them lifted their gazes.

"Ask and it shall be given," Salomeh's voice resounded. "Seek and you will find. Believe and Elyon shall grant you extraordinary power. Greater faith in Elyon unleashes deeper trust in one another."

78

WILL HELD THE JEANS HE'D WORN on Shelter Island and ripped into a pocket seam. He removed a small blood-filled syringe stitched within the fabric. For a moment, he stared at the blood of Oliver and Winnie Bennett, curious to know whether their gifts would fully heal his wound from the Windstrikers. As the needle pierced his skin, Cherub blood entered his bloodstream. He was certain his gifts were becoming even more powerful as he watched the wound fade into a scar. Footsteps echoed in the hallway, so he quickly pulled his shirt down, wrapped his jeans around the syringe, and stuffed the denim behind a bookcase.

"One's life was cut short, while the other grew old." Will's gaze remained fixed on a framed black-and-white snapshot of Sir James Nightingale and Sir Alfred Crozier in their military uniforms.

They stood side by side in a muddy trench. The gleam in their eyes was evidence of a proven bond between friends. "Now that I'm back, it feels like I'm on the outside."

"You are not alone, Will." From the doorway, Emma offered a disarming smile as she stepped into the quaint office stacked with boxes and rolled-up maps. "You are loved."

"Truth is, I wasn't sure you'd come."

Will glanced around the room, which looked more like a storage space than the original headmaster's office. He had nicked the key from his father's desk drawer downstairs and escaped to Beacon Hill's history so he could write his future. *Wonder if Nightingale kept any clues locked away in here.* Messaging Emma wasn't part of Addison's plan, but Will couldn't stop himself. He turned his attention toward color photos of Nightingale and Upsdell riding camels in the desert, then another of an aged Nightingale hunched over on the steps of Beacon Hill, posing for a shot with Headmistress Rowell. *Whatever happened to Rowell?* Nightingale's cold blue eyes were haunting, no matter the age of the legendary headmaster.

"Doesn't matter now." Will inhaled remorse and exhaled bitterness. "The past will always remain history."

Emma took another step forward. "We learned on Karābu to find healing in Elyon."

"You mean before I was kicked off the island after I failed to make the cut? I was gone before you even arrived. Maybe if I had met you then, we could have stopped all this from happening." Will shifted his weight, suddenly uneasy in Emma's presence. "My father kept this place locked up for years, but I've seen the maps he's taken from here and stored in his office. Whatever he was looking for didn't help him find me."

"I cannot imagine what you have gone through," Emma replied softly. "But it is over."

"We'll see if you're right." Will's eyes narrowed. "So, are you and Jack together?"

"It is complicated." Emma started to reach out but hesitated. "I care for you both."

"But you care for him more." Will refused to hide his disapproval. "He has taken it all."

"You need time to heal, to be restored by Elyon."

"The Cherub way hasn't stopped the pain from ripping my family apart. There is no healing in my future." Will grabbed Emma's hands and squeezed tight, imagining her parents' blood flowing through his veins. "What if we escaped from here and left all of this behind? Let the Cherub and Merikh destroy each other."

Emma pulled back as Will leaned in. "You are asking the impossible."

"There is another way to be free." Will's cheeks flushed as he let go of her hands, rejected once again by someone who claimed to care for him. "We can use our gifts to discover the world instead of being held back by the rules of those who want to control us."

"I cannot leave Jack and the others to fight this war alone."

"You know, you don't stand a chance against his father and the Merikh."

"Allowing darkness to rule," Emma retorted, "means surrendering the light."

"Darkness is all that's left." Will brushed past before stopping for a moment with his back to Emma. "After my mum died, you were there for me. I won't forget it."

79

QUARRY BAY, HONG KONG ISLAND

"I HAVE NEVER EXPERIENCED ANYTHING like it before."

Since leaving through the basement tunnel and grabbing the MTR, Tim hadn't stopped talking about what happened earlier in the Lion's Den. Normally, Jack would've tuned him out, but he was reliving those moments for himself in utter amazement.

"You know my parents would never believe me if I told them how I felt at that moment," Vince admitted. "When everyone got on their knees, it was like someone else was with us."

"Of course someone was with us." Amina smiled. "Elyon never leaves us."

"No way I thought I'd ever believe in Elyon," Vince confessed. "Now there's no doubt."

Tim shifted the conversation. "Emma, have you heard anything about your parents?"

"Timothy." Amina nudged him hard. "I am sure Emma would have told us."

"Nothing yet," Emma answered. "But like Amina said, Elyon never leaves any of us."

"We will find your parents," Jack promised.

"Thank you. I have faith I will see them again."

In the courtyard, the five were surrounded by eighteen-story buildings with multicolored floors guarded by the faction. The bright-red lanterns that had captured Jack's attention the first time he was here were absent now, leaving the area looking more run-down.

"What do we do now?" Tim asked, impatient. "Where is the faction?"

"Keep your voice down," Jack replied. "It's a secret hideout, remember?"

"Definitely not the Batcave," Vince retorted. "Why are we here, Jack?"

"We need to pick up a few things we left behind." Jack was caught off guard when Eliška stepped out from one of the buildings, along with another member of the faction. "Perfect timing."

"You brought everyone with you," Eliška said. "Professor Burwick will not approve."

"The faction's secret is safe with us," Jack reassured. "We've been together since the beginning. After last night, I think we've proven ourselves to be trustworthy." He nodded toward the other faction member. "Are you going somewhere?"

"One of Professor Burwick's sources within the HKPF informed her the Merikh have a shipment arriving tonight in Aberdeen."

Eliška glanced over her shoulder. "We will be there when it arrives, and we will—"

"What kind of shipment?" Tim asked, oblivious. "Drugs? Weapons?"

Vince nudged Tim twice as hard as Amina had. "The shipment is Cherub, dumpling head."

"Whoa . . ." Tim raised his brows at Jack. "You and Emma should go with them."

"Maybe we should all go," Vince suggested. "Eliška, do you need our help?"

"Look at you two," Amina mused. "Now you are searching for a fight."

"Only if you are willing," Eliška replied. "We do not know how many are being trafficked, or whether we will be able to get close enough to rescue them."

"Can't be worse than Shelter Island," Vince said.

Jack was eager to strike again. "It's settled then."

"Two nights in a row," Tim added. "Pretty soon we *will* need our own Batcave."

"Easy, crime fighter," Vince laughed. "You don't get more than one life in this game."

"Is that what you were thinking when you and Eliška turned into Aquaman and pulled the life raft all the way to the ferry?"

"Okay," Jack interrupted. "Less talking. More walking."

Tim and Vince exchanged a puzzled look, but before either could ask for an explanation, their attention shifted to Professor Burwick, who walked across the courtyard without her cane. Her stride seemed less labored than in Kyoto. *Maybe she's got a few healers of her own.* Everyone grew quiet as she approached.

"Eliška, you have some new recruits?"

"I am sorry, Professor. I did not expect—"

"You abandoned us last night," Jack interrupted. "We needed the faction."

"A mistake I will not make a second time." Burwick offered a disarming smile. "As far as this evening, I was hoping you and Emma could assist me with an important matter."

"If you need someone to stay behind," Tim offered, "I'm the one you should ask."

"I am afraid what is required is rather—dangerous."

"Roger that. I am *definitely not* the right person then. My specialty is more tactical."

"Are you listening to yourself?" Vince bantered. "Tactical? Now you're Jason Bourne?"

"Jack and Emma would be useful in Aberdeen," Eliška pointed out. "Professor?"

From the tension between Burwick and Eliška, it was clear there was something even more important than rescuing Cherub in Aberdeen. *I haven't seen either of them on edge with one another, but it's possible Eliška is sore because the faction bailed on us.* Jack kept quiet and listened closely, not only to what they said but to the words left unspoken.

"We should stay together," Emma suggested. "Aberdeen first, then we will help you."

"Time is of the essence," Burwick urged. "We risk losing a window of opportunity."

Jack was intrigued. "What opportunity?"

"To ambush your father," she replied flatly. "And strike a blow against the Merikh."

Adrenaline rushed through his veins. "Emma goes to Aberdeen, and I'll go with you."

"Jack," Emma protested. "We are stronger together."

He leaned in closer to Emma. "There are battles I need to fight for myself."

"What she is suggesting is not a battle," Emma whispered. "It is suicide."

"Suicide? You don't think I can handle myself after today?" Jack turned toward Burwick and ignored a disapproving glare from Emma. "Professor, I will go with you."

"Very well," Burwick replied. "Best we leave immediately."

Jack held out his hand until Emma gave him a handful of silver coins. He nodded at Tim and Vince, then followed Burwick as they walked through the courtyard. He wanted to look back and reassure Emma that he would be fine, but he knew it would only make things worse. *Was that our first fight? We're not even together, officially.* Just hours earlier, they'd been elated when the Rod of Elyon displayed its magnificent power. And now they were at odds, when all he'd done was repeat the same words Emma had once said to him. Ducking between buildings, Burwick led the way to a waiting van. He slid into the back seat and gazed straight ahead as the door closed.

"Jack, we need to make one stop on the way."

80

REPULSE BAY, HONG KONG ISLAND

ADDISON FUMED WHILE BLOOD taken from Oliver and Winnie Bennett streamed into his veins. Shortly after the prisoners on Shelter Island had disappeared, he'd received word and decided it was time to raise the stakes. Whether or not the transfusion worked, he knew he needed to retaliate. If one showed weakness when attacked, then one became the prey. He watched the clock until the scientist entered the room and completed the procedure.

Before leaving the penthouse, Addison grabbed Dragon Soul from one of the bedrooms and boarded his private elevator. When the doors opened, he crossed the rooftop as if he were out on a leisurely stroll. Beneath the stars sparkling extra bright in the night sky, he was certain the transfusion worked—which meant he was more lethal than the most gifted Cherub. Tonight, however, his retaliation would not be directly against them.

"Fear is the spark of any revolution," he whispered.

He gazed toward the lights across the bay, illuminating the wealthiest district in the world. Hong Kongers. Expats. Politicians. Celebrities. Global elite. The influential who shifted and coerced the culture, then escaped to their hideaways to separate themselves from the rest of society. Addison removed Dragon Soul from its scabbard and gripped the sword as if he were reuniting with an old friend.

"Far too long my gifts have remained stolen by the Cherub." He pointed the edge of Dragon Soul toward the full moon as a black flame engulfed the blade. "Tonight, I am the greater thief who lurks in the shadows stealing hope from the enemy."

With a swift swipe of the blade, flames streaked across the night before exploding against a building near a sandy beach. A blaze erupted and spread violently. Addison swiped the blade again, and another blast of fire struck a luxury apartment building. He moved with purpose across the rooftop, dancing in the darkness while escalating his destruction with precision. One building and mansion after another burned across Repulse Bay as those who believed they were protected from the world became the target of Addison's wrath.

At first, he laughed loudly, believing the energy flowing through him meant his gifts were being resurrected. But soon after he unleashed his attack, he was left winded on his knees, bracing himself by digging the point of Dragon Soul into the rooftop. Even after all the Cherub who were captured, and dozens of transfusions, a twinge of fear struck the Merikh leader. His gifts might never fully return, and he'd be left a mere shadow of the executioner he'd once been.

81

THE PEAK, HONG KONG ISLAND

A VAN RACED UP THE WINDING MOUNTAIN until the vehicle pulled over at The Peak, a famous tourist spot. Burwick climbed out and headed in the opposite direction from the restaurants, gift shops, and iconic viewing platform overlooking the city. Jack kept on her shoulder, surprised by how quickly she moved. Burwick turned left and took the stairs down to a concrete path winding along the ridge of Mount Austin. More than once, Jack gazed out on the sparkling lights of Hong Kong Island, Victoria Harbour, and Kowloon.

"Professor Burwick, where are we going?"

"The Cherub pride themselves on following the commands within the Eternal to the letter." Burwick continued her quick pace. "The Elders taught if one were to break the commands of Elyon even once, there would be consequences."

"I don't understand what that has to do with tonight. Aren't we going to ambush Addison and take the fight to the Merikh?"

"When Peter Leung took Eden's Star and used the compass to search for the artifacts, he committed the greatest sin since Asiklua and the legion were cast by Elyon from Charis." Burwick ignored Jack's question about Addison as she stepped off the concrete path and headed up the side of the hill along a narrow dirt trail. "In that moment, Peter broke the Mercy Covenant—which promised followers of Elyon peace within a dark world. We have all sinned against Elyon—however, grace and forgiveness restore our faith. I will confess, there have been moments when temptation knocked on my door. But I have always been curious about what the great Elder found after he stole Eden's Star and vanished."

"I have thought the same thing," Jack admitted. "Do you know?"

"While the Elders, Cherub, and Merikh have searched for Eden's Star and the artifacts, I have found the answer to my question—and I am not the only one who knows."

"Who else knows what he found, Professor?"

"Fang Xue, for one," Burwick replied. "And who knows which other highest Cherub."

"Why haven't they told anyone?"

"If they were quick to condemn his sin, they would unveil their own shortcomings." Burwick stopped in a small clearing and held out her open palm. "Another gateway—another offering."

Jack reached into his pocket and retrieved two silver coins, handing one to Burwick. He was on the edge of his seat, hoping she was about to uncover one of the mysteries he'd wondered about himself. *What did Peter Leung find with Eden's Star?*

"I must warn you, Jack . . ." Burwick dropped the coin onto the dirt. "Addison is part of the mystery."

The dirt beneath her feet began to swirl, so Jack quickly dropped his coin. Within a few seconds they were surrounded by quicksand and pulled beneath the earth. In a blink, Jack found himself standing on the shore of a lake with the sun setting behind the summit of a vast mountain range.

"Where are we?" Jack asked. "It's beautiful."

"Lake Brienz, Switzerland." Burwick pointed across the water. "During the age of Ryder Slybourne, whom you have known as the greatest Cherub warrior, many battles were fought and many treasures were taken. Slybourne was no different from any other man. He fought valiantly, and he gained great riches. In fact, the treasures he possessed were far greater than those of any other king or queen during his era—the world's only quintillion."

"I don't know how much a quintillion is, but I get the point." Jack kept his eyes glued to the boats floating in the lake. "Salomeh told us about Slybourne and Upsdell taking their treasure from Sakkhela and hiding it inside the Exodus Mines."

"Salomeh is very wise." Burwick nodded. "However, do you know why Dragon Soul is so important to both Cherub and Merikh alike?"

"Headmaster Upsdell found it on Everest centuries after Slybourne used it to fight against the Nephilim king." Jack had his own suspicions from what he'd heard, but he asked the question anyway. "Why is it so important?"

"Along with its supernatural powers in battle, there are those who believe the sword is also a key to the Exodus Mines." Burwick paused. "Peter Leung possessed many gifts; however, he was not able to wield Dragon Soul. Before his gifts were taken by Elyon, he wanted nothing more than to find Ryder Slybourne's treasure."

"Are the Exodus Mines here?"

"The mines are not in Lake Brienz, but the Cherub are keeping their own secret beneath the surface." Burwick pointed toward the boats at the center of the lake. "Before Eliška and Darcy traveled to Vietnam, I gave Eliška the only silver coins I had left—given to me by Dabria—and asked her to seek an answer. While she never found the Exodus Mines, she followed Peter Leung and several others to this place—including Fang Xue."

"What are they guarding here?"

"Eliška swore she witnessed Bau Hu using Dragon Soul to move the waters until the bottom revealed itself. And she watched as crates were loaded onto semitrucks—crates retrieved from the bottom of the lake."

"Professor, you already know what I'm going to ask."

"Yes, I believe it is perhaps a small fraction of Slybourne's treasure."

"Now Peter Leung is dead, so they are using the treasure for themselves." Jack hesitated. "Professor, the Merikh found Slybourne's shield—which could be from the Exodus Mines."

"How do you know this?" Burwick asked, surprised.

"We stole it from them," he admitted. "And we left it with someone—an ally."

"If you are correct, the Merikh must have secured the mines for themselves."

"Makes this place even more valuable to the Cherub if it's all they have left of Slybourne's treasure. With the sword missing, even if they were able to find the Exodus Mines, they wouldn't be able to get to it." Another puzzle piece was fitting into place. "And the only person left who can control the sword seems to be Bau Hu." A twinge of fear struck him. "Is Bau the shadow who attacked on Mount Hareh, killed Charlotte Taylor, and found us in Sakkhela?"

"Unless there is another from the past," Burwick suggested.

His encounter in the Zakhar flashed in his mind, but he remained quiet. *Addison.*

"The time to strike draws near." Burwick eyed Jack steadily. "Are you certain Bau is the only one you have seen use Dragon Soul at the school?"

Jack nearly snapped back an answer, but he stopped cold. "There is someone else who held Dragon Soul the night of the Sword and Fan."

82

ABERDEEN, HONG KONG ISLAND

IN ABERDEEN, known as the "Son of Hong Kong" since the Qing Dynasty, the floating village and seafood restaurants were highly sought after by tourists and Hong Kongers alike. A number of guarded warehouses were situated a few blocks inland from Aberdeen Harbour. Once an area of the fishing village where Aquilaria trees were exported to China, most of the warehouses were now controlled by the Merikh to traffic fentanyl—and people.

A double-decker plastered with digital screens displaying the top Hong Kong hot spots was parked near a dock where gamblers and foodies waited to board sampans for a night of indulgence within the colorfully lit harbor. Inside the double-decker, everyone stayed in the shadows and watched the activity at the warehouses, as well as those who waited in line at the docks.

"Let me get this straight," Tim said in a hushed voice. "We are going to waltz in there, somehow avoid those men with semi-automatics, then make our escape aboard this double-decker?" His gaze shifted between them. "Doesn't that sound a bit—bonkers?"

"At the right time we will need a distraction," Eliška replied confidently.

"It's okay if you're scared," Vince jabbed. "No shame in your game."

"Making it through the night without being shot sounds like a reasonable request." Tim turned toward Emma. "You have your hands full tonight, literally."

Since leaving Quarry Bay, Amina and Emma had remained relatively quiet. A shadow knocked on the bus door, startling everyone. Vince didn't hesitate as he moved toward the front and peered through the window. With a broad smile, he pulled a lever, and the door opened wide enough for the shadow to slip aboard.

"How did you find us?" Vince asked.

"Find My settings for Tim's cell." Will stood in the aisle. "Remember, last semester he lost his phone for nearly a month before he found it in the cricket clubhouse? He set up the phone to find it on mine if it ever happened again."

"And now you've found us," Tim chimed in. "Shouldn't you be resting?"

"And let you lot do all the heavy lifting?" Will looked past them at the others on the bus, who were armed with weapons. "Doesn't look like Beacon Hillers to me. Who are they?"

"Cherub faction." Tim nodded toward Eliška. "Will, meet Eliška. She's in charge."

"Nice to meet you." Will grinned. "What's a Cherub faction, anyway?"

"All you need to know," Vince replied, "is that our opponent is the Merikh."

"That's good enough for me." Will found a seat beside Emma. "Hey."

Emma smiled warmly. "I am glad you are here."

"You were right earlier. I survived for a reason, but sitting around in Crozier isn't the way for me to heal." Will paused. "Where's Jack?"

"There was somewhere else he needed to be that's just as important."

"Right . . ." Will's voice trailed off.

Twenty minutes passed before a semitruck approached a gated entrance to one of the warehouses. Heavily armed men stood guard as the gate opened and the semi rolled through. Eliška checked a message on her phone, then beckoned the others from the faction.

"Time to go," Eliška whispered. "Vince, Tim, and Will—you are our distraction."

"Huh?" Tim blurted. "What are you saying?"

"We got this, Eliška." Vince slapped Tim on the back. "Game time."

"Now we're cooking with fire," Will added. "We are the perfect *gweilos*."

Emma and Amina followed Eliška and the armed faction out the rear of the bus and disappeared into the night. Will led the way out the front with Vince and Tim on his heels. All three crossed the street and headed straight toward the armed men near the warehouse entrance. Will stumbled forward as if he were drunk, then started talking loudly. With the attention of the armed men turned in their direction, Tim and Vince followed Will's Oscar-winning performance and shouted at the top of their lungs as they nearly bumped into the two guards, who cursed as they passed.

Tim whispered, "Now what?"

"We become the heroes," Will answered.

Will spun around and darted toward the entrance to the warehouse, launching himself onto one of the men who had his back turned to him. Vince was right behind, pouncing on the other while Tim stood frozen as a statue. With several quick blows, Will and Vince disarmed the men and moved into the warehouse. Tim hurried to catch up.

Slipping through the warehouse, they moved stealthily between stacks of crates until they rendezvoused with the others. Will crouched behind a crate and placed his hand on Emma's shoulder with a look of determination as voices shouted outside.

"We need to split up." Eliška nodded toward the faction. "Search the bottom floor."

As the faction moved quickly, gunfire erupted. Bullets splintered wooden crates and ricocheted off metal beams. All of them crouched low until Eliška turned and raced upstairs. One by one they followed until only Will and Tim were left behind.

Will grabbed Tim's arm hard. "Did Jack find any other artifacts?"

"Seriously?" Tim replied, wide-eyed. "Look around. Now is not the time."

"Answer the question," Will seethed. "Has he found any more?"

"C'mon, we cannot get left behind."

"Where is he keeping the Rod of Elyon?"

"Look, enough chin-wagging. We need to stick with the others like glue or else we'll end up on Shelter Island—or even worse, Shek Pik."

Tim shoved Will backward and darted up the stairs. On the second floor, Vince guarded the hallway while Emma, Eliška, and Amina checked the rooms on both sides.

"No one is here," Emma said. "Eliška, are you sure this is the place?"

"Professor Burwick was certain—at least a hundred were to be trafficked."

"Do you hear that?" Amina asked, concerned. "The bullets stopped."

"Maybe we should get out of here," Tim suggested. "I got a bad feeling about this."

A royal purple burst of light flashed from out of nowhere through the hallway, striking Emma squarely in the chest. She collapsed to the floor while the others stood in shock. From the other end of the corridor a group of Merikh assassins moved in formation with weapons raised. Vince scooped Emma up in his arms just before the Merikh forced them downstairs. Those who were part of the Cherub faction were already disarmed and on their knees with hands interlaced behind their heads. As the Merikh assassins poked and prodded, Vince laid Emma on the floor beside him. Will was the last one to be pushed onto his knees.

Tim whispered loudly enough for all to hear. "Emma . . . wake up."

83

FROM THE SHADOWS, Addison Reynolds appeared with Dragon Soul firmly in his grasp. While the Merikh assassins kept their positions inside the warehouse, Addison strolled freely in front of his captives, relishing the moment.

"Your loyalty and faith in Jack is admirable," he said coldly. "But he has led you astray, so I am offering you a way out."

"We will not tell you where he is," Eliška said, fearless.

"Burwick's prized pupil speaks." Addison's soulless eyes grew darker. "You have cost the Merikh far more than you are worth—such a naive girl without any gifts. How easily I have rooted out the faction's mole within the HKPF." Addison pointed the sword within an inch of her nose. "You have survived longer than you deserve, but perhaps you will fetch a decent price—again."

"Enough with the speeches," Will blurted. "If you are going to kill us, then get it over with so we don't have to listen to one more second of your endless rant."

"Will, stop talking," Tim urged. "You're making it worse."

"What a disappointment you must be to your father." Addison stepped in front of Will and eyed him with contempt. "Jack caused you a great deal of pain—one might say he cost you everything." He waved Dragon Soul around them. "Where is he when you need him?"

"Jack is stronger than you'll ever be," Vince taunted, "even without the artifacts."

"And yet he continues to be a failure and danger to all of you." Addison stepped over to Amina and pressed the blade against her neck. "Tonight, he has abandoned you to suffer the consequences of his actions—alone." Amina bit her lip while tears rolled down her cheeks. "If you want to save your lives, it is very simple—tell me where to find my son and where the artifacts he has found are hidden. One . . . two . . ."

"He keeps the Rod of Elyon wrapped around his arm," Tim confessed, terrified. "We don't know what other artifacts he's found, or where he's keeping them."

Addison eased up on the blade's razor-sharp edge. "One of you has some sense."

"Don't say another word," Vince argued. "Not one more word, Tim."

"We have found the weakest of the misfits," Addison noted. "And the strongest."

Will stood as the others watched, confused and stunned. He joined Addison and grabbed Dragon Soul from the kingpin's grip. Without a word, he punched Tim so hard in the face his black-rimmed glasses shattered and flew across the floor. Vince lunged toward him, but Will moved quickly and blasted him with a burst of lightforce. He roundhouse-kicked Vince squarely in the jaw, leaving him unconscious beside Emma. Will didn't hesitate as he turned toward Tim and pierced with precision, pushing the blade into Tim's side. Amina grabbed hold of Tim as his eyes rolled back and his body slumped forward. She placed her shaking hands over the open wound and prayed earnestly.

"A Cherub healer," Addison said with a twinge of contempt. "Can she heal all of them at once?"

Amina glanced up, horror reflected in her eyes. "Will, you are a traitor."

"He is more loyal than any other," Addison rebuked. "And his revenge is justified."

Will unleashed another burst of energy, sending Eliška rolling across the floor. A smirk twisted his lips, as if he were enjoying the torture. "You are the traitors. Every last one of you."

"No mercy, my boy," Addison ordered. "You are one of us—the stronger one."

"We are your friends," Amina pleaded. "Vince and Tim are your brothers."

Will pointed Dragon Soul at Tim again. "They picked sides when they disappeared with Jack and left me behind."

"Jack is not the cause of your pain." Amina kept one bloodied hand on Tim's side and pointed another finger at Addison. "Whatever he has told you is a lie."

"She is the liar," Addison barked. "Kill them and send a message to the Cherub."

"I am telling you the truth." Amina stood her ground. "Stand with us."

"You don't know what I have done," Will said, glassy-eyed. "Who I have become."

"It is never too late for forgiveness, but you need to stop."

With gritted teeth, Will plunged Dragon Soul deep into Tim's chest while Addison unleashed deathly flames, engulfing the faction operatives and turning them into ash. Amina uncaged a bloodcurdling, bone-chilling scream that pierced the realms of light and dark. Emma's eyes opened, and she rolled onto her knees. Streaks of light burst from her glowing palms, consuming the Merikh assassins. She struck as quickly and as deadly as Addison. Her eyes turned stark white as she lifted her hands toward the heavens, sending crates flying across the warehouse. Will countered with his purple lightforce, exploding the crates in midair, while black flames swirled around Addison. Emma darted across the warehouse before pinning Addison against the wall with her power, struggling to keep him from breaking free. She braced for an onslaught as Will swung Dragon Soul back and forth—but he wavered.

84

A TORNADO SWIRLED INSIDE THE WAREHOUSE, a powerful force tearing apart walls and ripping the metal roof from its iron beams. In the center of the twister, Jack and Professor Burwick appeared out of thin air. Before the spiral evaporated, Jack moved swiftly, spinning Soulweaver with a righteous vengeance. Energy pulsed, then shot like a cannon from the rod, exploding against his best friend. Will never let go of Dragon Soul as he flew through the air and slammed against a stack of crates.

He's knocked down, but he's not out.

Jack couldn't comprehend the unthinkable as he battled between fear and rage. He swung Soulweaver as hard as he could, but Will blocked every strike. Before he could switch his tactics, Will swept his legs out from under him. Dragon Soul flashed against the heartwood of Soulweaver as Jack lay on his back, desperately trying to defend himself. The blade moved like lightning and landed like thunder. Jack rolled as quickly as possible, then scrambled to his feet as the blade sliced across his scarred arms. Pain seared through him, but he knew if he stopped it was over.

"Will, you better put Dragon Soul down." Jack grimaced as he steadied himself. "Before it's too late."

"You have taken everything from me," Will hissed. "Now it is my turn."

"Only the strong embrace revenge," Addison shouted. "No weakness."

A searing inferno spread across Jack's chest as Soulweaver twisted between his fingers. *Elyon, you are in control of the rod. Help me put an end to this.* Emma blitzed from the opposite side, keeping Addison pinned against what was left of the warehouse wall. She closed in with a barrage of energy pulses. Will wielded Dragon Soul as if he were Ryder Slybourne, deflecting her attack without harm. Jack took advantage of the distraction and stepped closer. Will glanced over his shoulder at Emma, then back to Jack.

"Turn from the darkness," Jack ordered Will, "and this will all be over."

"Jack!" Vince shouted, now fully conscious. "Tim's in bad shape, bro."

"He needs to get to Windsor," Burwick called out. "Right away."

"Please!" Amina screamed. "He is dying!"

Blood dripped down Jack's arms as he stabbed Soulweaver into the ground as a warning, cracking the concrete foundation into pieces. Emma took another step closer, harnessing her power in the palms of her hands. Will lowered Dragon Soul, and for a split second Jack thought he was going to surrender.

"This is not the end," Will promised. "It is only a new beginning."

He raised his hand, and in a cloud of brilliant purple light, the headmaster's son vanished. Addison remained pinned against the wall as he laughed hysterically. Vince stormed across the warehouse with clenched fists. He swung with every ounce of anger, knocking Addison out cold.

"A wound caused by Dragon Soul is not of this world," Burwick said urgently. "He needs Windsor and more experienced healers if he is to have any chance of surviving."

While Emma kept an unconscious Addison up against the wall, Jack hurried over and slid on his knees, stopping next to Amina. With his own arms covered in blood, he placed his hand over hers and grabbed Tim. He closed his eyes and tried to settle his spirit, which seemed impossible since his heart was beating a thousand times per second.

How was Will able to disappear? I thought it was only possible with Eden's Star, or through a gateway. C'mon, Jack. All that matters right now is getting Tim to Windsor.

Breathing in deep, the warmth in his chest boiled into a searing heat. A split second later, he, Tim, and Amina were on the grass of the quad at Beacon Hill. He picked Tim up in his arms and carried his limp body toward the Main Hall. Amina raced ahead as she shouted out for Professor Windsor.

By the time Jack reached the entrance, he'd lost a lot of blood and was losing consciousness. Bau appeared at the top of the stairs and slid down the handrail. He grabbed Tim from Jack, then carried him up the stairs two at a time into the Main Hall. Jack struggled to keep up as his vision closed in on him. He stopped, pressed his elbows into his knees, and vomited on the ground. He stumbled up the steps before falling facedown on the marble floor.

Professor Windsor was working methodically by the time Jack

shuffled into Crozier Hospital. Amina and Bau rushed out past him. He guessed they were going to find more healers. Windsor worked to slow the bleeding from Tim's chest and side. She glanced up for a second and eyed Jack.

"Best put pressure on your wounds," she instructed. "How did this happen?"

Jack wiped his bloodied hands on his clothes. "He was stabbed with Dragon Soul."

"The wounds are very deep, and I cannot stop the bleeding." Windsor kept her eyes glued to the task at hand as she grabbed a surgical stapler and attempted to close each wound. "If this is from Dragon Soul, infection will be our greatest concern."

Jack's legs weakened as he slumped against an empty gurney. His surroundings turned to tunnel vision as blood flowed from his open gashes. Professor Windsor grabbed him before he could fall to the floor and guided him over to another bed. She hurried back to Tim and hooked him up to an IV, then returned to Jack with what she needed to suture the wounds on his arms.

"Are these from Dragon Soul as well?" Windsor asked calmly.

In a daze he mumbled, "I'm sorry . . ."

"Hold still, Jack."

Windsor weaved the needle and nylon thread beneath his skin. He winced in pain, but it was nothing compared to the agony in his soul. A lump lodged in his throat and tears flowed. He couldn't stop, and he didn't care whether Windsor was present. A flood of remorse burst from every ounce of his flesh. He struggled to stay conscious until he knew for sure whether Tim was okay, but once Windsor hooked up the IV, the world around him faded.

85

IN THE EARLY MORNING HOURS, before daybreak peeked over the earth, a steady rhythmic beep woke Jack, who'd been moved to another room. He tugged at an IV inserted into his arm pumping a strong dosage to ease the pain. He grunted as he struggled to sit up, head swimming while he tried to keep his balance. Emma was curled up in a chair beside his bed. He gazed at her body rising and falling, convinced he was falling even harder.

"Don't suppose you would rest until morning," Professor Windsor said softly.

Jack turned his head, surprised she was standing there. "How's Tim doing?"

"The next forty-eight hours are critical." Windsor's gaze eased, a contrast to her matter-of-fact demeanor. "Cherub healers were here earlier, and now they are gathered in the House of Luminescence."

Jack reached for the IV. "I need to speak to the headmaster."

"Hold on a minute, Jack. I stitched and bandaged your wounds as best I could. However . . . well . . . I am certain you are aware of what is on your arm." Windsor grabbed his other arm and removed the IV, then unhooked the devices monitoring his vitals. "Best someone goes with to keep an eye on you."

Emma stretched her arms and legs. "I will go with him, Professor."

"Jack needs to take it slow." Windsor locked eyes with him. "I want to run more tests later."

"Slow and steady." Jack realized Windsor knew his secret. "I promise."

"I will come find you if you are not back here this afternoon."

Professor Windsor left them alone in the room and disappeared down the corridor. Emma set a pair of jeans, a T-shirt, and a burgundy hoodie on the bed. Normally, Jack would have been embarrassed by the serpent wounds on his arms, the crude scarring from Eden's Star on his chest, and the purplish-red bruises crisscrossing his body. But there were more pressing concerns on his mind. With his arms partially bandaged, he realized the cuts from Dragon Soul were yet another reminder of what was at stake.

A wound caused by Dragon Soul is not of this world.

He winced as he pushed the bedsheet aside and slipped on his jeans. Only then did Windsor's comments fully register—Soulweaver remained wrapped around his right arm beneath the bandages. As he gingerly stepped onto the cold tile floor, Emma helped him pull the T-shirt over his head and wrap the zip-up hoodie around his shoulders.

"Healing is in Elyon's hands," Emma said. "We must wait for his timing."

"I thought only Eden's Star could make someone disappear." He shuffled out of the room with Emma by his side. "On Mount Hareh, the same purple lightforce made you disappear too."

"Will was at the Sanctuary of Prayer," Emma agreed. "Along with Peter and your father—they are the ones responsible for the massacre. Honestly, it is hard for me to accept."

"For a long time, I suspected the headmaster was keeping something from me." Jack stopped in the doorway of another private room in the wing and stared at Vince and Eliška, who were asleep in their own hospital beds. "How bad are their injuries?"

"Will's lightforce is extremely powerful, and your father's abilities are unlike any I have ever seen. Vince and Eliška are extremely fortunate. Professor Windsor sedated them as a precaution, but she expects they will be on their feet soon. Both are fighters."

"What happened after I brought Tim and Amina back?" Jack asked.

"Professor Burwick reached Fang Xue while I kept your father contained. His powers were so strong I was not sure I would be able to keep him under control." Emma paused. "He has the gifts of a Cherub—in the same way as Michael Chung—but there is something far darker raging within him. Fang Xue told Burwick that his powers are weakened, which means there was a time when he must have been unstoppable."

"I thought if he had gifts, they would've been taken after what he did to my mom, Rachel, and me—and who knows how many Cherub he's killed. If he still has his gifts, is that because he's an outlier?"

"Somehow, the Merikh took my gifts from me before I was

restored in Sakkhela. Perhaps they know how to return one's gifts apart from Elyon. We will need to ask the highest Cherub whether this is actually possible, especially for an outlier." Emma squeezed his hand. "More than a dozen Cherub arrived in Aberdeen with Fang Xue and took Addison away. Your father is no longer a threat to the Cherub—or to you. He will be imprisoned for eternity."

"What about Will?" Jack struggled to accept that his best friend was more powerful than he'd ever realized. "He still has his powers *and* Dragon Soul."

"Two of the strongest Merikh leaders have been defeated. We do not know what tomorrow will bring, but in this moment the Cherub are victorious."

"Victorious?" Jack repeated, incredulous. "Emma, this is not a victory."

Jack continued down the corridor until they reached another doorway. He peered inside, where Elis and Beca Lloyd were huddled around the bed of their son. Guilt shredded what was left of his spirit. Before either looked up, he stepped back and kept walking—ashamed.

"What am I supposed to say to them?" Jack mumbled. "All of this is my fault."

"Sometimes there are no words to comfort others," Emma replied. "Your presence is what matters most—and your love for them."

"Elyon was supposed to protect us. We risked our lives, and look at us."

"We are still alive, for which I am grateful. Now is not the time for doubt."

"Professor Burwick must've known Addison would be there—or at the very least whoever stole Dragon Soul. She took me to a place hidden by the Cherub and waited until the right time. I'm not sure whether Eliška knew what the professor was up to, but she was right—we ambushed Addison and struck a blow."

"At a heavy cost," Emma replied. "I warned you about trusting the faction."

"I don't think we can trust Fang Xue either. Not after what I've seen."

"Then we can only trust each other."

Jack and Emma left Crozier Hospital and took the stairs as whispers echoed off the concrete walls. Those whispers grew stronger once they reached the solid oak doors leading to the House of Luminescence. A myriad of colors emanated from the room, no longer a singular turquoise but a spectrum of Elyon's creation. Beneath the wood beams and around the thick vines, this forbidden place overflowed with Cherub on their knees in prayer.

"Faith of a mustard seed," Jack whispered.

"Parts the seas." Emma grabbed his hand. "And moves the highest mountains."

Out of the corner of his eye, Jack noticed Headmaster Fargher in the back of the room with his arms crossed. When Fargher looked in his direction, their exchange confirmed to Jack what the headmaster had kept from him. He squeezed Emma's hand tight and tried to keep himself from collapsing.

Amina approached with tears in her eyes, yet with a radiant glow as she hugged Emma. "So many are praying—not only here but everywhere the Cherub remain."

"Elyon promises to heal the sick," Emma said, "and bring peace to the broken."

Jack let go of Emma's hand once he realized Fargher was headed for the doors. By the time Jack reached the hallway, the headmaster had neared the steps. He wanted to call out but kept his distance instead. Fargher climbed the steps to the Main Hall, and Jack followed. Both walked at a slow pace through the halls, past the wall of heroes, before exiting out into the quad. Fargher continued down the steps, striding along a stone path until he reached the Oasis of Remembrance.

Chinese elm hedges and wisteria vines were barren. Plum blossoms, roses, lilies, daisies, and hydrangeas were withered on the ground. Jack crunched across the dry grass while Fargher stood in front of a ginkgo tree, its leafless branches looming over a concrete stone. Jack read the plaque in silence while he mustered up his nerve.

"All this time," Jack said, "did you know?"

Fargher answered with his back to Jack. "Is my son alive?"

"He was there with Addison, but then he disappeared." Jack harnessed his anger. "But not before he attacked with Dragon Soul *and* his lightforce. Right now Tim is fighting for his life, and all you've done is run from the truth. Rachel helped you return to your faith, and all along you knew the evil within your own house. I deserve to know, Headmaster."

"When William was rescued from Shelter Island, I hoped it was over." Fargher turned around with a sorrowful gaze. "I trusted Peter to teach him the Cherub way—against the concerns of Olivia. She worried about William and feared he was unable to control his abilities. It seems she was the wise one—and I am a fool."

"Did you tell Will it was Michael Chung who killed her?" Jack waited impatiently for an answer, then fired off one more. "Does he know it was because of Addison?"

"My son returned." Fargher shook his head slowly. "Too broken to know the truth."

"Who told Peter about Will? Was it my father?"

"We instructed William to never reveal his supernatural ability to anyone." Fargher sat on a stone bench and dug his elbows into his thighs. "However, one afternoon he was caught on the roof of Nightingale House testing his lightforce. He was afraid his secret would be revealed to everyone, including you. Instead of exposing him to the world, we were introduced to Peter and sworn to secrecy. Weeks later, William was invited to train on Karābu Island with the Elder."

"He was caught by one of the chosen," Jack said, dumbstruck. "Is he one of them?"

"We thought he would become one." Fargher stared hard at the concrete stone. "His abilities were not strong enough during those days. He was devastated and angry. Peter offered to continue teaching him how to control his gifts. At the time, we did not know the Elder's true intention."

"Did you know who the chosen were at Beacon Hill?"

"Throughout the years, not all of the names have been disclosed to me. Most recently, Amina was a bridge between the Elder and myself to help keep certain identities and purposes from being known. Still, I remained faithful to the Cherub and believed the Elder would ensure the protection of the students within the grounds—including William. However, we feared one day Cherub or Merikh would arrive to take him away."

"'We knew this day might come,'" Jack whispered. "That's what you said to McDougall."

"After Olivia's death it was inevitable, I suppose."

"Headmaster, who caught Will on the roof of Nightingale?"

"Dear boy . . . it was Rachel."

86

REPULSE BAY, HONG KONG ISLAND

DROPS OF BLOOD SEEPED DOWN the inside of a glass tube and dripped onto the original Treaty of Nanjing. Will had watched the Russian scientist perform the procedure several times before, so he followed the steps as he remembered. Next to him, Dragon Soul was laid across a table with streaks of Jack's blood on the blade—and Tim's too.

Why didn't he tell me what I needed to know? It's his fault, not mine.

Crimson spread across the map of the Highlands, revealing the areas of Sakkhela and a path to the Valley of Grace. Will had been with the Merikh assassins when they ambushed Jack and the others in Sakkhela, but Addison called him back before he could continue. Chung led the assassins through the gateway to the Valley of Grace. When Tim had told Will about Charis and how Jack killed Chung with the Rod of Elyon, Will's only regret was not being the one to stand before Jack.

A swaying bridge in Vigan flashed in his mind—the night Will had killed another Cherub Elder. Addison sent him, but it was Chung who trained him. Now there was only one Elder left alive. Blood seeped toward the edge of the parchment, crossing over the boundaries of the map to reveal an ancient text marked beyond the Highlands.

Will stabbed the glass with his finger. "That's where you're going next."

He grabbed Dragon Soul and entered the opulent living room of the penthouse. He swung the sword recklessly, shattering glass and shredding everything in sight. He smashed the case displaying the Windstrikers, then snatched them up. Broken glass was scattered across the marble floors as he gripped Dragon Soul and the Windstrikers, stabbing the pointed blade into the center of the painting depicting ancient Merikh ships floating in Repulse Bay.

Arrogance led Addison into the hands of the Cherub. I will not make the same mistake.

Alone in the Merikh fortress, he stormed from room to room in a rage of uncontrolled destruction. Addison had brought him there after he chose betrayal to protect his father, but there was only one room where he'd slept whenever he wasn't hunting the Cherub with Chung. He stuffed the Windstrikers and a handful of clothes into the same backpack he'd found in the bushes at Fortress Hill. He'd kept the drawings hidden from Addison inside a zippered pocket. He'd pulled them from the backpack only a handful of times—late at night when he was alone.

The first drawing was the Clock Tower in Tsim Sha Tsui. The second sketched rolling hills and a stone wall, then another was a wooden shack with a tiled roof along a mountain. In the next, he recognized a lion's head with a magnificent mane as the mascot of Beacon Hill. But it was a steep mountain with a pointed peak and a sprouting tree on the summit in the last drawing that caught his attention most, as he imagined it must be Elyon's Vine in Charis.

What other secrets to the artifacts are these drawings hiding?

Will slid Dragon Soul into the scabbard and slipped the backpack over his shoulders. He left Charlotte Taylor's and Addison Reynolds's lair and swore never to return.

On the rooftop of the penthouse, a helicopter waited with blades spinning. Will climbed aboard and the pilot lifted off, heading in the direction of Lantau Island. Twenty minutes later, the skids landed within the barbed wire fencing of Shek Pik Prison.

The prison warden approached. "I was expecting Mr. Reynolds."

"He sent me instead." Will remained stone-cold. "Is there a problem?"

"Not a problem—follow me."

The warden escorted Will across a concrete yard, then through a maze of security doors. Will recognized the building as the place where Cherub were stripped of their gifts through transfusions, leaving those who survived the procedure powerless. He passed rooms filled with empty beds and stacks of folded-up body bags waiting to be used.

The warden unlocked another door with a key card. "As instructed."

Inside a steel-enforced room, a hooded inmate stood shackled inside an iron-barred cage. Half a dozen armed and masked Merikh surrounded the space. Will stepped forward and eyed the inmate, looking for any reaction to his presence. *Nothing.* He pulled a lever on the wall, and the floor beneath lifted while the ceiling above opened wide.

Under starry skies, the barred cage appeared on the rooftop of the building. The Merikh assassins stepped away and took their positions while Will stayed close. His instincts fired in overdrive as he reached through the bars and yanked the hood away. Xui Li stood there with graying hair and pale skin, glaring at him with intense brown eyes.

"You are the last of the Elders—and you are helpless." Will paused. "I am the one responsible for the massacre at the Sanctuary of Prayer. I am the one who killed Charlotte Taylor and the Elder in Vigan." He noticed her gaze flicker, then return to a deadpan stare. "The Cherub told me I was not gifted enough, but the Merikh are not strong enough to control me. You see, I am the shadow who lurks in the nightmares of those who believe."

"Elyon is patient with all who seek forgiveness," Xui Li replied coolly. "Even you."

"I am not a blind follower—not anymore." Will stepped back so Xui Li could get a look at what was behind him—hundreds of Cherub prisoners zip-tied and on their knees. "I will spare their lives if you tell me what lies beyond the Highlands."

Xui Li shifted her gaze toward the prisoners. "Beyond the Highlands lies a nether realm concealing the most powerful of all artifacts ever formed with Elyon's hand—stolen by the darkest of betrayers."

"Does Jack know about this artifact?" Will asked point-blank.

"I can only speak the truth, and the truth is he has chosen his path."

Will pressed harder. "Can he use Eden's Star to enter the nether realm?"

"Eden's Star is a compass meant to hide the artifacts, but for some it has been used to take what does not belong to them. Only the darkest of souls may cross over into the nether realm." Xui Li hesitated. "Jack will die if he searches for what lies beyond."

A low thumping from the helicopter grew louder as the aircraft hovered directly overhead, a thick cable swaying beneath. Will grabbed hold of the cable and latched it to the top of the barred cage. He stepped back as the helicopter ascended, bearing Xui Li inside the cage. Several of the Cherub prisoners lunged forward, but the Merikh assassins reacted with lethal force. Will moved swiftly through the chaos as black flames ravaged the blade of Dragon Soul.

87

BEACON HILL

In the stillness of the morning, the clock tower remained quiet as a vision swarmed through Jack's mind, beyond the ones he'd seen before. Innocence was stolen with Dragon Soul. Dark silhouettes whipped across a night sky, unleashing vile squeals over the dead. Blurred sketches shifted into focus to reveal ancient text on a map of the Highlands. *Will has uncovered the rest of the Treaty of Nanjing.* A sea of thousands were desperate to enter through the gates of Beacon Hill. Jack couldn't determine which parts of the vision were in real time, and which had not yet occurred. With his head lowered and arms wrapped around his knees, the vision vanished once he opened his eyes.

A wooden door creaked, and McNaughton called out, "Jack, are you up there?"

"Yeah." He pulled himself to his feet and stepped back from the gaping hole in the floor, noticing that the brass clock remained stuck on 11:47. "Needed a few minutes to clear my head."

McNaughton appeared at the top of the steps. "Fang Xue is requesting a meeting."

"I'm not going anywhere until Tim wakes up."

"It is about Addison—and Emma's parents."

Jack's brows furrowed. "What about her parents?"

"I heard from Detective Ming an hour ago." McNaughton hesitated. "There was an incident last night at Shek Pik Prison."

"Were they being held there with the other Cherub? Are they alive?"

"Slow down, Jack. Fang Xue is willing to shed some light and answer questions."

"You know what they will do, especially if they find out Eden's Star is inside me." Jack paced back and forth, attempting to discern whether this was a trap or an olive branch. "If it will help Emma then I'll do it, but she needs to be there too."

"Come on then." McNaughton started down the stairs. "Everyone is waiting."

By the time they entered the auditorium, a group was gathered. Headmaster Fargher. Professors McDougall, Windsor, and Burwick. Salomeh and Faizan. Fang Xue. And Emma. All eyes turned toward Jack, which left him feeling as if he were on trial. He found a spot next to Emma while McNaughton kept her distance and remained near the door. His gaze shifted among them before he realized who was missing—Bau.

"Beacon Hill remains neutral ground," Fargher said pointedly. "Understood?"

"We have sworn to protect the school for many years," Fang Xue replied. "However, what has unfolded is unprecedented. Headmaster, you are harboring the one who killed Peter Leung, and the highest Cherub demand justice."

"No student of Beacon Hill will be forcefully removed by anyone."

"We will do what is necessary to protect the Cherub." Fang Xue turned her attention toward Emma. "You continue to disobey all you have been taught, and you have thrown Elyon's calling on your life away. After what you have done, you will never become our leader. In fact, there is much discussion among the highest Cherub regarding your role in the mayhem."

"Fang, give it a rest, for the love of Elyon," Burwick interrupted.

"What happened at Shek Pik?" Jack asked. "Isn't that why we're here?"

"Last night the Merikh slaughtered Cherub in the prison," Salomeh stated. "One of the faction's sources has confirmed some of the identities of those who were killed."

"Emma, your parents have not been identified, but we are still receiving names of the deceased," Burwick said. "Our source within the prison confirmed the last name Bennett was found on a list kept in a medical wing. Between Fang, Salomeh, and myself, we recognize most of those so far who are confirmed dead. We believe others may still be imprisoned at Shek Pik. However, transport buses have left the prison since the attack—before we received word."

Fang Xue held up her hand, anticipating an outburst. "Until

we have a plan to rescue the other Cherub being held, it is unwise to provoke further aggression."

"Are you serious?" Jack argued. "Merikh are killing people and you do nothing?"

"William was seen last night arriving at the prison," Burwick continued. "Our source is one of the prison guards who also confirmed sighting of a woman inside a solitary cage on the roof where the Cherub were killed. He struggled to describe the swiftness of death that occurred, but we will continue to seek more details."

"Based on what we have heard from the guard since last night, the woman inside the cage was Xui Li," Salomeh added. "She was taken by helicopter immediately before the massacre. Jack, clearly the headmaster's son is far more dangerous than Cherub or Merikh imagined—perhaps surpassing Michael Chung and your father."

"If William kept Xui Li alive," Burwick interjected, "there is a reason."

"Addison is willing to speak." Fang Xue's gaze shifted to Jack. "But only to you."

"He cannot be trusted," Burwick objected. "It is all a game to him."

"We are better off staying focused on rescuing the Cherub from Shek Pik," Salomeh suggested. "Besides, what could you offer him that would force him to tell the truth?"

"Elyon's mercy," Fang Xue replied. "There is no other way to be free from endless torment."

"And if he lies?" Burwick retorted.

"He will suffer eternal pain—beyond our world in another realm."

Headmaster Fargher cleared his throat. "Jack, the choice is yours."

With all eyes on him, Jack weighed his decision. "I'll go, but everyone else stays."

"Professor Burwick," Emma said softly. "I will go to Shek Pik Prison."

"The faction is ready to fight alongside," Burwick replied, resolute. "You have my word."

"I must warn you—" Fang Xue began.

"You cannot control everyone all the time," Salomeh retorted. "Take Jack to see Addison, and pray for a miracle."

Jack pulled Emma aside while the others remained in a circle, their heated discussion escalating. Clearly, the faction and Cherub were being held together by a thread.

"We each will fight our own battles today." Emma removed the bangle Salomeh had given her and slipped it onto Jack's wrist. *In raging seas and surging tides, Elyon draws close to all who call upon eternity's glory.* "Be careful, Jack."

"Bring your parents home, Emma. And I'll deal with my father."

McNaughton stepped over. "Which one of you needs a shadow?"

"Boys are always the ones who find trouble," Emma teased half-heartedly.

"You're stuck with me then," Jack said.

88

WHEN JACK HAD TRAVELED through the gateway to Lake Brienz with Burwick, the sun was setting and night wrapped around the lake. This time it was daylight, and he saw a number of boats circling in the center of the lake.

"You two are acting like this is normal," McNaughton said. "A gateway?"

"I've gone through a few of them," Jack replied. "You never get used to it."

"Gateways allow us to travel across this world and into other realms." Fang Xue motioned a boat drifting near shore to approach. "Within the Golden Triangle, journeying through gateways has proven to be increasingly perilous."

Jack tried to catch Fang Xue off guard. "How much of Slybourne's treasure are the Cherub keeping underwater?"

"The faction continues to find ways to cause division among Elyon's followers," she replied without hesitation. "However, in my role as Cherub leader, the truth is my guiding light. So I will share with you a secret kept from many of the Cherub—a secret it seems you may already know. Many years ago, Peter Leung found the Exodus Mines and used Slybourne's riches to rebuild the Cherub, strengthening our foundation and equipping us with the resources to defend ourselves against the Merikh."

"Do you know how he found the mines?" Jack asked.

"Elyon guided him along his journey and revealed the mines to him for this purpose."

"He stole Eden's Star and one of the maps hiding the artifacts from the Elders." Jack couldn't deny a twinge of satisfaction. "He found the Exodus Mines because he was searching for what Elyon commanded must remain hidden. Then somewhere along the way—I don't know where or when—he lost Eden's Star and it ended up in the Temple of the Nephilim in the City of Gods."

Fang Xue's brows furrowed. "How can you possibly know this to be true?"

"He was nothing more than a thief and a fraud." Jack knew he'd knocked Fang Xue off balance. So he continued. "He stole Slybourne's treasure to stay in power and allowed the existence of the Elders to remain a myth so he could keep control of the Cherub. He deceived all who swore allegiance to him and Elyon—including you."

"Are you keeping Addison in the Exodus Mines?" McNaughton asked.

"The Exodus Mines aren't here," Jack interrupted. "Isn't that the truth?"

"No Cherub alive knows where the mines are located—and I assure you the mines are not at the bottom of Lake Brienz." Fang Xue shifted her weight uncomfortably. "We have brought Addison here to keep him under watch—among others."

"If the treasure was buried beneath a lake like this one," Jack pressed, "Peter would have needed someone strong enough to control Dragon Soul." He was putting the pieces in place as the words left his lips. "Bau or Will weren't born back then—and the only other person I've seen with the sword in his hand is my father."

"Addison and Peter Leung stole the treasure together?" McNaughton asked.

"That is a question I intend to ask him."

"Where is Eden's Star?" Fang Xue demanded. "Show it to me."

"We are keeping it hidden, like how you are hiding the truth from the Cherub about this place." McNaughton shot Jack a quick glance. "But I have seen it."

Fang Xue eyed McNaughton. "Eden's Star and the artifacts belong to the Cherub."

"The compass belongs to Elyon," Jack retorted. "And I am the Protector."

"That explains why Emma has remained by your side," Fang Xue chided. "She has chosen her love for you over her allegiance to the Cherub. You have turned her against us."

"She has sacrificed far more than you realize, and she is far more loyal than you can imagine. Deep down, you know what I'm saying about Peter Leung is true."

"You need Jack's help with Addison," McNaughton redirected.

"We should stay focused on that for now. It is important we know what the Merikh have planned next."

The speedboat approached the shore, and a young man behind the wheel docked at a small wooden pier. Jack followed Fang Xue and McNaughton aboard as the engine revved and the speedboat headed toward the center of the lake where the other boats drifted. He breathed deep, attempting to rein in his anger.

"I am afraid only Jack will be allowed beyond this point," Fang Xue said.

McNaughton protested, "That is not part of the agreement."

"It's okay," Jack replied. "Natalie, I'll be fine."

McNaughton grabbed his shoulder. "I should go with you."

"I need to face Addison—and if this is the only way, then so be it."

Fang Xue leaned over the side of the boat and placed her hand beneath the surface of the water. A ripple swirled while the rest of the lake remained calm. Jack peered over the edge and noticed a hole appear inside the swirl and grow wider. Fang Xue wasted no time as she climbed over the side of the boat and dropped into the abyss.

"Surrender is not a choice that is made once. It is a decision made thousands of times."

With Xui Li's voice echoing in his soul, Jack climbed overboard and jumped in. He slid down a waterfall within the lake. Even though he was sliding rapidly, he landed softly on the bottom. Fang Xue stood over a brass vault door as the rushing water swirled around them.

"Let's hope there's not a Nephilim king inside," Jack mumbled.

Fang Xue ignored his sarcasm and unlocked the vault. He followed her down a ladder, deeper beneath the earth. The vault door sealed shut, and they were surrounded by a bluish illumination. Jack stayed on Fang Xue's heels as she moved briskly through a cavernous space, which reminded him eerily of the Cave of Prophets. He noticed ancient relics stacked on both sides as if they were mountains of gold—too many to count.

This is only a fraction of Slybourne's treasure? The Merikh will use the Exodus Mines to gain greater power, which is trouble for the rest of us.

A warmth spread across his chest, and his instincts sharpened. He wasn't prepared for Eden's Star to flare, so when the heat magnified, he knew one of the artifacts may be nearby. *Does Fang Xue know what's being kept down here?* He didn't trust her, but he knew once he was back on the surface he'd be sure to tell McNaughton. He stopped next to Fang Xue in front of an unguarded iron door.

"Those who pose a great threat to the world are on the other side," Fang Xue explained. "No matter what Addison reveals, it must never go beyond these doors."

Jack nodded. "Understood."

89

Fang Xue placed her palm against the iron door, and an orange glow spread until the lock clanked open. Jack followed her inside and tried to make sense of why Addison would only speak with him. His mind flashed to the rainy day when he'd stood over the mound of dirt where Rachel was buried. *I've failed to deliver on my promise. Elyon, I don't deserve to be trusted with Eden's Star or Soulweaver.* Jack snapped back to the present when the bluish hue was replaced by a dull glow hovering in a narrow corridor with iron doors lining both sides.

"Since the victories of the Great Wars, the defeat of Slybourne in the Battle of Everest, and the Age of Trepidation, we have fought against enemies of this world and other realms." Fang Xue walked at a deliberate pace as an eerie silence lingered. "Enemies captured by the Cherub are kept here in the depths of the Dungeon of Savages."

Jack felt Soulweaver squeeze tight around his forearm. "Are there prisoners here now?"

"Not as many as during the Great Wars," Fang Xue admitted. "Jack, unless we know which artifacts the Merikh have found, we face the wrath of darkness in this world and beyond."

"Do you really think Addison will confess?" Jack asked, unconvinced. "Think about it. You've locked him in an underwater dungeon because he is a *savage*."

"Before Addison was captured in Aberdeen, I stood face-to-face with him and offered a truce. In exchange, I promised to give you to him. Still, he refused to agree even though judgment against you would be his reward. Then I looked into his soul and understood his sins go far beyond the Merikh." Fang Xue stopped in front of another iron door. "The highest Cherub see you as an enemy, so this is your opportunity to prove your loyalty to Elyon. In this moment you can end the nightmares and stop this war from stealing more souls."

"Your plan is to hand me over to him?" Jack replied. "A sheep led to slaughter."

"With Addison imprisoned, there is another way. A truce has not yet been sealed, and if you are able to prove yourself to the Cherub, then I will use my authority to help you avoid the judgment that is coming."

"Then let's get this over with before I change my mind."

Fang Xue turned around and held her arms wide. A low rumble vibrated through the earth beneath his feet. Then, with a deep groan of rolling metal, the iron door divided. Fang entered an inner chamber where flaming torches encircled Addison. When Jack saw his dark eyes glaring with pure hatred, his heart almost pounded through his chest. His fingers balled into fists as he fought the temptation to use Soulweaver's powers to end his father's life.

Jack stepped forward until he stood as close to the torches as possible. Addison lunged forward with his fists swinging, then slammed into an invisible force field that knocked him backward. He charged again and again. Then he unleashed what was left of his powers, and black flames struck against the force field. He was unhinged, even more than Jack remembered from his childhood in Sham Shui Po.

"Do you not know what the Cherub have stolen from me?" Addison seethed.

"And you have taken everything from me." Tears welled up in Jack's eyes. "You beat us when we were kids, and you tried to kill Mom because of your selfishness. From where I stand, you have gotten what you deserve."

"On that night, the highest Cherub ordered your mother to bring me to them and return Dragon Soul. When I refused to obey, she attacked and stole my gifts." Addison's eyes narrowed, and Jack was certain his father was skirting the truth. "I was the only one strong enough to control Dragon Soul, and the remaining Elders trusted me to guard the sword. Then they betrayed me. Don't you see? It is their fault I am who I am, Jack."

"You traveled with Peter after he betrayed the Elders and used Dragon Soul to open the Exodus Mines." Jack's lip quivered. "Why didn't you tell Mom the truth?"

"I sacrificed everything to stop the Cherub from stealing the gifts of others." Addison's jaw clenched, and then his gaze softened as if he were on the verge of surrendering.

Jack, don't let down your guard. He's playing you.

"I am an outlier, same as you, Son. Surely you will not allow them to keep me in this dungeon or kill me when Elyon teaches that all who believe must show mercy."

"Tell them which artifacts you have found, and where Will is going next." Jack dug deeper and battled against his childhood fear. "Whether they pass judgment on you is out of my hands."

"Coward!" Addison's eyes turned fiery. "A disgrace—like your sister. You should know I have kept one of the artifacts for myself, and there will come a time when it will set me free."

"You wanted me to come so you could say that to my face."

A sly grin twisted Addison's lips. "And it was worth the wait."

"After all the lives you've destroyed, not an ounce of remorse. Did you know it was Michael Chung who murdered Rachel?" Jack dropped the bombshell, and he noticed his words left his father stupefied. "Maybe one day I'll forgive you for what you've done—but not today."

From the shadows, angelic beings emerged and floated across the chamber. They wore pure golden armor and carried silver swords. *Elyon's army of Cherub from Charis—those who didn't betray him.* Jack remembered Asiklua being restored with one touch from Soulweaver. He stepped back as the angels stood guard near the flames. Addison shouted at the top of his lungs, but inside the chamber his curses were muted. Fang Xue led Jack out through the Dungeon of Savages and across the underwater vault where Slybourne's treasure remained piled high.

Jack wiped the tears from his eyes with the back of his sleeve. His chest was on fire, but he kept it to himself.

One of the artifacts is definitely down here—but it'll have to wait.

Once they reached the surface and climbed aboard, he could tell McNaughton was relieved. He wanted to tell her everything, but he was unnerved by Addison's words. *How much do I believe, and how much of what he said are lies?* He sat beside McNaughton as the boat headed for shore. Once they reached the bank, an awkward moment passed before Fang Xue broke the silence.

"You have done what was asked of you," she said.

"Does that mean the Cherub will stop hunting me?" Jack asked.

"For now, our effort remains on stopping the Merikh and William Fargher. However, I will speak to the highest Cherub on your behalf." Fang Xue exchanged looks with McNaughton, then pointed toward the forest. "The gateway is straight ahead—do you remember?"

"I remember," McNaughton replied. "You are not going with us?"

"My path leads me elsewhere." Fang Xue eyed Jack curiously. "The artifacts and Eden's Star are not yours to keep. While it seems you are the Protector, when this is over you must return them. If you choose not to, then we will hunt you like your father."

Jack and McNaughton headed into the forest without so much as a goodbye. A few minutes passed before they reached the gateway. Jack dug into his pocket and retrieved two more silver coins. He wanted to tell her about the artifact hidden somewhere in the vault and the Dungeon of Savages. Instead, he dropped the coins to the dirt. They sank beneath the surface and reappeared inside the clock tower at Beacon Hill.

"I am around if you want to talk," McNaughton said. "When you are ready."

"Might be never." Jack offered a half-hearted smile. "Thanks, Natalie."

"I will go check with the headmaster about Emma and the others."

"I'll be right behind you—just need a minute."

McNaughton took the stairs and left Jack alone in the clock tower. A clicking noise caught his attention as he stared at the back of the clock. He noticed the gear train engage and the main wheel rotate. At first he thought his eyes were playing tricks, but then he stopped cold when the minute hand moved.

It's counting—backward.

90

LANTAU ISLAND

BY LATE AFTERNOON, a sweltering heat mixed with thick humidity left a heaviness in the air. Emma, Eliška, and Vince crouched together on a lush hillside overlooking the maximum security facility surrounded by a razor-wire fence. Before leaving Beacon Hill, Emma stopped by Crozier Hospital and was surprised to find Vince and Eliška on their feet, ready to go. All three stopped by Tim's room and offered encouragement to his parents and Amina—who suggested spreading the word to reach those Cherub who were on Messagezilla.

Emma swiped her finger across the phone screen, and her face appeared. She pressed a red button and stared directly into the camera while Vince and Eliška watched quietly.

"Last night we captured the Merikh leader, yet our brothers and sisters remain imprisoned. For too long we have relied on the Mercy Covenant to protect us, but that covenant is now broken. Many of you are hiding underground, afraid the Merikh and their assassins will find you. Another within the Merikh will rise up if we do not find the strength and courage to stand against them. Today, Elyon promises freedom, but we must fight for it. He promises victory against our enemies, but we must stand united. We cannot allow this moment to pass. There is too much at stake." Emma turned the camera toward the prison for a few seconds, then back to her face. "Stand with me, and together we will set the captives free."

She tapped the red button a second time, then uploaded the video to Messagezilla. All three stepped back from the edge of the hillside and disappeared into the overgrown bushes near the Shek Pik Reservoir.

"Any idea how we get inside without being caught?" Vince asked.

"We need a miracle." Eliška eyed Emma closely. "Like on the *Eastern Dragon.*"

"For now, we will wait until night," Emma replied. "And yes, pray for a miracle."

"I wonder how Jack's doing," Vince said. "After what Will did . . ."

"He will get the answers we need and will do what is necessary to protect us."

"From what Professor Burwick told me about Addison Reynolds," Eliška said, "hoping he will cooperate with the Cherub or listen to Jack is wishful thinking."

They reached a clearing and found a group of forty men and

women huddled together—members of the faction handpicked by Burwick, Cherub from Beacon Hill, and Fang Xue's personal security team. Each one turned toward them, waiting for the green light. Emma found a spot and knelt on the grass. She bowed her head, clasped her hands, and closed her eyes. The others—including Eliška and Vince—joined her in prayer, and for a long time she didn't move.

Hours passed before Emma opened her eyes when she heard a low murmuring in the distance. She stood and headed back through the bushes, then crawled across the grass closer to the edge of the hillside. Eliška and Vince inched forward on their stomachs until they were beside her. An extraordinary sight met their eyes—hundreds were now gathered outside the gates of the prison, each one on their knees. Prayers from the depths of their souls resounded toward the heavens.

"Looks like your message struck a chord," Eliška said.

"I wonder how many of them are lightforcers, benders, or healers," Vince murmured.

"When darkness falls, we will see," Emma replied, resolute.

Late into the afternoon, the sun slowly lowered toward the horizon while minibuses, double-deckers, and taxis lined the only road winding around the reservoir to Shek Pik Prison. Passengers disembarked and joined the others at the gates while vehicles pulled U-turns and left the area at full speed. As the sun disappeared, the crowd grew to thousands, shoulder to shoulder, spilling out onto the blocked road. Armed HKPF and prison guards stood on the other side of the gates, waiting for someone to step out of line.

"In our time of need," Emma said softly, "Elyon promises to stand with us in the fire."

Night fell over Lantau Island as they climbed down the hillside with the faction and Cherub flanking them. All the attention remained on those at the gate and on the packed road directly outside of the prison walls. No one noticed as they made their way through the crowd closer to the entrance.

Helicopters arrived from HKPF and news channels, a sign that word had spread beyond Messagezilla. Chanting erupted from inside the prison, echoing the prayers of those gathered outside. What began hours earlier with a single voice intensified until a roar caused the guards to move in formation closer to the prison entrance.

"You must leave the premises immediately," the warden growled from a bullhorn, but his voice could barely be heard. "If you do not cooperate, you will be arrested."

"Emma, whatever we are going to do," Eliška urged, "best we do it now."

"Tonight, the walls of the Merikh will crumble." Emma ordered the lightforcers who were with them to spread out, then directed the benders closer to the barbed wire fence. Members of the faction who were skilled in extraction remained on her shoulder. She turned toward Eliška and Vince. "When the chaos erupts, stay by my side."

"You don't have to say that twice," Vince replied. "We're your shadows."

Cherub from Beacon Hill followed Emma as she pushed her way through the massive crowd until she stood at the front while the guards shifted their aim in her direction. Her palms glowed with a bright-white light, and she recognized the fear in their eyes. Cherub with Emma, along with others in the crowd, followed in the same way, and a rainbow of colors emerged. Emma harnessed her power and controlled the light from bursting into a ball of pure energy.

"I am the authority here," the warden shouted. "Do not come any closer."

Emma took another step with boldness. "In the name of Elyon, let his people go."

The benders lifted their hands toward the buildings, and seconds later a thunderous crack split one side of a building open. Chunks of concrete crumbled, but none smashed against the ground. Tons of rubble hovered in midair, to the shock of the warden, guards, and HKPF officers. Emma raised her glowing hands and signaled the lightforcers to release their power.

Vibrant bursts of burgundy, gold, orange, and purple streaked across the night before exploding against the buildings. With eyes glowing a fiery white, Emma unleashed a pulse of power and incinerated the fence surrounding the prison entrance. Guards scrambled and fired shots, yet none struck a single Cherub. Emma waved her hand toward the warden, guards, and officers near the entrance, leaving them imprisoned within an invisible force field.

The extraction team moved past Emma and darted toward the building with weapons raised. Lightforcers stood beside Emma, using their power to control the force field. Emma pulverized the iron gates with another pulsing volley, then raced through the entrance and across the prison yard. Vince and Eliška kept on her heels. From inside the split building, Cherub captives crawled out into the yard, disoriented, as the extraction team guided them toward the entrance. Beneath the spotlights swooping across the prison yard, additional HKPF officers and guards appeared, firing semiautomatic rounds—but the bullets slowed in midair before dropping to the ground.

91

Emma, Eliška, and Vince caught up with the extraction team, which operated methodically, moving from one cell to the next. Lights flickered inside the building where Cherub were imprisoned after their blood transfusions. The captives stepped out in shock—men and women of all ages and races wearing orange jumpsuits. They were ordered to move quickly through a gaping hole in the building.

"We do not have much time," Eliška urged. "Reinforcements will arrive."

Emma pushed her way forward through the packed hallways and waved her hands toward the cell doors that were still locked. She freely used her force, and all at once the doors burst open.

"Now that's impressive." Vince's brows raised as he helped a woman to her feet. "You two keep going—I'll be okay."

Emma and Eliška continued while Vince joined the extraction team. Captives poured out from their cells and were immediately escorted down the hallway. Emma eyed each one as they rushed past, searching for her parents. Elyon's spirit flowed through her veins, even though doubt lingered beneath the surface.

"They are not here," she said under her breath.

Eliška squeezed her shoulder reassuringly. "Emma, we will find them."

From one cell to the next, their pace quickened as the urgency reached a boiling point. Emma poked her head into one of the last cells, and the world stopped until she heard her name.

"Emma . . ."

"Mum," she exhaled in disbelief. "Dad."

Huddled in one corner were Oliver and Winnie Bennett, bruised and gaunt yet mostly unharmed. Her mother lunged forward and grabbed hold of Emma tight, as if she were never going to let go. Tears streaked down Emma's cheeks as her dad wrapped his arms around them both.

"After Mount Hareh," Emma said, "I feared you were both dead."

"We escaped from the Sanctuary of Prayer into the desert." Emma's mum squeezed her face with both hands. "One gateway to the next led us to Los Angeles, where we thought we were safe. Of course we wanted to reach you, but we were uncertain about the risks."

"Mount Hareh was beyond explanation," her father said somberly. "But we still believe."

"Emma—" Eliška stopped in the doorway. "Sorry . . ."

"Mum, Dad . . . this is Eliška." Emma wiped her face with her sleeve. "She is one of us."

"We need to leave," Eliška urged. "Right now."

Emma's father nodded at Eliška. "Lead the way."

By the time they reached the gaping hole in the building, they were among the last ones out. Emma and Eliška helped her parents climb down the rubble. Tear gas filled the prison wing as reinforcements breached the barricades that the extraction team left piled inside.

Hundreds of Cherub raced across the yard. Some were carried, while others gripped the hand of the person next to them. Vince scooped up an elderly man and carried him in his arms. Emma glanced ahead as the lightforcers remained focused among the commotion, keeping the warden, the HKPF, and the prison guards trapped inside the force field.

"If we are going to make it," Eliška shouted, "we need the lightforcers with us."

"Watch over my parents," Emma called back. "I will be right behind you."

Emma split off and darted toward the lightforcers. She ordered them to follow the thousands who were now an army on the road outside Shek Pik Prison. With her hands extended, Emma kept the force field strong. Each of the lightforcers peeled away until she was the only one left.

Sirens blared across the prison grounds while more helicopters hovered overhead. Emma stayed focused, knowing she wouldn't be able to hold the force field forever. She glanced over her shoulder and realized a heavily armed HKPF tactical unit had arrived near the prison entrance. While thousands of Cherub darted past, the unit's focus was strictly on Emma. The guards trapped in the force field readied their weapons. She sensed she was being cornered. Red lasers cut through the night, sweeping across the yard. As rapid-fire shots rang out from heavy-caliber weapons, Emma braced herself, certain she was about to die.

An iridescent light appeared out of nowhere—a blazing radiance, rapidly spinning. Surprised, Emma glanced over her shoulder and realized Jack was beside her with Soulweaver glowing between his fingers—defending them from a barrage of bullets. Jack grabbed her arm, and in a blink they vanished into thin air.

Emma's feet landed on a rooftop beside Jack, whose nostrils were bloodied. She wiped the crimson from his chin and stared into his eyes. Soulweaver wrapped around his forearm, and he pulled his sleeve down, covering the scars and hiding the weapon he was quickly learning how to use. He wiped another trickle of blood from his nose as Emma hugged him tight.

"My parents are alive," she cried. "We found them in Shek Pik."

"That's the best news I've heard all day." Jack smiled warmly, then added with a tinge of sarcasm, "I've probably broken a hundred Cherub commands by now, but I think I'm getting the hang of Eden's Star—or maybe the compass is getting the hang of me."

"Elyon's timing is perfect." She gently pushed herself away. "What about your father?"

"He's under the Cherub's watch in the Dungeon of Savages," he replied. "No way he's getting out of that place—and I made it without being abducted by Fang Xue." Jack stepped over to the edge of the rooftop and looked down on the street below. "Looks like we're in Wan Chai."

"Why would Eden's Star bring us here?"

"Each time I've used it, there's been a shift in time." Jack glanced toward a wooden plank laid flat on the rooftop. In the distance, colorful lights radiated across Gloucester Road while helicopters pointed spotlights down on a sea of people. "Let's get to the street."

Jack and Emma found a stairwell and bounded down one floor to the next. Jack was out of breath when they reached the ground floor, but Emma was ready to run another ten miles. As they stepped onto the street, the crowd approached, surrounded by luminescent burgundy, gold, orange, and purple lightforces. Cherub. Faction. United as one. At the front marched Eliška and Vince while a chanting melody echoed across Hong Kong Island.

"Vince's parents are definitely going to see him now," Jack said. "Maybe you should—"

Emma stepped back. "Eliška is right where she needs to be."

In the night sky, a brilliant full moon sparkled off the waters of Victoria Harbour, as if Elyon were revealing a path for them to follow. Double-deckers, minibuses, trams, and other vehicles stopped as the Cherub passed. Jack and Emma ducked into the crowd. A few miles ahead, HKPF guarded barricades blocking the entrance to Cross-Harbour Tunnel. While the sound of the melody grew stronger, tension remained thick as the Cherub headed straight toward riot police lined up shoulder to shoulder.

"Eliška needs help." Jack's brows raised. "She needs you, Emma."

"Elyon has called Eliška to set the captives free. He will lead the way."

As the Cherub approached, HKPF helicopters and news reporters on the ground captured every moment. Eliška held up her hand, and the massive crowd slowed, but the melody resounded even louder. Then, to everyone's surprise, the HKPF pulled the barricades aside and allowed the Cherub to continue into Cross-Harbour Tunnel.

Eliška and Vince never broke stride as they led the way beneath Victoria Harbour. Emma and Jack were in the middle of the pack when they neared the tunnel. Emma wondered how close she might be to her parents, but she knew they were safe within the crowd. Glancing over to her left, she recognized Professor Burwick and Detective Ming standing beside the HKPF commanders.

Emma imagined millions of Hong Kongers glued to their screens while the next few hours unfolded. Eliška and Vince would lead the Cherub through Cross-Harbour Tunnel, emerge onto Princess Margaret Road in Kowloon, then proceed through the gates of Beacon Hill.

92

MOUNT HAREH, EGYPT

PERCHED ATOP A MOUNTAIN IN THE MIDDLE of an endless desert, the charred ruins of the Sanctuary of Prayer were scattered across the ground. Once a picturesque oasis within a lush garden, this hallowed place for the Cherub was left desolate. Fang Xue stood before those summoned for the ceremony. She wore a red-and-white hooded robe, the same robe worn by all who were gathered. Among the highest Cherub summoned by Fang Xue were Salomeh Gashkori, Jin Qiaolian, and Aki Katsuo.

"With the capture of the Merikh leader, we have restored peace to the world and the other realms." Fang Xue's rigid jaw tightened. "We have committed and sacrificed our lives to defend the light of Elyon, and we have stood united in conquering the Merikh once again." Her gaze shifted between Salomeh, Jin, and Aki. "The battles we fight place us at odds with those who profess to believe in Elyon yet refuse to obey the Cherub commands. In the days and years to come, our greatest challenge will surface from within as the faction threatens to divide us with false prophecies. We have reached a moment when we must choose our future leader, one who possesses powerful gifts to protect and lead us against our enemies." She pointed toward the rubble. "We cannot forget what occurred because of an outlier—one who will be shown mercy for now, yet will never be one of us."

Fang Xue motioned for Bau Hu to step forward in his violet-hooded robe. He obeyed her instruction and stood in the center of the circle. Most who surrounded him had known him since his dedication inside the hallowed sanctuary before it became the sacred grounds of the dead. Among them were his parents, Winston and Betty Hu, highly respected by their peers.

"Bau is the future of our tribe," Fang Xue continued. "His character and leadership are unmatched, especially considering his youth. His bravery during the attack at Beacon Hill, as well as during the rescue of our brothers and sisters from Shelter Island, gives only a glimpse of his gifts and abilities. When I accepted my role after our great Elder was murdered, it was with the understanding that a new leader would soon be named."

One of the Cherub around the circle held out an original scribed edition of the Eternal, dating back many centuries. "Rest your hand and your heart on Elyon's Word."

With one parent standing on each side, Bau followed her direction and placed his right hand on the worn leather. Fang Xue dipped her index finger into a jar of oil, then anointed his forehead.

"Elyon has prepared you for this day—this moment. He has given you the gifts and abilities to lead all who follow in the Cherub faith. If you are to accept this responsibility, you will face great challenges that require even greater wisdom." Fang Xue placed her hand on the Eternal too. "From this day forward, you will be the leader of the Cherub—and I will remain by your side offering guidance along your journey. Do you accept Elyon's calling?"

"Yes." Bau's voice was barely above a whisper. "I accept."

"Praise be to Elyon." Fang Xue smiled. "It is done."

Bau's parents embraced him while others offered congratulations. Fang Xue stepped back and watched as the newly crowned leader was welcomed by the most influential of the highest Cherub. Before they left for their gateways, Salomeh, Jin, and Aki retreated to a spot near where the entrance to the Sanctuary of Prayer had once been. Fang Xue eyed them closely as she approached, knowing she had failed to gain their support.

"Your presence sent a reassuring message," she said. "Cherub *and* faction respect each one of you. Thank you for accepting my invitation."

"After all he has done"—Salomeh kept her gaze fixed on the rubble—"you chose to leave a target on Jack's head, and you left an opening for the Merikh to attack again."

"You have also questioned the legitimacy of the prophecy," Jin said. "Even though you know the lineage that precedes Eliška."

"Emma Bennett was believed to be the chosen one, and now you wish to choose Eliška." Fang Xue's brows furrowed. "Many before me have questioned the prophecy and chosen an heir they believed was right for the Cherub. I will not change my decision."

"Why anoint a leader in secret?" Aki asked. "Is that Elyon's will?"

"All three of you were invited because of your influence, and as a courtesy." Fang Xue started to leave. "What has been anointed by Elyon cannot be undone."

93

BEACON HILL

THE HELICOPTERS THAT HAD FOLLOWED the Cherub from Shek Pik Prison continued circling above Beacon Hill. Dozens of news vans were parked outside of the gates amid a massive HKPF presence surrounding the school.

Lightforcers returned to their positions around the grounds as they had done in the days before the prison break. Professor McDougall stood on the steps of the Main Hall wearing a colorful coat—a gift sewn by the children of Kati Pahari—rather than his tattered Burberry.

"Right this way," McDougall announced. "In an orderly fashion, please."

Oliver and Winnie Bennett waited at the top of the steps

searching for Emma. Jack didn't realize who they were until Emma smiled wide. Butterflies attacked his stomach.

"Mum . . . Dad . . ." Emma began. "I want you to meet Jack."

Oliver held out his hand. "Hey, how are you?"

"I'm good, thanks." Jack's cheeks flushed as he shook hands. "Glad you both are safe."

"I do not remember Emma mentioning you to us," Winnie teased.

"We've gotten close since—" Jack felt Emma nudge him in the ribs. "I mean, nothing is going on—well—strictly trying to save the world, I guess."

"I'd like to hear more," Oliver mused, "about saving the world."

"Okay, well . . ." Emma replied awkwardly, then hugged them both tight before letting go. "We need to check on one of our friends, so I will find you a bit later."

"Of course, dear." Winnie glanced around, then added in a lowered voice, "We were on Mount Hareh during the attack—we know the truth."

"Nice to meet you, Mr. and Mrs. Bennett," Jack said shyly.

"Likewise, Jack," Oliver replied cordially. "Watch over Emma."

"Dad!" Emma blurted.

While Oliver and Winnie stood in a long line, Jack and Emma broke away and entered a side door to the Main Hall. Classrooms were opened, and all the lights were on. Others were setting up each room with cots, blankets, and pillows. Racing upstairs, Jack and Emma entered Crozier Hospital and found Vince and Eliška waiting outside Tim's room with Amina.

"How is he doing?" Jack asked. "Any word?"

"Timothy has not regained consciousness." Amina's eyes were bloodshot, a clear sign she hadn't slept the night before. "Professor

Windsor is doing all she can, the healers stopped by throughout the day, and Cherub are in the House of Luminescence interceding. I cannot understand why I was able to heal Vince, but my gifts are failing Tim." She was on the verge of tears as Emma stepped forward and hugged her tight. Between sobs, she whispered, "Why has Elyon not healed him?"

A lump filled Jack's throat, and a knot twisted in his stomach. He swallowed hard, trying to stop himself from hyperventilating. *Elyon, do something, please. You can't let Tim die, not this way.* For a while they stayed outside the room while Elis and Beca Lloyd remained by their son's bedside. Amina slipped into the room and pulled up a chair next to Tim. She squeezed his hand tight and lowered her head. Jack was helpless as he struggled to accept what was unfolding before his eyes. Another hour passed as the four paced the hallways, mostly in silence.

Jack approached Eliška. "You were the Pied Piper today."

"I never intended to be the leader. It should have been Emma."

"You were right where you needed to be—and so was Vince."

"Quite unexpected. I felt stronger when he walked beside me."

"Yeah . . . he has that effect on people."

"When we left Emma, she was the last one holding the force field. How did she escape?"

"Eden's Star brought me to her. Somehow the compass knew she was in trouble."

McNaughton walked down the hallway with Detective Ming by her side. One look at the grim expressions on their faces, and Jack knew they didn't have good news.

"Jack," McNaughton said, "there is a situation."

"Seriously, what else can happen tonight?" he replied.

"News networks across Asia covered the prison break and the march across Hong Kong." Ming looked toward Vince and Eliška.

"HKPF and the PRC have identified the four of you as being responsible for leading the assault. And it seems they are fully aware of the *security* that exists at Beacon Hill."

"You know as well as anyone it wasn't a breakout of criminals," Jack argued. "They are Cherub who were unjustly imprisoned by the Merikh, most likely with the help of the government."

McNaughton held up her hand. "Detective Ming is here to help, Jack."

"I know—we saw her with Burwick at Cross-Harbour Tunnel."

"Joseph and Imani Tobias watched their son return to Beacon Hill," Ming explained. "We need to take Vince to them immediately, which is their right as his parents."

"You are the only one who can convince him," McNaughton said. "I have tried before."

Jack knew this day would come. He'd sensed the struggle from Vince to keep the truth from his parents, knowing they must be heartbroken by his disappearance. Vince had put them through so much, and Jack knew it was all because of him. No question, Vince was as faithful a friend as anyone—a true steadfast brother. He expected Vince to put up a fight against leaving them or the quest to find the artifacts behind. At first Jack wanted to debate with McNaughton and Ming, but in his spirit he knew they were right. He turned away and shuffled toward Vince, whose stare was a dead giveaway he'd been eavesdropping.

Jack pulled Vince aside and searched for the words. "You heard what they said?"

"Most of it," he admitted. "But I'm not going anywhere."

"You are wanted by the government—the Chinese government."

"I'm in the fight with the rest of you. I won't leave you guys."

"Vince, think about what your parents are going through. It's my fault."

"You said we each had to make a choice," Vince argued. "I'm not gonna cut and run."

"It won't be forever—just until all of this blows over."

"We both know this isn't blowing over. I've never walked away from a fight."

"And you're not doing that now. It's for your mom and dad." Jack hesitated. "Go see them so they know you're good, and then I'll reach out with where we're going next."

"Promise?" Vince's eyes narrowed as Jack nodded. "Honestly, I'm scared of what they're going to do to me after what I've put them through."

"I'll go with you," Jack offered. "Your mom and dad like me."

"Not sure that'll work, but it feels better knowing both of us will be on the firing line."

Jack walked back over to McNaughton and Ming, who waited patiently. "Let's go."

"What do you mean?" Ming asked. "I planned on returning Vince to his parents."

"He wants me to go with him to break the ice."

"I'll go with you too," McNaughton answered. "Ming will bring us back afterward."

Jack glanced over his shoulder and caught Vince and Eliška standing close together. Emma raised her eyebrows, and he did the same as he approached and leaned toward her.

"I'm leaving in the morning," he whispered, "to go beyond the Highlands."

He stepped away from Emma at the same time as Vince did the same with Eliška. Jack and Vince wore similar frowns as they followed McNaughton and Ming out of Crozier Hospital.

94

A WHITE TOYOTA PRADO WITH FLASHING LIGHTS exited through the gates of Beacon Hill and moments later screeched down the streets of Kowloon Tong. Ming was behind the wheel with McNaughton in the front passenger side. Jack and Vince slouched low in the back seat, hidden from the cameras and helicopters overhead.

Ming accelerated and swerved through traffic until the SUV disappeared into Lion Rock Tunnel. On the other side, she turned on the blue flashing lights on the dashboard. HKPF officers at each checkpoint pulled the barricades aside, allowing the SUV to speed past.

Jack was exhausted and running on pure adrenaline. In a matter of days, they had freed the prisoners on Shelter Island *and* in

Shek Pik Prison. It would have been an impossible task left up to them, so it must have been a miracle orchestrated by Elyon. Still, he couldn't shake a haunting feeling all they had done was poke a hornet's nest. The Merikh would never stop trying to seize control of the Cherub and the artifacts by any means necessary.

With his powers, Will might be the greatest threat—especially with Dragon Soul. If he finds the artifact that exists beyond the Highlands, then he will be capable of ruling the world and all other realms.

"I can't believe it's ending this way," Vince said, dejected.

"It's not the end." Jack tried to assure himself as well as Vince. "Think of it as halftime."

"You're not going to sit back and wait for me. What are you going to do?"

"There's only one way forward." Jack paused. "I'm going to try and save Will."

"You know he wasn't in his right mind in Aberdeen. Did you see the look in his eyes? Since when did he get supernatural powers?"

Jack nearly poured out the secret Fargher had revealed, but then he second-guessed himself. "All we can do is hope there's good left in him."

Ming slammed on the brakes and made a sharp turn, skidding around a corner onto a one-lane road headed for Three Fathoms Cove. She parked near One-thirtyone, a European restaurant that overlooked a pier jutting out from the beach. A speedboat was docked there, while a mega yacht drifted in the deepest part of the cove alongside a fishing farm with dozens of submerged cages. Illuminated along the bow of the vessel was the word *Pathfinder*.

Ming's walkie-talkie on the console squawked as a voice rattled in Cantonese. She listened for a moment, then retrieved her Glock from a holster. "HKPF is on their way."

"We better hurry." McNaughton retrieved her Glock too. "Boys . . ."

Jack and Vince climbed out of the SUV while McNaughton watched their backs. A quick walk turned into a sprint toward the pier as Ming waited near the SUV. Jack glanced over his shoulder and watched flashing lights race down the one-lane road. Pumping his arms and legs, he tried to keep up with Vince, whose stride was longer even though he was a step slower than before Eden's Star had nearly sliced him in half. As they reached the pier, a dim light shone down from a wooden post bright enough for him to recognize Joseph and Imani Tobias racing toward them.

They both called out in unison. "Vince!"

Jack slowed his pace and waited while Vince's parents grabbed hold of their son with tears flowing. McNaughton kept her weapon by her side as she stopped beside Jack. Gunfire rang out from behind, and they all ducked for cover. Jack glanced back as the HKPF moved in quickly on Ming, who dropped her weapon and lowered to her knees.

"Quickly, everyone on the boat." An engine revved as McNaughton grabbed Jack's arm and pulled him forward. "Move!"

Joseph and Imani Tobias were stunned for a moment before Vince shoved them toward the waiting speedboat. There was no time to think, only react. As everyone jumped aboard, the captain behind the wheel of the boat wasted no time spinning the craft around and racing across the water toward the yacht.

"What is going on?" Joseph exclaimed to McNaughton. "Who are you?"

"She's my guardian," Jack answered. "Natalie McNaughton."

"Why are the police shooting at us?" Imani asked, frightened. "Vince—"

"All of this is my fault," Jack interrupted, ashamed. "Vince has kept me alive, Mr. and Mrs. Tobias. I'm sorry for everything that's happened. I am the one to blame, not Vince."

The speedboat slowed as it approached the yacht, where more crew waited to guide it into a custom-designed slip within the hull of the multimillion-dollar vessel. Within seconds, the mega yacht lurched forward, heading straight for the open waters of the South China Sea. Jack climbed the steps and entered a world of luxury. McNaughton holstered her weapon and remained near the stern.

"Mr. and Mrs. Lloyd, there will be lies told about Vince," Jack explained. "But you have to know, none of what you will hear is true. Your son is a hero, and the most loyal of friends."

Vince's eyes were glossy. "You and Natalie can come with us."

"You've watched my back since the first day we met at Beacon Hill. I think that's why Rachel liked you so much. She knew when she wasn't around, you'd be the one." Jack glanced toward McNaughton, sensing she was amping to leave. "We will see each other again."

Vince grabbed Jack and hugged him hard. "We better."

While Joseph and Imani Tobias watched in silence and utter bewilderment, Jack stepped back and nodded toward McNaughton. Eden's Star awakened within and scorched the tears that were on the verge of erupting. McNaughton squeezed his shoulder as the energy of the compass surged through him. At the last second, Vince reached out and tried to grab Jack, but they were gone.

Inside the Main Hall atrium, Jack and McNaughton reappeared, surprising those who continued to wait in a long line. McNaughton pulled him aside until they were standing near the family tree's worth of photos commemorating the roots of Beacon Hill.

"So, I'm your guardian?" McNaughton asked.

Jack grinned. "I've got no other family left, Natalie."

"Well, for the record, you know I was right from the start. You are part of a house of heroes." McNaughton nodded toward the wall where the names of those who fought in the Battle of Hong Kong were listed. "No matter what happens from this moment forward, you are the Protector." He started to deflect, but McNaughton held up her finger and stopped him. "Blood or no blood—we are family."

95

QUARRY BAY, HONG KONG ISLAND

BENEATH THE COURTYARD, wooden crates lined the walls of a gloomy space that stretched the length of the housing estate above. Rows of fluorescents illuminated the hundreds who were gathered. In the center of the circle, Professor Burwick eyed those loyal to the faction. Beside the professor, Eliška's gaze shifted from one person to the next and to the Chinese characters painted on the walls.

真理. *The Truth.*

"Quiet down, please." Burwick's voice cut through the whispering. "We have witnessed the courage of Elyon's followers rescuing thousands from Shelter Island and Shek Pik Prison. But we have also seen the devastation and death left by the Merikh in Repulse Bay. Tonight, I am more committed to the fight than ever before.

You have trusted me to guide the faction, and I am humbled by the privilege. Now the Merikh leader has been captured, but the Merikh have only grown more dangerous. Many of you know the grief and challenges I have faced since losing my daughter, Darcy. I am not the only one. No matter what darkness comes against me, my allegiance to Elyon and the faction will always remain. However, the days ahead will require more, which is why I can no longer be your leader."

Gasps and stunned whispers echoed off the walls. Eliška pointed her chin toward the floor and stared intensely at her boots while keeping her fingers clasped.

Professor Burwick raised her hand to restore order. "We have always stood by one another in unity to defend the name of Elyon." Burwick limped back and forth while the crowd hung on every word. "The days of fighting on the front lines are behind me. But there is one who has risen through our ranks, who has proven her loyalty to the faction. She is a descendant of the bravest warrior to ever battle against the darkness—Sir Ryder Slybourne. In the days ahead, she will be the one to lead us in this great war, to an even greater victory." Burwick wrapped her arm around Eliška's shoulder and pulled her close. "I have tried to convince the highest Cherub the prophecy is alive; however, they refuse to listen. So we must free those who have been captured and unleash our righteous anger against the Merikh. Eliška is the one destined to lead us. And she will need every last one of you by her side. Are you willing?"

Concrete rumbled as the faction roared. Eliška glanced up long enough to see the determination in the eyes of each one. She swallowed the lump in her throat, knowing she'd rather be standing there beside Darcy—and she knew Burwick felt the same. As the faction cheered her on, she realized she had a responsibility greater than just honoring her lineage. She knew she must fulfill her calling in the name of Elyon. She stepped away from Burwick and harnessed the resolve boiling within.

"I am honored to serve and fight alongside each one of you," Eliška said boldly. "I am no higher than any other—I am your equal." She nodded toward the wooden crates behind those who were gathered, then paced around the circle. "Many see us as the last ones worthy of this fight, yet we have been chosen by Elyon, who gives the hardest battles to the bravest warriors." Her voice grew even stronger. "Elyon will fight alongside us, and we will fight alongside one another. In the end, there is no greater calling. Tomorrow we will begin our offensive against the Merikh, and it starts with freeing all who are being hunted or held against their will—by any means necessary."

Another roar rumbled beneath the housing estate, even more intense than before. Eliška followed Burwick through the crowd as the faction buzzed with excitement. Together they entered a narrow corridor and caught their breath.

"You were brilliant, Eliška. Absolutely brilliant."

"Thank you, Professor, for believing in me and guiding my path."

"No one else has proven themselves worthy of the responsibility you now carry." Burwick wiped a tear from her eye. "I will be with you for as long as you need and do my best to bridge the gap between faction and Cherub."

"I need to tell Jack," Eliška said, pointedly. "And Emma."

"Along a silk road this secret will one day return . . ."

"What about the artifacts? Should we continue searching for them?"

"Wars are fought on two battlefields." Burwick paused. "One faces the enemy on a road to freedom, while the other travels a narrow path to bring ruin against the darkness."

96

BEACON HILL

AFTER A RESTLESS NIGHT, Jack rolled out from the bottom bunk in Rowell House and stuffed his backpack full of clothes. He removed the bandages from his arms, carefully grabbed a shower as he winced through the stinging pain, then dressed while trying to keep his thoughts from drowning his spirit.

It's impossible to get my head around everything that's happened since Rachel died—and I can't shake the feeling that the loss will stay with me forever.

Jack wanted nothing more than to bury it all before it buried him. He noticed the wounds from Dragon Soul were slowly healing—at least, that's what he hoped. With all that he'd been through, he realized he was strong enough to fight through the pain. He grabbed a roll of fresh bandages and carefully wrapped them around both arms.

A knock startled him. He shuffled over and opened the door but found no one in the hallway. Before he shut the door he glanced down and noticed a box on the floor. He checked the hallway again, then picked up the box and brought it into the room. Curious, he set the box on one of the empty desks and slowly lifted the lid. Inside, he found a dark-burgundy hoodie with a thin light-blue stripe. His fingers touched the fabric, which was unlike any normal cotton material, and then he slipped the hoodie on.

A perfect fit—as if it was made for me. Hold on—the tailor on Carnarvon Road.

Before leaving the room, he placed the small wooden box he'd found in Sham Shui Po inside one of the zippered pockets on his sleeve and slipped his backpack over his shoulder. He took one last look around at the plain room. *Life will never return to the days with Will, Vince, and Tim in Nightingale.*

The quad was quiet as he crossed the grass and entered the Main Hall. He shuffled his feet down the corridor, then climbed the stairs slowly, as his muscles were shredded. He knew he needed to leave, and even though he'd done it before, the decision wasn't any easier.

As he passed Rowell Library, Jack noticed the door was open. He poked his head into the library and found Headmaster Fargher, Professor McDougall, McNaughton, Salomeh, Faizan, Emma and her parents, as well as several others he didn't recognize. His anger lingered against the headmaster for keeping the truth from him. All eyes were on a flatscreen that showed the chief executive of Hong Kong behind a cluster of microphones.

"We must accept the attack at Shek Pik Prison as an act of

terror against Hong Kongers and the People's Republic of China. HKPF and our counterintelligence agencies are working vigorously to identify those responsible and those who escaped. When they are found, they will be held accountable. We are dealing with an unprecedented event, one we witnessed in real time. There is no denying we are facing enemies who are not of this world."

The chief executive glanced down at her notes, then stared directly into the camera.

"So far there are four suspects whose identities will not be released to the public until our national security determines it is advisable. However, we have arrested Susan Ming, an HKPF detective we believe helped one of the suspects escape last night and provided intelligence to these terrorists. While we will not be releasing any additional names at this time, it is important for these criminals to know justice is on our side."

Jack shivered as he listened intently. Of course with all the news cameras, Shek Pik security cameras, bystanders' cell phones, and the HKPF helicopter footage, the whole world knew Eliška and Vince led the revolt and Jack and Emma were freaks. *If Hong Kongers don't know our names now, they will soon.* He shoved his hands into his pockets and exhaled long as the chief executive continued.

"Thousands of inmates from Shek Pik Prison are now being protected within the grounds of Beacon Hill. We urge Headmaster Fargher to obey the rule of law and allow us to retrieve those who escaped. After what we witnessed yesterday, it is too great a risk to send law enforcement in without his assurance of their safety. Lastly, to avoid the riots and civil unrest we encountered only months ago, we are implementing a strict curfew. No one is to be on the streets after 8 p.m. This will go into effect immediately and will continue until we deem our city safe. If there is any further unrest or any other act of violence, we will execute a full lockdown."

Jack left the library without anyone noticing, then hurried down the hallway before entering through the double doors of Crozier Hospital. Just before he reached Tim's room, a beeping tone broke the silence and remained constant. Piercing screams shuddered his bones, followed by cries and wailing echoing off the walls. Amina stepped out from the room with tears streaking down her cheeks and locked eyes on him.

Jack stormed out of Crozier Hospital, enraged and broken. Stunned, he refused to listen to Elyon's voice as he spoke two simple words—"Guardians life"—and slipped through the basement tunnel.

A few blocks away from the tunnel exit, he was still in a tsunami as he pushed through the turnstiles at the MTR station. A lump in his throat choked every breath. With his tailored hoodie pulled over his head, he kept his face pointed toward the floor until he slipped off the train in Tsim Sha Tsui and picked up the pace down the sidewalk.

Jack reached the Clock Tower near Star Ferry and watched the minute hand tick. *Like the clock tower at Beacon Hill, it's counting backward—which means I'm running out of time. I won't accept Tim is gone—no way.* He walked around the side of the Clock Tower, searching for any clues. He turned toward Victoria Harbour and looked across at the skyline of Hong Kong Island. He noticed something different about the water—a shade out of the ordinary.

His eyes darted between the tourists and locals who waited in line at the bus depot and those headed for the ferry. Everyone was in a hurry, so no one paid him any attention. He walked beneath the palm trees of the promenade, then climbed over the railing and dropped down to a concrete platform barely wide enough for him to stand on. He knelt down, nearly level with the water, expecting to find murky yellowish-green, but instead it was pitch-black.

A twinge pricked the back of his neck as he stood and slowly turned. His gaze narrowed as he glared into the soulless eyes of his former best friend. Will dipped Dragon Soul into the harbor. When he pointed the razor-sharp blade toward Jack, flaming dragons were wrapped around the etched silver. Soulweaver slipped from Jack's forearm, extending with a glowing white fire spitting from both ends. Gripping the rod, Jack steadied himself as Will seethed with hatred.

"You have stolen everything from me." Will reached behind his back and retrieved the Windstrikers with one hand. He raised the war fans above his head as the dretium glowed with an engraved phoenix. "Now the world knows who you are, Jack."

"I'm sorry about your mom—I'm sorry for everything."

Jack's head spun as fighter jets screamed over Victoria Harbour. Fear clawed at every ounce of his faith. He looked past Will and realized the black water in the harbor was rising up like a tidal wave. He gripped Soulweaver firmly, unsure of how to stop the inevitable. The massive wall of tarred water rose higher until it loomed over Star Ferry and the promenade of Tsim Sha Tsui. Even though he couldn't see anyone else from the platform below, the panicked screams and shouting erupted with a chilling intensity.

Will waved the Windstrikers, and the black waters circled into a spinning vortex. He threw the war fans, and each one soared into the sky, drawn toward the water tornado. The twister whipped across the harbor, rapidly growing in size.

Dread surged through Jack's veins when explosions blasted

across Victoria Harbour—from Cross-Harbour Tunnel to Eastern and Western Harbour Crossings. All three underwater tunnels to Hong Kong Island were destroyed as concrete and steel ruptured from beneath the surface, launching through the skies before splashing into the pitch-black water.

Will gripped Dragon Soul with both hands and bounced from one foot to the other, eager to attack. Jack had seen this look in Will's eyes only once—when he pummeled him in Upsdell Dining Hall. At the same time, the heartwood vibrated and hummed in his grasp.

Soulweaver defeated Dragon Soul on Everest.

"I won't let you find any more artifacts or hurt anyone else," Jack promised as Elyon's presence shattered his dread and fear. "Even if it means we both die in the end."

Will's venomous glare darkened. "Then get ready for a battle, mate."

Acknowledgments

A SPECIAL THANKS TO READERS around the world who have journeyed along with me in this epic adventure captured in the pages of the Beacon Hill series. What began as a spark of an idea has evolved into a universe I've always dreamed of writing with characters we have all grown to love. To those readers who continue to dive deeper with Jack and his friends into this quest, a sincere heart of gratitude for your encouragement and support.

To Don Pape, the one who was first to ever hear about Beacon Hill. I've said it before, and I'll say it again—thank you for believing in this series and in me as a storyteller. Most of all, I'm grateful for your wisdom and friendship. Let's keep the dream alive.

To my Wander family, who have been in the trenches with me over the last few years. Your unique creativity and expertise have brought the Beacon Hill series to life. While most will never know the countless hours you have sacrificed, I've had a front-row seat. And in *Secrets of the Highlands*, we have navigated the peaks and valleys together. To each one of you, my deepest thanks for all you have done.

Two books down, more to go.

About the Author

D. J. WILLIAMS was born and raised in Hong Kong, igniting an adventurous spirit as he ventured into the jungles of the Amazon, the bush of Africa, and the ancient cities of the Far East. His global travels submerged him in a myriad of cultures, giving him a unique perspective that fuels his creativity. Providing a fresh voice in mystery and suspense, his novels have climbed the charts on Amazon Hot New Releases, and his books *The Auctioneer* and *Hunt for Eden's Star* received stellar reviews from *Kirkus Reviews*. *Secrets of the Highlands* is book two in his new Beacon Hill series. Williams has also been an executive producer and director on over five hundred episodes of broadcast television.